GEMINI

Mark Burnell

HarperCollins*Publishers*

HarperCollins*Publishers*
77–85 Fulham Palace Road,
Hammersmith, London W6 8JB

www.harpercollins.co.uk

A paperback original 2003

1 3 5 7 9 8 6 4 2

A catalogue record for this book
is available from the British Library

ISBN 0 00 715264 7

Set in Meridien and Castellar

Printed and bound in Great Britain byClays Ltd, St Ives plc

ACKNOWLEDGEMENTS

I would like to thank the following in Hong Kong, Philip Layton, Carolyn Fong, James and Juli Bryson, Victor Hu; in Singapore, Dominic and Miranda Armstrong; in Berlin, Alexander Eichner, Olivier Butin, and especially Tilmann Funck.

Those who I'd like to thank but can't name know who they are and I'm grateful for their help.

I would also like to thank Toby Eady and Susan Watt for their constant guidance, expertise and encouragement.

Most of all, I would like to thank Isabelle for her love and support. And patience.

For Ivan with love

Marrakech

The first time I came to Marrakech I was a French tourist. I was also one half of a couple in love. Or so it must have seemed to those who saw us together. He was a lawyer from Milan, who told me that he'd been married but was now divorced. He never mentioned his second wife, though, or that she still considered their marriage idyllic, blessed, as it was, with three children, a house by Lake Como and a villa in Sardinia. Then again, I never mentioned that I intended to steal Russian SVR files from the wall-safe in his company apartment in Geneva. Or that having an affair with me might cost him his life.

Dishonesty was the blood that surged through the veins of our brief relationship. Without it there would have been no relationship. Without dishonesty I can never have a relationship because, after the truth, who in their right mind would have me?

The lawyer from Milan knew me as Juliette. The man who will meet me on the roof terrace of Café La Renaissance in seven minutes will know me as Petra Reuter. Around the world my face has many names, none of them real. Long ago, when I was a complete person – a single individual – I was someone called Stephanie Patrick. But almost nobody remembers her now.

Sometimes, not even me.

Dressed in black cotton trousers, a navy linen shirt and a pair of DKNY trainers, Petra Reuter crossed Avenue Mohammed V and took the lift to Café La Renaissance's roof terrace, which overlooked Place Abdel Moumen ben Ali. Sprawled before her, Marrakech shimmered in the parching heat; eleven in the morning and it was already close to forty centigrade. She took off her sunglasses, swept long, dark hair from her eyes and was forced to squint. Above her the sky was deep sapphire, but the horizon remained bleached of colour. Beneath her, drowsy in the scorching breeze, the city murmured: the rasp of old engines, the squeal of a horn, of a shuddering halt, the bark of a dog from a nearby rooftop. She was surprised how much green there was among the terracotta and ochre, full trees throwing welcome shade onto baking pavements. She put her sunglasses back on.

There were some tables on the roof terrace with cheap metal chairs, their turquoise paint chipped and faded. At one table two soft, pear-shaped women were hunched over a map. Petra thought they sounded Canadian. At another table an elderly man in a crumpled grey suit sat in the shade, reading an Arabic newspaper. His walnut skin was peppered with shiny pink blotches. On a section of roof terrace overlooking Place Abdel Moumen ben Ali there were three large, red plastic letters hoisted on blue poles: b – a – r. Four French tourists were taking photographs of themselves with the reverse side of the letters as a backdrop.

Petra bought a Coke and sat at a secluded table. A fortnight had elapsed since her TGV had pulled into Marseille. She'd felt uneasy on that muggy afternoon, but she felt worse now. She'd arrived in Marseille from

Ostend, via Paris. In Ostend she'd gone to the bar where Maxim Mostovoi had once been a regular. A charmless place with bright overhead lights and two dilapidated pool tables, one with a torn cloth. With a shrug of regret the proprietor said that Mostovoi hadn't been in for at least six months; the traditional first line of defence. But Petra had come prepared, and a phrase contained within a question yielded an address in Paris: an apartment on the Rue d'Odessa in Montparnasse which, in turn, led to Marseille. From Marseille she'd travelled to Beirut, then Cairo. In Cairo two addresses – a Lebanese restaurant on Amman Street in Mohandesseen and a contemporary art gallery on Brazil Street in Zamalek – had finally delivered her to this rooftop terrace in Marrakech.

With each city, with each day, her suspicion hardened: that she was no closer to Mostovoi than she had been in Ostend. Or even in London, for that matter. Not that it made much difference. The pursuit might be pointless, but she knew that she would not be allowed to abandon it.

'Petra Reuter.'

He'd lost weight. His hair was long, lank and greasy, greying at the temples. The whites of his bloodshot eyes were a sickly yellow, his skin waxy and loose. His red T-shirt hung limply from his skeletal frame, dark sweat stains marking points of contact. Creased linen trousers were secured by a purple tie threaded through the belt-loops. His fingers were trembling. Through cigarette smoke, Petra smelt decay.

She had only met Marcel Claesen twice before. The last time had been in a dacha outside Moscow. That had been less than two years ago, but the man in front

3

of her appeared ten years older.

'You look sick.'

'Nice to know you haven't lost your charm, Petra.'

'Do you want to know what I really think?'

His feeble smile revealed toffee-coloured teeth. 'It must be the water here. Or the food, maybe ...'

'Or the heat?'

He missed the subtext and shrugged. 'Sure. Why not?'

'What are you doing here?'

'They sent me to make contact with you.'

Claesen, the Belgian intermediary. That was what he had been the first time they met. Then, as now, he'd radiated duplicity. He was a man who materialized in unlikely places for no specific reason, a man who didn't actually *do* anything. Instead, he simply existed in the spaces between people. A conduit, Claesen was the stained banknote that hastened a seedy transaction.

He sat down opposite her and crossed one bony leg over the other. 'Mostovoi thought it would be better to have a familiar face. You know, someone you could trust ...'

Petra raised an eyebrow. 'So he thought of you?'

He wiped the sweat from his brow with the heel of his hand, then shook his head and attempted another smile. 'The things I've heard about you, Petra. They say you killed Vatukin and Kosygin in New York. They say you killed them for Komarov.'

'How exciting.'

'Others say you killed them for Dragica Maric. That the two of you are in love, each of you a reflection of the other.'

'How imaginative.'

4

'How true?'

'You'd like that, wouldn't you? The idea of me and another woman. Especially a woman like her.'

Claesen's shrug was supposed to convey indifference but his eyes betrayed him. 'You mean, a woman like *you*, don't you?'

A black Land Cruiser Amazon with tinted windows was waiting for them at the kerb. Petra sat in the back, keeping Claesen and the driver in front of her. They headed for Palmeraie, to the north of the city centre, where extravagant villas were secreted in secure gardens. Most of the properties belonged to wealthy Moroccans, but in recent years there had been an influx of rich foreigners. At one of the larger walled compounds the driver pulled the Land Cruiser off the tarmac onto a dirt track. Ahead, heavy electric gates parted. Above them, two security cameras twitched.

Outside the compound the ground had been arid scrub between the palm trees. Inside it was lush lawn. Sprinklers sprayed a fine mist over the grass. Men tended flowerbeds, their backs bent to the overhead sun. On the right there were two floodlit tennis courts and a large swimming pool with a Chinese dragon carved from stone at each corner.

The villa was centrally air-conditioned and smelt like an airport terminal. There were two armed men in the entrance hall. Both were fair-skinned, their faces and arms burnt bright red. One carried a Browning BDA9, the other a Colt King Cobra. Without a word they led Claesen and Petra down a hall, the Belgian's rubber soles squeaking on the veined marble floor. The room they entered had a thick white carpet, four

5

armchairs – tanned leather stretched over chrome frames – positioned around a coffee table with a bronze horse's head at its centre and, in one corner, an enormous Panasonic home entertainment system. Wooden blinds had been lowered over the windows. A curtain had been three-quarters drawn across a sliding glass door that opened onto a covered terrace. The door was partly open, allowing some natural air to infiltrate the artificial. Beyond the terrace she saw orange trees, lemon trees and perfectly manicured rose beds.

'That's far enough.'

He was sitting on the other side of the room, his back to the source of partial light, a man reduced to silhouette. Dark trousers, a white shirt, open at the neck, dark sunglasses. Petra was surprised he could even see her.

'You want something to drink? Some tea? Or water?'

'Nothing.'

There were two men to his right. The shorter and leaner of the two had a bony face like a whippet: a mean mouth with thin lips, a pointed nose, sharp little eyes. His hands were restless but his gaze was steady, never leaving her. With Claesen and the pair behind her, the men numbered six, two of them definitely armed.

'Where's Mostovoi?'

The man in the chair said, 'Max has been detained.'

'Detained?'

Incorrectly, he thought he detected anxiety in her tone. 'Not in that sense of the word.'

'I'm not interested in the sense of the word. If he's not here, he's not here.'

'He sent me instead.'

'And you are?'

'Lars. Lars Andersen.'

Her eyes had adjusted to the lack of light. Andersen had short, dark, untidy hair, prominent cheekbones and olive skin that was lightly pockmarked; a Mediterranean look for a Scandinavian name, Petra thought.

'No offence, Lars, but I don't know you.'

'You don't know Max, either.'

'I know what business he's in. Which is why I'm here. But I'm starting to think I made a mistake. I'm running out of patience. That means he's running out of time. It's up to him. There are always others. Harding, Sasic, Beneix ...'

'They're not as good.'

'As good as what? A man who never shows? What could be worse than that?'

Andersen appeared surprised by her contempt. He glanced at the short one and said, in Russian, 'What do you reckon, Jarni? Not bad, huh?'

'Not bad.'

'You think she could play for Inter?'

'No problem.'

'Where?'

'Anywhere, probably. That's what I hear.'

Also in Russian, Petra said, 'What's Inter?'

Raised eyebrows all round. Andersen said, 'You speak Russian?'

'Judging by your accents, better than either of you.'

Andersen grinned. 'Max said we should be careful with you. Watch out for her, he told us, she's full of surprises.'

7

Outside, a lawnmower started, its drone as nostalgic as the scent of the grass it cut. It reminded her of those summer evenings when her father, back from work, would mow their undulating garden. A childhood memory, then. But not Petra's childhood. The memory belonged to someone else. Petra was merely borrowing it.

'What's Inter?' she asked again.

'You don't know?'

'Should I?'

He shrugged. 'Inter Milan.' When she made no comment, he returned to English. 'You've never heard of Inter Milan?'

She shook her head.

'The football team?'

The name *was* faintly resonant but she said, 'I have better things to do with my time than watch illiterate millionaires kissing each other.'

'Inter is more than a football team.'

'Is there any danger of you straying towards the point?'

Andersen looked as though he wished to continue. He leaned forward and opened his mouth to speak – to protest, even – but then appeared to change his mind. An awkward silence developed. Petra sensed Claesen squirming behind her.

Eventually, Andersen said, 'Tomorrow morning, the Mellah.'

'Mostovoi will be there?'

'Someone will be there. They'll take you to him.'

'If he's not there I'm going home.'

'Place des Ferblantiers at ten.'

The Land Cruiser drove her back to the city centre

and came to a halt on Avenue Hassan II, just short of the intersection with Place du 16 Novembre. Claesen turned round. An inch of ash spilled down his red T-shirt. His creepy confidence had returned the moment they left the walled compound.

'Until next time, then?'

'How did they know that you knew me?'

'I have no idea.'

'You didn't ask?'

'I received a message, an air ticket and the promise of dollars.'

'And that was enough for you? It never occurred to you to check it out first?'

His reply was bittersweet. 'These days that's a luxury I can't afford.'

'You know something, Claesen, I'm amazed you've made it this far.'

'Me too.' Smiling once more, he waved his Gitanes at her. 'I used to think I'd never live long enough to die from lung cancer. Now I'm beginning to think I have a chance.'

The Hotel Mirage on Boulevard Mohammed Zerktouni was in the Ville Nouvelle, not far from Café La Renaissance. Mid-range, it mostly catered for European tourists. Which was precisely what Petra was: Maria Gilardini, a single Swiss woman, aged twenty-nine. A dental hygienist from Sion.

There was a message for her at reception. She took the envelope up to her room, at the rear of the building, overlooking a small courtyard, opposite the back of an ageing office block. She sat on the bed and opened the envelope. As expected, there was nothing inside.

Petra had heard of Maxim Mostovoi long before he became a contract. A former air force pilot, he'd emerged from the rubble of the Soviet Union with his own aviation business. His military career had been restricted to cargo transport. At the time, that had been a source of regret. Later it proved to be the source of his fortune.

Among the first to recognize potential markets for the Soviet Union's vast stockpile of obsolete weaponry, Mostovoi was able to commandeer cargo aircraft from what remained of the Soviet air force. Then he formed partnerships with contacts in the army who were able to supply him with arms. In the early days he based himself in Moscow, taking comfort from the chaos that bloomed in the aftermath of the collapse of the Soviet Union. There were few laws to contain him. Those that existed were not enforced; bribery tended to ensure that. Failing bribery, there was always violence.

Mostovoi's first fortune was made in Africa. Rebel factions sought him out, eager for cheap weapons. Using huge Antonov cargo aircraft, he delivered to Rwanda, Angola and Sierra Leone, frequently taking payment in conflict diamonds, depositing the gems in Antwerp. Soon Mostovoi decided he would prefer to be closer to them. In 1994 he moved to Ostend, establishing an air freight company named Air Eurasia at offices close to the airport. As his reputation grew, so did demand for his services. He established an office in Kigali, the Rwandan capital, at the height of the genocide perpetrated by the Hutu militia. He bought a hotel in Kampala, in neighbouring Uganda. The top floor was converted into a luxury penthouse, marble flown in from Italy, bathrooms from Scandinavia, hookers from Moscow. Twice a year Unita rebels travelled from Angola to the hotel in Kampala with pouches of diamonds. The stones were valued by Manfred Hempel, a leading Manhattan diamond merchant, who was extravagantly rewarded for his time. Despite this, Hempel hated the trips to Uganda. To ease his discomfort Mostovoi used his Gulfstream V to ferry the diamond dealer directly from New York to Kampala and back again.

By 1996 his fleet of aircraft, mostly Antonovs and Illyushins, had grown to thirty-eight and had attracted the attention of the Belgian authorities. In December of that year he relocated Air Eurasia to Qatar, opening associate offices in Riyadh and the emirates of Ras al Khaimah and Sharjah. In February 1997 he met senior representatives of FARC – the Colombian rebel army – at San Vicente del Caguan, but failed to come to an agreement. From Colombia he travelled directly to Pakistan. In Peshawar he struck a deal to supply weapons to the Taliban in Afghanistan. Here he was paid in opium, which he sold for processing and onward distribution in Kazakhstan and Uzbekistan.

Born in Moscow in 1962, Mostovoi had been destined for mediocrity. An unexceptional pupil, a poor athlete, he longed to fly fighters for the Soviet air force but lacked the necessary skills, and was thus relegated to the cargo fleet. To those who knew him best, this would have seemed entirely predictable. As charming and amusing as he could be, it was accepted by everybody that Max would never amount to much. His wife used to tease him in public, and all Mostovoi would muster in his defence was a resigned shrug. Still, a decade and two hundred million dollars later, the memory of his heavy-hipped ex-wife had been eclipsed by the finest flesh money could buy. As a younger man he'd often dreamed of taking his revenge upon those who had humiliated him over the years. Now that he was in a position to do so, he found he couldn't be bothered. He didn't have the time. It was enough to know that he could.

Petra knew that had Mostovoi been content to confine his business interests to Africa, he would never have become the subject of a contract. The reality was that nobody cared about Africa. Afghanistan, however, was different. Through his relationship with the Taliban, Mostovoi was connected to al-Qaeda. Before 11 September 2001 he'd been an easy man to find, confident of his own security, keen to expand his empire. Since that date he'd been invisible.

Dusk descended quickly upon Djemaa el-Fna, the huge square in the medina that was the heart of Marrakech. Kerosene lamps replaced the daylight, strung out along rows of food stalls.

Petra found the café on the edge of the square. The outdoor tables were mostly taken. Inside, she picked a table with a clear view of the entrance. A slowly rotating fan barely disturbed the hot air. To her right, beneath an emerald green mosaic of the Atlas mountains, two elderly men were in animated discussion over glasses of tea.

She ordered a bottle of mineral water and drank half of it, checking the entrance as often as she checked her watch. At ten past seven she got up and asked the man behind the bar for the toilet. Past the cramped, steaming kitchen she came to a foul-smelling cubicle, which she ignored, pressing on down the dim corridor to the door at the end, which was shut. She tried the handle and it opened, as promised. She found herself in a narrow alley, rubble underfoot. At the end of the alley she saw the lane that she'd identified on the town map. She unbuttoned her shirt, took it off, turned it inside out and put it back on, trading powder blue for plum.

At twenty-five past seven she emerged from a small street on the opposite side of Djemaa el-Fna to the café. This time she melted into the crowd at the centre of the square, trawling the busy stalls, until she found one with no customers. She sat on a wooden bench beneath three naked bulbs hung from a cord sagging between two poles. The man on the other side of the counter was tending strips of lamb on an iron rack, fat spitting on the coals, smoke spiralling upwards, adding to the heat of the night. Petra passed fifteen *dirhams* across the counter for a small bowl of *harira*, a spicy lentil soup.

The woman appeared within five minutes, a child in tow. Short, dark and squat, she wore a dark brown ankle-length dress and a flimsy cotton shawl around her shoulders. The child had black curls, caramel skin, pale hazel eyes. She was eating dried fruit. They sat on the bench to Petra's right. The woman ordered two slices of melon, which the man retrieved from a crate behind him.

In French, she said, 'Someone was in your hotel room today. A man.'

Petra nodded. 'What was he doing?'

'Looking.'

'Did he find anything?'

'It's not possible to say. He spent most of his time

13

with your laptop. I think he might have downloaded something. It wasn't easy to see. The angle was awkward.'

'From across the courtyard?'

The woman shook her head. 'That view was too restricted. I had to try something else. A camera concealed in the smoke detector.'

'I hadn't noticed there was a smoke detector.'

'Above the door to your bathroom. It's cosmetic. A plastic case to satisfy a safety regulation. Actually, I'm surprised. A bribe is easier and cheaper.'

'Where was the base unit?'

'Across the courtyard. In the office.' The woman finished a mouthful of melon. 'He went through your clothes, your personal belongings. He took care to replace everything as he found it. He searched under the bed, behind the drawers, on top of the cupboard. All the usual hiding places. You have a gun?'

'Not there. Anything else?'

'A Lear jet arrived at Menara Airport early this morning. A flight plan has been filed for tomorrow afternoon. Stern wants you to know that Mostovoi has a meeting in Zurich tomorrow evening.'

I lie on my bed, naked and sweating. When I came to Marrakech with Massimo, the lawyer from Milan, we stayed at the Amanjena, a cocoon of luxury on the outskirts of the city. There we indulged ourselves fully. On our last evening we ate at Yacout, a palace restaurant concealed within a warren of tiny streets. We drank wine on the roof terrace while musicians played in the corner. A hot breeze blew through us. Mostly, I remember the view of the city by night, lights sparkling like gemstones against the darkness. Later we ate downstairs in a small courtyard with rose petals on the floor. That was where Massimo took my hand and said, 'Juliette, I think I'm falling in love with you.'

I gazed into his eyes and said, 'I feel it, too.'

I think he was telling the truth. At the time, that never occurred to me because everything I said to him was a lie and I assumed we were both playing the same game. When he said we should meet again in Geneva I said that would be lovely, that I couldn't wait. Which was as close to the truth as I ever got with Massimo; I needed unforced access to his company apartment. Later, when he told me he thought I looked beautiful, I just smiled, as I wondered whether I would be the one to kill him. As it turned out, it was somebody else: Dragica Maric.

When Claesen mentioned her name, the memory of the last time we were together was resurrected: about two years ago, at the derelict Somerset Hotel on West 54th Street in Manhattan. We were in a narrow service corridor down one side of the hotel. It was dark and damp, the sound of the city barely audible over the rain. She was armed with a Glock. She told me to kneel. There was nothing I could do but obey. Then she asked me questions, which I answered honestly. Certain that I was about to die, there had seemed little point in lying. Finally she fired the Glock. Above my head. By the time I realized I was still alive, she was gone.

Place des Ferblantiers, ten in the morning. Petra's guide wore the traditional white *djellaba* with a pointed hood. Inside the Mellah, the Jewish Quarter, they entered a covered market. In the still heat, smells competed for supremacy: fish, body odour, chickens, rubbish and, in particular, a meat counter with oesophagi hanging from hooks. The hum of flies was close.

Beyond the market the guide led her through a maze of crooked streets, some so narrow she could press her palms against both walls. There were no signs and no straight lines. They passed doors set into walls, snatching occasional glimpses: a staircase rising into darkness, a moving foot, a sleeping dog. Lanes were pockmarked with tiny retail outlets: a man selling watch straps from a booth the size of a cupboard, a shop trading in solitary bicycle wheels, Sprite and Coke sold from a coolbox in the shallow shade of a doorway.

They came to an arch. Beneath it a merchant was arranging sacks of spices. Behind the sacks, on a wooden table, were baskets of lemons and limes. Garlands of garlic hung from a wooden beam. They passed through the arch into a courtyard. Beneath a reed canopy two women were weaving baskets.

They headed for a door on the far side of the courtyard, took the stairs to the upper floor, turned left and arrived at a large, rectangular room. It was carpeted, quite literally: carpets covering the floor and three walls. Other carpets were piled waist high, some exquisitely intricate, with silk thread shimmering beneath the harsh overhead lighting, others a cruder style of kilim, in vivid turquoise, egg-yolk yellow and blood red. The fourth wall contained the only window, which looked out onto the courtyard.

Maxim Mostovoi was at the far end of the room, sprawled across a tan leather sofa as plushly padded as he was. He wore Ray-Ban Aviator sunglasses and a full moustache. His gut stretched a pale green polo-shirt that bore dark sweat stains in the pinch of both armpits. Fat thighs made his chinos fit as snugly as a second skin.

Jarni, the whippet-faced man from the villa at Palmeraie, stood to Petra's right. Beside him was a taller man, a body-builder perhaps, massive shoulders tapering to a trim waist, black hair oiled to the scalp, his skin the colour and texture of chocolate mousse. He had a gold ring through his right eyebrow.

'I feel I know you,' Mostovoi murmured.

'A common mistake.'

'I'm sure.' He nodded at the body-builder. 'Alexei...'

Petra said, 'I'm not armed.'

'Then you won't mind.'

Petra had been frisked many times. There were two elements to the process that almost never varied, in her experience: the procedure was carried out by men, and they took pleasure in their work. More than once she'd had eager fingers inside her clothes, even inside her underwear and, on one occasion, inside her. The man who'd done that had gorged himself on her discomfort. Later, when she crushed both his hands in a car door, she took some reciprocal pleasure from the act.

'You should be more careful where you put your fingers,' she'd told him, as he surveyed what remained of them.

Petra had dressed deliberately. Black cotton trousers, a black T-shirt beneath a turquoise shirt tied at the waist and a pair of lightweight walking boots. Suspended from the leather cord around her neck was a fisherman's cross made of burnished mahogany, the wood so smooth that the fracture line at the base of the loop was almost invisible. She wore her long dark hair in a pony-tail.

Among friskers she'd known, Alexei the body-builder was about average. In other words, tiresomely predictable. Petra knew that behind his sunglasses Mostovoi wasn't blinking. His face was shiny with sweat. As he took in the show, she took in the room. Apart from his mobile phone, the table was bare. A lamp without a shade stood on an upturned crate at the far end of the sofa. By the door she'd noticed a box containing a wooden paddle for beating the dust from carpets. Next to the box there was a portable black-and-white security monitor on a creaking table, a bin, a ball of used bubble-wrap and an electric fan, unplugged. She'd been in rooms that offered less. And in situations that threatened more. Until now she hadn't known whether Mostovoi would be viable.

Alexei reached between her legs, but Petra snatched his wrist away. 'Take my word for it, you won't find an Uzi down there.'

He glanced at Mostovoi, who shook his head, then continued, skipping over her stomach and ribs before slowing as he reached her breasts. His fingers found something solid in the breast pocket of her shirt. Petra took it out before he had the chance to retrieve it himself.

'What's that?' Mostovoi asked.

'An inhaler,' Petra said. 'With a Salbutamol cartridge. I'm asthmatic.'

He was surprised, then amused. '*You?*' It was the third version of the inhaler Petra had been given. She'd never used any of them. Mostovoi's amusement began to turn to suspicion. 'Show me.'

'You put this end in your mouth, squeeze the cartridge and inhale.'

'I said, show me.'

So she did, taking care not to break the second seal

18

by pushing the cartridge too vigorously. There was a squirt of Salbutamol from the mouthpiece, which she inhaled, a cold powder against the back of her throat.

The frisk resumed, until Alexei stepped away from Petra and shook his head. Mostovoi seemed genuinely amazed. 'You don't have a gun?'

'I didn't think I'd need one. Besides, I didn't want your friend to feel something hard in my trousers and get over-excited.'

A barefoot boy entered the room, carrying a tray with two tall glasses of mint tea and a silver sugar bowl. Fresh mint leaves had been crushed into the bottom of each glass. He passed one to Petra and the other to Mostovoi, before leaving.

Petra said, 'That was a neat idea, using Claesen as an intermediary yesterday.'

'It was a matter of some … *reassurance*.'

'I know.' She caught his eye. '*Your* reassurance, though. Not mine.'

Mostovoi inclined his head a little, a bow of concession. 'Your reputation may precede you, but nobody ever knows what follows it. Within our community you're a contradiction: the anonymous celebrity.'

'Unlike you.'

'I'm a salesman. Nothing more.'

'Don't sell yourself short.'

Mostovoi smiled. 'I never do.' He lit a Marlboro with a gold Dunhill lighter. 'This is a change of career for you, no?'

'Not so much a change, more of an expansion.'

'I know you met Klim in Lille last month. And again in Bratislava three weeks ago.'

'Small world.'

'The smallest you can imagine. You discussed Sukhoi-25s for five million US an aircraft. For fifty-five million dollars, he said he could get you twelve; buy eleven, get one free.'

'What can I say? We live in a supermarket culture.'

'Or for one hundred million, twenty-five. Which is not bad. But you weren't interested.'

'Because?'

'Because the Sukhoi-25 isn't good enough. The MiG-29SE is superior in every way. That's what Klim told you. And that they can be purchased direct from Rosboron for about thirty million dollars each. However, good discounts can be negotiated, so …'

'But not the kind of discounts that you can negotiate. Right?'

Mostovoi took off his sunglasses and placed them beside his phone. He wiped sweat from his forehead. 'That depends. I understand you're also in the market for transport helicopters. Specifically, the Mi-26.'

'Actually, the Mi-26 is all I'm in the market for. Klim got over-excited. We discussed the Sukhoi and the MiG, but that's all it was. Talk.'

Mostovoi looked disappointed.

The Mi-26 was a monster: 110 feet in length, almost the size of a Boeing 727, it was designed to carry eighty to ninety passengers, although in Russia, where most of them were in service, it was not uncommon for them to transport up to one hundred and twenty.

'How many?' Mostovoi asked.

'Two, possibly three.'

'That's a lot of men.'

'Or a lot of cargo.'

'Either way, it's a lot of money.'

'I'm not interested in running a few AK-47s to ETA or the IRA.'

Mostovoi pondered this while he smoked. 'Still, a deal this size ... normally I would hear about it.'

'Normally you'd be involved.'

'True.'

'Which would leave me on the outside.'

'Also true.'

Petra took a sip from her tea, letting Mostovoi do the work. Casually, she wandered over to the window, which was open, and looked out. There was no hint of a cooling breeze to counter the stifling heat. The canopy covering the basket-weavers was directly below. She glanced at Alexei and Jarni. They'd relaxed; Jarni's eyes had glazed over. The wooden grip of a Bernardelli P-018 protruded from the waistband of his trousers. Alexei was wearing a tight white T-shirt that revealed his chiselled physique to maximum effect. And the fact that he was unarmed.

The immediate future was coming into focus. She returned her attention to Mostovoi, who was talking about the nature of the clients she represented. A rebel faction of some sort, perhaps. Or drug warlords. From Colombia, maybe, or even Afghanistan.

'What's your point?'

'Maybe there is no deal.'

He made it sound as though the idea had only just occurred to him. Petra felt her damp skin prickle with alarm. 'Klim thinks there is.'

Mostovoi snorted with contempt. 'That's why Klim flies economy while I have a Gulfstream V ...'

Petra spun to her left, sensing the movement behind her: Alexei advancing, swinging at her. The blow caught her on the ribs, not across the back of the neck, as intended. But it was enough to crush the air out of her. She tumbled onto the mustard carpet, her glass of tea shattering beneath her. Alexei came at her again, brandishing the wooden paddle like a baseball bat.

Jarni yanked the Bernardelli from his waistband. Petra rolled to her right, fragments of glass biting into her. The paddle missed her head, crunching against her shoulder and collar-bone instead. Moving as clumsily as she'd anticipated, his bubbling muscularity a hindrance, not an advantage, Alexei attempted to grasp her, but she slithered beyond his reach.

Jarni aimed a kick at her. His shoe scuffed her left thigh. She made a counter-kick with her right foot, hooking away his standing leg. He toppled backwards. As his elbow hit the ground the gun discharged accidentally, the bullet ripping into the ceiling, sprinkling them with dusty rubble.

Before she could get to her feet Alexei's boot found the same patch of ribs as the paddle. Winded and momentarily powerless, she couldn't prevent the body-builder grabbing her pony-tail and dragging her to her knees. Jarni was on his side, stunned, the 9mm a few feet away. Alexei hauled her to her feet and threw several punches, each a hammer-blow, the worst of them to the small of her back, the force of it sending a sickening shudder through the rest of her. Then he attempted to pin her arms together behind her back. Which would leave her exposed to Jarni. Or even Mostovoi. Through the fog, she understood this.

Petra curled forward as much as she could, then dug her toes into the ground and launched herself up and back with as much power as she could muster. The crown of her head smacked Alexei in the face. She knew they were both cut. His grip slackened and she wriggled free as he staggered to one side, dazed and bloody. Petra grabbed the inhaler from her breast pocket, pressed the cartridge, felt the second seal rupture and fired the CS gas into his eyes.

Jarni was on his feet now, the gun in his right hand rising towards her. With a stride she was beside him, both hands clamping his right wrist. Unbalanced, he wobbled. She drove his hand down and nudged the trigger finger. The gun fired again, the bullet splitting his left kneecap.

Gasping, Alexei was on his knees, his face buried in his hands, blood dribbling between his fingers. Jarni started to scream. And Mostovoi was exactly where he'd been a few moments before. On the sofa, not moving, the complacency of the voyeur usurped by the paralysis of fear.

There were shouts in the courtyard and footsteps on the stairs. She picked up Jarni's Bernardelli and aimed at Mostovoi's eyes.

Resigned to the bullet, he matched her stare.

'*Why?*'

As good a last word as any, Petra supposed. She pulled the trigger.

Nothing.

Mostovoi blinked, not comprehending. She tried again. Still nothing. The weapon was jammed. And now the footsteps were at the top of the stairs and approaching the door.

She dropped the gun and took the open window, an action that owed more to reflex than decision. She shattered the fragile wooden shutters and fell. The canopy offered no resistance, folding instantly. Her fall was broken by the bodies and baskets beneath. From above, she heard a door smacking a wall, a rumble of shoes, shouts.

Instantly she was on her feet, accelerating across the courtyard towards the arch. Behind her, shots rang out. Puffs of pulverized brick danced out of the wall to her right. From another door in the courtyard two armed men emerged in pursuit. Then she was in the gloom of the arch, safe from the guns behind, but not from the threat ahead.

Even as her eyes adjusted to the shade she saw the merchant reacting to her, bending down to pick up something from behind a stack of wooden boxes. With her left hand Petra reached for her throat and tugged the cross. The leather cord gave way easily. The merchant was rising, silhouetted against the sunlight flooding the street. Her right hand grasped the bottom of the cross, pulling away the polished mahogany scabbard to reveal a three-inch serrated steel spike.

The merchant raised his revolver. Petra dived, clattering into him before he could fire. They spilled across sacks of paprika and saffron. In clouds of scarlet and gold she aimed for his neck but missed, instead ramming the spike through the soft flesh behind the jawbone up into the tongue. He went into spasm as she grabbed his revolver, clambered over him, spun round and waited for the first of the chasing pair to appear. Four shots later they were both down, and Petra Reuter was on the run again.

The Hotel Sahara was between Rue Zitoune el-Qedim and Rue de Bab Agnaou, the room itself overlooking the street. Petra closed the door behind her. Deep blue wooden shutters excluded most of the daylight. It was cool in the darkness.

There was a small chest of drawers by one wall. Petra opened the top right drawer. She'd already removed the back panel so that it could be pulled clear. She dropped to a crouch, reached inside and found the plastic pouch taped to the underside. The pouch contained an old Walther P38K, an adaptation of the standard P38, the barrel cut to seven centimetres to make it easier to conceal. She placed the gun on top of the chest of drawers.

Her pulse was still speeding and she was soaked – mostly sweat, some blood – the dust and dirt of the Mellah caking her skin.

There was a loud bang. She reached for the Walther. The bang was followed by the drone of an engine. A moped, its feeble diesel spluttering beneath her window. A backfire, not a shot, prompting a half-hearted smile.

Across town they would be waiting for her at the Hotel Mirage; Maria Gilardini's clothes were still in her room, her toothbrush by the sink, her air ticket wedged between the pages of a paperback on the bedside table.

Petra opened the shutters a little, dust motes floating in the slice of sunlight. In the corner of the room was a rucksack secured by a padlock. She opened it, rummaged through the contents for the first-aid wallet, which she unfolded on the bed. Then she stripped to her underwear and examined herself in the mirror over the basin. Her ribs were beginning to bruise. Among the grazes were cuts containing splinters of glass.

Mostovoi had known there was no deal; not at first

– he'd agreed to meet her, after all – but eventually. The more she considered it, the more convinced of it she became. He hadn't asked enough questions about Klim to be so sure of his doubt. The fact that he'd allowed himself to be met proved that he was interested – with so much money at stake, that was inevitable – and yet he'd known. Or suspected, at least.

She used tweezers to extract the shards of glass, then dressed the worst cuts. Next she took the scissors to her hair, losing six inches to the shoulder. Not a new look, just an alteration. She put in a pair of blue contact lenses to match those in the photograph of the passport: Mary Reid, visiting from London, born in Leeds, aged twenty-seven, aromatherapist. Rather than Petra Reuter, visiting from anywhere in the world, born in Hamburg, aged thirty-five, assassin.

The hair and the contacts were useful, but Petra knew there were more significant factors in changing an identity; deportment and dress. When Mary Reid moved, she shuffled. When she sat, she slouched. The way she carried herself would allow her to vanish in a crowd. So would the clothes she wore, and since Mary Reid was on holiday they were appropriate: creased cream linen three-quarter-length trousers, leather sandals from a local market, a faded lilac T-shirt from Phuket, a triple string of coral beads around her throat.

She abandoned the rucksack and the Walther P38K, taking only a small knapsack with a few things: some crumpled clothes, a wash-bag, a battered Walkman, four CDs, a Kodak disposable camera and a book. Even though her room was pre-paid, she told no one she was leaving. She caught a bus to the airport and a Royal Air Maroc flight to Paris. At Charles de Gaulle she checked in for a British Airways connection and then made a call to a London number.

Flight BA329 from Paris touched down a few minutes early at ten to ten. By ten past, having only hand-luggage, she was clear of Customs. The courier met her in the Arrivals hall. He was pushing a trolley with a large leather holdall on it. She placed the knapsack next to the holdall and they headed for the exit.

'Good flight?'

'Fine.'

'Debriefing tomorrow morning. Eleven.'

At the exit Petra picked up the leather holdall and the man disappeared through the doors with her knapsack. She turned back and made for the Underground. As the train rattled towards west London she opened the holdall. Her mobile phone was in a side pocket. She switched it on and made a call. When she got no answer she tried another number.

She knew it was unprofessional, but she didn't care. She was tired, she was hurt, what she needed was rest. But what she wanted was something to take away the bitter taste.

After the call she went through the holdall: dirty clothes rolled into a ball – *her* dirty clothes – and another wash-bag, again hers. In another side pocket she found credit cards, her passport and some cash: a mixture of euros, sterling and a few thousand Uzbek *sum*. There was a Visa card receipt for the Hotel Tashkent and an Uzbekistan Airways ticket stub: Amsterdam–Tashkent–Amsterdam. In the main section of the holdall there was a plastic bag from Amsterdam's Schiphol Airport, a bottle of Veuve Cliquot inside, complete with euro receipt.

Much as it hurt her to admit it, she admired their craft. If nothing else, they were thorough.

At the bottom of the bag was a digital voice recorder with twenty-one used files in two folders. Also a Tamrac camera bag containing six used rolls of Centuria Super Konica film, a Nikon F80, a Sekonic light meter, three lenses and a digital Canon. She knew what was on the Canon and the rolls of film: details from the Fergana valley, home to an extremist Uzbek Islamic militia.

At Green Park she swapped from the Piccadilly Line to the Victoria Line, and at Stockwell from the Victoria Line to the Northern Line. From Clapham South she walked. It took five minutes to reach the address, which was sandwiched between Wandsworth Common and Clapham Common, a street of large, comfortable semi-detached Victorian houses. Volvos and Range Rovers lined both kerbs.

Karen Cunningham let her in. They kissed on both cheeks, hugged, left the holdall in the hall and made their way through the house to the garden at the rear. A dozen people sat around a wooden table. Smoke rose from a dying barbecue in a far corner of the garden.

'Stephanie!'

Her fourth name of the day.

From the far side of the table Mark was coming towards her. He wore the collarless cotton shirt she'd bought for him, the sleeves rolled up to the elbow. They kissed. She noticed he was barefoot.

They made space for her at the table. Someone poured her a glass of red wine. She knew all the faces in the flickering candlelight. Not well, or in her own right, but through Mark. After the welcome the con-

28

versation resumed. She picked at the remains of some potato salad as she drank, content not to say too much. Gradually the alcohol worked its temporary magic, purging her pain. Purging Petra.

From Marrakech to Clapham, from Mostovoi to these people, with their careers, their children, their two foreign holidays a year. From a steel spike to a glass of wine, from one continent to another. Two worlds, each as divorced from the other as she was from any other version of herself.

It was after midnight when Mark leaned towards her, frowning, and said, 'It's not the hair. It's something else …'

'What are you talking about?'

'There's something … *different* about you.'

'You're imagining it.'

He shook his head. 'Got it. It's your eyes.'

For a moment there was panic. Then came the recovery, complete with a playful smile, while the lie formed. 'I was wondering how long it would take you to notice.'

'They're blue.'

'Coloured lenses. Found them in Amsterdam. Pretty cool, don't you think?'

1

Mark Hamilton was lying on his front, snoring into his pillow, one foot hanging over the end of a bed that wasn't built for a man of six foot four. Stephanie looked at the scar tissue running across his central and lower back. She had scar tissue of her own – on the front and back of her left shoulder – but, unlike Mark's scars, hers were cosmetic, surgically applied to mimic a bullet's entry and exit wound.

She glanced at Mark's bedside clock. Five to six. She tiptoed to the kitchen to make coffee. A bottle of Rioja stood by the sink, two-thirds drunk. Which was how they'd felt by the time they'd returned to Mark's flat shortly after one. Despite that, he'd opened the Rioja, put on a CD, *Ether Song* by Turin Brakes, and they'd talked. About nothing in particular. After three weeks, it was enough simply to be together again. Normally her trips abroad only lasted a few days.

When he'd said he was going to bed, just after three, she'd said she wouldn't be far behind. But she'd waited until he was asleep, even then keeping her T-shirt on as she lay beside him; she was too tired to answer the questions he would inevitably ask when he saw her naked.

Mark owned a place on a corner of Queen's Gate Mews, off Gloucester Road. The ground floor was a garage, which he used for storage. A steep, narrow

30

staircase led to the first floor, where he lived, and a stepladder that doubled as a fire escape led to the roof, which was flat, and which was where Stephanie took her mug of coffee, having pulled on a pair of ripped jeans.

Above, in a pale pink sky, intercontinental flights lined up for Heathrow. Below, an Alfa Romeo rumbled over cobbles. In the distance, an alarm bell was ringing. She cupped the hot mug with both hands and smiled.

One year to the day.

She'd gone to the Dolomites to unwind. Stephanie had always found that climbing cleared the mind of clutter. It had become part of her routine after a Magenta House contract: a few days away by herself, the local climbing guides her only source of social interaction. By the time she returned to London, more often than not, she'd rinsed the contract from her system.

Mark was staying at the same hotel in a party of six. She noticed him the first day they arrived, her ear drawn to the group by language; they were the only English in the hotel. Over two days, she crossed them in the dining room, at the bar, in the lobby and outside on the observation deck. He was the tallest and least obviously attractive of them, with a storm of dark hair and a perfect climber's face: craggy, marked with ledges and ridges.

On the third day Stephanie lost her grip during an afternoon traverse of an uncomplicated face. The rope snagged her, twisting her sharply to the right. Her left toe was still locked into a small hold. She felt a sharp pinch in her left hip and chose to walk back to the hotel to try to work off any stiffness. Later she took a cup of hot chocolate onto the wooden observation deck. Mark was in a deckchair, reading a Robert Wilson paperback.

Not wanting any conversation, Stephanie walked to the far end and leaned on the rail. It had been a hot, sunny day, but late afternoon brought with it the first hint of a sharp chill. She drank the chocolate and the mountain air, and watched shadows creep as the sun slid. When she'd finished, she walked back along the deck. They were still the only people on it and he was looking straight at her. Not at her eyes, but at her body. Without any attempt to disguise it.

Irritated, Stephanie said, sharply, 'You're staring.'

'You're limping.'

Not the apology she'd anticipated. 'Hardly.'

'Does it hurt?'

'It's nothing. It's just my hip.'

'Actually, it's your sacro-iliac joint.'

'Sorry?'

'To you, your lower back.'

'What are you? An osteopath?'

'A chiropractor.'

'And a man with an answer for everything.'

'Do you want me to prove it to you?'

She tilted her head to one side. 'Are you for real?'

'Are you?'

Half an hour later they were in her bedroom; stained floorboards, thick rugs, ageing cream wallpaper with rural scenes in a pale blue print. She could smell the dried lavender in the frosted glass bowl on the chest of drawers. Beside a lacquered table there was a full-length mirror. Stephanie stood in front of it with Mark behind her. Only now did she appreciate how large he was. He completely framed her in the reflection. She'd pulled off her jersey and shirt, and could see her black bra through the thin cotton of her T-shirt.

Mark reached out and touched her, two fingers pressing softly at the base of her neck. It was barely contact, but it sent a pulse through her. Slowly, he walked the fingers down her spine.

'Why do you climb?'

'It's in my blood,' Stephanie said, her voice no more than a murmur. 'My mother was a fantastic climber, more at home in the mountains than at home. What about you?'

'To relax. And because I have friends who climb.'

'I don't have *any* friends who climb.'

'Then you're worse than us. In a monogamous relationship with the rock-face? I don't think I've ever heard of anything so self-centred.'

'You might be right.'

To relax, he'd said. Not for the thrill, or the sense of achievement. That was how she felt. Besides, as Petra, Stephanie found herself in situations where the adrenalin flowed faster than it ever could clinging to the slick underbelly of a precarious overhang.

'Here we are.' His fingers stopped, just above the top of her jeans. Very gently, he pressed against a point. Stephanie felt heat bloom beneath. Then he placed a forefinger on either shoulder. 'Look in the mirror. You've dropped a little through the left.'

It was true. She could see a marginal difference.

'Can you do something about it?'

Mark looked around the room. 'Well, normally I'd use a bench for something like this, but I'll see what I can do.'

33

'See what you can do?'

He smiled, a fissure forming in the rock-face. 'I'm joking. You'll be fine. You don't have a desk in here, so we'll use your bed.'

Stephanie felt she ought to say something but couldn't.

Mark said, 'Let's hope it's not too soft. I'd like you to undo your jeans.'

She raised her eyebrows at him in the mirror.

'You're lucky I haven't asked you to take off your T-shirt.'

She really couldn't gauge him at all. 'Do you want me to?'

'You don't have to.'

But she did, before undoing her jeans. 'Is that better?'

'That's fine. But you really didn't have to.'

He moved closer to her and laid a coarse hand on one hip. Then the other hand settled on the other hip. She felt radiated heat on her naked back.

When he manipulated her, the conversation dried up. She let his hands guide her, let him turn her, position her, let him use his weight against her. His fingertips seemed to carry an electrical charge.

Any moment now ...

There was no reason for it. It was just a feeling. An assumption. That whatever was happening was mutual. One part of her felt wonderfully relaxed while another part burned in anticipation. But of what, exactly? She closed her eyes and waited. For a kiss, perhaps. Or for a moment when his fingers deviated from the professional to the personal.

Instead, his hands left her body. 'That's it. You're done.'

She opened her eyes. 'What?'

'You've been manipulated.'

Said with a grin. Stephanie wanted to be annoyed, but wasn't. 'Well ... thank you, anyway. Do I owe you something?'

He shook his head. 'There's no charge.'

'I wouldn't say that.'

He smiled, a little embarrassed, it seemed. 'I'll be going.'

'Why?'

'I'm sorry?'

'Stay.'

Mark said nothing.

'Stay.'

The smile had gone. 'Are you sure?'

'I'm sure.'

'What time is it?'

'Why?'

'I just want to know the time.'

Stephanie looked at her watch. 'It's eight minutes past six.'

The first time they made love it was as though the manipulation had never stopped. More than anything, it was his hands that made love to her. Stephanie was almost entirely passive. There were moments when she didn't feel she had a choice.

Two-thirty in the morning. Stephanie ran her fingers over the scars on his back. With scars of her own and a library of scars inflicted upon others, she had to ask.

'It was eleven years ago on Nanga Parbat, coming down the Diamir Face. With hindsight, we shouldn't have been there at all. It was a bad team, no cohesion, no leadership. But, being arrogant, we went up anyway. During the descent there was an avalanche. Afterwards we were all over the place. Two of our group died. I would have died too, but I was lucky. Dom stayed with me. He kept me from freezing to death. As for Keller, our team leader, he was close to us but never tried to reach us. He didn't even attempt to communicate with us. We watched him disappear.'

'He died?'

'We assume so. His body was never recovered.'

'And you?'

'Again, in a strange way, I was lucky. Broken ribs, crushed discs, two hairline fractures, muscle separation, some nerve damage, but no permanent spinal damage.'

'That's a painful kind of luck.'

'It led me to my career.'

'I'm not sure I'd have reacted to a back injury in the same way.'

'A lot of people say that. For me, I think becoming a chiropractor was a Pauline conversion. It's what I'm supposed to do.'

'And climbing again – how hard was that?'

'It was gradual, rather than hard. I didn't think about it for three years. Now it's not an issue. The only thing that's changed is my ambition. Before the accident I had a hit list of climbs and peaks. These days those things don't matter to me.'

By the time they fell asleep daylight was seeping through the curtains. When Stephanie opened her eyes Mark was no longer in bed. He was on the far side of the room, almost dressed.

36

'Where are you going?'

'Back to where I came from.'

'Where's that?'

He shrugged. 'You tell me. You're the only one who knows.'

Which was true. Although it took her a while to realize it. By then, he'd gone. She'd chosen him, not the other way round. He'd understood that and had accepted it. Had been *happy* to accept it. She found him after lunch, on the observation deck again, reading his paperback, cloned from the day before.

'Is that it?'

He put down the book. 'Wasn't it what you wanted?'

'What did *you* want?'

'I thought we understood each other.'

'After one night?'

'I thought we understood each other yesterday afternoon.'

He was right. 'We did. But that was then. What about today?'

'Today?'

'Yes. And tomorrow.'

Now, standing on Mark's roof, rather than some remote roof of the world, it was hard to believe a year had passed. As far as Mark was concerned she was still Stephanie Schneider, a lie so slender she could sometimes convince herself it wasn't a lie at all; Schneider had been her mother's maiden name. Instead, she had been born Stephanie Patrick. But in a windswept cemetery at Falstone, Northumberland, there was a gravestone bearing her name, date of birth and date of death. Her stone was the last in a row of five that included her parents, Andrew and Monica Patrick, her sister, Sarah, and her younger brother, David. They'd all died together, but there was nothing of them in the cold ground. Their vaporized remains had drifted towards the bottom of the north Atlantic with the incinerated wreckage of the 747 they'd been in. Christopher, the eldest child, was still alive, still living in Northumberland, a wife and family to care for. The last time Stephanie had seen him had been at her own funeral. Through a pair of binoculars she'd watched him cry for her – for the last of his family – and had found that she'd been unable to cry herself.

Her coffee finished, she climbed down the stepladder and went into the bedroom. Mark was stirring. He looked a little groggy. She put the empty mug on a bookshelf and began to undress. He propped himself up on one elbow to watch the performance. And she watched him as she pulled the T-shirt over her head.

'God, Stephanie, what happened to …?'

'Don't ask. Not yet.'

London might have been fifteen centigrade cooler than Marrakech but the climate was far less agreeable with reeking humidity trapped beneath a hazy brown sky. Stephanie reached the corner of Robert Street and Adelphi Terrace, overlooking Victoria Embankment Gardens which, itself, overlooked the Thames. A pair of barges crawled upstream, overtaking the tourist coaches congesting the Embankment.

The brass plaque beside the front door was original: L.L.Herring & Sons, Ltd, Numismatists, Since 1789. The firm still occupied a small part of the building. The other companies fell under the umbrella of Magenta House. An organization without designation, it had no official title and was not registered anywhere. There was no secret code of reference for it. It formed no part of MI5 or SIS, or any of the other security services. Magenta House was the name of the dilapidated office block on the Edgware Road that the organization had first occupied. Subsequently the building had been demolished to make way for a hotel.

Existing beyond existence itself, Magenta House was not constrained by law, by the fluctuating fashions of politics or by scrutiny from the media. It was established as a direct consequence of increased transparency in the intelligence services. Its creators regarded accountability as an alarming intrusion by an ignorant public whose right to know needed to be restricted to information they could digest. They felt that politicians, in thrall to the short term, should be bypassed. They believed there were areas of national security too vital to disseminate, and they knew, with evangelical certainty, that there were some threats that could not be countered by legal means. Stephanie had no idea who these creators were, but they had invested control of the organization in one man: Alexander. If he had a first name, Stephanie had yet to meet anyone who knew it.

She pushed the second button on the intercom, which was marked Adelphi Travel. The lens on the overhead camera turned before she heard the click of the lock. She pushed open the door and entered a parallel world. In the aftermath of 11 September 2001 Magenta House's area of responsibility had been expanded. So had its budget, which was bled from the military. Some of the changes were macro, some micro; the new smoke detectors, for instance, were a precaution with a difference. They functioned conventionally but were also capable of delivering an anaesthetic gas to counter hostile intrusion.

Soft pools of muted light fell onto the reception area: two sofas, two armchairs, newspapers and magazines in half a dozen languages spread across a coffee table, fresh flowers in a china vase on an antique sideboard. The paintings were nineteenth-century landscapes, oil on canvas, each individually lit. Even the receptionist had been overhauled: gone was the weary middle-aged chain-smoker of years gone by, replaced by a younger model with good cheekbones, a chic grey suit and cold zeal for eyes.

Stephanie said, 'Which room are we in?'

'Mr Alexander wants to see you before you go down.'

Alexander's large, rectangular office overlooked Victoria Embankment Gardens. In the winter he had a view of the river and the south bank. Now all he could look onto was the lush foliage of the trees in the garden.

The room was persistently old-fashioned: parquet floor, Persian carpets, a Chesterfield sofa, wooden shelves groaning beneath the weight of leather-bound books. At the centre of this office stood Alexander, in a navy chalk-stripe suit, a pair of black Church's shoes, a white shirt with a double-cuff secured by gold cufflinks, a silk tie. Which, appropriately, was magenta. When Mark wore a suit, Stephanie saw an animal trapped in a cage. Alexander, by contrast, wore a suit as naturally as skin. And in this environment he looked at home. But it was an environment that belonged to another era.

'I wanted to see you alone before we meet the others for the debriefing.' He was standing by the window, smoking a Rothmans, his back to her. The windows were open, rendering recently installed mortar-proof glass redundant. 'Were you injured?'

Not the first question she would have expected. It almost sounded like concern. Which made her suspicious. 'Nothing serious.'

'What went wrong?'

'They knew. *He* knew.'

'Mostovoi?'

'Yes.'

'But he saw you.'

'I know. When he agreed to see me, he must have thought the deal was valid. Or, at least, potentially valid. In the end, though, the deal was too big. It wasn't realistic. Not for Petra.'

'That was the point. He'd been invisible for a year. It needed to be something extraordinary to draw him out. To be honest, I was beginning to wonder whether he was still alive.'

'Well, now you know. Was and still is.'

'How close did you get?'

'Closer than I am to you.'

He turned round. 'You were in the same room as him?'

'Yes.'

'Face to face?'

'Yes.'

'And you didn't manage an attempt of any sort?'

Stephanie resented his tone. 'Actually, I did. After I'd handled his protection.'

41

'What happened?'

'The gun jammed.'

'You *fired* at him?'

'I tried to.'

'Then what?'

'There wasn't time for anything else. I had to exit immediately.'

Alexander shook his head in disbelief, then sat down at his desk. 'How can you be so sure about Mostovoi?'

'They had me tagged from the start. The day before yesterday they went through my hotel room while I was out and ...'

'How do you know?'

'It was witnessed.'

'By?'

'Independent cover.'

'Presumably you didn't go back there.'

'I didn't need to. I'd already established a second identity.'

Alexander frowned. 'Was that sanctioned?'

'Under the circumstances I thought it better to act on instinct.'

'You're supposed to respond to instruction, not instinct.' He took a final drag from his cigarette, then ground the butt into an onyx ashtray. 'Let me guess. The independent cover and second identity were provided by Stern.'

Stern, the information broker, the ghost in the machine. His business was conducted over the internet. Nobody knew his – or her – identity, but Stephanie had used him since her days as an independent and he'd never let her down. Nor she him. In Stern's virtual world, information was both product and currency. Sometimes, as Petra, Stephanie had bought information with information. Alexander hated the idea of Stern because he was beyond Magenta House's control and because his electronic existence allowed Stephanie a form of freedom.

'As fond as you are of Stern, has it ever occurred to you that he might not be reliable?'

'Compared to?'

He stiffened, then tried to shrug it off – a pointless victory, perhaps, but sweet nonetheless – before changing tack. 'You didn't go home last night.'

'That's not home. It's a film set.'

'Did you go straight to his place after you left the courier?'

'None of your business.'

'If it concerns your professionalism, then it's my business.'

'We made a deal after New York. I gave you my word. Since then I've never given you any reason to worry.'

'Your private life is a worry.'

'Grow up.'

'One of us should, certainly. You don't just place yourself in jeopardy, Stephanie. You place everyone who comes into contact with you in jeopardy. That includes Hamilton.'

'Leave him out of it.'

'I'd love to. Really, I would. But your behaviour won't allow me to.'

'I've taken precautions.'

'Not good enough.'

'You have no idea whether they're good enough.'

43

'Perhaps,' he conceded. 'But what I do know is this: one slip is all it'll take.'

The first time I met Alexander he held the power of life and death over me. He saved me, then turned me into the woman I am today. Before him I was a drug-addict, a prostitute, a grim statistic waiting to happen. He could have hastened the predictable end. But he didn't. Instead he let his people loose on me. Now you can drop me anywhere in the world and, like a cockroach, I'll thrive, no matter how harsh the environment. I am any woman I need to be at any given moment, fluent in four foreign languages and able to scale a building like a spider. I can kill a man with a credit card ... and not by shopping. I'm more than a woman, I'm a machine, and the man who made it happen – Alexander – is the man I detest most in this world.

The feeling is mutual. He can't abide me, despite the fact that I am probably his greatest technical achievement and his single most potent asset. Like magnets, we repel but are also drawn together. The deal we made after New York ensured that. At the time I could have walked away from Magenta House. Nothing would have given me greater pleasure. But I chose not to.

His name was Konstantin Komarov, and I was completely in love with him. Even though I am now with Mark, there is a part of me that is lost to Kostya and always will be. A complicated man, certainly. A man with a past, most definitely. But where Magenta House saw a threat, I saw a future. Alexander had promised to set me free after New York and was true to his word. But Kostya was a Magenta House target. I pleaded with Alexander to let him live even though I knew it was pointless. In the end I had only one thing to offer him. So we struck a deal.

44

A truly Faustian pact it was, too. I returned to Magenta House and Alexander suspended the order on Komarov. As long as I remain here, he's alive. The moment I leave, he dies. It's hard to imagine anything more perverse: I kill people to keep alive the man I used to love.

I haven't seen him since we kissed goodbye at JFK in New York. That was the final condition that Alexander insisted upon: I could save him but I couldn't be with him. I've thought about this so many times since then and have always come to the same conclusion: there was no good reason for this condition. I believe Alexander imposed it upon me simply to prevent me from being happy. In that, at least, he's failed. Kostya is alive, somewhere out there, and I'm in love again.

Mark has no idea about any of this. He's in love with a woman named Stephanie Schneider, a freelance photo-journalist, who is secretive about her past and whose work takes her to some of the world's riskier regions.

When we were falling for each other, I had no idea how complicated this arrangement would become. When Alexander first discovered that I was seeing someone – as opposed to just having casual sex, which would have been fine – he was furious and ordered me to drop Mark.

'How do you know about this?' I'd countered.

His initial silence was confirmation of a suspicion that he tried to justify. 'Everyone here is subject to periodic security review. You know that.'

'Even you?'

'You can't play this game, Stephanie.'

'It's not a game.'

'All the more reason to call it off, then.'

'Forget it.'

Eventually Alexander relented, even though he was right. A relationship is completely incompatible with my profession.

To make it work I had to create an artificial environment for
it. At first I was complacent; a few lies here, a few half-truths
there, I thought. And since lying was never a problem for me,
I imagined it would be relatively simple.

Now I have two lives. I am Petra Reuter and I am
Stephanie Schneider, with Stephanie Patrick stranded in
limbo somewhere between them. I have my flat. This is the
only interface between the two versions of me. It's Stephanie's
flat – it contains all the paraphernalia of her life – but it's
where Petra goes to and from. I think of it as an airlock. There
are two environments, one on either side, and the airlock
allows me to acclimatize from one to the other.

My relationship with Alexander is a balancing act that is
constantly tested. Here was a battle he couldn't win, so, for the
sake of the war, he withdrew. He even contributed to the cover.
My assignments as a photo-journalist come through Frontier
News, an agency that specializes in sending freelancers to the
kind of trouble-spots where no one offers you insurance. The
company was established ten years ago by three former sol-
diers. Two of them are dead; the first was beheaded by Tamil
Tigers in Sri Lanka, the second was shot by Chechen rebels in
Georgia. Alexander knew the third and put me in touch.
Which is not to say he's happy about it. He's like a father who
hands his daughter a pack of condoms because the idea of her
repellent boyfriend getting her pregnant is even more revolting
to him than the idea of them having sex.

I know it's crazy to see Mark, but Alexander should con-
sider the alternative. Mark gives me stability. Through him
I've made friends; normal people living normal lives coloured
by normal concerns. They have become an emotional cushion
that makes it easier for me to continue to do what I do for
Alexander at Magenta House.

Last night, after too many drinks at the Cunninghams'

house in Clapham, we played the Kevin Bacon game. This is a movie version of the Six Degrees of Separation theory, which suggests you can connect any two people in the world in six moves. It occurs to me that there could easily be a Stephanie Patrick game. I can play Six Degrees of Separation without ever having to leave my own skin.

After a four-hour debriefing Stephanie went to her own flat, a third-floor walk-up on Maclise Road with a view of the rear of the Olympia exhibition centre. There was mail on the floor, dust in the air, nothing in the fridge. She opened several windows but there was no breeze to counter the humid heat. Then she checked the sensors: two micro-cameras, one in the living room, one in the bedroom, connected to an exterior base-unit that sent a coded message to her desktop. The cameras were activated by movement, the sensors detecting changes in air temperature and density. She'd bought the equipment from Ali Metin, a Turk who owned a computer shop on the Tottenham Court Road. According to her monitor, neither camera had been triggered. There were no images.

Later she took the dirty clothes from the leather holdall to the launderette next to the Coral betting shop on Blythe Road. Back at the flat she made green tea, put on a CD she'd borrowed from Mark – *Is This It?* by The Strokes – and sorted through her post. Circulars and bills, mostly. There were two statements: one from HSBC, the other from Visa, both in Stephanie Schneider's name. The current account showed two credits from Frontier News for stories filed during the previous three months. The savings account held just less than fifteen thousand pounds. In a box-file beside her desktop computer, there were receipts for hotels she'd never visited, flights she'd never caught.

The flat was run down: a bucket beneath the sink in the bathroom because the pipes leaked, patches of damp on the kitchen ceiling, rotten window-frames. Stephanie never attempted to address these problems. On the contrary. She left dirty plates in the sink, unironed clothes on her bed, used clothes on the floor. There were papers across the table in the living room, books on the carpet, camera equipment in the kitchen.

By inclination, Stephanie was organized and tidy. Stephanie Schneider, however, was by her own admission a 'domestic slut', which had the intended benefit of discouraging Mark from spending time at her flat. As the portal connecting her two worlds, it was the one place where she felt uneasy with him. Consequently they spent all their time at his flat. Occasionally this was an issue he attempted to address by suggesting she move into Queen's Gate Mews.

'It's not that I don't want to live with you, Mark. It's just that I don't want to give up my own place.'

'But we don't spend any time over there. It doesn't make sense.'

'It doesn't make *financial* sense. But it makes a different kind of sense. Besides, what about all my stuff? You've hardly got enough space for your stuff.'

'We could convert the garage downstairs.'

'It's full.'

'Only of old climbing gear. I could put that into storage. Or sell it. Or throw it out. Then you could have an office. Or we could sell both flats and get somewhere bigger.'

Which was exactly what one half of her wanted.

But the other half wouldn't permit it. Not yet. Conversations like this offered Stephanie glimpses of a possible post-Petra world, and she'd found them far more seductive than she'd ever imagined.

The evening made way for night. They drank wine and watched a DVD, content not to speak. Later, a little drunk, they made love. Afterwards, damp with perspiration, Mark found the cut on the top of her head.

'Is it sore?'

'A little.'

He ran a finger over her bruised ribs, and along parallel grazes over her right shoulder. 'Do you want to tell me?'

'We went off the road. Coming back from the Fergana Valley.'

It was impossible to tell what he was thinking. 'Anyone else hurt?'

'The driver cut his head quite badly. I had to drive the rest of the way. I think he must have fallen asleep. It was about three in the morning.'

As slick as glycerine. Even now Petra could still surprise Stephanie. She watched Mark get up. He had a climber's physique. There was no bulk to his strength; his power lay in sinews and suppleness. Naked, he disappeared into the kitchen. He walked as he climbed, moving like liquid, his feet sometimes seeming barely to touch the ground. A smaller man, Komarov's physique had been equally lean but his had been fashioned by the years lost to the brutal prisons of the Russian Far East.

After Komarov there had been other men before Mark, but no relationships. She'd used them to scour herself. It wasn't making love, it was barely sex. It was just fucking, as emotionally charged as an hour on a treadmill: aerobic, sweaty, occasionally sore, with only a dull muscular ache for a memory. Mark was supposed to have been the same, the next anonymous man in the queue. When she realized she was falling for him she'd actually resented him for the way he made her feel. She'd never wanted a relationship to replace Komarov. She'd wanted him to be her last.

She could have stopped it, she told herself. But she hadn't. Lately she'd come to believe that was because she couldn't.

Mark returned from the kitchen. He was carrying a small box wrapped in silver paper. He handed it to her.

She said, 'I didn't get you anything. I wasn't sure you'd remember.'

Inside, there was an antique watch with a chain. She picked it up. Gold, to judge by the weight. There was a crack across the glass.

Mark said, 'It doesn't work. And never will.'

Stephanie wasn't sure how to react. 'It's lovely, though.'

'The hands are frozen. That is the only time it will ever tell.'

Eight minutes past six. As it had been the first time they kissed.

One year to the day.

Frontier News shared a building on Charlotte Street with KKZ, a graphic design agency. KKZ's offices were graphite and glass, central air-conditioning and espresso machines. Employees worked at the latest Apple Mac flat screens on ergonomically designed

50

chairs from Norway. Frontier News's office was an attic with three fans, a leaking roof and second-hand furniture bought at a government auction from a bankrupt insurance company.

Gavin Taylor was on the phone, bare feet on the desk, his tilting chair at a precarious angle. He waved Stephanie into the office. Open-plan was how he described it. In other words, he couldn't afford partitions.

Taylor's assistant, Melanie, was at her desk, talking to a broad-shouldered red-headed man as she examined a chipped fuchsia fingernail. A lit Lambert & Butler was going in a green glass ashtray stolen from a pub. The heat hadn't prevented her from applying her customary mask of make-up. 'Hiya, Steph.'

The man turned around and Stephanie recognized him. David Craig, a Frontier News regular, for whom no assignment was too hazardous.

'Haven't seen you for a while. Been away?'

'Uzbekistan.'

Craig raised an eyebrow. 'And how is the brother Karimov these days?'

Since the collapse of the Soviet Union in 1991 Uzbekistan had been a *de facto* dictatorship under the rule of Islam Karimov, a man who once claimed that he would personally rip off the heads of two hundred people to protect his country's freedom and stability.

'It's business as usual in Tashkent.'

'And outside Tashkent?'

She faked innocence. 'How would I know?'

'All room service at the Holiday Inn, was it?'

Taylor finished his call and wiped sweat from his forehead. 'Give her a break. At least she comes back

51

with the goods.' Turning to Stephanie, he said, 'Last time out, David came back empty-handed from Pakistan. Made it across the border with nothing more than the clothes he was standing in.'

Stephanie knew the bitterness in Taylor's voice was genuine. Craig was a reckless glory-hunter, a minor public-school product whose lacklustre army career had left him lusting for some kind of heroic validation. In Taylor's view, the actions of adrenaline junkies like Craig demeaned the lives of men like Andrew Duggdale and James Hunter, co-founders of Frontier News. There were photographs of each dead man on the far wall.

Taylor stepped into a pair of worn docksiders and took her to lunch at an Italian bistro on Charlotte Street. By the time they were inside, sweat had stuck moist patches of his frayed cornflower blue shirt to his shoulders and belly. They settled into a gloomy corner at the rear, beneath a noisy fan. Taylor struggled to light a cigarette, then ordered a bottle of Valpolicella.

'How's business?'

He shrugged. 'The ponces downstairs don't want us sharing a communal entrance any more. They even offered to pay for one of our own.'

'That sounds okay.'

'Bloody pony-tails and polo-necks.'

'Let me guess. Articulate to the last, you invited them to reconsider.'

He grinned, smoke leaking from his teeth. As far as Stephanie knew, Gavin Taylor was the only person outside Magenta House who knew what she was. Overweight, profane, a heavy drinker it was hard to see what Alexander saw in Taylor. The only thing they had in common was a taste for Rothmans cigarettes. Taylor's past was in the military and Stephanie had always assumed that Alexander's was too but she didn't know that for certain.

'I'll put your Uzbekistan stuff out to tender. We might get a nibble. If not, I'll give it a week or two before I get him to send the cheque. It'll be the usual amount, I expect, five to seven. It'll take about a week to rinse it through our books. Is that okay?'

'That's fine.'

Stephanie pushed the bulging manila envelope across the table. Inside were the Uzbek photographs and files that she had received from her Magenta House courier at Heathrow.

'I heard Marrakech wasn't all it was cracked up to be.'

'Alexander told you?'

He nodded, then contemplated the tip of his cigarette. 'I met Mostovoi a couple of times.'

'Really?'

'In Berlin, then Dortmund. I was with John Flynn.'

The name rang a bell but the chime was distant. 'Remind me ...'

'Sentinel Security.'

An arms-dealing firm. With that, a face returned to the name. 'He had to leave the country, didn't he?'

'That's right. Lives in Switzerland now. But Sentinel's still going. Doing well, too. Anyway, we were in Berlin. It was before I started Frontier News. John was putting a deal together with some Russians. Mostovoi was the broker. We met a couple of times. Nothing came of it in the end.'

'What was he like?'

'Mostovoi? Nice bloke. Good company, especially after a drink. Mind you, even I'm good company after a drink.'

'Is that what you've been told?'

'Oh, very funny.'

'What else?'

'Nothing much, really. To be honest, I was too busy eyeing his girlfriend. Russian, I think she was. An absolute cracker. Hard as nails, mind, but a real eyeful. Can't remember her name. Still, no matter. I can remember all her important bits.'

'Have you ever considered joining the twenty-first century, Gavin?'

He slid the cigarette back between his lips. 'Now why would I want to do that?'

Maclise Road, four in the afternoon. Stephanie let herself in, dumped two bags of shopping on the kitchen table and checked the answer-machine for messages. Nothing.

'Hey ...'

Rosie Chaudhuri was standing in the living room. Magenta House's rising star and the only female kindred spirit Stephanie had encountered in Petra's world.

'Christ! Don't do that!'

'Sorry.'

'You'll give me a heart attack.'

She smiled apologetically. 'Yes, that would be inconvenient.'

'What are you doing here?'

'I didn't want to give you the opportunity to put the phone down on me.'

'Why would I?'

'We need to talk.'

'About?'

'Marrakech. Mostovoi.'

'How did you get in here?'

Rosie went into the living room, reached into her bag and produced a key, which she offered to Stephanie. It looked familiar. She checked the kitchen drawer where she kept the only spare. Which was still there.

Rosie said, 'When you first started seeing Mark, Alexander had this copy made. He used to have the place swept once a week.'

'*What?*'

'Until I found out about it and insisted that he put a stop to it.'

Stephanie's own security had only been in place six months. At the time she'd wondered whether she was being paranoid.

'I don't believe it.'

Rosie smiled. 'Come on. What don't you believe?'

A fair point.

'What was he looking for?'

'Anything, I guess.' Stephanie gave Rosie a look. 'I promise you, I don't know.' She handed over the key. 'Anyway, here it is.'

The peace offering. Offered in advance of whatever was coming. Stephanie made green tea as Rosie leaned against the sink, her arms folded. She was in a sleeveless chocolate linen dress that she would never have worn when they'd first met. She wouldn't have had the confidence. The change in shape was pronounced: the curves a little sleeker, breasts merely large rather than huge, legs and arms toned, stomach flat, one chin,

55

not several. Her skin was clear and her hair, now short, framed her face rather than concealing it.

When the tea was ready they went into the living room. Stephanie sat cross-legged on the carpet, in a gentle draught between the door and window. 'So, what's on your mind?'

'Mostovoi. Alexander asked me to come over and run through a couple of things. For clarification.'

'Go on.'

'You were in the room with him. You had a gun. He survived.'

'I thought I'd made it clear at the debriefing. The gun jammed.'

'At that point the two bodyguards were incapacitated?'

'Pretty much.'

'And Mostovoi was doing what?'

'Nothing. He was sitting there, scared stiff.'

'What about the spike?'

'I used it on the trader.'

'Couldn't you have used it on Mostovoi?'

'What's going on, Rosie?'

Alexander needed to be sure. That's what she said. Except Stephanie could see that wasn't it. There was a subtext. With each question, Stephanie grew more evasive, the truth no longer a comfort.

When Rosie had finished, Stephanie said, 'What now?'

'Nothing.'

'Nothing?'

'Take some time off. Go on holiday.'

'Am I okay?'

'You're fine.'

But Stephanie's antennae were still twitching. 'Rosie, if there was something serious you'd tell me, wouldn't you?'

'Don't worry about it.'

'Wouldn't you?'

'It's nothing like that, Steph.'

'You know as well as I do, you're the only one I trust.'

Rosie smiled. 'I know.'

2

Summer drifted by, long, hot, empty. And, eventually, lovely. Once I'd learnt to relax. It wasn't easy. The doubt persisted. Was I under review? That was the word they generally used instead of 'suspicion'. If I found myself on the outside, what would that mean? There'd be no pension or gratitude, that was for sure. I told myself I was being paranoid. But that didn't mean I was wrong.

However, as the weeks passed, that anxiety receded and I fell into a lazy routine. Late starts, a visit to the gym to maintain fitness, afternoons free, evenings and nights with Mark. For two months I was happy. It was carefree and uncomplicated. The days merged, the weeks lost their shape. I raced through half a dozen paperbacks a week. I went to the cinema in the afternoons. Or slept. Or lay on the grass in Kensington Gardens, listening to Garbage on my Walkman, the volume turned up. When Mark got back from his practice in Cadogan Gardens we'd have a drink on the roof terrace, or make love, or take a bath together. We went out, we had people over. We were a couple.

In late August we went to Malta for ten days. We stayed in a cheap hotel and did nothing, apart from a trip to Gozo and Comino. We sat in the sun and swam in the sea, we read, ate out, drank cheap red wine, went to bed early and got up late.

The day after our return to London I realized I'd missed my period. I didn't tell Mark. I didn't take the test, either. Not straight away. I wanted to sort out my head first. If it was pos-

*itive, what would that mean? Alexander would assume I'd
done it deliberately. But what would he do about it? The
prospect of telling him had a lighter side – Does Magenta
House have an active maternity leave policy? When I come
back as a working mum, will the hours be flexible? – but the
reality was more chilling. Most likely he'd prescribe an abor-
tion and try to find some way to force me to accept it. Which I
never would. That much I knew.*

By the time I took the test I wanted it to be positive.

It was negative.

*I decided not to tell anyone. What was there to say? Guess
what – I'm not pregnant? Mark noticed a change. I said I was
feeling down but it was nothing to worry about. Two days
later I was with Karen. After a sweltering hour in John Lewis
on Oxford Street, we were having a cup of coffee at a nearby
café, sitting at a table on the pavement, just in the shade,
shopping bags at our feet. We were having a good time when,
out of the blue, Karen asked me if everything was all right.*

'I'm fine. Why?'

*She looked at me, suddenly serious. 'I don't know. I just
felt … something.'*

'What?'

'Nothing. Forget it.'

*Which was when it hit me. A pain in my chest that began
to spread.*

*She seemed to sense it. She put her hand on my arm.
'Stephanie?'*

When I looked at her, she was blurred.

'What is it?'

*I told her. When I'd finished she hugged me, kissed me on
both cheeks and wiped away the wetness from my eyes with
her handkerchief.*

'I'm sorry.'

I tried to laugh it off. 'Don't be. It's ridiculous. I don't know what I was thinking. I mean …'

'Stephanie.'

I sniffed loudly. 'What?'

'You're not fooling me. Does Mark know?'

'No.'

'Are you going to tell him?'

I bit my lip. 'Not yet.'

'Later?'

'Maybe. I don't know.'

The following week Magenta House called. Summer was over.

The subterranean conference room was deliciously cool. Dressed in a maroon T-shirt, black linen trousers and trainers, Stephanie felt goose-bumps on her arms. She sat at the most distant point of the oval table to Alexander.

'Let's talk about Lars Andersen. Remind me what he said to you.'

He opened the folder in front of him and began to scan printed pages. She wondered whether it was her debriefing transcript. Such transcripts had short lives. When Magenta House signed off on a contract, all trace of it was erased. That was the nature of the organization: to kill you, then once you were gone to deny you'd ever existed.

'Any part in particular?'

'The Russian conversation you had with Andersen and the man you later shot through the knee … what was his name?'

'Jarni. I'm not sure there's much I can add to what I've already said.'

'This reference to Inter Milan, could you tell me something about that?'

'Like what?'

'The tone of the reference, maybe?'

'It was just banter, I think. At least, it was until they found out I understood Russian. Even then the atmosphere was relaxed.'

'Russian speakers but not Russian ...'

'My Russian was better than theirs.'

'And you told them you hadn't heard of Inter Milan.'

'As I understand it, Inter Milan is an Italian football club. What does this have to do with Mostovoi?'

Alexander slid a selection of photographs down the table to Stephanie. There were a dozen, five in black-and-white, none of great quality. She flicked through and saw versions of a younger Lars Andersen: climbing out of a Mercedes with Dutch plates, wearing a leather jacket, faded jeans and trainers; exiting a glass office-block in a suit that was too tight; hunched over a plate in a crowded pizzeria, the photo taken through the window. In three shots his hair was collar-length, in the rest it was shorter. She stopped at the final photograph. He was standing in front of a dark forest in dirty camouflage combats, heavy boots caked in mud, webbing, with an AK-47 in his right hand. His scalp had been shaved more recently than his jaw; he was grinning through a week of stubble. The grain and crop of the image suggested it had once formed part of a larger picture. The irony was not lost on Stephanie.

Alexander said, 'Ever heard of a man named Milan Savic?'

'No.'

'You're looking at him. He was a Serb. During the Balkans conflict he was a paramilitary warlord. Before that he was a gangster, a black-marketeer in Belgrade.'

'You said Savic "was" a Serb.'

'Correct. He was shot dead by the Kosovo Liberation Army during an ambush outside Pristina on 13 February 1999. Three other members of his paramilitary unit were killed. The deaths were confirmed by two UNHCR representatives on a fact-finding mission to Kosovo. Before Kosovo, Savic and his paramilitaries were active in Croatia and Bosnia. Which means he was involved at the start and nearly made it to the end. That's almost a decade. This photo was taken in woods not far from Banja Luka.'

'How does Lars Andersen fit into this?'

'Rumours have persisted suggesting Savic is still alive. We know that Lars Andersen is one of the aliases Savic is supposed to have used since 1999.'

'And Inter Milan?'

'It's the nickname for the paramilitary unit he ran. The true title of Inter Milan – the Italian football club – is actually Internazionale. Savic's paramilitary unit had an unusually high number of non-Serbs in it. He actively recruited foreigners – mercenaries, mostly – hence the name. Internationals became Inter Milan, Milan Savic's private armed militia. They even took to wearing the club colours, black and blue.'

Stephanie re-examined the photograph from the woods. Wrapped around Savic's throat and tucked into the top of his camouflage jacket was a black and blue football scarf.

'Savic was a real bastard. Not that he was alone in

that. There were plenty of others. Some of them have been indicted by the International War Crimes Tribunal in The Hague while others haven't and never will be. Some died, some disappeared. At the time, Savic's death was greeted with relief not only because of what he did but because of what he knew.'

'Like what?'

'In this matter, the International War Crimes Tribunal operates two types of indictment: the declared indictment, like those issued against Slobodan Milosevic or Radovan Karadzic, and the "sealed" or "secret" indictment, like the one used to bring General Momir Talic to justice. But there's also a third list. Completely unofficial, it contains names of those war criminals who can never be permitted to see the inside of a courtroom. It's not a long list, but Savic's name is on it.'

Stephanie understood the nature of such lists. 'I can see where this is heading. It sounds like a face-saving exercise.'

'It doesn't really matter what you think.'

He pressed a button on the console in front of him. The overhead lights dimmed and the wall-screen to her left flickered to life.

Alexander said, 'Our arrangement has always been a hideous thing, I'm sure you'll agree. Then again, we're hideous people. Ever since New York, you and I have coexisted under the terms of an uneasy truce. As you know, the contract on Komarov was never rescinded. It was merely suspended. Consequently, we left our file on him open, amending it from time to time, when S3 came into possession of relevant material. Such as this ...'

An unfamiliar black-and-white face formed on the

wall: puffy cheeks, clipped hair, a neat goatee beard, rectangular glasses.

'This is David Pearson. One of ours, Section 5, Support. In January, under S3 guidance, he went to Turkmenistan to make preparations for an Ether Division contract on Yuri Paskin, a Russian smuggler whose network is particularly strong through Central Asia. For the right fee Paskin will transport anything. Guns, drugs, prostitutes. Or Islamic terrorists. Out of Afghanistan, for instance. Which was what brought him to our attention and earned him a well-deserved contract. Based in Ashgabat, he runs a network that stretches in the east from Pakistan, Tajikistan and Kyrgyzstan to the western shore of the Caspian Sea. And from Iran and Afghanistan in the south, up through Turkmenistan, Uzbekistan and Kazakhstan into Russia in the north. In the international scheme of things Paskin's a nobody. Regionally he's a giant. Which was why I took the decision to retire him discreetly, rather than the blunter approach.'

'You mean, someone like me.'

'Precisely. Anyway, Pearson went to Ashgabat. Paskin's a heavy smoker and drinker – not to mention casual cocaine user – so we'd decided an induced heart attack would be best. Nobody who knew him would have been surprised. We had an Ether Division unit standing by in Baku, ready to cross the Caspian. But at the last minute Paskin was tipped off. He fled to Irkutsk, and Pearson was shot twice in the head in his room at the Hotel Oktyabrskaya. That crucial piece of information came from Komarov.'

Don't say a word. Not now.

Alexander looked strangely weary, almost resigned.

'I'll be frank with you, Stephanie: in the past I've activated contracts for less, and I make no apology for it.
My choices are based on hard, factual analysis. It can't
be any other way. Which is why Komarov should be
dead. Twice, in fact. Once in New York, and once for
Pearson.'

'Killing him for Pearson would be revenge. That's
emotional.'

'Not true. Revenge is an instrument. It sends a message: kill one of ours and we'll kill one of yours. Take
my word for it, as a policy it works.'

She opened her mouth to speak but he raised his
hand to silence her. In the past she would have ignored
such a gesture. But not now.

Alexander said, 'I'm considering closing the file on
Komarov.'

For a moment, she didn't understand. *Closing the file*
– it sounded terminal. But it wasn't. On the contrary.
Like a Caesar, Alexander was granting life. Gradually
Stephanie realized what was happening. His tone made
sense, the anecdote made sense: it was the carrot and
the stick. And so far it had all been carrot.

She chose to probe a little. 'If that's true, there's no
reason for me to stay. Not under the terms of our
agreement.'

'I said "considering". I didn't say it was done.'

A succession of images filled the screen. Komarov
was coming out of the Turkmenistan Ministry of
Foreign Affairs on Magtumguly Prospekt. The date, 5
January, the time, 17:43. Next he was with a shorter
man. They were only visible from the shoulders up,
their bodies blocked by a black Mercedes. The caption
read: *Y. Paskin and K. Komarov outside Ak-Altyn Plaza*

Hotel, 7 January, 19:57. There were two more shots of Komarov in Ashgabat, one walking past the Azadi mosque, the other getting out of a dusty Toyota outside the Russian Embassy on Saparamurat Turkmenbashi Prospekt. The final image of the sequence saw both men either side of a stunning blonde in a sable coat. *K. Komarov, L. Ivanova and Y. Paskin, leaving the Lancaster hotel, rue de Berri, Paris, 19 March, 17:08.*

'Technically you're right, of course,' Alexander was saying. 'Without the threat to Komarov, what's to keep you here?'

Mark filled her mind. 'I'm sure you could find something.'

'I'm sure I could. But I'm not inclined to. In fact, quite the opposite. I'm inclined to let you leave Magenta House.'

She wasn't sure she'd heard correctly. 'Leave?'

'That's right.'

There would be a condition. 'But?'

'But first, Savic.'

'That's it? Then I walk?'

'Yes.'

'And the threat to Komarov is lifted?'

'After Savic, yes.'

'What aren't you telling me?'

'I don't want you to kill Savic. I want you to get close to him.'

'Why?'

'Because of this.'

From his folder he took a crumpled piece of paper and pushed it across the table. Stephanie had to get up to retrieve it. She sat back down and smoothed the creases with her palm.

The paper had been torn from a notebook. Some of the blue ink had run. There were two dark splashes on the top left-hand corner. It was a list. There were nine names before the rip, which severed the tenth. Six of the names appeared to be from the Balkans. The other three were French, English and German.

'Recovered by Pearson three days before he died.'

'What is it?'

'Before his death in Kosovo, Savic was rumoured to be running an exit pipeline for war criminals. Four of the names on that list have International War Crimes Tribunal declared indictments against them, two have sealed indictments against them and the other two are on the third list. None of them have been seen since 1999.'

'Savic spirited them away?'

'It's possible. One thing's for certain: they're not on this list by coincidence.'

'What am I supposed to do?'

'Locate Savic and find out if this so-called pipeline ever really existed.'

'Savic is definitely alive, then?'

'Yes.'

'Where is he now?'

'The Far East. We're still collating. You'll be fully briefed when we're ready.'

'Why me?'

'Because you have a way in.'

'Marrakech?'

'Correct. You were looking for Mostovoi. They know each other. You can make that work to your advantage.'

Stephanie shook her head. 'This isn't what I do. You

know that. I'm S7, an in-and-out girl. This is something for S3.'

Section 3 was the intelligence section. Section 7 was Operations (Primary), one of two assassination sections. In total, Magenta House had ten sections, including Control, Archive, Resources, Support, Finance, Security (Internal), Security (External), Operations (Invisible).

'S3 is fully stretched supporting the Ether Division. Besides, this will require an external presence.'

'There must be somebody else.'

Still staring at her, Alexander said, 'I'm not asking you.'

The carrot and the stick – it didn't matter which Alexander used. In the end they came to the same thing. A choice with no alternatives.

I don't bother picking the fight. In the past I would have. And Alexander would have expected me to. But we're beyond that now. These days I know what I am and I don't bother to deny it. I've accepted myself. I'm a professional woman of twenty-nine, trying to balance my work with my private life. On the Underground, in the supermarket, at home or in the office, most of my concerns are the same as everyone else's. It's only the nature of my work that marks me out.

Upstairs, on the ground floor, I run into Rosie Chaudhuri. I haven't seen her since she came to Maclise Road after Marrakech. The fact that we're friends is strange because we're so different. She truly believes in Magenta House. She heads S10, Operations (Invisible), the newest section, which was established after the terrorist attacks of 11 September 2001. S10 leaves no traces. Its victims die from natural causes, or accidents, or they simply vanish, ensuring they don't become martyrs. Initially it only targeted Islamic extremists. Not a politically correct remit, to be sure, but then Magenta House has never been too concerned with political correctness. Now S10 targets anyone who merits their talents. Among Magenta House staff, S10 is always referred to as the Ether Division.

'Hey, Steph. I didn't know you were due in today.'

'Nor did I.'

'Something new?'

'He wants me to chase a ghost.'

'Savic?'

'You knew?'

'He mentioned it. I wasn't sure how far he'd take it.'

'Apparently your lot are soaking up everyone in S3.'

'You don't sound thrilled.'

'I feel like a three-star Michelin chef who's been asked to scrub dishes.'

We take the lift to the top floor to Rosie's new office with its view of the Adelphi Building. When I was first recruited Rosie was a member of the support staff with limited security clearance. It was her talent for analysis that won her promotion. With promotion came full clearance. I've never discovered Rosie's flaw, but I know there is one. Somewhere, lurking in a file, she has a weakness that's been documented. We all do. Magenta House insist upon it. Personally I have too many to count so it's never bothered me the way it bothers others. Rosie has never mentioned hers to me. It is, perhaps, the only taboo subject between us.

In her early thirties, Rosie could be the picture of a successful modern woman. Before she started up S10 she spent a spell in S7 with me. That was when she lost weight and toned up. Like me, she was reincarnated.

She moves behind her kidney-shaped desk and settles into

her Herman Miller chair. 'What kind of tea would you like?'

'Green, if you have it.'

She pushes a button on the phone base. 'Adam, two teas, when you're ready. One green, one lemon and ginger.'

'What do you know about Savic?'

'Not much. He hasn't strayed across my desk. But I've heard the rumours, naturally. There've been alleged sightings of him in Germany, Belgium and Holland. Some say he runs a chain of call-girls in Prague and Budapest.'

'How original.'

'Others say he's gun-running down to Maputo. Or was it Harare?'

'That sounds more like Mostovoi's line of work.'

'There have been reports of him in Pyongyang, Osaka and Shanghai.'

'How long can it be before he's spotted working with Elvis in a fish-and-chip shop in Scarborough? Anything concrete?'

'Not until you landed Lars Andersen. By the way, I'm sorry about S3. I'll get somebody to put some stuff together for you. Give me a couple of days.'

'Thanks.'

'How's Mark?'

'He's well. We're starting to plan a big climbing trip for next summer.'

'Where?'

'El Capitan.'

'Never heard of it.'

'It's in California. What about you? How was your date with that architect? You never said. Did he have any designs on you?'

Rosie winces. 'Oh Steph, that's really lame. Even for you.'

'Couldn't resist it.'

'Put it this way. He made me go halves at dinner and then

70

wanted to go the whole way afterwards.'

I laugh loudly. As gorgeous as she is, Rosie has little luck with men. I suspect it's because she intimidates most of them. She wants to be dazzled and so assumes they do too. If she was more like me she'd understand that most men don't want a competitor in a woman, or even an equal.

'Are you taking precautions?' she asks me.

'God, you sound like my mother.'

'You know what I mean.'

I tell her I am. The door opens and Adam, Rosie's assistant, enters the room carrying two steaming mugs. He's older than she is, in his mid-forties, perhaps. Stereotypically, it would be easy to imagine that he was Rosie's boss. But then there's nothing conventional here.

Rosie's parents are first-generation immigrants. Both are doctors, both still practising; her mother is a GP, her father is a chest specialist. They live in north London and have three other children, all boys. Two work in the City, one shoots commercials. None of them have any idea what she does. Like me, she lies. Like me, she's so good at it, it's as natural to her as telling the truth. They believe she's a security analyst at the Centre for Defence Studies at King's College, London. Elsewhere it might seem strange that a young second-generation Indian woman is heading an outfit like the Ether Division. But in our world it seems perfectly normal because we can be anybody we need to be at any given moment.

They drove south-west in Mark's fifteen-year-old slate grey Saab, reaching the Saracen Arms, a fifteenth-century manor house with a twenty-first-century interior.

Saturday was hot and still. They climbed at Uphill Quarry, a Site of Special Scientific Interest on account of its rare flora. A westerly crag set beneath a village church and a graveyard, Uphill's challenges were technical rather than strength-orientated. Mark climbed smoothly, but Stephanie felt heavy-limbed and was frustrated to be stumped by A Lesser Evil on the Great Yellow Wall. Mark completed The Jimi Hendrix Experience – the route had recently been bolted – and then both of them completed Graveyard Gate, the arête furthest to the right of the Pedestal Wall.

In the evening they soaked for an hour in the giant freestanding bath in their bathroom, then ordered room service. They ate looking out to sea, as the bloody sun set. They drank a bottle of Mercurey and Stephanie expected they would make love. Instead, somehow, they fell asleep without either of them noticing. When Stephanie awoke she was face down on the bed, cocooned in a white dressing-gown, Mark beside her, snoring and sunburnt.

Sunday was hotter but with a breeze. They drove to Brean Down, a limestone peninsula protruding into the Bristol Channel, not far from Uphill Quarry. Boulder Cove was a five-minute walk across the beach from the car park. They warmed up on Coral Sea and then proceeded up Achtung Torpedo, through the face's black bulge, before moving on to Chulilla, Casino Royale and Root of Inequity. Stephanie climbed effortlessly, the clumsiness of Saturday falling away from her as lightly as sweat. Mark finished with Anti-Missile Missile, a girdle traverse.

From Brean Down they drove straight back to London, simultaneously spent and energized. They were sitting in a traffic jam on the M4, not far from Heathrow, when Stephanie said, 'I might have a new job lined up.'

'Oh yeah?'

'It might be longer term than usual.'

'Longer than Uzbekistan?'

At three weeks, the journey from Ostend to Marrakech had been her longest contract since she'd started seeing Mark by more than a fortnight. Usually she was only away for two or three days. That made the deception a lot easier.

'Could be. I don't know yet.'

'Where?'

'I'm not sure.'

'You don't sound very happy about it.'

'Well, to be honest, I'm considering a change of career.'

He gave her a quick glance. 'Really?'

'After this job, yes. Maybe.'

'How long have you been thinking about this?'

'Not long. That's why I haven't mentioned it.'

'What will you do instead?'

Stephanie smiled. 'That's the good part. I have no idea.'

Magenta House was two different buildings that had been merged laterally. The building that overlooked Victoria Embankment Gardens had been erected by a wealthy sugar trader who had insisted on a large cellar. When Stephanie had first come to Magenta House the cellar had still housed wines, brandies, damp and dirt. It had been a smaller organization, then. No less venal, but more personal, it had been Alexander's private fief-dom. Now it was growing and Alexander was more of an anonymous corporate chairman, while the wines in the cellar had made way for an expanded intelligence section.

The staircase had been removed. Section 3 could only be accessed by a lift, which required security clearance on entry and exit. Rosie led her through the main cellar, which was now an open-plan department with state-of-the-art work stations for its permanent staff of five, and into a vaulted sub-cellar made of brick. The original wooden doors had been replaced by sliding glass.

Stephanie sat at a swivel chair in front of a keyboard and three flat screens. 'Have you seen any of this material?'

'Just the basics,' Rosie said. 'It's not pretty. I'll leave you to it.'

The door whispered shut and Stephanie was cocooned in soundproofed silence. She stroked the keyboard and the central screen came to life. She typed in her security code, MARKET-EAST-1-1-6-4-R-P, and the other two screens illuminated. The one on her right subdivided into thirty-six boxed images, the one to her left into sixteen boxes containing text headlines. She started with a general profile.

Milan Savic was an only child. His father, Borisav, left home when Milan was six. A year later his mother committed suicide. Thereafter he lived with his maternal grandparents in Belgrade. A teenage thug, then a black-marketeer, by 1989 Savic was well known to the police in the Yugoslav capital, not only for his criminal activity, but also for the generous bribes he paid to them.

After January 1989 there was a gap in the files. A two-year blackout. When it was over, early in 1991, Savic was running a paramilitary unit in Croatia. The file claimed that in conjunction with the SDB, the Serb secret police, Savic was instrumental in preparing Serb communities within Croatia for insurrection. These activities were coordinated by Colonel Ratko Mladic, commander of the Knin garrison. Despite this Savic remained under the direct control of Franko Simatovic, known to everyone as Frenki, and Radovan Stojicic, known as Badza, numbers two and three at the SDB.

Frenki and Badza – pronounced *Badger* – were familiar names to her. They'd both known Zeljko Raznatovic, also known as Arkan. As Petra, Stephanie had known Arkan too, if only for a moment. On 15 January 2000 both of them had been in the lobby of the Hotel Inter-Continental in Belgrade. So had Dragica Maric. But Stephanie had only discovered that later, inside the derelict Somerset Hotel on West 54th Street, New York. It had been raining, she remembered, the downpour drowning the sound of Manhattan's traffic. That was when Dragica Maric had told her that she was there too, watching, as Arkan walked towards Petra Reuter, unaware.

Arkan had founded the Serbian Volunteer Guard, later known as the Tigers, just as Savic had founded Inter Milan, his Internationals, a group of outsiders, hungry for violence and money. Between Arkan and Savic existed Frenki and Badza, on behalf of the SDB.

At first Savic worked in areas of the Krajina, stirring the ghosts of the Second World War, resurrecting the spectre of the dreaded fascist Ustashas. Arkan was doing similar work, as well as making arrangements to arm the local Serb population. Once the Serb Autonomous Region – the SAR – had been set up in the Krajina, Savic's unit was instrumental in purging it of non-Serbs. This formed a behavioural template that was to last for eight years. In Croatia and Bosnia, then Kosovo, villages were attacked, cattle slaughtered, crops burnt, houses looted, innocents brutalized, then murdered.

From the screen to her left she picked another title: Inter Milan. There were photographs and brief biographies. She scanned them.

Savic's right-hand man within Inter Milan was Vojislav Brankovic. His name was one of the nine on the list that Alexander had shown her. A native of the Krajina, Brankovic came from the small town of Titova Korenica, not far from the beautiful Plitvica National Park in Croatia. The son of a baker, he'd done military service with the JNA, the Yugoslav National Army, before returning home. In early 1991, when Savic went to the Krajina, Brankovic was apparently contented, working in the family business, living with his parents, surrounded by friends from childhood. His girlfriend, Maria, was a beautiful Croat whose parents lived in a house four doors away. The file did not disclose how Brankovic had been recruited by Savic. It only documented those activities accredited to him.

Brankovic was known as the Spoon because he wore a JNA army-issue canteen spoon on a chain around his neck for good luck. There was a picture to prove it, Brankovic in a tight-fitting olive T-shirt, the battered teaspoon worn like a set of dog-tags. He had a broad, agricultural face, a fuzz of fair hair, pale skin and a physique that radiated power through scale rather than menace. Here was a chopper of trees, Stephanie felt, rather than a baker of bread. Along with Savic, Brankovic had been one of those allegedly killed by the KLA outside Pristina on 13 February 1999.

She looked at some of the internationals. Barry Ferguson, British, from Gateshead, ex-SAS, ex-husband to a battered wife, ex-father of three, ex-inmate of Durham Prison. Troy Carter from Maine – unlike Ferguson, he'd never made the grade as a professional soldier. He'd gone to the Balkans to prove himself. And had failed again. Within a fortnight a landmine had scattered him over his colleagues. Fabrice Blanc, a native of Marseille, had deserted the French Foreign Legion specifically to go to the Balkans.

'I need to fight to live,' he'd claimed.

It was a phrase with resonance among the Inter Milan hard core. How did mild-mannered Vojislav Brankovic, the baker's son, become a vicious murderer? How did a boy with a beautiful Croat girlfriend end up stabbing other Croats in the face simply for being Croat? Stephanie knew part of the answer: in war, some men found themselves.

There was a picture of Harald Gross kicking a severed Bosniak head into a makeshift goal with spent shell cases for posts. In the background there were several blurred onlookers, their grins smudged. The rest of the mercenaries were European apart from a Canadian, two Australians and a South African. At any given moment the internationals accounted for between thirty and forty per cent of the Inter Milan force. Mercenaries they might have been, but one thing was clear: they were there for the fighting, not for the money.

On the screen to her right Stephanie touched a box with a woman's face. She came to life, her expression as harrowed in motion as it had been frozen. A box of text in the right-hand corner informed Stephanie that

77

the woman was from a small village close to Foca, in eastern Bosnia, a town that had been ethnically cleansed in 1992. Over her testimony, another woman translated into English.

'They came in the morning. They beat up anybody who got in their way. One of them shot a farmer in front of his wife and children. When the wife attacked the gunman, another one intervened and cut her throat. The children were hysterical. Their mother was in a pool of blood in the dirt. Other men took the children away. The leader told us we were to be transported to Foca, where we would join the people of the town, and then we would all leave the district together. They said we had one hour to make our preparations. We went home. An hour later we gathered in the market square. I had a bag, packed with ... I don't know what ... anything ... I couldn't think. My husband carried a sack with bread and clothes. Then there was a delay, a lot of confusion. They made us sit down in the square. It was very hot. We were there for some hours.'

Stephanie reckoned the woman was in her late forties. The interview was taking place in an institutional room: cream gloss walls, a smooth concrete floor with a single table at its centre. She was talking to another woman whose back was to camera. Stephanie paused the footage and checked the directory; the interview had been conducted in a Bologna police cell. When the action resumed, so did the clock in the bottom left-hand corner: 14.14 on 11 April 1997.

'They asked me what I did. I said I was a teacher. The one with no teeth told me to show him where the school was. He said they would need a place to keep us

78

for the night because we would not go to Foca until the next day. I got up from the ground to take him to the school. That was the last time I saw my husband alive. Four other men came with us. It was a small building with one large classroom and two small utility rooms. The man with no teeth told me to take off my clothes. I refused and one of the others hit me across the cheek with the butt of his rifle. Then they stripped me and raped me.'

The other woman asked a question that Stephanie couldn't hear. The first woman shook her head defiantly and continued, her voice a sobering monotone.

'No, it was all of them. The man with no teeth went first. When he was finished, the others followed. I tried not to make a sound because I knew they would hear me outside. Later some of the men went out, then others came in. Sometimes it was one of them, sometimes two or three. They brought in other women. Some of the women were older than me, some were just girls.

'They brought in the doctor's wife late in the afternoon. After four or five men had raped her, they brought in her husband. They made him watch as more men raped her. Then they slit his throat in front of her. Like me, she survived the massacre the next day. I know that because she made it to Athens where she had some family. But she's dead now. She killed herself.

'During the night they were drinking. We heard screams and shouts in the square. We didn't know what they were doing until the morning when we saw the bodies. They'd knifed some of the old men and hung some of the boys. One of them was six. By the end I don't think I felt a thing. I don't know how many of them raped me, or how many times. It doesn't matter.

'When they left they shot some of those who were still in the square. But not all of them. It was the same in the school-house. They murdered a few and let the rest live. To tell others what had happened, to spread the fear. I can't forgive any of them for anything. But in particular, I can't forgive them for not shooting me. For letting me live. I don't care what any of the other survivors say, that was the worst thing they did to me. I think about suicide every day, but I can't do it. It's a sin. I want to die, though. As soon as possible so I won't have to remember.'

She was staring, unblinking. Not at the woman opposite her, but at the camera. At Stephanie.

Another box on the right-hand screen, another face, this one a man's, an Albanian from Kosovo. The interview was recorded in a community centre in Hamburg on 13 June 2001. There were other immigrants in the frame. The man spoke slow, clear English.

'They kicked us out of our houses, robbed us, then beat us up. They separated the men of fighting age from the rest and told us they would be taken to a secure camp. They said they would be well treated, but we didn't believe them. We already knew they were butchers. There was panic, women clinging to their husbands. The terrorists – that is what they were, not soldiers – beat the women back. But there was no controlling them. There was one woman, she was on her knees clinging to her husband's legs with one arm and her little boy with the other. The leader of the terrorists, a big man with a shaved head, tried to pull her off her husband. I could see how angry this monster was. His eyes were dead. He grabbed her by the hair and pulled but she would not let go. Instead she spat at him. And so he shot her husband. Just like that. As though he was taking the top off a bottle.

'Before the woman had time to react, he grabbed the little boy, his face splattered with his father's blood. The savage held him tight, put a gun to his head and threatened to shoot unless there was order. Nobody said anything. Nobody protested any more. The men who had been singled out got on the bus and were driven away. Those of us who were left – the sick, the old, the women and children – we watched, some crying, some too terrified to cry.

'The man said we had to pay for the trouble we had caused. Fifteen thousand deutschmarks for the boy. I was one of those detailed to collect the cash. He gave us half an hour to find the money. What could we do? They had already robbed us. But they knew we would find cash that was hidden. We went from house to house, collecting what we could. When we returned we had just over ten thousand deutschmarks, much more than I expected. I was the one who handed the money to him. He counted it and said, "Ten thousand is not enough. I said fifteen." Somebody else said there was no more, that it was all we had. He shrugged and said, "Okay. I'm a fair man. A deal is a deal. You give me two thirds of the money, I give you two thirds of the boy." He decapitated the child in front of us. When they left they took their third away – the head – and left his little body on the ground next to his father.'

*   *   *

The windows are open. I can hear the distant murmur of traffic on the Gloucester Road, a phone ringing, the dull drum-roll of a helicopter passing overhead. Mark looms over me, enters me and kisses me. I can taste myself on his tongue.

Already flushed, I break into a sweat, our skins soon slippery, the sheets beneath us crushed and damp. I push my fingers through his dark hair and they come away wet. At first I'm content to let his weight pin me to the bed; I snake my arms around his neck and pull him down onto me. Later we roll over and I'm in charge, swiping away his hands from my hips so that I decide how hard we go, how deep, how fast. Which is when I seize up. Suddenly I'm no longer in his bedroom and I have no idea how it's happened.

I try to escape his grasp but he doesn't get it. He hardens his grip so I grab the fingers of his right hand and twist violently. I lurch forward and we separate. Still clutching his fingers with a force that amazes both of us, I wrench again, clamping my other hand over his, straining the tendons in his wrist.

'Jesus … Stephanie …'

He rolls with the pain. He has to, otherwise the wrist would snap. I know that for certain. It's a move I've used often. I let go just in time, but he's hurt. And in shock. For a second or two neither of us does or says anything. Then I stumble off the bed and scramble to the bathroom, where I lock the door.

I'm trembling but I'm not sure whether it's anger, sorrow or surprise. I lash out at the shelf above the basin, scattering two plastic mugs, a can of shaving foam and a half-used bottle of Listerine.

I don't know what to think. Or what I can say to him. Because whatever I do, I can't tell him the truth. I can't share

my day's work with him. I can't say what I've learnt after ten
hours, or excuse my behaviour by telling him that all I could
see was a Bosnian school-teacher being gang-raped by a Serb
paramilitary unit. Or a little boy lying in the dirt next to his
father, his head severed.

There's a knock on the door. My breathing is slowing but
my skin still gleams with sweat. He murmurs my name. I
stare into my reflected eyes – my most potent weapon – and
take control again.

Then I turn round and open the door.

Mark had pulled on a pair of cotton trousers. Stephanie
was still naked. Her voice was barely a whisper. 'Do
you want me to go?'

'I want you to talk.'

'It would be easier to go.'

'I'm sure it would.'

He offered her an old shirt of his. She pulled it
around her damp body. When she said she was sorry,
she couldn't bring herself to look him in the eye. He
asked if she needed a drink. She did but she declined.
Then she sat on the edge of the bed, her back to him.

'You know that feeling, when you're almost asleep
but not quite? And you're not actually sure whether
you're awake or not. And then you picture yourself
tripping or falling, and even though it's your imagination your whole body lurches … that's what it was like.'

'I know the feeling. But I don't know what you're
talking about.'

'I can't. I'm sorry.'

Mark said it was okay. When it clearly wasn't. Or, at
least, shouldn't have been. He should have asked questions. Or shouted. Something. *Anything*. But he didn't

because he didn't have to. He understood without the details.

From the very start there had been a condition, laid down in her bed in the hotel in the Dolomites. *Don't imagine you'll ever get too close to me, Mark. No matter what happens to us, there are whole areas of my life that I will never be able to share with anyone*. He'd said he didn't care.

Now, despite what she'd said, he had got close. Far closer than she could have anticipated. But not to her past. The condition remained intact.

He opened a bottle of wine to soothe the tension. Later, he cooked for them and they relaxed a little, a second bottle helping.

They went to bed just before midnight. With the curtains open, a street-lamp washed the ceiling dirty orange. They lay tangled together, her head on his chest, his fingers in her hair.

He said, 'You're the strangest person I've ever met.'

'I'm not half as strange as you.'

'I don't think I'm strange.'

She looked up at him. 'Do you really think *I* am?'

'One moment you're one person, the next moment you're somebody completely different. That seems to me to be strange. Then again, it is who you are.'

'Trust me, Mark. You have no idea.'

3

The first week of September brought the first storm since mid-July. Volleys of rain lashed the carriage windows as the District Line train wheezed to a halt at Olympia. As the doors parted, Stephanie turned up her collar. Maclise Road was just a minute away but she was dripping by the time she kicked her front door shut. She shed her raincoat and draped it over a chair, leaving her in grey sweatpants with a green stripe, a chunky black V-neck over a purple long-sleeved T-shirt and yesterday's underwear. In other words, the clothes that had been closest to her side of the bed.

She switched on the Sony Vaio in the living room and sent a brief message to a Hotmail address. I'm back from my travels. I've got a couple of questions for you. Let's get in touch.

In the kitchen she made herself coffee and turned on the radio. The news bulletin was finishing with an item of gossip about some soap star she didn't know. It was five past seven. Mark had been asleep when she'd left him. By contrast, she'd been awake since three. Worrying, wondering.

It had taken several days to absorb Alexander's deal fully. At first she'd only seen the carrot and that had blinded her to everything else. As intended, she supposed. It took longer to analyse the detail, the reality, the potential consequences. The more she considered it, the more anxious she'd become. Above all, there was one thing she knew: Alexander was not a man who liked to give.

There would be a subtext. There always was. Offering her a future free of Magenta House was not credible by itself. Alexander had prohibited her from seeing Komarov after New York out of nothing more than spite. Why would he let her go now? There was no obvious answer.

And what of the contract itself? It wasn't what she was trained for. Despite Mostovoi and Marrakech, there were others who'd be better suited to the task. Was it a demotion? Did Alexander feel she no longer had the cutting edge to survive in S7? She'd never heard of anyone being demoted at Magenta House. Those who left did so without fanfare and never returned.

The deal and the contract itself, neither was right.

She checked three Hotmail addresses of her own, as well as her five AOL addresses. Over the years she'd developed a system for e-mail management. The Hotmail addresses were permanent and belonged to Petra. Consequently very few people ever used them, and she couldn't think of anyone who knew more than one of them. Nearly all her Hotmail traffic was spam: tacky offers for cheap loans, penis or breast enhancement and off-the-shelf diplomas. The AOL addresses were spread across five of her established identities, Stephanie Schneider among them. Finally there were those addresses that were set up for one contract only. Or even one message.

Stephanie Schneider had mail. Steffi – it's ready for collection, Ali.

At nine she left the flat. After an hour of Pilates with

a private instructor at a studio in Earls Court. She found Pilates useful for maintaining core strength and flexibility. Her instructor, an Australian from Adelaide who was also called Stephanie, had become a close friend and they often had lunch together after class.

On her return there was a message waiting. I've heard such exciting stories about you. You must tell me everything. Shall we meet at the usual place? I'll be there for three hours, starting now.

Stern. More than Rosie ever could, Stern belonged to the Ether Division. Or should have. Because that was where he – or she – existed: in the ether. A virtual being, Stern had provided Petra with more concrete information than Magenta House ever had. The 'usual place' was a virtual café in the stratosphere. Stephanie checked the time of transmission: two hours and thirty-five minutes ago.

Hello, Oscar.

Stephanie had always used the name Oscar. It personalized Stern, and he'd never objected.

Well, well, all that blood in Marrakech and Mostovoi is still alive. I think I can guess why we're talking.

I doubt it. What does the name Milan Savic mean to you?

The Serbian paramilitary warlord?

Yes.

I think you'll find he's dead.

That's a popular assumption. What if he wasn't?

What basis do you have for suspecting otherwise?

Humour me. Call it rumour and conjecture.

Ah, the names of my two most valuable employees. Give me an hour.

It was still raining. Stephanie took a carton of Tropicana from the fridge, then put on a CD, the third, untitled album by Icelandic band Sigur Ros. None of the eight tracks had titles either but she fast-forwarded to the fourth, her favourite. From her wet window she gazed at the rear gates of the Olympia exhibition centre.

She looked at a photocopy of the names on the list that David Pearson had recovered. Goran Simic, Milorad Barkic, Robert Pancevic, Fabrice Blanc, Vojislav Brankovic, Dejan Zivokvic, Milutin Nikolic, Ante Pasic, Lance Singleton. There had been a tenth, but the tear in the paper had rendered the name illegible. And if there was a tenth, why not an eleventh? Why not a hundred? Who could say how many there were?

Alexander had given her his word but she still didn't trust him. Rather than break his word, which he considered his bond, Alexander was the type of man who redefined the terms of the deal so that he didn't have to. Which was why Stephanie had maintained Stern. She needed independence. She needed insurance.

Forty-five minutes later Stern was back. Quid pro quo, Petra.

What do you suggest?

No need for cash, a name for a name. And you go first.

Stephanie offered a name provided by Magenta House, an alias that Savic was rumoured to use.

Martin Dassler.

Hong Kong?

Correct.

Carleen Attwater.

Never heard of her. Also Hong Kong?

No. London.

Six thirty in the evening. The persistent rain had rinsed away most of the people who usually clogged Leicester

Square. The pub was packed, after-work drinkers unwinding with tourists and the pre-cinema crowd. It had less atmosphere than deep space: bright overhead lights, Linkin Park on the sound system competing with a chorus of cheesy mobile ring-tones and a football match on the screen at the far end.

Ali Metin was at the bar, nursing a pint of lager. 'Steffi ... looking foxy, as usual.'

'Ali ... looking shiny, as usual.'

Metin was proud to be bald by design and ran a hand over his mercury-smooth scalp. Beneath a long leather coat he wore a shimmering silk shirt and pleated trousers with a suspiciously high waist-band, both black. From his coat pocket he produced a silver mobile phone and handed it to her. It was a Siemens.

'Talk me through it.'

'It's a beauty. Two things you got to remember. None of the calls you make can be traced. There are no records in the phone or on the SIM card. Anybody tries to return your call, they get blocked. If they got the facility to bypass, they won't get the real number. They get a different number. You can use the memory but it won't show right. The first time you put in the number you want to save, the phone will show you another number. It's up to you to remember that. There's no other way of knowing without ringing.'

She took an envelope out of her bag. Metin opened it and fanned through the dirty twenties inside. 'Fancy a drink? I reckon I could stand it.'

Three days later Carleen Attwater says, 'So, you're one of Stern's ...'

'Yes.'

'I've never met one before.'

'Is that why you agreed to see me? Out of curiosity?'

'Aren't journalists supposed to be curious? Or even ex-journalists ...'

'You're retired?'

Her smile is as enigmatic as her reply. 'At the moment.'

'How come?'

'Burn-out. Too much jet-lag, too much alcohol, too much CNN.'

'I thought those were part of the deal for war correspondents.'

'Then too much Balkans.'

'The straw that broke the camel's back?'

'Exactly. Besides, I was never a war correspondent. I was a journalist who just ended up in a lot of wars. Take Croatia. I went to cover a human interest story about murals in a monastery and I stayed until the end of Kosovo. The best part of a decade. Or, should I say, the worst part?'

We're standing on the roof terrace of Attwater's top-floor flat in Poplar Place, off Bayswater Road. She's watering her plants, which occupy two thirds of the available space.

She's in pastel blue three-quarter-length linen trousers, a large buttercup T-shirt that falls to the thighs and a wide-brimmed hat. Not quite the flak-jacket she used to wear in Beirut or Baghdad. Or the Balkans. Now in her fifties, her career is etched into her skin but she still exudes an earthy sex-appeal. According to Stern, that was an asset she used to use freely.

'Who were you working for?'

'Nominally, I was freelance. But the New Yorker was good to me. So was Vanity Fair, when they could find it in their hearts to squeeze some serious stuff between puff pieces for Hollywood's latest airheads. Drink?'

'Thanks, yes.'

'I hate London when it's hot. Amman, fine. Damascus, fine. Here it's horrible. Jim used to feel the same.'

'Your husband?'

'Like my career, my ex ...'

'Sorry.'

'Lord, don't be. We aren't. We get on much better now we're divorced. Of course, it helps that he's back in New York.'

Her laugh is a sultry smoker's laugh. Her ex-husband is James Barrie, a foreign correspondent for *Time* for more than twenty years. They surfed the world's troubles together.

We go down the iron fire-escape and enter Attwater's kitchen. She pours me fresh lemonade from a glass jug that has chilled in the fridge.

'You met Savic?' I ask her.

'Many times. Especially during Bosnia.'

'He trusted you?'

'I think so.'

'Why?'

Attwater sighs. 'Because I don't think he saw me as an American. In fact, I don't think he saw me as a journalist. I don't believe he felt I'd taken a side.'

'And had you?'

'By the end, no. With most of the others who were there, I think it was the other way round. They tried to be impartial, then crumbled.'

'Why was it different for you?'

'I don't know. After a while you begin to lose your sense of perspective. Sides don't seem to matter that much. Who's right? Who's wrong? Who cares? You just go from day to day, village to village, carcass to carcass.'

'Surrendering responsibility?'

'Give me a break. Nobody takes responsibility for their actions any more. It's outdated, like good manners, or the slide-rule.'

'That's a rather cynical view.'

'Talking about responsibility in relation to what occurred in the Balkans is the worst sort of window-dressing.'

'Are you excusing what Savic did?'

'Not at all. I'm just saying that to judge it against the standards you and I take for granted is absurd. War is a different form of existence. It's heightened living. Survive or die, hour to hour. I apologize if I'm making it sound glamorous in some way. It isn't. It's dirty and disgusting. But every time I tried to leave, something held me back. By the end of Croatia I was already dead. And still I stayed, through Bosnia, through Kosovo. I hated being there. But when I wasn't there I hated wherever I was even more. It was a kind of addictive madness. Heroin for the soul ...'

Heroin for the soul. There's a phrase that has resonance for me.

'What about the ones he was supposed to have helped?'

She nods vigorously. 'The project was called Gemini. It was well organized. Milan was impressed by the Homeland Calling fund run by the KLA. Gemini was financed along similar lines. It had a proper command structure, too.'

I point out that most people dismissed the rumour as a conspiracy theory. She counters by pointing out that none of them were there.

We move into the coolness of her sitting room; heavy plum curtains, dark green damask wallpaper, photographs in silver frames on a piano.

'How did Savic rise so quickly? One minute he's a street-thug in Belgrade, the next he's in with the SDB and Frenki and Badza.'

'A street-thug? Who told you that?'

'I thought it was common knowledge.'

Attwater shrugs. 'He started on the street, but he outgrew it. Quickly, too. Milan was a rich man by the time Croatia started. He had a good business brain.'

'What was he into? Drugs? Guns? Girls?'

'Televisions.'

As she has clearly anticipated, that stops me in my tracks. 'Televisions ...'

'Cheap ones, Chinese made, imported from Hong Kong.'

'Hong Kong?'

'In the early eighties he made a contact out there. I don't know who. But they started with TVs, then moved into other electronic goods: stereos, computers, cell phones. Some legitimate, some fake, all of them cheap enough to find a market in Yugoslavia. That was how Milan made his first fortune. But it wasn't just financial. It was political, too.'

'How?'

She pauses for a moment to take a sip from her glass. 'Okay. I'll give you an example. On May 29th 1992 a shell killed sixteen people in a bread queue in Vase Miskina Street in Sarajevo. The next day, through resolution 757, the UN Security Council imposed a total economic blockade on Serbia and Montenegro. Total meant total, too. It covered all exports with the exception of medical supplies. Crucially, it included oil. Which Serbia needed desperately. In the end Serbia got round the problem by striking a deal with China, buying Chinese-bound imports at a premium, some of it paid for by barter. It was Milan who put that deal together, acting directly on behalf of Slobodan Milosevic.'

Next I ask her if she thinks Savic is still alive.

'I know he's alive,' she says. 'I saw him last November.'

'Where?'

'Zurich. At the airport.'

'Did you speak to him?'

She laughs. 'God no! I made damn sure he didn't see me. I mean, I guess he could've died since then. But then you wouldn't be here, would you?'

When I phoned Carleen Attwater, I told her I was a journalist. She hasn't said anything to challenge that since I've been here. She doesn't need to. I can see she doesn't believe me. Which means she has her own reasons for being so forthright.

'Do you know where he is now?'

She shakes her head. 'I don't know and I don't care.'

'One last thing. Why didn't you do something on Gemini?'

'What do you mean?'

'You're a journalist. What a scoop Gemini could have been.'

'Come on. More like a death warrant.'

It was worth a try. 'I suppose so.'

'Although that isn't the reason I didn't do it.'

'Oh?'

'I refrained out of courtesy. Milan knew that I knew about Gemini. The safest thing for him would have been to kill me. And that wouldn't have bothered him at all, believe me. But he didn't. He took that risk because he thought he understood me. That we understood each other.'

'And did you?'

'Absolutely.'

Barefoot, dressed in scarlet Bermuda shorts and a primrose T-shirt, Karen Cunningham poured two glasses of chilled Pinot Grigio. Stephanie carried the glasses and Karen carried Fergus, her seven-month-old son. The garden was an oval of grass cushioned by well-tended flowerbeds contained within a fence. There was a mature cherry tree at the far end. They sat at a bleached wooden table in the shade of a large red and blue umbrella.

Fergus, on Karen's knee, gurgled then let out a high-pitched squeal of glee before grabbing a handful of her T-shirt and stuffing it into his mouth.

'How's it all going?' Stephanie asked.

'It's wonderful. Knackering but wonderful. We've been very lucky, though. He's been such a good boy. Do you want to hold him?'

'I'm not sure.'

The sentence slipped out before she could vet it. Karen had already picked Fergus up. Now she settled him back on her thigh. The baby smiled at Stephanie, then turned coy, dribble coming off a fleshy lower lip.

Flushed, Stephanie said, 'God, I'm sorry, Karen. That sounded awful.'

'It's okay.'

Stephanie could see that it wasn't. 'I don't know why I said that.'

'It really doesn't matter. Actually, it's rather presumptuous of mothers to expect …'

'The thing is, I've never held a baby before.'

Karen's laugh was dismissive. 'Come on …'

'I'm serious.'

'Never?'

She supposed she might have held her younger brother or sister, but she didn't know. Besides, they belonged to a different Stephanie. The one that Karen knew had no brothers or sisters.

'Not that I can remember.'

There was an awkward pause before Karen said, 'Do

you want to? I mean, if you'd like to … you don't have to …'

Stephanie thought of all the reasons she'd never held a baby and felt disgust more than regret. When the moment passed, Karen was offering him to her. Stephanie took Fergus and sat him on her lap. He squirmed a little, looked up at her and broke into another toothless smile. Warm and fat with wisps of gold hair, he clutched Stephanie's wrist with podgy hands.

'Did you tell Mark about the test?'

'I couldn't see the point.'

'You must have thought about the possibility before that.'

'Of course.'

Stephanie had only ever allowed herself to consider the issue in the most conceptual fashion. Of all women, how could she bring a child into the world? More practically, she wasn't sure she was maternally inclined. Considering the life she'd led, nobody could accuse her of an overdeveloped instinct to nurture.

Mark was lighting a barbeque on the roof terrace – the last of the year, he said – the first oily flames dancing over the charcoal. Stephanie carried a tray of glasses across the decking to the table in the far corner. She put the tray on the table, picked up her glass of wine and plucked a bottle of beer for Mark from the turquoise cool-box.

'What time did you ask them?'

'Eight, eight-thirty.'

There were six coming. True friends of his, friends-by-proxy of hers. But they felt real enough most of the time. With a warm evening sun on his shoulders, dressed in a loose navy T-shirt and a pair of faded knee-length cotton shorts, with his hair suitably dishevelled after an active hour in bed, he couldn't have looked more relaxed.

'You know who called today?'

'Who?'

'Cameron Diaz's people.'

Said as though this was a common occurrence. Although it wasn't *that* unusual. The practice in Cadogan Gardens did attract a number of high-profile clients. In her darker moments Stephanie sometimes wondered whether they were drawn by the quality of the treatment or by Mark himself.

'Cameron Diaz?'

'Apparently she's in town to promote a new movie. Or to start filming one. I can't remember …'

Right.

His back was turned to her. Quite deliberately, Stephanie knew, though he'd maintain he was tending the charcoal.

'What's wrong with her?'

'I think it's her hip flexor.'

'I see. And you'll be treating that yourself, will you?'

'It's my practice. I think I should, don't you?'

'Naturally.'

'It'll probably require some subtle manipulation followed by some deep, penetrative massage.'

Stephanie picked up a piece of French bread from the wooden bowl on the table and threw it at him. It hit him between the shoulders. He turned round, feigning angelic innocence.

'Her hip flexor?'

He shrugged. 'Who knows? If I'm lucky …'

97

'I hope you'll charge her the full rate.'

'I'll probably charge her double.'

'Then it better be a successful movie.'

'That's a bit harsh.'

Julian Cunningham, Karen's husband, had once told Stephanie that chiropractors were like lawyers and bookies: you never saw a poor one. She reminded Mark of that.

He put up his hands in mock defence. 'All I'm doing is charging the going rate. Same as you.'

'True.'

Which was why, in a numbered dollar account at Guderian Maier bank in Zurich, Petra had just over three million eight hundred thousand dollars. Not a cent of which had found its way into the life she shared with Mark.

'I'm going to Hong Kong.'

He took it in his stride. 'It's agreed?'

'Pretty much.'

'For how long?'

'I'm not sure.'

'What for?'

'Organized crime in the Far East.'

That was the cover Gavin Taylor at Frontier News had decided upon. It was a little conventional for his taste, but Stephanie had decided to tell Mark she was going to Hong Kong. Normally she would have lied about her destination, as an added precaution. This time, with the contract open-ended, she was worried about complications. Taylor had agreed; keep it simple and keep it as close to the truth as possible.

'When are you leaving?'

'The date isn't fixed. But soon.'

'Are you still thinking about quitting afterwards?'

'Definitely.'

'So everything's fine?'

She nodded. 'Very much so.'

He looked at her, saying nothing. With most people Stephanie was the master of silence. Not with Mark. She never had been.

'You don't believe me, do you?'

'I believe you're going. And that you'll come back.'

'And the bit in between?'

He considered this for a good while. 'Given the choice between not knowing and being lied to, I'd prefer not to know.'

'And you're happy with that?'

'I'm happy with you.'

'But?'

'But nothing. I've always accepted you as you are, Stephanie. Other people might find that strange. That there are things about you that I don't know. That I don't insist on total disclosure. But it's just the way I am. You're different. I'm different. We strike chords in each other. And if we have to make allowances, we make allowances.'

'Don't your friends find that odd?'

'My friends don't know. Nobody knows. It's just us.'

Stephanie pressed her palms together, then sandwiched them between her thighs. 'The thing is, I'm not sure I could do the same, if our positions were reversed.'

Mark shrugged. 'But they're not, are they?'

That was the point. She got up, walked over to him and kissed him. 'Every morning, when I wake up, I look at you and wonder why it's you. And then I give up. Do you know why?'

'Yes, I do.'

'Go on, then.'

'It's because you don't care why.'

Inevitably, he was right. The more he diminished Petra, the more Stephanie loved him. It was the calmness. At first she'd mistaken it for indifference. And even arrogance. Later she recognized it as strength. Inner strength, not the show of strength that Petra preferred. Only once had she seen a side of him that could have been attractive to Petra.

The previous December they'd been mugged in a poorly lit side-street off Battersea Park Road. It was just after nine on a wet Wednesday evening. They were scurrying back to the Saab when three youths emerged from a soggy patch of waste-land fringing a tower-block.

Stephanie's first reaction was disbelief. It couldn't be happening. Not to her. It was such a cliché: black teenagers with their hoods up and gold around their necks. Her second instinct was to let Petra loose on them. Of the two, that proved harder to contain.

Knives out, they demanded money and Mark's car keys. The one closest to her was glaring at her, his switch-blade glinting in the wetness. For all of her that was Stephanie, the part of her that was Petra would not allow her to give him the fear that he wanted.

Mark was handing over his wallet. The one nearest her wanted her watch. Still staring at him, she unfastened the strap.

Petra was straining at the leash, trembling inside Stephanie.

She held out the watch. The mugger reached for it.

Quite deliberately, she let go of it, her eyes still riveted to his. The watch fell to the pavement. She thought he'd tell her to pick it up. Or take a swipe at her. Instead he spat at her.

As a spectator, the seconds that followed seemed to play in slow motion. Mark attacked all three of them. Too stunned to be Petra, Stephanie stood by and gawped, helpless and useless. Even when one of them slashed the palm of Mark's hand, she did nothing.

They never stood a chance. It wasn't really self-defence. Not after the first blow to the mugger nearest him sprayed shattered teeth into the gurgling gutter. And certainly not later, when the mugger who'd tried to steal Stephanie's watch found himself being propelled face first through a rear passenger window, then hauled back to receive a kick in the balls powerful enough to strain the tendons in Mark's ankle.

When it was over, he took back his wallet and keys, then picked up her watch. Stephanie was completely speechless. As she should have been. Except it wasn't an act. It was genuine.

Mark drove them home, his hand wrapped in an oily rag they found in the boot of the Saab. Neither of them said anything. In the kitchen at Queen's Gate Mews, Stephanie examined his hand. She said he should go to hospital. He said he wouldn't.

'You can't afford to damage your hands, Mark.'

'Just do what you can.'

So she did. Afterwards he opened a bottle of Calvados and collected two tumblers from the draining board. An hour later the mist began to lift and the man she knew started to drift back to her.

He said, 'I should call the police.'

'What's the point? I mean, we were the ones who were attacked. Let's not forget that. But the way the law works, you'll be the one who gets charged.'

'If I don't call, I'm no better than they are.'

'I understand that.'

'What I did – I shouldn't have …'

'I understand that too, Mark. And I know that you're not going to be persuaded by notions of natural justice. But hear me out.'

He drained his glass and poured himself another couple of fingers.

Stephanie played the fear card. 'If you call the police there'll be a record. Especially if you're charged with something. That means names written down, addresses, phone numbers … they could find out where we are.'

Reluctantly, he'd relented. And she'd been more grateful than he could possibly have imagined.

Stephanie shrugged off her leather coat to reveal a lime cut-off singlet that just covered her cosmetic scar but left her stomach exposed.

Cyril Bradfield said, 'If a daughter of mine dressed like you, I'd ask her what she thought she looked like.'

'And if a father of mine asked a question like that, I'd ignore it.'

'I'm sure you would. Tea?'

'Funny you should ask.' She reached into the plastic bag she was carrying and handed him a box from Jackson's of Piccadilly. 'For you.'

'Russian Caravan. My favourite.'

'Of course.'

'The sweetener before the pill?'

Stephanie nodded.

'Where to this time?'

'The Far East.'

They took creaking stairs to the attic; the forger's lair or the artist's studio, depending on your point of view.

'You've been fiddling about.'

Bradfield worked off two large wooden benches running down the spine of the attic. The shelves on the far side of the room had been rearranged: solvents, inks and adhesives in their own sections, with documents and reference books also partitioned. There were two shelves of photographic make-up, although Bradfield no longer permitted clients to come to his house. With the single exception of Stephanie.

'What's that machine?'

There was a dull beige unit on the bench closest to her, next to two lamps fitted with natural daylight bulbs.

'You didn't see it when you were last here?'

'No.'

'I used it on your Mary Reid document. Purchased from E.R. Hoult & Son of Grantham, Lincolnshire. Printers, in case you didn't know.'

'That doesn't look like a printer.'

'It isn't. It laminates. And with it I can replicate with absolute precision the way the UK Passport Agency laminates all new passports. Including placing a UKPA watermark over the face of the document holder. Which, as you may have noticed, makes identification harder, not easier. It's connected to my computer so that I can pick up a signature, scan it in and download it to this machine. Then it's lasered onto the page.'

'Computers, lasers, machines that laminate – you're selling out, Cyril. Where's the art?'

'In the perfection of the document. As always.'

He switched on the paint-spattered kettle at the end of the other work bench, tore the seal from the box of tea and took two mugs from the sink.

'So, the Far East – what do you need?'

'Nothing too fancy. One to get me there and back, one substitute.'

'Nationalities?'

'I'm going direct, so the first can be British, if that makes life easier. The second can be anything else.'

'Let's keep it within the European Union, then. German?'

'Fine.'

When the kettle had boiled he warmed the brown ceramic teapot before preparing the tea. Then he rolled himself a cigarette from a pouch of Sampson tobacco.

'The same as usual, is it?'

Stephanie shook her head. 'Not this time.'

In the years they'd known each other Stephanie had never actually said what it was that she did. She hadn't needed to. From the start Bradfield had known something of its nature. Why else would she need him? Gradually the full extent of her profession had become clear. Although his feelings for her bordered the paternal, he'd never moralized. Or tried to caution her against it. As fond of each other as they had become, their relationship was built upon professional foundations. The only other 'civilian' who knew of her work was her personal banker in Zurich: Albert Eichner of Guderian Maier. And he differed from Bradfield in one vital respect. In Zurich, with Eichner, she was always Petra, never Stephanie.

*   *   *

Alexander said, 'As Martin Dassler, Savic has been to Hong Kong seven times in the past year. We know this from immigration records. In that time he's spent nearly nine months there.'

'What we don't know,' Rosie said, 'is where he's been staying, or what he's been doing. Through the Hong Kong police, S3 has turned up only one Martin Dassler from hotel records: a sixty-five-year old Swiss architect from Lausanne. We've checked and it wasn't him. Dassler has some registered commercial interests in Hong Kong but doesn't seem to lavish much time on them.'

The Far East was an obvious destination, Stephanie supposed. He'd had contacts in Hong Kong and China for years. Where better to disappear to after the Balkans collapse? With money at his disposal, reincarnation would not have been difficult.

'Your contact in Hong Kong will be Raymond Chen,' Alexander told her. 'Anything you need, go through him. He's a strange one, but he's one of ours.'

'Aren't they all? Anyway, I wasn't aware Magenta House ran operatives abroad.'

Alexander shifted uncomfortably. 'Technically we don't.'

'Technically? What does that mean?'

'It doesn't matter.'

'What he means,' Rosie said, 'is that we retain him.'

Stephanie looked at her, then at Alexander. She was waiting for him to slap her down. She could barely believe what she'd just heard. But he didn't. He just sat there, behind his desk, with his recently clipped snow-white hair and his watery blue eyes, staring at her, never blinking, not moving. The buttons of his double-breasted jacket were still fastened; he looked like a waxwork in a strait-jacket. Not for the first time, Stephanie had the sensation that Alexander had become fossilized, stranded in the amber of the era of the dead-letter drop.

'You mean you pay him?'

Suddenly Alexander was reasserting himself. 'What *she* means is that we look the other way. Chen has a variety of business interests in Hong Kong and over here. From a legal point of view, few of them would tolerate much scrutiny.'

'What a surprise.'

'There's a lawyer in Chinatown. Thomas Heung. He has a legal practice on Gerrard Street, on the first floor above a Chinese supermarket. The firm is actually owned by Chen. Heung's a soft touch with an equivalent in Hong Kong, also controlled by Chen. Between the two of them they provide documents for Chinese wishing to come to Britain.'

'False documents?'

'On the whole, yes. But for those who can afford it, legal documents are also available.' Alexander gave her the thinnest of smiles. 'As they always have been.'

Which she knew to be true. There didn't seem much point in arguing about the morality of retaining a contact by contributing to the country's illegal immigration problem. That was the least of Magenta House's ethical crimes.

Stephanie had already digested Chen's profile, as provided by S3, and had come to the conclusion that she needed a contact of her own. The same anxiety had persuaded her not to mention her meeting with Carleen Attwater. Or Gemini.

Alexander said, 'We believe the list that David Pearson recovered is incomplete. We believe there may be many more names on it.'

'Why?'

'During research, S3 came across some of the names on the list but there were also other names. Same context, different identities, suggesting Pearson's list could be incomplete. We might be talking one, or a dozen...'

'Or none?'

'Possibly. But it's wiser to assume the worst. We also believe that there is another list. A reciprocal list, if you like. A list of new identities for the names on the original.'

She looked at Rosie. 'Do you believe this?'

'Of course.'

It was impossible to tell whether she did or didn't. Her tone and expression could not have been more neutral.

Stephanie turned back to Alexander. 'Assuming I get hold of these names, then what? Is Savic a contract?'

'Not yet. He's on the Limbo list. Nothing happens to him until we know, one way or the other, about the names.'

So many lists. Life was a long list of lists. She wondered how many she was on. And whether she was on one or more of Magenta House's. Probably. The Limbo list was rather like a credit rating; you never knew there was a problem with your own status until it was too late.

'Supposing I find Savic but can't get close.'

'You'll think of something, I'm sure.'

'I'm serious.'

'If all else fails, use your charm.'

'The way you use comedy?'

'A man like Savic will always find a use for a woman like Petra.'

This is the worst part. Before Mark it never bothered me that much. Once I'm Petra I'll be fine. Rosie once compared it to being an actor preparing for a role. She said that once you are performing you become the character. That's not true for me. Petra isn't a role. She's me. And when I'm her I won't have time to worry about Stephanie, which will be a relief.

We're in Kensington Gardens. It's a beautiful, warm evening. Branches creak and leaves shuffle in the breeze, their tips just beginning to rust. The air cools quickly and has a taste to it, a sure sign of an imminent change in season.

Mark's arm is around my shoulder. I find its weight reassuring. I'm holding onto his fingers. My hand looks ridiculously small next to his.

'Will you miss me?' *I ask him, immediately regretting it because it makes me sound needy.*

'From time to time.'

I look up at him. 'From time to time?'

'Well, I'll be pretty busy, I imagine. Pub crawls, football, poker nights …'

'Not to mention Cameron Diaz's hip flexor.'

'Exactly.'

'Bastard.'

'Bitch.'

We stop to kiss.

We've had an idyllic day: a lazy morning in bed with Bloody Marys for breakfast, lunch at E&O, a restaurant on Blenheim Crescent, then a movie. This evening, when we get home, Mark will cook something simple for me. The wine we drink will be special: Cos d'Estournel 1989. This has become part of the pre-Petra routine. Mark knows how tense I get the night before I leave, even though he has no true idea why. We've never talked about it. We've never had to.

When I was a child my mother did the vast majority of the cooking at home. Occasionally, though, my father, who was a poor cook, would make my favourite dish, spaghetti bolognese, for us. Except it wasn't for us. It was for me. And he did it when he knew I was upset. He didn't do it for the others when they were upset. Just me. And it was never because I'd made a scene. On the contrary. It was always when I was doing my utmost to hide it. Yet he could always tell. And spaghetti bolognese was his way of putting his arm around my shoulder without letting the others know.

In the same way, this ritual is Mark's way of letting me know that he knows what I'm feeling, without having to drag it up for discussion. It's understood and understated. Just the way it was with my father. They're the only two who've made me feel this secure.

It's not the only thing they have in common, either; they both chose healing professions. My father was a doctor. I'd love to be able to tell Mark this. Not that I think it's particularly significant – they're completely different men – but it would be nice for him to be able to put me in proper context. Sadly, that can't happen. At least, not yet.

I expect my father had private signals for all of us. I don't believe it was just me. I hope it wasn't. It was such an important thing. Then and now. And once he'd gone, those were the moments I missed the most. The little ones. The silly ones. The completely unrepeatable ones.

4

The clouds began to part. Her face pressed to the window, Claire Davies caught glimpses of Hong Kong beyond the massive, groaning wing: lush green peaks, glass skyscrapers, the polluted waters congested with tankers and tugs. Twelve hours in the rear of a Cathay Pacific 747, half of it turbulent, the taste of recycled air coating her mouth, her skin parched of moisture, yet still there was a frisson of anticipation that bordered plea-sure. As Claire Davies, Stephanie was Petra Reuter again.

Every time she returned to London – to Mark – she was happy to leave Petra behind. But now, as Petra once more, the feeling was back: the suspicion that her alter ego was a superior creature, not just to Stephanie, but to almost anybody. A cyborg, part human, part machine.

Stephanie's struggle was to be routine. To blend in. To be normal and to be accepted as such. Petra's quest was for perfection. Cold and clinical, devoid of super-fluous emotion, uncluttered by conscience. The truth was this: Stephanie enjoyed being herself, but she took pride in being Petra.

Into the quiet, empty spaces of the cavernous air-port at Chek Lap Kok, as great a contrast to the sordid crush of Heathrow as it was possible to imagine within the numbing world of commercial aviation. A sleepy official examined her passport and immigration form: Claire Davies, aged twenty-seven, single, born

110

in London, accountant turned tourist, wearing a plain white T-shirt beneath a tatty denim shirt tied at the waist, a pair of three-quarter-length khaki cotton trousers and black canvas plimsolls. She collected her luggage from the carousel – an old rucksack secured by cheap padlocks with a large peeling sticker on the main flap – *G'Day from Perth, WA* – then made her way through customs. She withdrew Hong Kong dollars from an ATM then boarded the Airport Express.

It was raining in Kowloon. Torrential, vertical, deafening. People huddled beneath canopies and in doorways. Vehicles crawled along streets, their windscreen-wipers rendered redundant. Stephanie waited at Jordan station until the worst of it had passed, using the time to buy an Octopus card for the MTR.

Nearby she found a cheap place to stay on Nanking Street, just off the junction with Shanghai Street. Up two flights of stairs, the Majestic Guesthouse was fraudulently named. In a lobby the size of a suitcase she registered her details. The room was one floor up. A damp cube of heat with a bed that was barely a single: a narrow mattress on a metal frame with a sag at the centre, covered in a lemon bedspread. There was a sink in the corner, a toilet and shower in a cupboard just large enough to fit a coat-hanger, and a small TV bolted to a wall-bracket.

She opened the dirty window. Wires and cables snaked across the street at the upper levels. Hanging out of a fourth-floor window, a woman was retrieving sodden laundry from a neighbour's wall-mounted television aerial. To her left a cat tiptoed across a visor of corrugated iron, scratching through rotting rubbish. Below, the street was almost empty, soaked pedestrians congregating in the 7-Eleven, lighting cigarettes, making calls.

She left the window open, enjoying the sound of the rain, and hauled her rucksack onto the bed. Out came Claire Davies's clothes: cheap underwear, faded jeans, walking shoes, old T-shirts, a bulging wash-bag. The side pockets contained her passport and air ticket, the second leg of which was due to take her to Sydney in three weeks. In her wallet she had a Visa card, activated less than forty-eight hours earlier. It came complete with a five-year financial history. That had been Magenta House's touch, not Bradfield's.

The second passport – Eva Hartstein, a dental technician from Stuttgart – was housed in the foam comfort pad on the back of the rucksack, between the straps. Stephanie left it there. At the bottom of the main part of the rucksack was a new compact Sony Vaio, courtesy of an old acquaintance of Cyril Bradfield's. Less of a laptop, more of a knee-top, it was impregnated with a dormant virus. Stephanie had to go through a three-step procedure in order to use the machine safely. It also contained a measure of last resort: Semtex ribbons beneath the keyboard, coated in a resin to avoid detection. The explosive could be set as a tamper device or switched to a timer, employing the computer as the countdown mechanism.

Stephanie had left Mark a number of the place where she'd told him she was staying, but the Zhuhai Hotel on Nathan Road was merely a figment of someone's imagination. If Mark tried the Kowloon number, he would get through to reception and then be put through to her room. But after a dozen rings the call would revert to the receptionist, who would conclude, in an English accent coloured by Cantonese, that Miss

112

Schneider was out. It would be a conversation that occurred entirely in London.

Stephanie switched on the Siemens phone she'd bought from Ali Metin. She also switched on a Nokia. That was Petra's.

It was almost dark by the time she went out, neon flickering in compensation: slabs of red and yellow, blue dragons with twitching emerald tongues, winking arrows pointing to depressing nightclubs. From Nanking Street she looked up. Not far from her bedroom window there was an illuminated billboard with two young girls pouting at punters below, dressed in skimpy underwear, the name of a karaoke bar flashing above them.

She found a small restaurant on Canton Street. Nothing fancy. Hard plastic, blood red and butter yellow, with lots of bright light overhead. An ultra-violet lamp zapped flies over a cooker, while a family of six at a table for four were shouting to make themselves heard over each other. She slid into a booth along one wall and ordered noodles and vegetables with chicken.

She looked at her watch. Eight minutes past six. The time of her life.

Despite two tablets of Melatonin, Stephanie slept poorly. The gossamer curtains were no defence against the neon outside and her mattress might as well have been stuffed with gravel. Now, naked, she went through an exercise regime that she'd devised with her namesake from Adelaide: a series of conventional stretches combined with elements of Pilates. By the time she'd finished, her skin was damp with perspiration. After a long, cool shower she dressed and left the

Majestic. As she walked onto Nathan Road she called a memorized number.

At the fourth ring, a man answered. '*Nî hâo.*'

'*Wô xìng* Petra.'

The man turned to English. 'Have we met?'

They never had. Stephanie said, 'In Seattle.'

'When?'

'August. Two years ago.'

'Where are you?'

'Kowloon.'

'Where do you want to meet?'

'I'll come to you. Where are you?'

'Windsor House, Causeway Bay.'

Stephanie walked to the tip of Tsim Sha Tsui and caught the Star Ferry to Central. She took a seat on the upper deck, reversing the wooden bench, leaning on the rail. Victoria Harbour was smothered by brown fog; pollution rolling in from the Chinese mainland. The heat and humidity were soaring, so it was a small pleasure to have ten minutes in the breeze of the open water.

She took a taxi from the ferry to Windsor House, a shopping mall as soulless as any other. Star Electronics sold computers like every outlet on the tenth and eleventh floors. There were about a dozen customers inside. A skinny boy in jeans approached her. His white T-shirt had Star Electronics emblazoned across the chest.

'Can I help?'

'I'm here to see Raymond.'

The boy vanished into the back office. The man who emerged, moments later, was barely five foot tall, almost as wide, dressed in a tight grey suit with an open-necked cherry silk shirt. His long, lank black hair had been pulled into an ill-advised pony-tail. Raymond Chen's office was smaller than her room at the Majestic and had no window. A black MDF desk partitioned the room. Chen was only just able to squeeze behind it. He was sweating despite the artificial chill. Petra tended to have that effect on men. Especially where her reputation preceded her.

'Nice business you've got here.'

'It's ... it's ... a sideline,' he stammered defensively. 'I'm here two – maybe three – mornings a week.'

'And what do you do with the rest of your time?'

It wasn't a question she expected him to answer honestly.

'A bit of this. A bit of that.'

'And a bit of the other?'

Chen was an American citizen, although it was now unlikely he would ever return there. He regarded himself as a refugee. Not from America, though, but from another nation entirely: the American intelligence community.

With a budget approaching twenty-five billion dollars, it employed more than a hundred thousand people around the world. It had spy satellites powerful enough to read the number off a credit card from space, but had failed to predict the attack on the World Trade Center. Just as it had failed to foresee the Soviet invasion of Afghanistan, or the collapse of the Berlin Wall. There were many reasons for these failures, but primary among them was an over-reliance on technical intelligence rather than human intelligence, or HUMINT.

Over a quarter of a century the CIA's decline had

been particularly marked, some of it self-inflicted, some of it imposed. The constraints placed upon the agency hadn't helped. During the nineties the CIA had been prevented from recruiting anyone with a criminal record, or who had been found guilty of violating human rights. As Alexander had consistently pointed out, where would Magenta House have been without such people?

Chen had fallen foul of this requirement on two counts: first, for having a criminal record and, second, for illegally concealing it. It took internal security at the CIA seven years to catch up with him. When they did, he fled, ending up in Hong Kong. Which was when Alexander stepped in. Belief in Magenta House had never been a prerequisite for working for it. People were hired for their talent and kept in check by their history. Chen was ideal; gifted and tarnished in equal measure.

Multilingual, he was far happier in the far-flung corners of the world than behind a desk, which was another quality that had set him apart. Too many of his former colleagues at the CIA had complacently believed that technology could reduce espionage to a desk job. That spies could become analysts without any drop in performance.

Stephanie had always been rather amused by this. If the most sophisticated listening devices in the world were monitoring your phone calls, you didn't use the phone. It was well known that Saddam Hussein had used motorbike couriers to distribute intelligence. The IRA passed information orally. If mobile phones were necessary, one used pay-as-you-go, like any drug-dealer, or customized units, like the Siemens that Ali

Metin had sold her. For the internet, as Petra had found out, Hotmail was perfect – the new one-time pad.

For all the technology in the world, there was no substitute for people on the ground. A good human asset took a second to axe but years to replace.

'You have something for me?'

Chen took a key from his pocket, unlocked the bottom drawer of his desk and produced a CD in a cardboard sleeve.

'Is that it?'

Normally there was a bulging envelope, printed pages, poorly developed photographs. Chen nodded. 'It's all there, but you can call me any time if there's something else you need. I'm available twenty-four hours a day.'

Stephanie took the disk from the sleeve and examined both sides. 'I can't believe it. Alexander's finally joining the late twentieth century.' She put the disk back. 'Just after everyone else has left it.'

I break the seal on a large bottle of water, drink a quarter of it, then sit down cross-legged on my bed. I switch on the Vaio and insert the disk.

Milan Savic, Lars Andersen and now Martin Dassler. Dassler has no address in Hong Kong but he's been here nine times in the past fifteen months. S3 had concluded he was either using another identity for hotels or staying with contacts. But the person who compiled this disk knows better: Dassler has access to a corporate apartment at the Dragon Centre, a skyscraper in Central.

The Dragon Centre is an astonishing piece of architecture. A reflective glass skin housed within a polished steel endoskeleton, it doesn't look like one building. Misleadingly, it

117

appears to be three, all different in circumference and height. There's an aerial shot, peering directly down. To me it looks like three sections of a honeycomb. I zoom in on one of the sections, the second highest. Within a protective fence, the roof is a tiled terrace with tended flowerbeds, manicured trees and a swimming pool. I check the notes. It belongs to a corporate apartment, registered to a company called Golden Harvest Property Services, based in a one-room office on the ninth floor of a run-down block in Wan Chai. There are three other businesses at the same address: another property company, a limousine service and a firm of flower importers.

Dassler's false passport details are provided. German, born in Rostock, Mecklenburg-West Pomerania, in 1958. I scroll down the page to see if there's a home address. There's a rented flat in Moscow, another in Berlin, neither of them current. For a while he was living with a girlfriend in Hamburg, a Slovakian lap-dancer named Krystyna. There's a picture of her: lots of dyed blonde hair, green eyes set against ruby lips, a fabulous body.

Dassler's involved with three nightclubs in Kowloon: Gold Cat and Kiss Kiss, a pair of cheap dives in Mong Kok, and Club 151 in East Tsim Sha Tsui, one of Hong Kong's most expensive nightspots. The in-house girls at the clubs in Mong Kok are all local, the ones at 151 tend to be imported, mostly from Europe. I wonder if Krystyna from Slovakia ever made it as far as East Tsim Sha Tsui.

It's not clear what role he plays regarding the clubs, which are owned by a company called Victoria Entertainment International. His other business interests include two restaurants, a travel agency, a container leasing company, two flower shops, several bureaux de change *and a haulage firm in the New Territories. The balance of the portfolio strikes me as peculiar.*

There's a file listing Savic's known Hong Kong associates. These include Tony Parker, a former British soldier, who now fronts a security consultancy. In his world that's the equivalent of a non-executive directorship. For more than twenty years Parker was a mercenary, mostly in Africa. I recognize the name of the Jahari brothers, Indian diamond merchants, and Mikhail Andreyev, a Russian: once a lowly clerk for Intourist in Vladivostok, now a hotelier worth three hundred million dollars. Andreyev was in the early running for the Macao gambling licence that eventually went to Steve Wynn, the Las Vegas casino king. The other names in the file are Chinese and mean nothing to me.

I look for lingering traces of Milan Savic's early links with this part of the world but there aren't any left. Just as Hong Kong itself has, he's left behind his reputation for being a cheap television trader. Along with his name, his nationality, his homes and Krystyna from Slovakia. They all belong to a different era. Like me, Savic seems to be a man who's spent much of his life getting a divorce from himself.

Claire Davies was ideal for footwork. A tourist doing the sights, some on the backpacker's beat, some not, but a tourist nevertheless. A knapsack, sunscreen and sunglasses, the obligatory bottle of mineral water. Perfect fodder for the Indians along the lower reaches of Nathan Road, trying to flog cheap suits and fake Rolexes.

It was early afternoon when she walked up Shanghai Street to Mong Kok. Kiss Kiss was on Fife Street. Gold Cat was on Portland Street, just off Mong Kok Road, barely a couple of hundred yards from one to the other and not much to choose between them. In the daylight their exteriors were depressingly dreary.

Set in glass display cases, one on either side of the entrance, Gold Cat had photographs of girls in bikinis. Time had bleached most of the colour from the shots; sultry pouts, bad make-up, eighties hair. Kiss Kiss had a huge set of neon lips above the entrance. With the sign switched off, the lips were grey with grime. Club 151, in East Tsim Sha Tsui, was set back from the street in the basement of a prestigious commercial building with uniformed security, valet parking and CCTV.

Back at the Majestic, Stephanie returned to the disk that Chen had given her. Savic didn't seem like a nervous man. He had no permanent protection, although he was sometimes accompanied by Sun Tai, nominal head of security for Victoria Entertainment International. There was a poor photograph of Sun. Obese, shaven-headed and tattooed, Stephanie knew the breed; slovenly and slow, with only a scowl for impact. Savic also had a driver, a Macanese named Figueiredo.

The following morning she returned to Hong Kong and headed for Central and the Dragon Centre. She'd identified the building from the Star Ferry, but it was even more impressive close up. The tallest of the three sections rose seventy-eight seamless floors within the endoskeleton. The mirrored glass had been put in place so precisely it was impossible to see the joins between the sheets; three smooth cylinders forming one glittering building. There was a vast atrium, six storeys high, with hundreds of halogen spots lowered on barely visible threads so that, in the evening, one could look up from the polished granite of the lobby and see the night sky perfectly replicated inside the building.

Set into the stone of one wall was a digital screen.

Stephanie touched the directory and brought down a list of the companies renting space in the skyscraper. Then she went to the Central Government Offices on Queensway, where the Registrar of Companies oversaw the Companies Registry, and where a member of the public was able to examine the statutory information about any company on the list. Providing one had details of an identity card or a passport, it was also possible to conduct a search to see if a named director was on the board of any other company. Stephanie was armed with Martin Dassler's passport details and a copy of a document allegedly used by Lars Andersen.

Using Victoria Entertainment International as a starting point, Stephanie instigated a search to see how many companies were operating under the Dassler flag of convenience. Three, it turned out, all of them questionable. All had six directors, and in each case Savic was the only non-local. Not a sure sign of a front company but a fairly reliable indicator. Apart from Dassler, there was one man common to all three. Tsang Siu-chung. And it was this name, half an hour later, that stopped her in her tracks.

Among many business interests in the SAR, Tsang Siu-chung was also a director of a company called Primorye Air Transport. Based in Vladivostok, with a subsidiary office on Sakhalin, but registered in Hong Kong, there were five directors, four of them Chinese. And one Russian.

Konstantin Komarov. *Kostya.*

A coincidence, Stephanie told herself. Nothing more. Besides, she knew Kostya as well as anyone. Or had, at any rate. A man with connections everywhere.

Moscow, New York, London, so why not Hong Kong? He knew the Russian Far East too, if being left to languish in its grotesque prisons could constitute regional knowledge. And yet she still couldn't quite believe it. In Petra's world, what was a coincidence? Alexander would say that it was an oversight.

In her room at the guesthouse there were two pieces of e-mail for her. The first was for Stephanie Schneider at AOL. There was no text, just an attachment. She opened it, a familiar face forming on the screen: Cameron Diaz looking radiant, smiling for the camera at some film première. Beneath the picture, the message: Dear Stephanie, My hip flexor feels a lot better now. Please thank Mark for all his love and attention. It only took him a night or two. He's *soooo* good. Your grateful new best friend, Cameron, xxx.

Stephanie sent Mark a reply. Dear Cameron, Think nothing of it. If you happen to see Mark before I get back, please tell him that his hip flexor's going to feel a lot worse than yours. And it won't take me a night or two, either. In brutal anticipation, Stephanie, x.

The second message was from Stern. He had a name for her. Not Komarov, but another Russian. Another coincidence? It didn't feel like it. And when she saw who it was, she was sure he wouldn't feel it was a coincidence either. She tapped the keyboard back to Stern.

The Fat Man? I thought he was in Moscow.

He was. But Moscow was never permanent. His powerbase has always been the Far East. In Hong Kong he can be a big fish in a small pond. In Moscow he was a minnow. And as you can imagine, that never suited the Fat Man. The only thing larger than his waistband is his ego.

Stern gave her the address, then Stephanie telephoned Albert Eichner at Guderian Maier in Zurich on the Nokia. The bank had no electronic banking facilities. As Eichner had once told her over an eighty-year-old glass of cognac in his office on the Bahnhofstrasse, 'Our clients wouldn't … *appreciate* … that sort of service.'

The word *appreciate* had made him wince. But he'd been right. Petra had electronic access to accounts in Europe, the United States and Mexico, all of which she knew to be vulnerable, no matter what the banks claimed. For the same reason, all of Magenta House's most sensitive information was housed on computers that were hermetically sealed from the outside world. They weren't even connected to one another. There were no phone sockets in the rooms that contained the terminals. Just accessing a CD-ROM required special clearance, the disks themselves having been configured so that they could never be used on conventional equipment.

'For some of our clients,' Eichner had said, 'the technologies of the future are a thing of the past. They're looking for something much more remarkable: human trust.'

In that respect, banking with Guderian Maier was an expensive luxury that came cheap at the price. Just like the information she bought from Stern.

The Thomson Commercial Building in Wan Chai was wedge-shaped. Stephanie stepped out of the sun into the poorly lit lobby. Twenty-two floors of rented offices were listed on two notice boards. None of the plastic name plates looked permanent: Top Mind Promotion Ltd, Flourishing Engineering Co Ltd, Excellence Business Service Co Ltd, Friendly Press and Book Binders.

Polar Star Holdings shared the nineteenth floor with three other companies. The door was shut. Stephanie knocked on a pane of etched glass. No response. She tried the handle. It opened and she found herself in a small reception room: two cheap chairs against a flimsy partition, a desk, a computer terminal with no one behind it. A freshly lit cigarette was burning in a glass ashtray. To her right there was a grey door. Behind that, the sound of running water. She tried the door on the left and didn't bother knocking.

'Hello, Fat Man.'

Their eyes met. Instinctively he stood, as his jaw dropped. 'You? *Fuck!*'

'I hope that's not an offer.'

Viktor Sabin looked past her and saw the vacant desk. Stephanie smiled coldly, then closed the door.

'What are you doing here?'

'I'm on business.'

His mouth was still slack, and the colour began to drain from his soft cheeks. For a moment Stephanie thought he might collapse.

'Relax, Viktor. *You're* not the business.'

It took a moment for the assurance to register. 'No?'

She shook her head. 'The last time we met I saved your life. Remember?'

Panting, he sat, the chair squealing in protest beneath him, his bulk consuming the arm-rests. 'I remember. Just like I remember what you do. It's not easy to keep the two apart. One's status can change in a heartbeat.'

'How true.'

'I always imagined if I ever saw you again, you'd be the last person I'd see.'

'You must have made more enemies than I thought.'

'Sadly, in my line of work, that's an occupational hazard. We all live with the fear that one day a client will bring something more than custom to the door.'

'Today's not that day.'

'How did you find me?'

'Stern.'

Sabin's brow furrowed. 'The internet man?'

'That's right.'

'I've heard the name but I thought he was just … a *rumour*.'

'He'd die of pride to hear you say that.'

'How did *he* find me?'

'If I knew that I wouldn't need him, would I?'

Sabin's nickname was well earned. To describe him as obese seemed utterly insufficient. Standing, he looked like a mountain reflected on the surface of a still lake, his belt marking the shoreline. Chins sloped out of his head onto his chest. He wore chunky bracelets of fat on his wrists and ankles. No slack remained in his aubergine slacks and his navy polo shirt could have doubled for a spinnaker.

It was a crummy office: three grey filing cabinets, shelves stuffed with box-files, their edges frayed, a nylon carpet – once green but never cleaned – with faded sun-patches. On the desk, a Compaq monitor with brown cigarette burns marking melted plastic, two mobiles, an unconnected land-line, paperwork, two ashtrays, a glass and a large plastic bottle of Diet Coke.

'Classy place you got here. What does Polar Star do, Viktor?'

'Import–export.'

'Of course.'

He lit a Camel Light with a trembling hand.

Stephanie sat down and said, 'I meant what I said. It's not you.'

He began to look as though he might, in time, believe her. 'What do you want?'

'Hardware. Discreetly delivered.'

He puffed out his chest. *It goes without saying.* They discussed details, then he punched a number into one of the mobiles and put it to his ear. The Rolex on his wrist looked tight enough to stem his circulation.

The last time they'd been together had been nine months earlier in a room at the Hotel Lisboa in Macao. There had been two other men in the room. An Algerian and a Saudi, both clerics. The Ether Division had followed them from Hamburg to Damascus, then to Beijing and beyond. They'd recruited Sabin clandestinely, setting up a ghost deal, factoring him into it to give the proposition legitimacy. As bait, he'd been a success; the men had been lured to Macao from their safe haven in China.

With no need for subtlety, the Ether Division had handed Stephanie the job. *Make it messy so that it looks good for the papers.* In other words, it wasn't enough to kill them. They had to be discredited too.

And so they were. Two Islamic extremists who'd slipped down to Macao for a weekend of gambling, prostitutes and alcohol. That was how it had been reported. The papers preyed on the gross hypocrisy of the clerics and weren't too concerned with the police investigation that followed. Local organized crime took the blame, but nobody faced a charge. Including Sabin, who, having been the only witness, was released in

126

return for his silence. The alternative he was offered made it no choice at all. Within thirty-six hours he'd arrived in Moscow, badly shaken. Now he was back in Hong Kong, his nerve partially restored.

When he'd finished the call, they didn't negotiate. Instead Stephanie asked for a price, Sabin gave it and she agreed to it. Unlike Mostovoi, the supermarket arms trader, Sabin was a specialist. There were no bulk purchases, so no discounts.

'Let me ask you something.'

'What?'

'Your presence out here … is there a German in the equation?'

Stephanie aimed for inscrutability but fell short.

'A fake German?' Sabin persisted. 'From the Balkans?'

'You should be careful, Viktor. You might lose your reputation for discretion.'

Relaxing into a smile, Sabin said, 'I heard about Mostovoi and Marrakech.'

'From?'

'This is a small community. Everyone talks.'

'Go on.'

'I've known Max for years. After all, although we operate in different areas, we're in the same trade. It's inevitable.'

'You've spoken to him?'

'Not since then. He's gone even deeper into hiding than before. But I spoke to an associate of his. Marcel Claesen.'

'Ah …'

'You know each other?'

'He'd say we did.'

'And you?'

'I've had the misfortune to be in his presence on two or three occasions.'

Taking his cue from Stephanie's expression, Sabin nodded. 'I have to confess I feel much the same way about him.'

'What did he tell you?'

'That Mostovoi was a cat who used up eight lives when you were with him.'

'Claesen said that?'

'Yes.'

'How poetic. Especially for a man who wasn't there.'

'Is it true?'

'The basic facts, maybe.'

'He also told me that Lars Andersen was in Marrakech. And that the two of you met.'

'You know about Andersen …'

'Being Savic? Of course.'

'And Claesen?'

'No, I didn't get that impression.'

'So your conclusion is … what?'

'Well, it's so soon after Marrakech. First you're there. Now you're here. And it can't be for Mostovoi. So …'

'So you add two and two together and come up with any number you like.'

Sabin's secretary wandered into the room without knocking and seemed astonished to find Stephanie sitting opposite her boss. She blushed, then apologized. Sabin waved her out of the room. Once the door was closed he said, 'Can I ask you something else?'

'If you choose your subject more carefully than your last, sure.'

128

'That night at the Lisboa. What stopped you?'

'You weren't the target.'

'I could have identified you.'

'You could have, yes …'

'Most of those in your profession wouldn't have taken that risk.'

'Probably not.'

'So why did you?'

The answer, she suspected, depended on a point of view that could change in a moment. Because she was human, after all? Because Sabin fell outside the strict remit of the contract? Because her instinct told her that he wouldn't betray her?

'I don't know.'

The answer seemed, nevertheless, to satisfy him. 'Whatever the reason, I feel I owe you something, so let me offer you this: a little information, free of charge. Whether it is of any use to you, I have no idea.'

'One can never be too well informed.'

'You're not the only one here looking for Savic.'

Whatever she was expecting, that wasn't it.

'Go on.'

'A Bosnian, I think. Certainly from the Balkans.'

'How did *he* find Savic?'

'I don't know.'

'Does he have a name?'

'Like you, he probably has many.'

'Where can I find him?'

5

Viktor Sabin's Bosnian, Asim Maliqi, was staying in room 512 at the Shanghai Hotel on Nathan Road in Yau Ma Tei, an establishment run by the China Travel Service. The head-and-shoulders photograph of Maliqi provided by Sabin looked official; gaunt, with several days of stubble adding to a shadow cast by sharp cheekbones, black eyes staring directly at her, messy black hair shot through with silver.

The Shanghai's lobby – a brown zigzag carpet, smoked glass tables, a tinted chandelier – was too small to allow her to linger anonymously, so she loitered on Nathan Road. An hour later, at half past eight, Maliqi appeared. A couple of inches shorter than her, with a sinewy build, he was dressed in jeans and a khaki T-shirt. He carried a small knapsack over his left shoulder.

Stephanie followed at a discreet distance. First stop, Flower Market Road, flower shops running down one side of the street, the large, blue corrugated iron perimeter fence of the Mong Kok Stadium along the other side. The scent of flowers struggled against the stench rising off an open drain belonging to the Drainage Services System. Half way along the street Maliqi stopped and opened his knapsack. Stephanie pretended to examine the stall closest to her: lilies, carnations, azaleas and sunflowers assorted in orange and green plastic tubs. Out of the corner of her eye she saw Maliqi photographing shop fronts. Once he'd moved on, Stephanie inspected the two he'd picked: the Good World Flower Trading Company and Wing Fat Flower Wholesaler. Neither looked particularly different to any of the others: smallholdings opening onto the pavement, interiors crushed with colour and fragrance, residential blocks above street level, the concrete cracked and stained.

After Flower Market Road, Maliqi visited a jewellery store on Lock Road. From the street Stephanie watched the silent conversation between Maliqi and an old man behind the counter. It became increasingly animated. There was a sign stuck to the window: *Hippopotamus tooth and mammoth tusk carvings a speciality – CITES legal export certificates available*. All Stephanie could see was jade.

Later Maliqi crossed to Hong Kong and headed for the mid-levels, where he spent two hours in the bustling grid of Lyndhurst Terrace, Peel Street, Gage Street and Graham Street. Here he was easy to follow, the congested markets offering natural cover, squatting women stacking vegetables, butchers up to their elbows in blood, hacking cuts of dripping meat on wooden slabs. She noticed a pharmacist selling traditional Chinese remedies, modern medicines *and* cigarettes. In the time it took Stephanie to pass his shop, a fishmonger reached into a polystyrene tank, grabbed a grouper, decapitated it and began to scale it. With every step the smells changed: poultry, incense, fruit, diesel.

Maliqi dipped into three buildings but Stephanie was unable to follow him for fear of being noticed. It was after midday before he emerged from the last of them. Late in the afternoon he headed for the Hong Kong–Macao Ferry Terminal at Sheung Wan. When Stephanie entered the terminal she saw there weren't enough passengers boarding the TurboJet hydrofoil to offer her cover, so she dropped him.

Hot and frustrated, she was returning to her hotel when it occurred to her that she could visit his. The crossing to Macao took about an hour. Even if he caught the first return he'd be away for at least a couple of hours.

Back at the Shanghai the lobby was crowded: a package tour from the mainland, two dozen or so, all wearing red plastic name badges. Unchallenged, Stephanie took the lift to the fifth floor and found room 512, two doors from the end of a gloomy corridor lit by dim wall-lamps; the frosted glass was green, giving off a creepy glow. The lock was operated by a Ving card. Stephanie looked around. There was a small plastic hemisphere protruding from the corridor ceiling; a security camera, most likely. With no chance of a direct entry, she passed by his door, made a pretence of discovering that she was on the wrong floor and turned back, memorizing the position of his room.

Out on Nathan Road again, amid the roaring traffic, Stephanie looked at the front of the Shanghai. 512 was at the rear. There was no break in the frontage so she headed for the nearest turning, which was to the left, and discovered, almost instantly, another left turn. More of a passage than an alley, it was so dark that at first she thought she was inside. The two buildings backed onto each other so closely that where air-conditioning units protruded from both at the same level, there was barely a metre between them. Looking up,

132

her view was obscured by water-pipes, outlets for old ventilation flues, electric cables, swaying cord. Through this filthy lattice, fifteen storeys above her, she saw fragments of grey sky, the afternoon descending into dusk.

She trod cautiously, the ground ankle-deep in rubbish and alive with rats. There were doors set into both walls. Most were bolted shut, but she passed two that were open; the first offered only darkness, the second opened onto a kitchen, heat surging out. She paused in the shadows and caught glimpses of three men, one of them smoking. It sounded like an argument. Her back against the wall, she drifted past the door and came to the rear of the Shanghai.

As a climb, it could hardly have been easier for her; there were so many gaping toe-holds, so much clutter to cling to. But there was no pleasure in it. Every pipe seemed crusted with bird-shit, every ledge coated in sticky grime. The air was not just still; it seemed to have died. She could taste decomposition. It was so dark she didn't worry about being noticed.

Looking for an implement, she was spoilt for choice, eventually selecting a piece of rusted pipe dangling from a section of net that had become snagged on an overflow outlet. She reached the fifth floor and perched on the slippery sill, one foot in front, one tucked beneath her.

Maliqi had left his curtains half drawn. Stephanie rubbed her fingers on the window and peered in. Empty. The bed had been made, his clothes piled on a chair in the corner. She swung the pipe against the window. In the confined space between the buildings the echo of breaking glass sounded unreasonably loud, but she knew the rumble of traffic on Nathan Road would swallow it.

She knocked fragments clear of the frame, then entered the room, her shoes grinding splinters into the beige carpet. It didn't matter to her whether Maliqi knew of the intrusion so she took no measures to conceal it.

It was a smoker's room, stale tobacco clinging to fabric. Peach walls, peach bedspread, peppermint curtains and plastic peppermint frames for prints of fishing boats navigating deep gorges. In the cupboard the safe was open and empty. Stephanie was surprised. She patted down the pockets of a brown jacket, went through the clothes in his drawer and checked his bathroom. Nothing.

His suitcase – shiny brown plastic imitating leather – was under the bed. She lifted it on top, felt the shift of objects inside, and used the mini-bar corkscrew to break its catches.

There were two large maps – one of Hong Kong Island, the other of Kowloon East and West – three used rolls of 35mm film, a plastic folder with a zip and a large guidebook. Stephanie spread both maps across the floor. There were markings in red ink on both, including the places she had seen in his wake: Flower Market Road, Lock Road and several in the mid-levels. On the Hong Kong map there was one circle at Deep Water Bay on the south side of the island, as well as crosses in Wan Chai, Happy Valley and Causeway Bay. The guidebook was German and well used. Maliqi's air ticket was inside the plastic folder, issued by a travel agency in Berlin, Dardania Tours; the return flight wasn't for a week.

Sabin might have been right about Maliqi. Equally, he could have been wrong. Between the places she'd followed him to and the belongings in his room, the only thing that could link the Bosnian to the Serb were the shops on Flower Market Road; as unlikely as it seemed, Dassler was involved in the flower business. On the other hand, perhaps Maliqi was in Hong Kong as a tourist.

She checked the room again, more thoroughly than before, and still came up with nothing. In the bathroom she washed off the worst of the dirt, having decided to leave by the door. Maliqi was a dead end. He'd report the broken window. And the fact that nothing was missing. As for the mystery woman coming out of his room – that was precisely what she'd remain.

She closed the door quietly behind her and headed for the lifts. There was a man walking towards her. In and out of the murky pools of light cast by the green frosted wall-lamps, he had a small knapsack over his shoulder, just like the one Maliqi had. The man stopped a moment before she did.

Stephanie thought she saw an instant of recognition before the panic. In her own mind there was confusion. Not enough time had elapsed. He should have been in Macao. He turned and ran. Even as he did so, the reaction struck her as perverse. She was coming out of *his* room yet he hadn't challenged her. He hadn't even shouted at her in protest.

Stephanie accelerated after him. Maliqi didn't bother to try the lifts. He crashed through the swing-door and down the stairwell. When they reached the ground floor they erupted into the lobby, carving a path towards the exit, scattering guests and luggage. By the time anybody was ready to react, Maliqi and Stephanie had gone.

Nathan Road, the principal artery feeding Kowloon, was packed. Cream and green double-decker buses processed slowly while impatient taxis darted between lanes. The pavements were generating their own heat, faces washed by the garish light emitted from sparkling stores. Above, neon shut out the night, illuminated billboards lighting up the street like a stage: Anna Kournikova sporting an Omega watch, George Clooney in Police sunglasses, Budweiser, Marlboro. Between these, the names of bars, clubs, rent-by-the-hour hotel rooms and eat-all-you-can restaurants. All set against the city soundtrack, the deep throbbing hum of engines, sirens, phones, shouted conversations.

Maliqi made little attempt to weave between people. He cut through pedestrians like a scalpel through soft butter, fear driving him on. Stephanie's path was no easier. In his wake he left bodies and dropped shopping.

At Kansu Street he veered right, skidding as he did so, colliding with an elderly woman yapping into her phone. She tumbled into the road, a taxi screeching to a halt just inches from her. Stephanie crossed the road on the diagonal, as Maliqi took the first left, Woosung Street, followed by another right and left. Now they were heading down Temple Street. In open flight she closed on him, but he seemed quicker through the human traffic. Not far ahead was Nanking Street, where she was staying, but before that, he turned right into Ning Po Street, then cut back, up an unlit alley.

In the musty darkness she snatched blurred images:

an old woman sitting cross-legged in the dirt, a clay pipe between her lips, a partially open door offering a glimpse of a thin girl picking her toenails.

Then she tripped, skidding as she tried to correct herself, the uneven ground slick underfoot, her ankle folding. A complete fall was prevented by the wall to her right. It buttressed her, scraping skin from her arm. She pressed on but Maliqi, diminishing ahead of her, had reached Saigon Street, where, briefly, he grew brighter.

She heard the squeal of locked tyres followed by the shrill cry of a horn and the cushioned thud of a body bouncing off a bonnet. By the time she reached Saigon Street the driver was out of his Nissan and Maliqi was off the ground, running again, but with a pronounced limp. Now she was closing in on him and Maliqi knew it, casting nervous half-glances over his shoulder. He ducked down another alley, Stephanie close enough to hear him panting.

Half-way along he spun round to face her, taking her by surprise. In the foetid darkness there was an arc of winking light as she tried to slither to a stop. A knife. Out of nowhere, it seemed. He lunged at her. Off balance, she twisted to her left and fell. Maliqi was above her immediately, thrusting downwards. Stephanie rolled to her right. The blade jarred against concrete. Stephanie lashed out with her foot, connecting with the left shin, just below the knee. He buckled but didn't fall, then was coming at her again.

It was Stephanie who fell but Petra who rose. She scrambled to a crouch, feinted right as he swiped at her and missed, then jumped at him, shoving him back. Unsteady on his feet, he threw a loose jab at her ribs that she dismissed with her left arm, opening up his front. As he struggled to retain his balance Petra took a step away, to give herself space, suddenly seeing clearly in the dark. Again his right hand was moving but she was ahead of him now, the weight transferred to her right foot, the left lashing out, cracking against his wrist. The hand splayed, the knife slipping from his fingers.

Petra was still moving, the sweep of the kick complete, her weight and balance shifted. Maliqi never saw the elbow that caught him between jawbone and cheekbone. The blow knocked him against the alley wall and he collapsed.

Petra retrieved the blade from the dirt. It was a paring knife. Bought locally, she presumed. She stood over Maliqi and reached down. Still stunned, he tried to beat her hand away. She punched him in the mouth then grabbed a fistful of khaki T-shirt, hauling him upwards. She thrust the knife forward until the blade was an inch from his left eye.

'What are you doing?' she hissed.

She wasn't sure what she was looking at. Fear, certainly, but something more.

His voice was a rasp, his English heavily accented. *'Who ... are ... you?'*

'What are you doing in Hong Kong?'

She could smell herself, a feral scent rising off the sweat that was running through her hair and down between her shoulder-blades. From the tip of her nose a drop fell, hitting Maliqi in the eye. With a drum-roll pulse, her body was fizzing with adrenaline. Yet she was under complete control, everything functioning according to design. These were the moments she could almost savour; Petra *über alles*.

She lowered her face to his. 'Tell me.'

Maliqi swallowed, then shook his head.

Petra pressed the knife into him. Just below the eye. A small slice, slowly drawn. Maliqi gasped, then froze, suppressing the squirm, the instinct to protect his eyeball superseding the pain. For several seconds Petra left the tip of the blade in the wound, her own eyes wide open, absorbing everything.

Then she withdrew the knife and brought it up to the left eyeball, holding it there, her grip steady, the bloody tip wiped by his eyelashes every time he blinked.

'Last chance ...'

'You thought you recognized me, didn't you?'

Maliqi made an exaggerated examination of the tip of his unlit cigarette.

'Who did you think I was?'

No answer.

'*Who?*'

Agitated, he lifted his stained khaki T-shirt to reveal a recent scar on the left side of his abdomen. 'The woman who did this to me. When I saw you coming out of my room, I thought it was her.'

'Why?'

'Because you look the same.' As though that was the most natural answer in the world. Her surprise prompted Maliqi to add: 'Well, not really. Not now. But in the corridor, in that light, for a moment ...'

Stephanie said, 'When did you get the scar?'

'Two months ago.'

'Here?'

139

'In Berlin.'

'Who was she?'

'I don't know. But she works for him.'

'Who?'

'Milan Savic.'

They were sitting in a franchised patisserie off Chatham Road South, far enough away from the alley of an hour earlier. Stephanie had given him a choice. They needed to talk, she'd told him, but it was up to him. He could walk away, if he wished. On the other hand, if he wanted to know what she'd been doing in his room...

He hadn't been sure at first. He'd sat there in the dirt, wiping blood from the cut beneath his eye, then massaging his bruised mouth. *Who are you?* he'd asked. She'd said that wasn't a question she was prepared to answer until she had answers of her own.

They'd cleared the immediate area quickly, later finding public toilets on the edge of Kowloon Park. As she had in his hotel room, she'd tried her best to wipe herself clean, scrubbing her arms, rinsing her face, running water through her hair, then slicking it back. In the mirror she'd seen a wreck, but it was still an improvement. Outside, she'd had to wait five minutes before Maliqi appeared. He'd asked her if she'd thought he might run. No, she'd replied, both of them knowing it was a lie. After that they'd headed for nowhere in particular, which was exactly where they ended up: a French patisserie as envisaged by a fast-food corporation. For all its charm it could have been a Burger King in Kansas City.

Maliqi said, 'You don't work for him, then?'

'Savic? No.'

'Why were you in my room?'

'Why weren't you in Macao, when I was in your room?'

He frowned. 'What?'

'You went to the ferry terminal ...'

'You followed me?'

'All day. Until you decided to go to Macao. Or rather, didn't ...'

Maliqi found a wallet of matches from the Shanghai Hotel in his pocket. They were still dry. He lit his cigarette and said, 'If you're not working for him, maybe you're *after* him. And you came after me because you thought *I* was working for him. Perhaps you thought we were the same.'

'Why would I think that?'

'What nationality are you?'

Good question. 'German.'

Maliqi looked a little startled, then broke into German himself. It was better than his English. 'I'm from Bosnia. Savic is a Serb. For you, maybe that is the same thing. Just another Balkan dog ...'

'Considering what you thought you saw in the hotel, I wouldn't be so quick to start jumping to conclusions. What's your interest in Savic?'

Maliqi drew on his cigarette. 'Simic.'

She understood the name was a probe. 'Simic?'

'Goran Simic.'

One of the nine names on the list that David Pearson had recovered.

Stephanie said, 'Never heard of him.'

'Simic fought under Ratko Mladic, first for the JNA, then for the Bosnian Serb Army.'

He left it at that, as though that was enough. And up

141

to a point, it was. Stephanie had known about Mladic long before she'd heard of Milan Savic. He'd been commander of the Yugoslav National Army (JNA) garrison at Knin until he was transferred to Sarajevo in 1992. Not long after that he'd become the first leader of the Bosnian Serb Army. His men had loved him while the media had characterized him as a soldier's soldier. As ever, the truth was more complex: Mladic was a psychopathic coward with a talent for organization.

As leader of the Bosnian Serb Army he presided over the flight of hundreds of thousands of unarmed civilians. It was Mladic's men who established the detention centres that became extermination camps. And it was his men, under his leadership, who committed atrocity after atrocity, culminating, in 1995, in the massacre of thousands at Srebrenica. For Mladic, though, as deluded as he was, such actions were always justifiable because he truly believed he was fighting for the very survival of the Serb people. In that sense he was a man forever marooned among the bodies at Kosovo Polje, the Field of Blackbirds, on 28 June 1389.

Maliqi said, 'I was at Omarska. You know Omarska?'

'No.'

'A Bosnian village, close to Prijedor, although at the time of the Second World War it was Serbian. There was a massacre there in 1941. Of Serbs. Some people say that is one of the reasons for the horrors that took place in the summer of 1992. Revenge ...'

'A Balkan speciality.'

Maliqi nodded. 'Omarska is a mining area, rich in iron ore. And it was the industrial facilities – the factory sheds, the compounds – that were turned into the camps. When my village was cleansed I found myself transported to Omarska. There were thousands of us there. We had little food or water, no facilities. Every night the guards would come and take away ten or twenty prisoners. We would hear them being beaten. Sometimes they used weapons, sometimes just their hands. When they were finished, a bullet in the back of the head made sure. I don't know what they did with the bodies. A truck used to take them away in the morning. At Brcko they used to get rid of them in the animal-feed plant.

'Sometimes they poured petrol over the prisoners and set them on fire. Sometimes they just knifed them. Or they'd take a dozen out, castrate them, cut off their ears, slit their throats. Maybe that would be enough, or maybe they'd come back for a dozen more. Some nights it was thirty or forty. They used to blood their army recruits with us. I watched a teenage Bosnian Serb knife a man old enough to be his grandfather. He was just a child. Crying like a baby, he pissed himself with fear. But the officers wouldn't let him off. They made sure he did it. *Go on, don't be a woman. The first is the hardest. The second is when the fun begins. After that, it's easy.* I won't ever forget his face.'

'That was common?'

'Sure.' Maliqi blew smoke out of the corner of his mouth. 'That boy was different, though. Most of the boys his age couldn't stick the knife in quick enough. For them, killing their first Muslim was better than losing their virginity ...'

'Goran Simic was at Omarska?'

'For a while, yes. Until the end of July 1992. While I was there. And he was among the worst. His favourite

143

way to kill a prisoner was with a hammer. He used to do it naked so that his clothes wouldn't become soaked in blood. And he wouldn't always stop once the victim was dead. It was incredible. I never saw anything like it. His insanity was a raging fever. He would turn a head into stew and not even realize it.'

'You saw this yourself?'

Maliqi nodded. 'He liked an audience. Many of them did. Especially when they were drunk, which was most of the time.'

'What happened to you?'

'I survived. My father, my brothers and one of my uncles – they didn't.'

'Was Simic involved with any of their deaths?'

Maliqi averted his gaze. 'My brothers. Both of them. In front of me. And neither said a word.' He looked back at her, nothing in his eyes at all. 'That's what saved me. He never knew I was the youngest of three ...'

For a moment the ghosts of her own family flared before her. When they were gone, it was back to the bad overhead lighting and piped music.

'Do you have anyone left?'

'In Sarajevo. My mother lives there with cousins of hers. One of my sisters is there too. The other went to Germany. I don't know where she is now.'

'What about you?'

'When I was freed I just wanted to go home. But there was no home to go to. They'd destroyed everything. In our village there wasn't a single building left. They removed it from the map.'

'What did you do before the war?'

'I was a teacher. But I never confessed to that when

I was detained. They killed members of the so-called intelligentsia first. I told them I was a labourer.'

'Then what?'

'For a while I did nothing. I drifted. Prijedor, Bihac, then into Croatia and down to Split. I worked in a bar for a year, getting worse.'

'Worse?'

'All I wanted to do was kill them. The men responsible: Mladic, Karadzic, Milosevic. Then any Serb at all. I couldn't sleep at night. I'd lie on my bed imagining what I'd do. Imagining what I'd use. A pitch-fork, electric cable, boiling oil. All the things I know they used. For those who weren't there, it's hard to understand the animal behaviour that occurred in the countryside that summer. It wasn't normal war. It was a psychopathic rampage. The work of devils done by librarians, farmers, bus-drivers.'

Maliqi drifted into a silence she understood. She left him to it. Five backpackers entered the place, bright rucksacks, shorts, baggy T-shirts, tanned skins and sun-bleached hair. Damp and merry, they shuffled and took their time at the counter. In their twenties, by the look of it, and totally carefree; she envied them. Her twenties had been stolen from her. Now, just a few months shy of her thirtieth birthday, she wondered what the next decade would bring.

Maliqi said, 'In the end I just ran out of energy. I changed jobs so many times, I don't even remember half the things I did. When I was awake I was asleep. That probably sounds stupid but ...'

'No. I understand,' Stephanie insisted. 'I understand perfectly.'

He looked up at her, wondering if she really did, and

145

saw something that convinced him. Which surprised her. Was it so obvious?

Maliqi tapped ash onto the floor. 'Finally I thought about the future. Not in a big way. Just – you know – getting some money. For my mother and sister in Sarajevo. I had friends working in Germany. And my younger sister was there too. So I contacted a family I used to know in Banja Luka and they told me to come. And I've been living and working there ever since.'

'So you became a *gastarbeiter*?'

'Yes. I have a job with Deutsche Bahn in Berlin. I check the track.'

'So what does that make this? A vacation?'

Maliqi managed a tired smile. 'Officially, yes.'

'Why Berlin?'

'That was where my sister was working. At least, that's what she said. I went there to find her but there was no club. No one had heard of it. The address she gave, it was just derelict offices. I don't know where she is now. To be honest, she was always the wild one in our family. It wasn't a surprise when I didn't find her. But I had to keep looking ... our mother, you know?'

'Of course.'

'So I kept going until I ran out of money. After that, I *couldn't* go anywhere else. I called the family from Banja Luka – they were living in Dortmund – and they sent a little cash and put me in touch with Farhad Shatri, a Kosovar living in London. He was with the KLA during the Kosovo conflict. He lives in London now but has strong links with Germany. He helped me get somewhere to live, a job, some documents.'

146

Stephanie drank some more of her sterile coffee. 'And you've been looking for Simic ever since?'

Maliqi fingered his cut. The blood wasn't flowing but the wound was still wet. Beneath it, a bruise was beginning to emerge.

'No. Only since last June.'

'Why did you wait so long?'

'Because before that there was no need to look for Simic. He was dead. Blown apart by a land mine between Banja Luka and Prijedor in 1995. He was in a vehicle with three others. They were all killed.'

'Just like Savic.'

'Yes.'

Stephanie considered the date. 1995. Four years before Savic's own death. If Gemini had existed as a coherent entity, when had it started?

'Tell me about Simic.'

'He was in Hamburg last June, staying at the Atlantic Hotel.'

'Are you sure?'

'He was recognized by one of the staff there. A friend of mine who was also at Omarska. He was doing the room service night-shift and got an order to take up some food to one of the suites. Simic opened the door. At first Hamdu didn't realize exactly who it was – Simic was dead, so why would he? – but he had this feeling, this instinct. Like a cancer, eating away at him. Anyway, he pushed the trolley into the suite. There were two whores on the bed, both laughing. There were empty bottles everywhere, a real party going on. It was while Hamdu was setting up the table that he realized who it was. Simic. Of course he couldn't believe it. Not at first. But there was no doubt about it. He called me straight away because I was in Omarska too. It was about midnight, I remember. I was already in bed because my shift started at six.'

'Are you sure he was right?'

Maliqi smiled sourly. 'I didn't take his word for it, if that's what you mean. How could I? I borrowed a car and drove through the night to get to Hamburg. I missed my work shift but I didn't care. Hamdu clocked off at nine. We hung around the hotel together. We would have waited for a week, if necessary. Anyway, around eleven Simic came through the lobby with the whores, all of them looking pleased with themselves. It was him, no question. The name on the room service check was Ullman. Hamdu checked his hotel registration for the complete details. Paul Ullman, a German from Bremen. I was completely stunned.'

Stephanie thought of Savic, another new German: Martin Dassler.

'Hamdu wanted to confront him. To *kill* him. In his suite, as soon as possible, and fuck the consequences! But I said no. I felt we should think about our options. The police, maybe. Even though I could have done it myself. *Easily* …'

'I'm sure.'

'But I was wrong. Hamdu was right. We should have done it then.'

'He ran?'

'He checked out early.'

'Was he tipped off?'

'Who knows? Anyway, that was when we went to the authorities. They contacted the hotel and the whores. They did what they could. But the address in

Bremen was a dead end. The credit cards, too. Like a ghost, he vanished in a moment.'

It was after nine. They were sitting in a cheap restaurant off Granville Road; red paper lanterns, plastic benches, steam and noise. Maliqi spooned fried rice into his bowl. The last dish sat between them; dumplings stuffed with pork and mushrooms. There was cigarette ash and plum sauce on the paper table-cloth.

At the previous place they'd managed to stretch their coffee over an hour. Not wanting to draw attention to themselves by staying anywhere for too long, Stephanie had decided they should move on.

Maliqi talked about life before, during and after the war. He talked about being a Bosnian, and the more he did so the more confused Stephanie became. Most of Bosnia's population were southern Slavs. Roughly, those who were Orthodox Christians fell into the Bosnian Serb category, those who subscribed to Catholicism were mainly Bosnian Croat, and the followers of Islam, the majority, were regarded as Bosnian Muslims. Also known as Bosniaks. Or, now that times had changed, simply Bosnians. Which was all Maliqi had ever regarded himself as anyway. But war had changed that. Cohesive communities had been divided whether they liked it or not. The old names resurfaced. The Serbs were Chetniks, living off the memory of Tito's Partisans. The Croats became Ustashas, the Fascist Nazi collaborators. And the Muslims simply became Turks, a term dating back to the rule of the Ottoman Empire.

'That's the kind of insanity there was. You think it's

149

strange that men were running around the country killing their friends, raping their friends' daughters, when this is their background? Their heritage? Their *blood*? The trouble with Balkan history is that it's never history.'

He talked about life as a teacher in rural Bosnia. About his community, his school, his friends since childhood. About his wife. About the fact that he now regarded her death from cancer, at the age of twenty-nine, as a blessing. He described the seasons of his past, the landscape, the pine forest that opened onto a meadow where he'd played as a child, the waist-high grasses of summer, the drone of insects, the air thick with pollen, the first frosts of autumn and the glinting hardness of winter.

Eventually he came to the search for Simic. After Hamburg he'd vowed to hunt him down, no matter how long it took. Then he described the process that had brought him to Hong Kong.

'Savic is the key,' he concluded.

'Why?'

'Because he helped all of them. Simic was one of the first – maybe even the very first – and Savic himself was the last.'

Stephanie played ignorant. 'What was his role?'

'He was in charge of it. He had the routes, the contacts, the *finance*.'

'Does the name Gemini mean anything to you?'

He took a while to consider it. 'No.'

'Why do you suppose Savic would go to all that effort? What was in it for him?'

Maliqi sat back and shrugged. 'I don't know. Money, I guess. If that's the kind of man he is. One thing I can tell you for certain is this: suites at the Atlantic Hotel in Hamburg are not cheap.'

Stephanie knew that. She'd spent a weekend with Kostya in one of them.

'Nor are the kind of whores Hamdu saw with Simic,' Maliqi added.

That, too, she knew. Or imagined she did. She felt Petra's cold presence when she asked him, 'So what are you planning to do? Kill him?'

Maliqi shook his head vigorously. 'Savic is the only one who knows. If I kill him I'll never find Simic.'

'You won't find Simic anyway.'

'I found Savic, didn't I?'

'True, but have you got close to him?'

Maliqi's pained silence confirmed what Stephanie had suspected: Maliqi had the desire but not the stomach. He was a passionate amateur, nothing more.

She said, 'The moment you open your mouth, he'll kill you. Or have you killed.'

'You don't know that. You don't know *him*.'

'Trust me, I know him a lot better than you do.'

'What does that mean?'

She ignored the question. 'You had your chance with Simic in Hamburg and you blew it. You won't get another one.'

Stephanie placed some cash on the table and got up.

'Where are you going?' Maliqi demanded.

'Take my advice, Asim. Go back to Berlin. Back to your job. Make a future for yourself and leave Simic in the past.'

'Wait. Who are you?'

* * *

151

The following morning she visited Viktor Sabin at Polar Star Holdings in the Thomson Commercial Building. The gun was a 9mm Browning Hi-Power Mark III. Sabin charged her fifteen hundred dollars for it.

'That must be twice what it costs, Viktor.'

He shrugged. 'Import duty. End-user tax. Freight. Storage. Not forgetting delivery, of course. It all adds up ...'

'End-user tax? That's a little lame, isn't it?'

'Could be worse. I once dispatched three hundred AK-47s from Singapore to Mogadishu packed in coffee crates. On the invoice I included a disinfectant charge against African Swine Fever. Nobody complained.'

'Could they read?'

'They paid, so who cares?'

'You're a classy act.'

'So they say. Was Maliqi useful?'

'A dead end.'

'I'm sorry to hear that.'

His secretary brought them a pot of thick Turkish coffee. Sabin spooned sugar into a miniature porcelain cup so that it was almost half full. Then he poured the coffee, which flowed like treacle.

'Don't you want any?'

'I'll just breathe the air.'

'Please yourself.'

'What does Savic do when he's here?'

'Nothing that makes a noise. There is a rumour that when he's here he's not here at all.'

'What do you mean?'

'He flies into Hong Kong, goes up to the New Territories, crosses over to the PRC without any record of his exit, then comes back the same way whenever it suits him, before flying out of here.'

'Giving the impression that he's been here for several weeks, perhaps, when he could have been anywhere else.'

'Exactly.'

'Do you know if he's here at the moment?'

'He is.'

'How can you be sure?'

'I have my sources at the Dragon Centre. He's staying in a corporate apartment there.'

'I need to meet him, Viktor.'

'I can find out his number. Then you can give him a call.'

Stephanie smiled humourlessly. 'I had in mind something a little more direct.'

Sabin winced, even though he'd known it was coming. 'I want your word that it never came from me.'

'Naturally.'

He picked up a pen and reached for a pad of paper. 'When he's in Hong Kong he goes here once a week. Same day, same time. Don't ask me why. I don't know and I don't *want* to know.'

She took the paper and read what he'd written. 'Tomorrow?'

'Tomorrow. At that time.'

Sabin looked anxious.

'Relax, Viktor. I just want to talk to him.'

'Like you wanted to talk to Mostovoi in Marrakech?'

Chungking Mansions, a teeming sub-city on Nathan Road. A high-rise slum of Hong Kong's cheapest guest

153

houses made from monstrous tower blocks perched unsteadily on top of a two-level arcade, it was as famous for its squalor as its prices. The true residents of Chungking Mansions were cockroaches, not people.

At five past eleven a dark green Jaguar slid to a halt beneath a large billboard advertising Guess jeans. Stephanie was loitering just inside the entrance to the arcade. Savic got out of the car first, followed by two other men. Stephanie recognized the one emerging from the front passenger seat – well over six foot tall, broad-shouldered, blond hair, bland face – but it took a moment to recall his name.

Vojislav Brankovic, the Spoon. Another dead man from the Balkans.

Stephanie was wearing black cargo pants, trainers, a sleeveless faded purple cotton shirt, sunglasses. A Lowe knapsack was slung over her right shoulder. As the men passed by her she turned her back to them and busied herself with cheap umbrellas. Then she followed them in.

Chungking Mansions swamped the senses. Retail units were jammed together, trading cheap electronics, clothes, luggage, haircuts, food, cosmetics. Over the bronchitic gasp of bad air-conditioning she heard garbled Russian, fat frying, African French, Cantonese pop, the percussion of barter, televisions, all of them set against the cacophonous backdrop of spoken Chinese. She smelt curry, body odour, sandalwood and patchouli, rotting rubbish, sulphurous perfumes.

Until now she didn't think she'd seen a single black face in Hong Kong. Here, bizarrely, she was spoilt for choice: north Africans, sub-Saharans, Jamaicans. There were also Arabs, central Asians, east Europeans,

Bangladeshis, Indians, Australasians.

Most of the *bureau de change* booths were on the ground floor, two Travelworld outlets among them. Savic visited both, chatting with the men behind the glass. Brankovic looked bored. On the mezzanine floor the three men entered Khalid Trading Co, which shared a unit with Samarkand Travel. There was a faded PIA poster in the window above an IATA sticker that was clearly fake.

Stephanie dropped back because there was no cover. The mezzanine level had a balcony that allowed a view of the ground floor. The gantries supporting fluorescent tubes sagged beneath the weight of years of accumulated rubbish. A peculiar odour seeped out of the stairwells leading to the blocks overhead. Pale cockroaches scuttled between the tables and chairs of an Indian café, one of many throughout the arcade. Nobody seemed to care; the place was busy, meals dispensed on paper plates by a woman with burn scars down one side of her face.

At five to midday Stephanie followed them back to the ground floor and to the two elevators servicing B block. Savic exchanged a few words with Brankovic and his companion before taking the lift alone. The men melted away. Stephanie waited for the other set of lift doors to open before making her move; just another tourist heading up to one of B block's notoriously grim guest houses.

When the doors rattled open she stepped into a corridor so narrow it seemed to taper. She could touch the loose ceiling panels above her head, piercing white light beating down from one bulb in five, with darkness between. She forked left, past the partially open door of the Taipei guest house, catching a glimpse of a plump middle-aged woman slumped on a chair, her lipstick smudged, an open rose gown revealing too much mottled thigh. A male voice was shouting at her. There was no mistaking the tone. Wang Fai X-Ray Service followed the Taipei, then the Evergreen, a Chinese restaurant crammed into a dimly lit alcove, before, finally, the Lucky Seven Guest House.

The reception area was brightly lit in orange. There was a TV behind the desk, a game show from the mainland playing at full volume. The woman beside it wore a blazer. Given the surroundings, it could not have looked more incongruous; brass buttons with a gold crest threaded through the breast pocket. Her hair was a solid mass of lacquered black above a face of puffy alabaster. Between chipolata fingers a menthol Marlboro was wedged into a tortoiseshell cigarette holder.

'You want room?'

Stephanie nodded.

'Very special room. One hundred seventy-five Hong Kong dollar. You stay three night, only one hundred fifty dollar a night.'

'Can I look?'

'How long you want to stay?'

'I don't know.'

'You pay one hundred twenty-five dollar.'

'Maybe.'

The woman summoned a man to show her. He was almost bent double; a lump rose off the back of his neck like a second set of shoulders, preventing him from looking up at her. Barefoot, he led the way, unlocking an iron grille that opened onto a creaking passage with accommodation on either side and a communal bathroom at the far end. The room had no windows; it was a box made from flimsy partitions. There was an air-con vent above the door, a narrow bed with maroon sheets, a green ashtray, a TV bolted to the wall, a naked bulb dangling from the ceiling.

The man hovered in the doorway. Stephanie worked out where she wanted to be. Not down this corridor where the rooms were numbered 7 to 12.

Back in the reception area she said, 'I want a room with a view.'

The woman screwed her face into wrinkles. '*What?*'

'A window. The room has no window.'

'No window, no window.'

'No windows anywhere?'

'No windows …'

Said with less conviction.

Stephanie looked apologetic. 'Thanks, then …'

She turned to leave. The woman cleared her throat loudly. 'Got a room. But more expensive. Two hundred dollar …'

Down the other passage, no more appealing than the first, and into room 4, a clone of the previous room apart from a filthy glass rectangle that looked across the narrow space between two tower blocks. It wasn't much of a view: dripping water-pipes, decaying concrete, damp washing strung on lines, weeds growing out of unlikely surfaces, all of it in perpetual shadow.

'I'll take it.'

She paid for one night, took the key and retreated to the room, where she locked the door before dumping the knapsack on the bed and opening it. She took out the Browning and checked the action.

Twelve twenty. She had forty minutes. She decided to wait ten. Just after half past, with her knapsack over her shoulder, she stepped into the corridor. The 9mm was in her right hand, pressed against her thigh. A quick glance left and right – she saw no one – then diagonally across the corridor to room 1. She knocked on the door and stood to one side.

Footsteps approached. The lock squeaked. Stephanie eased off the safety-catch and raised the Browning. The door opened. It wasn't Savic.

A young Chinese woman looked up at her in surprise, then horror. Her face was shiny with perspiration, strands of hair stuck to the skin. Before she could react, Stephanie had a foot in the door and a hand across her mouth. In place of a finger she raised the Browning to her lips for silence.

They moved inside. It was very hot and close. The air stank of kitchen grease. Flies circled the light bulb, bouncing off the burnt shade. The TV was on, music playing beneath Spanish dialogue. Room 1 was much larger than room 4. There was a small en-suite toilet and shower immediately to the left, which blocked her view of the bed. She pressed the door shut with the heel of her foot and spun the woman around, clutching the collar of her shirt at the base of the neck, the tip of the gun by her right ear. They inched forward.

'Who was it?'

A male voice, English with a European accent.

Stephanie nudged the woman into the room. Savic was sitting on the far side of the bed, hunched over something she couldn't see, sweat darkening the shirt between his shoulders.

'Hello, Martin.'

He sat up and looked round.

'Or should I say Lars?'

Stephanie shoved the woman forward. She spilled onto the mattress. For a second Savic looked utterly bewildered. Then he put a name to the face and his expression changed.

Stephanie's smile was the coldest Petra could muster. 'Or perhaps I should just call you Milan?'

6

The confusion I see is entirely justified. There's half a world between the Mellah and Tsim Sha Tsui. As Savic struggles to make sense of me I feel the bloody surge that keeps Petra alive. I look at the Chinese girl. Young, petite and very pretty, she's wearing a black mini-skirt and a damson T-shirt that looks like silk. Her skin is creamy and flawless but her make-up has run.

'Where's Maxim Mostovoi?'

Savic shakes his head. 'I don't know.'

I take a step forward, my teeth clenched, and point the gun at his face. I start to squeeze the trigger. Savic blanches, the girl squeaks.

'That's the last time you use that phrase as an answer. Nod if you understand.'

He nods.

'Good boy. Now where is he?'

'I haven't seen him since Marrakech.'

'I don't believe you.'

'I swear it.'

'You set me up.'

'No.'

'He tried to kill me. When we met, you were speaking on his behalf. That makes you guilty by association.'

'You have to believe me.'

'You think so?'

Savic pauses for a few seconds. 'After Marrakech he

vanished. He thought you would come after him.'

'Did he tell you that? Or did you figure it out by yourself?'

'It's what happened.'

'What were you doing in Marrakech?'

I watch him conjure up an answer that isn't the truth. 'It was business. Max and me – we go back a long way.'

Big-boned, he's heavier than in the photographs I've seen of him. In Marrakech he was sitting down in partial darkness so it was hard to tell. His hair is short, thick and black. His eyes are almost the same colour. He's sweating so hard I can watch it streaming down his forehead and cheeks. His shirt is drenched. I'd love to pretend I was the reason, but I'm not. It's like a sauna in here, my own skin prickling as the pores open up.

'Can I ask you something?'

His first move.

'Go on.'

'Why were you in Marrakech? Your deal – it never existed, did it?'

'It served its purpose.'

It takes him a while to work it out. 'Because it got you close to him?'

'That's right.'

'Someone hired you to kill him?'

'No. It was personal. He cheated me.'

'Ah.'

'I lost a lot of money because of him.'

'That's what this is about? Money?'

'Not really. He left me for dead.' That slows him down. I let it sink in for a moment. Then I say, 'He should have made sure when he had the chance.'

'I never heard about this.'

Which is when I drop the bomb. 'Claudio Argento.'

The effect is immediate: his spine stiffens, the eyes widen.

An Argentinian based in Paris, Argento negotiated a deal with Mostovoi in July 2001 for a cargo of arms and explosives to be shipped from Tirana to Marseille. At the exchange there was a shoot-out. Five people died, including Argento himself. Since Mostovoi's business has always depended on his reputation, the incident has been reworked. Revisionist history now plays it like this: Argento tried to cheat Mostovoi and so the Russian exacted a brutal revenge. *Thus a negative became a positive, allowing Mostovoi to emerge from a potentially damaging incident with his professional reputation not only intact, but enhanced.*

Except that Magenta House had discovered the truth.

'The shoot-out in Marseille was engineered by Mostovoi, wasn't it, Milan? As retribution. Argento was fucking Mostovoi's girlfriend. That's what it came down to. Not just fucking her but boasting about it too. He let everyone know just how much she loved to be degraded by him ...'

Savic's expression tells me I'm right.

'The trouble is, Argento never told him who the end-users were. Or that he wasn't negotiating the deal directly. I put up two million dollars when I hired Argento to talk to Mostovoi. It wasn't his deal, Milan, it *was* mine. And my partners put up another *two million*. That *was* our *deal*. So when Mostovoi walked off with *our* money and *our* cargo, that left me four million down.'

'If this is true, Max never knew.'

'Well, that's a great comfort. Sadly, my partners never saw it like that. They're not renowned for their tolerance. It must be the cocaine.'

'Narcotics?'

'Well, there are some people who regard them as Colombia's finest. FARC.'

162

'They were the end-users?'

'Would have been. Fortunately, I wasn't dealing with them directly. Unfortunately, the three-man contact group were not very understanding when I couldn't come up with their money.'

'Look, I don't know about any of this ...'

'They sent four men to take care of me in Miami. They didn't even bother trying to kill me for the first forty-eight hours. You know how it is. Boys will be boys. Entertainment first, business later ...'

Now he's beginning to get it, and he looks truly worried. I'm an unbalanced woman with a loaded gun. And not just any woman, either. A woman who enjoys her work, if her reputation is anything to go by. A woman with dead eyes.

'Anyway, I'm here and they're not. In case you're wondering, they experienced more pain than I did.'

I offer him a sickening smile. Why not? He's a man familiar with other people's pain. He might appreciate it. Except it doesn't look like that. If anything, he looks like he might throw up. Which is, in its own way, deeply satisfying.

'It took a lot of time and effort to track down the members of the contact group. Now they're dead, that just leaves Mostovoi.'

I move deeper into the room. There's a door on the far side of the bed, light seeping from beneath it. I can now see what he was bending over when I entered: a bulging canvas bag. I take another step forward and peer inside. Passports. A couple of hundred, I'd guess, many nationalities, mostly used by the look of it, the covers dog-eared and scratched. On the floor, beside the bag, lie bricks of cash: Hong Kong dollars, US dollars, euros, Chinese Yuan.

'Take some, if you want.'

I couldn't look more disgusted. 'Is that what you think of me?'

'I don't know where he is. I need time.'

There's a part of me that's itching to squeeze the trigger. I'm already exerting more pressure than I should. Savic is lucky I've got a steady hand.

'I can't tell you how easy it was to find you, Milan.'

This, perhaps, scares him more than anything else.

'If you shoot me you'll never get to Mostovoi.'

'Don't be absurd. Of course I would. You're simply a short cut.' I ease the safety-catch back on. 'But I'm not going to shoot you. I'm going to make it easy for you. I'm going to give you the opportunity to establish some trust.' I lower the Browning. 'You're going to make some calls. Tomorrow we'll meet. You pick a time and place and I'll be there. Come alone. If you don't show, I'll find you. Take my word for it.'

And with that, I'm gone.

Time for a change. First, new clothes. She went to Pacific Place, a slick shopping mall spread over several floors, where she bought a piece of Samsonite luggage and clothes to fill it. There were two hotels on top of Pacific Place, the Conrad and the Island Shangri-La. From a coffee shop on the ground floor, she rang them. Both had rooms available. She made a reservation at the Conrad, then returned to her room at the Majestic on Kowloon. She showered in tepid dribble, changed into some of her new clothes, gathered her belongings, then checked out and moved into the Conrad. Claire Davies, accountant turned tourist, had become Claire Davies, accountant, full stop.

Now there was nothing to do but wait. At seven she went downstairs for a drink. The bar at the Conrad offered the greatest possible contrast to room 1 of the Lucky Seven Guest House at Chungking Mansions: cool, open and airy, muted light, tables set apart, walls of glass offering a view of glittering skyscrapers. There was a singer, accompanied by a pianist. Slim, with glossy waist-length hair, wrapped in a figure-hugging dress of ruby silk, she brought 'These Foolish Things' to a close and launched into 'One For My Baby'.

Stephanie was the only single woman in the bar. The majority of the customers were on business, she estimated, plenty of single men among them. As Stephanie, that made her uncomfortable. More than once she'd been alone in a hotel bar only to be mistaken for a hooker. As Petra she couldn't have cared less. Except that there was a part of her that remained Stephanie: the Siemens phone that she'd brought down from her room. Petra's phone was still on her bed.

A waitress asked what she wanted to drink. She ordered a glass of champagne, then checked the phone. No messages. Not a spoken word, in fact, since she'd left London. Just the playful e-mail. The part of her that was Petra was delighted.

A short cut. That was what she'd told Savic he was. The more she thought about it, the truer it was. A short cut to the Gemini list. A short cut to the big prize; a future beyond Magenta House. A future where all the options were hers.

Her champagne arrived in a slender flute. She drank to Mark. Later, alone in her room, she dialled his number. But she never pressed the green button.

Lan Kwai Fong in Central, a steep sloping street littered with bars and restaurants popular with ex-pats and locals. Stephanie had checked it during the afternoon and had found it a suitably sterile environment. At five to six it was still relatively quiet, the after-work rush hour not yet in full flow. Stormy Weather was at the top of the street, on the corner; Moby playing on the sound system, English football on the TV overlooking the bar. Stephanie was amused to find Savic already there, a bottle of Blue Girl beer almost finished, two Salem cigarette butts in the ashtray. Clearly, missing the meeting had never been an option.

Apart from a white T-shirt, Savic wore black, including a black leather jacket. *They always do.* He drained his beer bottle, waved it at the girl behind the bar and asked Stephanie what she wanted. Mineral water, she said, sliding onto the stool opposite him. He lit a third Salem.

'Yesterday, for the first time in my life, I thought I was a dead man.'

'You're not looking too bad on it.'

'When I was growing up in Belgrade it never occurred to me. Even during the campaigns of the nineties there was never a moment where I actually thought I was going to die.'

'It's not great, is it?'

'It's happened to you?'

'Once.'

'Actually I'm surprised it hasn't happened to you more often.'

'In my business it usually only *ever* happens once. Just before the fear becomes a reality.'

'Maybe you should change business, then.'

'What I do is who I am.'

Stephanie didn't think she'd ever uttered a truer phrase as Petra.

Savic said, 'I guess it's the same for me. I've always been in business. In Belgrade, when I was a kid, I stole a rusty foot-pump from a garage. I used to let down car tyres, then charge people for inflating them again. At first one or two of them smacked me around the head. So I sneaked out in the night and slashed their tyres to ribbons. Everyone got the message. Pretty soon I didn't even have to bother letting tyres down. People paid me not to.'

'What about Croatia? Or Bosnia and Kosovo? Was that business?'

'I don't know what you've heard about me but I can guarantee you this: it won't be the truth. You should hear some of things people say about you.'

'I have. The difference is, they're mostly right.'

Savic said, 'What would it take to make you forget Mostovoi?'

'Amnesia.'

His smile didn't last long. 'Look, he and I are business partners. We have a shared history.'

'I know.'

'If I give him to you, I'm screwing myself.'

'If you say so.'

'What about a compromise?'

'The men in Miami weren't interested in compromise.'

'Max had nothing to do with them.'

'Don't be naïve.'

'We can make a deal.'

'You're not listening.'

Savic sat back and exhaled in exasperation. 'Okay.

So you kill him. Then what?'

Stephanie shrugged. 'I'll get to that when the time comes.'

'Killing him won't buy back what you lost.'

'You're overestimating me. My thrills come pretty cheap.'

'Come on. There has to be a way around this.'

Time to offer him a glimpse.

Stephanie waited, then softened. 'What have you got in mind?'

The Lexus was outside the Conrad at ten the following morning. Stephanie sat next to Savic in the back. Vojislav Brankovic was hunched in the front passenger seat. They took the Cross Harbour Tunnel to Kowloon and headed for Kai Tak, the airport that had served Hong Kong until July 1998.

They cruised past the old departure terminal, now a vast second-hand car showroom that also traded left-hand drive vehicles for the Chinese mainland, then headed out along the deserted runway, which protruded into Kowloon Bay. When they reached the tip they came to a driving range, Oriental Golf City. The rubber stains left by aircraft wheels were still visible on the cracked concrete of the car park.

Savic said, 'Go onto the range. He'll be down the far end.'

'Who?'

'The ugly bastard. You'll see.'

'You're not coming?'

'He'll want to talk to you alone.'

She got out and shut the door. The Lexus pulled away. She watched it bounce over sleeping policemen, then head back along the taxiway that ran parallel to the runway.

A fierce sun burnt in an unusually clear sky. A stiff breeze blew across the bay, churning the waters. At twenty past eleven on a mid-week morning, Oriental Golf City was almost deserted. There was no one in the shack that passed for a clubhouse. The driving range was the rough grass that had once fringed the end of the great runway. There were only three men practising, two nearby, one away to her right. She headed for him.

He had his back to her; a small man in tan trousers, white golf shoes, a black polo shirt and a towelling visor. Stephanie stopped and watched a shot. The ball looped into the air and fell short of the hundred-metre marker.

'Do you play?'

'No.'

'That's a shame. The idea of someone like you playing golf is amusing. The golfing assassin. It has a ring to it, don't you think?'

He turned round. His jaw was grossly undershot, his nose splayed to the face, hooded eyes partially concealed behind glasses with a heavy black frame and tinted lenses. The mouth sloped, his blubbery lips thicker towards the droop. Thinning black hair was oiled back over the scalp, the sun winking on the slick.

'My name is Gilbert Lai. I hope you don't mind if I practise while we talk.'

'Not at all.'

'I'm a member of the club beside my house at Deep Water Bay. Usually I play there. But when I have to come to town I always make sure I have an hour here. Especially at this time of the day, if I can.' He tapped another ball onto the mat. 'Standing here, at the end of the old runway, we are about as isolated as it is possible to be in Kowloon. Or Hong Kong, for that matter.'

Stephanie moved so that when he addressed the shot she was facing him. He raised the club and swung. The ball travelled further than its predecessor.

'Golf is the new heroin, Miss Reuter. Except it's better than heroin. Because it doesn't kill its addicts. And because its addicts have money. Which means they can be bled for longer and for more.'

'And it's legal.'

'Another advantage, yes.'

'On the other hand, it's not without its devastating social consequences.'

Lai looked surprised. 'Such as?'

'The clothes.'

She was as inscrutable as he was.

'I have many interests, property among them, and I can tell you this: entertainment is the future. The new Disney complex that is being constructed here is proof of that. In my own modest way I have contributed to the culture. Here we are restricted by lack of space. On the mainland, that has never been a problem. I own seven courses. My travel agencies provide package tours for people in Hong Kong. They book through my companies, they stay in my hotels, they play on my courses.'

He hit another ball. Badly hooked, it curved to the left. Shielding her eyes from the sun with a raised hand, Stephanie looked around. To her right, North Point and Quarry Bay on Hong Kong, to her left, across the Kwun Tong Typhoon Shelter, Kwun Tong itself, fronted by the old cargo working area. Large dredgers were moving along either side of the runway.

'Earth moving,' Lai explained. 'They're trying to decontaminate the land.'

'What's wrong with it?'

'Seepage from the massive underground tanks that used to store aviation fuel.'

'What follows decontamination?'

'Potentially, the greatest property development project we've seen here in years. But nobody knows what it will be.'

'Is that another reason you come here?'

He didn't answer immediately, preferring to play another shot. Then he changed the subject. 'I don't know what Savic has told you.'

'Next to nothing.'

'I have a proposition for you.'

'I'm listening.'

'I wish to hire you.'

Stephanie watched a dredger slope past them. 'When you said you had a proposition, I imagined you were talking about a financial settlement.'

'In a way, I am. I know why you're here. You want Mostovoi. But Savic doesn't want to give you Mostovoi because of the consequences he will face. Which, in turn, will present me with problems I could easily do without. The truth is this: killing Mostovoi isn't worth the trouble.'

'That's easy for you to say.'

He nodded. 'I understand you lost two million dollars when Claudio Argento was killed. And that your partners lost another two million.'

'That's right.'

'If you agree to my terms I will compensate you

fully. Three million dollars. Two for the money you lost, one for the job I have in mind.'

'Does Mostovoi know he's worth so much? To me he's always been a slug; something fat that leaves slime in its wake.'

Lai smiled for a moment. 'As a human being I'm inclined to agree. But you're in Hong Kong now, Miss Reuter. This is business. Sentiment we leave to others.'

Stephanie looked out to sea. 'What's on your mind?'

'One job, two targets.'

'Who?'

Lai slid his five iron into his golf bag and took out a seven. 'One of them is local. Chinese, rich, prominent in his own way, but nobody outside the SAR. The other is an American, based in Singapore, a lawyer.'

'Usually that would qualify you for a discount.'

'They're not political. It's strictly business.'

'Names?'

'Felix Cheung and Alan Waxman.'

'I'll need time to consider it.'

'Naturally. My driver will take you back to your hotel. He'll give you my personal number. You can call me any time you like.'

At the Conrad she sent an e-mail to Magenta House, asking for S3 profiles of Gilbert Lai, Felix Cheung and Alan Waxman. Shortly before seven she received a reply from Rosie Chaudhuri.

Please find attached a profile for one of the three. Speak to our contact regarding the other two.

Stephanie opened the file. Gilbert Lai's wealth was estimated at a billion dollars, primarily in real estate and shipping. His first fortune was made at sea and he continued to maintain a global cargo fleet and container business. In the seventies he'd moved into property, specializing in hotels and casinos, and had once enjoyed a close association with Stanley Ho, founder of the Sociedade de Turismo e Diversoes de Macau, the body largely responsible for overseeing Macao's transformation from provincial slumber to gambling glitz. A keen gambler himself, Lai had secured his own place in Las Vegas folklore when, during a one-week visit in 1991, he managed to drop $1.5 million in a single evening at Caesar's Palace, only to win $2.1 million at baccarat three nights later.

There were persistent rumours of a Triad connection. Many of them were fuelled by Lai's reluctance to deny them; he never spoke in public on any issue, a rule he'd maintained for over twenty years. He was a known associate of Lee Wing-fat, a money-launderer wanted by the FBI in San Francisco, and Yip Wai-fa, a heroin trafficker and immigrant smuggler busted by the DEA in New York in 2000, following a raid on one of his properties on Mott Street, Manhattan.

Lai himself had faced accusations of money-laundering on more than one occasion. Privately, according to S3 sources, this had always amused him greatly. 'Of course I launder money,' he'd been overheard to say, 'I'm a casino owner.' Running cash through casinos had always been one of the easiest methods of money-laundering. Lai's hotel-casino portfolio included properties in Australia, Malaysia, Indonesia and the Philippines.

These were his legitimate business interests and formed the first third of the file. The last two thirds documented his 'known' criminal activity.

Lai owned two companies on the mainland that were shells for software counterfeiting. For a long while the global centre for illegal software manufacture had existed on a single block in the Sham Shui Po district of Hong Kong, at the junction of Fuk Wah Street and Pei Ho Street. At the time this illegal activity had been controlled by Triads, which was one of the reasons Lai decided to establish factories in the southern province of Fujian, on the Chinese mainland. The other reason was scale; supply was being swamped by demand. By 2000 the software counterfeiting business had been worth twelve billion dollars annually. Lai had pioneered the transformation from an anarchic criminal enterprise into a streamlined industry. Since then the two factories at Fuzhou had diversified into CDs and DVDs.

Lai was also involved with the counterfeiting of spare parts for commercial airliners and the theft and resale of luxury cars worldwide, both being trades that made use of his global shipping business. But, as Magenta House pointed out, Lai himself was legally insulated from these activities by an impenetrable web of companies created by the sharpest legal minds money could buy.

Stephanie looked out of the window and wondered why Lai hadn't taken care of Waxman and Cheung himself. Particularly if his reputation for insulating himself from the sharp end of his interests was justified.

Just after two the following afternoon Stephanie boarded the Star Ferry bound for Kowloon. She took a seat to the rear of the Upper Deck. Just before the ramp was raised, Raymond Chen appeared. When they'd first met, Stephanie had thought his pony-tail was a bad idea. Seeing his hair fall freely, she was no longer sure. Wispy and greasy, the wind blew it around his head.

Chen waited until the ferry had pulled away from the pier, then handed Stephanie a photograph. 'Alan Waxman, fifty-one, born and bred in San Diego.'

'Not much of a looker.'

'Not much of a character, either. Waxman's on the Limbo list. Apparently that means something to you.'

File SA/13/RM/2.1, also known as the Limbo list, was a database containing names that had cropped up during Magenta House preparatory investigations into targets. Although not yet targets themselves, where the evidence merited it they had been added to the file. Where they languished, never to be deleted, ready for some future transgression that would allow Alexander to promote them to the bullet.

'What did he do? Fail to pay a parking fine?'

'Waxman has been conducting business on behalf of Osama bin Laden since 1991, setting up financial screens. Ghost accounts, off-the-shelf companies. Over the years he's provided the same service for Chinese criminal organizations, the Russian Mafiya and, in a private capacity, for government officials in Malaysia and Singapore.'

'He sounds good. I must take his number.'

Chen laid out the details that had earned Waxman his place on the Limbo list. On 6 September 2001 investors on the Chicago exchange bought two thousand 'put' contracts on United Airlines. That represented about ninety times the usual trading activity.

The deal cost $180,000. After 11 September it was worth $2.4 million. Through a tangled knot of companies Magenta House had traced the initial order back to Waxman. Subsequently other pieces of business had been placed next to him. There had been very high levels of short selling of Munich Reinsurance, which lost £1.3 billion after the Twin Towers attack. Swiss Reinsurance also suffered, as did Axa, not to mention American Airlines. In total, it was estimated that Waxman's invisible clients made about twelve million dollars out of 11 September.

'How interesting.'

Chen missed Stephanie's sarcasm and said, 'Not as interesting as this: Milan Savic has been a client, too. Last year Waxman was involved in a property deal with Chinese clients of Felix Cheung's. Hotels, two in Shenzhen, one in Guangzhou, the fourth in Macao. The reason the deal came together was because both parties had a mutual business acquaintance from the past.'

'Savic?'

'Correct. Back in the days when he was doing business with the Chinese, Waxman brokered some of his deals. They made money together. Waxman knew Cheung and introduced Savic to Gilbert Lai. Lai acted like an old-fashioned comprador when Savic first started coming to Hong Kong and China.'

'What's Felix Cheung's story?'

'Cheung is Triad through and through. At least, he *was*. Started out as a *fei jai* – just a kid hanging around on street corners looking for trouble – before becoming a 49, when he joined a Triad street-gang. He used to do the whole nine yards: pimping for hookers, running protection, loan-sharking, debt collection, narcotics. Pretty slick with a chopper too, though that never stopped him getting cut.'

Traditionally, choppers were the Triad weapon of choice, especially for street violence; kitchen cleavers, up to thirty centimetres in length, normally with a wooden handle. Most choppings were not intended to kill and were usually administered to the arms or legs. It was not uncommon for victims to lose fingers. Where death was the intention, the victim was cut all over the body and left to bleed.

'Didn't take him long to become a Red Pole, over-seeing his own group of 49s. That was when he first started to make serious money. The way it works is like this: 49s hand over the money they generate to a Red Pole, who then pays them their percentage, takes a larger percentage himself, before passing the rest onwards and upwards. During this period Cheung opened restaurants throughout Kowloon – good legiti-mate enterprises with lots of cash running through them. Since then he's diversified. Entirely self-made, he's no idiot. He's got a shrewd investment brain and an even shrewder team of advisors to back him up. These days he's got restaurants all over the territory, also in Shenzhen, Humen, Zhuhai and Guangzhou. He owns the transport companies that supply them and the farms that produce much of their food.

'Superficially he's cleaned up his act. A respected businessman, he's a minor celebrity. He gives a lot to local charities, sits on the boards of a couple of commu-nity projects – one of them an infant school – and throws parties that make the papers. Lives in a large house in a well-protected compound in Kowloon Tong, with his wife and three children; two sons and a daughter. He also owns an apartment on MacDonnell Road, which is where he keeps his mistress. He visits her three or four times a week, usually around lunch, or early afternoon. Often she imports a friend or two.'

'A busy man.'

'Very busy. Most of the ones who've made it the way he's made it like to leave the past behind. Not Felix. He still likes to get a little dirt under his finger-nails.'

The ferry began to decelerate as they approached the pier at Tsim Sha Tsui.

Chen said, 'Magenta House would like to know how they're involved.'

Stephanie smiled. 'So would I.'

7

Gilbert Lai sent a car for her: a black BMW X5 with black windows and a mute driver. They took the Aberdeen Tunnel to the South Side. Standing on concrete stilts, Lai's house at Deep Water Bay protruded from the hill behind, a sweep of pale pink set against dark green vegetation. The three storeys were staggered, the façade a curve. From the road there was a twisting drive that led to the rear of the house. Vehicles were parked along it, thirty or forty of them, gleaming and expensive. On the phone, Lai had mentioned that he would have guests. Stephanie had assumed that meant three or four.

The entrance was on the top floor, an open space with a wall of glass at the front, overlooking Deep Water Bay. A servant was waiting for her, dressed in black. Head bowed, eyes averted, he led Stephanie away from the steps that led to the terrace below, where Lai's guests had congregated. Instead she found herself being ushered into an enormous room with no windows.

'Mr. Lai will be with you as soon as he can.'

With that, the door closed and she was alone.

There were paintings on the walls, set well apart, each independently lit. Down the centre of the room were four glass display cases, two on either side of a sculpture that sat at the centre of the room: a smooth globe of a head by Constantin Brancusi, dated 1913, in bronze with gold leaf and dark brown patina.

Stephanie examined the paintings on the far wall: mostly Dutch, sixteenth and seventeenth century, they included works by Salomon van Ruysdael, Thomas de Keyser, Gerard Ter Borch and Johannes Lingelbach. The wall opposite contained only contemporary paintings; Karel Appel, Asger Jorn, Jean Dubuffet and Jean-Michel Basquiat. The display cases were a mixture of porcelain, glass and silver, and also included two Fabergé eggs.

The floor was the last thing Stephanie noticed. At first glance it appeared to be nothing more than a hard mottled surface, divided into large squares. But when she looked at it more closely she realized that what she was standing on was reinforced glass and that there was something beneath.

She dropped to a crouch. The speckle effect began to come into focus. They were tiny leaves, perhaps, of several colours: orange, rust, grey, ochre. But there was still something further beneath.

Gradually she saw. They weren't leaves. They were hands. Tiny hands, palms upward, supporting the glass panel on which she stood. Beneath the hands were arms and bodies. Small men, in work clothes, made from plastic or some kind of resin, all identical, packed tightly together. Thousands of them per square. She looked up and down the room and tried to guess how many there were in total.

A male voice said, 'One million, more or less …'

She looked over her shoulder. Gilbert Lai was standing in the doorway. She stood up and smoothed the creases that had appeared in her black linen skirt.

'Of all the pieces of art in this room, this floor is my favourite. And unlike every other piece, it's a copy. The Brancusi – at auction, that would probably sell for somewhere between eight and ten million dollars. This floor, built to fit this room, is worth nothing.'

'I've never seen anything like it.'

'The original was created by the Korean artist Do-Ho Suh. A true genius, despite being Korean. He has made entire apartments – accurate in every detail and to scale – out of diaphanous silk and nylon. He created wallpaper out of thirty-seven thousand miniature photographic portraits. Everything he does stimulates the mind. Take it from me, Miss Reuter, a man of my wealth can afford anything, and that can be a curse. It can leave you jaded. I find Do-Ho Suh is the antidote to that.'

Lai was wearing black trousers, a Gucci belt to go with his Gucci loafers – complete with matching gold buckles – and a silk shirt with stripes of black, lilac, chocolate and deep purple.

'Have you come to a decision?'

'Almost.'

'What else do you need?'

'Answers.'

He nodded slowly. 'You want to know what the condition is?'

When they'd spoken on the phone, Lai had said there was one condition that he would have to impose if she accepted the contract. She'd asked what it was and he'd declined to tell her, arguing that until she accepted, it was irrelevant.

'Is that the only answer you require?'

'Not quite.'

181

'What else?'

'I need to know the reason.'

'Why?'

'Because I don't walk into anything blind.'

'I give you my word …'

'I don't want your word. I want the reason.'

He chewed on this for a moment, then conceded. 'The reason and the condition are entwined. The condition is this: both men must die simultaneously.'

'I'm sure that can be managed.'

'Not as easily as you might imagine. They are never in each other's company.'

'Never?'

'Never. For precisely this reason.'

'Anywhere else and that might sound like paranoia.'

'I'm a rich man but I didn't start out that way, Miss Reuter. I had to fight to get where I am today. Over the years I've made deals, alliances and enemies. Mostly, over those years, I've been a predator but, as I've grown richer and older, I have become a target for other predators. Younger, hungrier, stronger – you could describe it as some sort of Darwinian cycle – they see age as weakness. But I have two advantages over them: experience, and the resilience that comes through experience.

'Felix Cheung is a parasite. He's enriched himself by feeding off others. He hasn't created anything. The restaurants he owns are simply vehicles for crime. The parties he throws, the donations he makes – they are cold and calculated. I don't pretend to be a virtuous man, but I have a code that I adhere to. Cheung doesn't. His only interest is money. He would sell his mother to a butcher.'

'In my line of work I've come across men like that before.'

'I'm sure you have. And men like me, I expect. I don't know how much you know about me but I imagine that in the past few days you have been finding out what you can.'

'Naturally.'

'Then let me ask you this. Last year my son – my only child, as it happens – was kidnapped. Did you know that?'

Raymond Chen hadn't mentioned it in his capacity as a Magenta House mouthpiece, or in his own right. 'No.'

'That is because it was never reported. Not to the authorities, not by the media. Yet if you ask me how many people in Hong Kong had heard something of the incident, I would say many thousands. If somebody told me that figure was as high as half a million, I wouldn't disbelieve it. Rumours preying on rumours based on a kernel of truth. Hong Kong operates on many levels, including those levels that are not open to your sources.'

'Evidently.'

'The kidnap was organized by Felix Cheung. My son was held captive for a month. Inevitably, there was a negotiation. As a father, all I can say is that I was prepared to meet the first demand instantly. But I couldn't. Because if I had, other demands would have followed. As you probably know better than I do, there is a process to go through. Neither side can acquiesce too swiftly, nor be too resolute in any given position. It's a dance. And a very brutal one, too.'

Lai moved into the room and paused by the

Brancusi, running his hand over the smooth, clean curves.

'When they sent the first demand, they also sent my son's severed right ear to prove how serious they were. The final demand, four weeks later, was accompanied by a videotape. It showed Cheung's men beating him with hose-pipe before cutting off the little finger from his left hand and forcing it into his mouth. Two days later he was released.'

'What did you pay?'

'A lot. But not very much at all, really.'

'And how is he?'

Lai was still caressing the Brancusi, but now he turned his back to her. 'He's living in Europe. At first he was in a clinic outside Stockholm. Now he lives in Geneva. He likes to ski. At one time I had hoped he would take over from me. Now I think he'll probably pursue our mutual interest in art. Before last year that would have made me angry. Now it makes me happy.'

'That's what this is about – revenge?'

'Sadly, it's rather more complicated. Part of the agreement I struck with Cheung was that once my son was returned, and once he'd received his money, there would be no further action on either side. This sort of arrangement is not unprecedented in this part of the world. Alan Waxman was brought in to negotiate the details on Cheung's behalf. When the money was paid, it was Waxman who handled it and who has subsequently been responsible for investing it. This I know through my own sources.'

'If it's not revenge, what is it?'

Lai turned again to face her. 'Despite the agreement, both Cheung and Waxman felt it necessary to take precautions. They let me know that if anything happened to either one of them, the other one would enforce retribution. I think you can guess what that means.'

'Your son?'

He nodded. 'In order to strengthen this position, they agreed not to meet again. This has not been a problem. Although Waxman has represented Cheung for a number of years, they had only met twice prior to my son's kidnap. It's not as though they are friends. Anyway, this was a measure they decided to adopt in order to protect themselves.'

'So if you're going to do one, you need to do both.'

'Exactly.'

'But if you'd all agreed that the matter was resolved, and if you insist you're not in it for revenge, why bother?'

'Waxman and Cheung have grown complacent. They feel secure. So secure, in fact, that they feel they can elicit more money from me. And, to be frank, they could. The trouble is, once they start, where will it end? My only priority is to protect my son from further harm. I take it you don't have any children?'

'No.'

'I don't mean to be condescending, but if you ever do, you'll understand. My fear is not that I shall bleed to perpetual blackmail. I can afford to. But I cannot – *will* not – allow the possibility of further harm to my son.'

'I understand.'

'Not fully, I'm afraid. It now transpires that they are actively planning to renege on our agreement.'

'When?'

'Some time within the next three months.'

'How do you know?'

Lai hesitated, but only for a second. 'Let us say … this: that one of Cheung's 49s transgressed in a local matter that came to my attention and that my people have questioned him thoroughly.'

'That sounds painful.'

'I believe it was.'

'Look, you don't need me for this. I'm sure you have access to blunter instruments who'd be a lot cheaper.'

'I want somebody who isn't connected to me. An outsider. And at the same time somebody who – if the connection ever *is* made – has the requisite reputation. Either way, I need somebody who can put an end to this matter. I need you.'

Time for Petra to show her true colours. 'Four million US dollars.'

Lai stiffened. 'Four? We agreed on three.'

'We didn't agree on anything. Three is what you offered. But four is what it's going to cost.'

If Lai was angry, it didn't show. After a protracted, contemplative silence, he said, 'Three point five.'

'This isn't a negotiating tactic. The price is four million. Or put another way, half a Brancusi head.'

That made him smile. 'I should have made you wait for me in another room, perhaps.'

As a courtesy, Stephanie returned the smile. 'It wouldn't have made any difference.'

I could have asked for five or six million, perhaps even ten. He had to agree, which is what I suspected, and which was why I raised the price.

He leads me out of the room, across the hall, through a gap

186

in the glass and onto the uppermost terrace. Out of dry, cool stillness into breezy, humid heat, yet there isn't a cloud in the sky. Far below us, to our left, is the exclusive Deep Water Bay Golf Club – Lai's local club – while in front of us, at the foot of the hill, stretches Deep Water Bay Beach, a narrow curve of golden sand running parallel to Island Road. It's a beautiful view. An expensive view.

Again, Lai seems to read my mind. 'This is perhaps the most desirable location in Hong Kong. The other houses around here belong to some of the richest and most powerful people on the island.'

'It's not hard to see why.'

'There's more to it than what you can see. The location has excellent feng shui. The houses all look out to sea. As you can appreciate, Deep Water Bay is horseshoe-shaped and the hill that we are on is at the base of that horseshoe. The hills and islands that form the rest of the curve on either side of us are like the arm-rests on an armchair. The hill behind is the back of the chair. It is important that we are half-way up the hill; not too high, not too low. The hill means we have something solid behind us, which is good. Looking directly ahead, we can see out of the mouth of the bay to the open sea beyond. There is nothing in the way. That is also good; it means there are no impediments to progress.'

The concept of feng shui is alien to me because I've come to associate it with the inane blather of intellectually shallow TV presenters. Gilbert Lai is the first man I've met who regards it as something more significant than a design accessory to lend cheap bathrooms a veneer of class.

Lai waves a hand over his guests who are on the lowest terrace. 'Why don't you come and meet some of my friends and associates?'

'Is that a good idea?'

'With these people, that won't be a problem. And after this we won't meet again.'

On the lowest terrace there is a large rectangular swimming pool with a dragon at each corner. It's an arrangement I've seen before.

'The villa in Marrakech – that belongs to you, doesn't it?'

Surprise makes way for curiosity. He's wondering how I know. Which means his ownership is concealed.

'It's Savic's villa.'

But his tone tells the truth: it's Savic's villa nominally.

I try another angle. 'Why is Mostovoi worth so much to you?'

'Beyond your personal involvement – for which you are now being generously compensated – does it matter?'

'I'm just curious. Where's the mutual interest?'

Lai thinks about this for a moment, then says, 'Global transport.'

Before I can ask anything else, we've reached the lower terrace and we're among people. But the answer does have a certain synergy: Mostovoi is in aviation and Lai is in shipping.

The first thing that strikes me about his guests is the number of them who are speaking Russian. Not just the European and Caucasian types, but some of the Orientals too; Mongols, Koreans and Asiatic Russians. Broad and squat with toughness etched into their faces, they might be wearing silk suits or designer casual wear, but they're not fooling anybody. The imported European clothes on their bodies look as out of place as the imported European girls on their arms. I look around and conclude that I'm the only female guest who isn't decoration.

Julia is a six foot tall Russian, with blonde hair, pale skin and cold, green eyes. She's smoking a Marlboro Light and

*drinking Krug 85 from a tall glass with a slender stem shaped
like a lily. She says she's twenty-five and almost looks it.
Which means she's probably still a teenager. Girls in Russia
grow up faster.*

*'I had to get out of Moscow, you know. My boyfriend …
crazy bastard …'*

*I can easily imagine her boyfriend. The young firebrand
with the most money. The kind of boyfriend who casually
hands out Rolexes and black eyes.*

'So you came here?'

'I was in Berlin.'

'Ah.'

*'Fucking all kinds of guys. You know how it is.' I'm not
offended by her assumption. I'm just disarmed by her blunt-
ness. 'It was good money but … there were too many of them.
I wanted to narrow it down, make it simple. Who are you
with?'*

'No one.'

*For a second there's hostility, as she wonders if I'm a
threat. It's a look I've seen too many times to count. From too
many Julias to count.*

*A waiter appears at our side, dressed in a white tunic with
gold buttons, bottle-green trousers and black slippers. He
refills our glasses from a magnum streaming condensation.*

'Who are you with?' I ask Julia.

*She points to the back of a bull-shouldered man in black
slacks and an iridescent black silk shirt. He's an ape; the black
hair on his scalp is cropped short and continues down the
back of his neck towards his shoulders, before disappearing
into the collar.*

'Aslan Shardov.'

'What's his story?'

'He's political.'

189

'Where?'

'Kazakhstan.'

'In Astana?'

'When he has to. But his businesses are mostly in Almaty.'

Business and politics being indivisible in Kazakhstan.

'What line of work is he in?'

'Construction. Transport. Banking.'

Anything and everything. Which explains why he's political: the wheels of commerce need constant lubrication.

'What's it like in Almaty?'

'At first I hated it. After Moscow it was so backward. But I like it now. The mountains are beautiful. We have a large house outside the city. It's quiet.' She takes a drag from her cigarette, blows smoke in my face, then breaks into a grin. 'Of course it helps that we go to Europe so often. I love London and Paris. Berlin's okay, too, but there's always that worry …'

She lets the sentence die but I know what she's thinking. 'That you're going to run into a familiar face?'

'Exactly.'

'And after Shardov?'

Just as I didn't take offence earlier, so she doesn't now. I'm not being rude. I'm being straightforward. We both know it.

She shrugs, then looks out to sea. 'Aslan's been good to me. I've got some money. When the time comes … I don't know. Spain, maybe. Or Italy.'

'Not back to Russia?'

She shakes her head. 'Every time I think of Russia, I think of all the men who fucked me. I can't separate the two. What about you? How come you're here?'

I tell her it's business. She giggles. Everyone's there on business, she replies. Not just the men. The women, too. Later I'm introduced to Ivan Simonov, another Muscovite, now

190

based in Hong Kong, working in shipping. He's talking to Dieter Hausmann, from Berlin, now living on Sakhalin, an oil man. He used to work in Vladivostok.

I say, 'Do you know Konstantin Komarov?'

The name rings a bell but he can't quite make the connection.

I give him a prompt. 'Primorye Air Transport.'

'Of course. Yes.'

'You know him?'

'I know of him. But we've never met. PAT I know. They have contracts with many of the oil and gas companies in the region because they have a reputation for reliability. In the Russian Far East that's more valuable than oil or gas itself.'

Hausmann introduces me to Zoran Antovic, a Serb from Moscow, a financier. When I ask him who he works for he looks at me as though I'm an idiot. 'Nobody.'

'You invest your own money?'

'Always.'

When he asks me what I do, I say, 'I'm a trouble-shooter.'

'Who do you work for?'

Now it's my turn. 'Nobody.'

He grins, splitting silver stubble with cosmetically enhanced tombstone teeth. And so it goes on for two hours. This peculiar gathering. I meet a sanitation engineer from Krasnoyarsk, a government official from Ürümqi, in the western Chinese province of Xinjiang, just a few hundred miles from the Kazakh border, and a Russian army officer based in Novosibirsk. I share a drink with another Serb who sells computers in Berlin and London.

'What brings you to Hong Kong?'

'My supplier is located in Fujian.'

'What kind of computers do you sell?'

'Any kind you like.'

191

'All the brands?'

'All the brands.'

'All supplied from Fujian?'

He raises his glass to me. 'Correct.'

We both smile at that.

When I decide to leave, Lai himself escorts me to the BMW X5. 'Have you enjoyed yourself?'

'You've got an interesting circle of friends.'

He seems genuinely pleased by this. 'It's what keeps me going. You'll let me know your arrangements for payment?'

'In a day or two.'

'Good. And thank you.'

'Before I go, can I ask you something?'

'Of course.'

'I know what you're getting out of our arrangement. But where does Savic fit in?'

'Milan and I have a bond.'

'You don't seem like the sentimental type to me.'

'I'm not. And nor is he. It's a business matter. He needs me more than I need him, so it's in his interest to see this done.'

'Why does he need you?'

'Do you know what guanxi is?'

'No.'

'Connections. Guanxi is a system of connections. It's the way business is conducted in China and among Chinese communities abroad. Its roots are in our agricultural past. It's a system of favours between families, between friends. It starts in infancy, exists in schools, through marriage, in secret and open societies, it runs through generations. It can be traded or inherited, but never ignored. It grew out of a system and an era where there were no legal controls. In that respect you could describe it as organic. With guanxi you have access to the best enterprises, the best people, the best prices. Without it

… well, you have nothing.'

'And your relationship with Savic allows him to tap into your connections, giving him an advantage denied to most outsiders?'

'Precisely. Whether it's buying cheap televisions for Belgrade housewives, or sanction-busting petroleum products for a discredited regime.'

'Presumably it's a two-way street.'

'Naturally.'

'So what do you get from him?'

Lai looks deep into my eyes for several seconds. I'm beginning to think I won't get an answer, when he says, 'I provide connections for him in this part of the world and he provides them for me in Europe.'

Savic is supposed to be based here, not in Europe. 'What connections?'

A sly smile spreads across his deformed lips. 'The best imaginable.'

As the lift rose or descended, so the interior lights altered their colour and brightness to match the ambience of either destination, top or bottom. It reminded Stephanie of Maclise Road. An airlock, the interface between two different environments; from Stephanie to Petra and back to Stephanie again. Or, in this case, from the lobby of the Peninsula, Hong Kong's finest hotel, to Felix, the Philippe Starck restaurant perched on top of it. Given the nature of their business, she didn't think the name of Savic's choice of restaurant was a coincidence.

A reed-thin waitress in black led her through the dining room to a massive table on a raised dais at the far end. The table was a slab, lit from inside. It glowed milky white, like illuminated marble. Milan Savic was waiting for her, a chunky tumbler in one hand, a cigarette in the other, his weathered face caught in a cone of falling light and rising smoke. He was wearing a dark blue V-neck T-shirt beneath a charcoal suit. It didn't look smart, or casual; it looked wrong.

Stephanie ordered a glass of sauvignon blanc from a passing waitress, then sat on one of the stools by the glowing slab and looked out of the two-storey wall of glass. Across Victoria Harbour the sparkling skyscrapers of Hong Kong lit up the night sky. Through the opposite window Kowloon glittered all the way to the New Territories.

Savic said, 'For my money, the best view in the world.'

It had been late afternoon when she'd returned to the Conrad. Within an hour he'd called to ask if they could meet. At nine he'd sent a car. The driver had been different from the one who'd driven them to Oriental Golf City. Stephanie recognized him from the Magenta House disk that Raymond Chen had given her: the Macanese named Figueiredo.

'I'm pleased you managed to work out something with Lai.'

'How much did he pay to get his son back from Felix Cheung?'

'Three hundred and sixty million Hong Kong dollars.'

Down the centre of the table there were lots of small glass cups, each containing a candle. Scattered among them were dozens of plastic beads, dark green or clear, like huge emeralds and diamonds. Savic began to play with a dozen of them.

Not one for small talk, he got straight to the point. 'In my world there are enormous possibilities for a woman like you.'

'For a woman like me there are possibilities everywhere. I'm never short of offers.'

He grinned. 'I can imagine. All the same, can I make a suggestion?'

'If you want, but there's no point. I'll say no.'

'How can you be so sure?'

'Look, I came here for Mostovoi. You're lucky that I'm going to let him live. You should leave it at that.'

'You're getting very well paid.'

'I'm not being paid to let him live. I'm being paid to work. And to look the other way. Anyway, money isn't the reason I took the job.'

'No?'

'No. I'm doing it for his son. I have plenty of money.'

'You forced Lai higher.'

'I also have a market value. I don't do discounts. When you hire me you pay a lot but you get what you pay for.'

'What about Mostovoi?'

'Until I met you, it was personal. When you said you needed him he became a commodity. I don't feel anything for him.'

'But you were going to kill him.'

'Again, that was a business decision. He damaged my reputation. That has a value too.'

Savic considered this. Then: 'You don't like me, do you?'

'I don't know you. So I don't feel one way or the other about you.'

195

'But you've heard things about me and you don't like *them*.'

She was going to qualify her answer, then chose not to. 'Why should I?'

'Because you have no idea who I am. Or what I've done.'

'Does it matter? If God exists, neither of us will see Him.'

The waitress brought Stephanie her glass of wine. Once she'd moved away Savic said, 'You're right. We're the same.'

She didn't deny it. He raised his glass, she raised hers to meet it. And saw something new. In Chungking Mansions he'd been afraid. At Lan Kwai Fong he'd been tense. In the car to Kai Tak he'd been cautious. Here, his confidence restored, she could see hunger.

His smile was conspiratorial. 'The things they used to say about me when I was alive. Savic, the Balkan butcher. Savic and his Inter Milan monsters. How many commentators were there? And the ones that were there, did they see both sides? Because I'll tell you this: it was war, not ethnic cleansing, or whatever the phrase for this week is. In war the boundaries between right and wrong become blurred. And until you've been at war yourself you don't know. Not the UN, not those parasites in The Hague and certainly not all the tourists from the media. Bastard journalists dropping into our misery for a working holiday, running around getting over-excited in their bullet-proof vests, then back to some fucking Hyatt with room service and CNN. *You* know what I mean.'

Stephanie hesitated. Not because of what he said – she recognized most of that was true – or even the force with which he said it, but because of what she was feeling. This was a pitch. A professional seduction handled by an amateur.

They ate at a table close to the window with the harbour view. Boats were crisscrossing the water, pin-prick lights marking them out against the oily darkness.

After they'd ordered, Savic said, 'Do you know what I do?'

'I know you used to sell second-hand TVs in Belgrade.'

'True.'

'Then you were in illegal oil.'

'Also true.'

'But until I found out who Lars Andersen really was, I didn't even know you were alive.'

'You didn't recognize me in Marrakech?'

'I'd never seen a picture of you.'

'So how did you find out I was Lars Andersen?'

'Like you, I have my sources.'

He let it drop. 'So?'

'Narcotics, maybe? The Balkans was always a pre-ferred courier route.'

'Not just for narcotics.'

'Tell me.'

'People.'

Their starters arrived; for Savic, honey-tempura prawns with Korean chilli and tobiko sauce. Stephanie had seared rare lemon-pepper ahi sashimi. The wait-ress opened a bottle of Chilean cabernet sauvignon and left it to breathe.

'People are the perfect commodity. You should understand that. I mean, assassination is a people

197

business too, right? The difference between us is that they pay me for a service but you ... you just kill them.'

He was pleased with himself.

'Why don't you say that a little louder? I'm not sure they heard you in Beijing.'

Savic couldn't have cared less. Here was a man who could be standing over the body, the smoking gun in his hand, the police coming through the door, and he still wouldn't have a worry in the world. No wonder he'd been in his element in the Balkans. He was never going to amble into a stray bullet. Stephanie had come across his breed before; rare, certainly, but never destined for extinction.

'Do you know how much human trafficking is worth, annually?'

She took a wild guess. 'Three billion dollars?'

'Add ten. And that's just the official estimate. I would say it's between fifteen and twenty billion a year. And it's not just the money that makes it attractive.'

'No?'

'The penalties are nothing compared to narcotics. Even better, the product works for you. A kilo of heroin incriminates you. An immigrant defends you.'

'Why?'

'Because they have a family back home.' Said without so much as a blink. 'There's one other thing. These people, it's what they want. In the West – in the media, especially – all you hear about is the exploitation. Well, sure, we like to make a profit. Just like General Motors or Airbus. But we're also providing a service. These people dream of making it to the States, or to Europe.'

'Please – I'm getting misty.'

'It's true. Nobody forces an immigrant to come to us. They come because they want to. Why? Because they know that if they stay they'll be condemned to poverty permanently. All they want is a chance.'

When Savic had finished eating he lit a cigarette. Stephanie drained her glass. 'Where do I fit into this?'

He was gazing out of the window. 'We're talking about a fifteen billion dollar industry where the most important qualification for success is not a certificate from Harvard. It's the will to do whatever is necessary. Making new markets, protecting established markets – it's never easy, it's often painful. You and I understand something that nobody else in this restaurant understands. That when you want something you have to take it. I didn't have the luxury of growing up in a society where you could ask politely and get something back. Or even where you could work for an eventual reward. Strip away the thin veneer of civilization and we all look after our own interests first. Call me a bastard, if you like, but at least I'm not a hypocrite.'

'I'm not like that.'

She could see he didn't believe it. 'Well, you may have had the privilege of being raised in Germany, but look at you now. What happened to make you who you are today?'

The main courses arrived: Stephanie's sautéed sea scallops on wasabi potatoes in a Singaporean black bean vinaigrette and Savic's double cut French veal chop.

'What, exactly, are you proposing?'

'Between here and Europe, we deal with Russians, Ukrainians, Georgians, Azeris, Chechens, Kurds, Afghans,

Croats, Bosnians and Italians. But in Europe itself, at the end of all the routes, we find ourselves in competition with two major groups. The Turks and the Albanians. The Albanians, in particular, are a problem for us.'

'Just like they were in Kosovo?'

He managed to restrain himself. *Just*. 'Do you have any idea what it was like for Serbs living in Kosovo before the conflict? Do you know what it is to be part of a persecuted minority?'

Five in the morning and I can't sleep. I've been tossing and turning for an hour. Now I get out of bed and draw the curtains. It's dark and raining.

I've got a headache. It was after one when I got back here. I drank too much with Savic. I feel a little confused. I'm satisfying Gilbert Lai to buy my way in to Savic but I suspect there's a more direct route available.

I switch on my Siemens phone. There's a text message from Mark. He misses me, he hopes it's going well, he hopes I'll be home soon, he loves me. That's it. No spoken message. I don't want to read it. I want to hear it.

I run a hot bath and soak for half an hour, drinking as much mineral water as I can. Then I call room service and get them to send me some coffee. I watch BBC World for a bit but I'm too agitated to concentrate.

At six I call him.

'Hello?'

He hasn't recognized the number. Then again, why should he?

'Mark?'

'Hello? Who's this?'

He's struggling against a noisy background: clinking glasses, laughter.

'It's me.'

'Steph?'

'Yes.'

'Hey – where are you?'

'In Hong Kong. Where else?'

A crass thing to say. I ask him where he is. In a restaurant, celebrating Julian Cunningham's promotion.

'He's been made a director.'

'Great,' I say, even though I can't remember what he does. Karen's told me many times but it never registers. Something in the City, I guess. Still, a bigger salary means better holidays and a new four-wheel-drive vehicle to clog up London's congested streets. Which is nice.

'Hang on, let me see if I can go somewhere less noisy.'

This was a mistake. I listen to Mark extracting himself from the table. He tells them it's me. Two or three people shout hello. Like me last night, they've had too much to drink. They're having a good time, which only reinforces the fact that I'm not.

'That's better.'

'Where are you?' I ask.

'Outside. It's raining but I'm under a canopy.'

'It's raining here too.'

'Small world.'

'Very funny.'

'You okay?'

'I'm fine. You?'

'Of course.'

I can't believe we're going through the motions like this. I ask him who's at dinner. They're all couples. Except him. And the girl Karen invited to balance the numbers. Justine Morgan.

'Justine …'

201

'Rob's in Paris this week, so she was on her own.'

Which is perfectly reasonable. Except that Mark once slept with Justine. Long before she married Rob. Long before he met me. Mark told me about Justine the first time I was due to meet her. It wasn't a problem. It never has been.

Until now.

I know it's completely ridiculous but I feel jealous. Actually it's worse than that. I feel suspicious. Which is unfair because I know there's no reason for it. But there it is. I can't deny it, and it stains the rest of my conversation with Mark. I barely hear what he's saying. At best, the questions I ask him are a waste of breath.

Eventually I say, 'You haven't asked me what I'm doing.'

Even as I say it I know it's reckless. I can almost hear Mark thinking.

'If I do, will you tell me?'

I'm standing at my window, my face pressed to the glass, sixty-one floors falling away below me. I gaze into the lit apartment windows in other skyscrapers. Other people, other lives, other secrets.

'No,' I whisper.

'Stephanie?'

'What?'

'It's okay.'

'Is it?'

'You know it is.'

Cathay Pacific CX715 left at eight in the evening, landing in Singapore at twenty to midnight. Stephanie checked into the Dragon Inn on Mosque Street in Chinatown. She had two days in Singapore. Both mornings, she tailed Waxman from his home in the grassy enclave of Alexandra Park to the skyscraper

202

on Raffles Place where his law firm was located. Waxman's offices were on the ninth floor. Stephanie didn't bother going up. Both days, he went for lunch at Jade, the extortionate Chinese restaurant in the nearby Fullerton hotel. On her first day he spent the afternoon at Oceantech Container Services, a storage facility for ship containers on Tuas South Street. That evening he went for dinner with a group of six at Au Jardin les Amis, a French restaurant in a colonial house by the Botanic Gardens.

The second afternoon was spent at a large house on the Mount Pleasant Estate. Shortly before dusk Waxman went for a walk with two men through the nearby Chinese cemetery. Stephanie followed at a distance discreet enough to render their conversation inaudible. It was a creepy place, almost empty, with paths curling through thick vegetation. Among rain trees, rampant undergrowth and dripping tendrils were Buddhist tombs; surrounded by incense sticks, made from stone or brick, most had a small portrait of the dead at their heart, either a photo or a painting.

She arrived back in Hong Kong on Friday evening. On Saturday morning, monstrous grey clouds rolled in from China, threatening rain. Stephanie headed for MacDonnell Road in the mid-levels, where she made several passes of the apartment block where Cheung kept his mistress, Daisy Yiu. Over the course of the following week Stephanie would witness Cheung entering and leaving the apartment four times.

On Sunday, around midday, she tracked Viktor Sabin to the Metropol Restaurant in the United Centre. A vast, brightly lit place with a low ceiling, it was packed, everyone eating *dim sum* and talking at full volume, the uproar as penetrative as a drill. Sabin was at a table with three Chinese and one of the Russians she'd seen at Gilbert Lai's house. They hadn't been introduced but she'd overheard him talking to the sanitation engineer from Krasnoyarsk.

Sabin looked ánnoyed, then smiled, the grease shining on all his chins. 'I'd forgotten I'd invited you.'

Stephanie played to his sarcasm. 'That's okay. I'm not staying.'

She pulled up a chair from the next table. The Chinese looked at each other while the Russian looked at her, making no attempt to conceal his hostility. He was whey-faced with thinning, mousey hair, pale blue eyes and bad teeth, in tracksuit bottoms and a black leather coat; Stephanie wondered if he resented the intrusion or whether they had, in fact, met in the past.

'Can you get me this?'

She handed Sabin the note. He took a few seconds to absorb the request. An old woman walked past pushing a *dim sum* cart. The Russian took two bamboo baskets from the top and opened them: steamed pork and shrimp dumplings and steamed mince beef balls. He extinguished his cigarette in the remains of a barbecued pork bun rather than use an ashtray, then picked up some chopsticks. Another woman appeared and four bottles of Tsingtao replaced the four empties. Also on the table there was tea, a plate of half-eaten crispy beancurd rolls and some vegetables, which had been largely ignored.

'The second item, easy. The first … I'll need to know the type of phone.'

'Motorola.'

'The exact type.'

'I'll have the precise specification for you in a day or two. But is it possible?'

Sabin nodded. 'I know someone who can do this. But it's work I have to contract out, you understand?'

'When can I have it?'

'When do you need it?'

'Come on, Viktor. You know the answer to that.'

'As soon as possible?'

8

Ten to ten on a soggy Tuesday morning in Mong Kok. Stephanie, Savic and Vojislav Brankovic were sitting at the bar in Kiss Kiss on Fife Street. By day the interior of the club was no less dismal than the exterior. A stained carpet on the floor, stale cigarette smoke for air, the hum of a diesel generator powering a pump to clear an overflowing toilet. There was a runway protruding into the room, four dancing poles along its length, an old barefoot man cleaning each of them with a wet rag.

'Girls come here all the time. They want to dance, to earn good money. We only take the good-looking ones. The best ones get sent down to Club 151 in East Tsim Sha Tsui. We'll go there later. Some of the ones who make it here are pimped under the protection of a Red Pole. Most of them want to go to America. If they can raise the money, we start the process. First, though, they have to buy out their contract from the Red Pole. Normally it's not a problem. But we have to check. The last thing we need is anything that draws attention.'

Brankovic was slouched over the bar, playing with a book of matches, turning them over and over, his eyes never straying from his fingertips.

'When you say you start the process, you mean here?'

Savic nodded. 'This place has a reputation. If you want to catch the wind that will blow you to the West, you come here. Or to Gold Cat. If they're going to fly, or travel overland, they need documents. They provide the photos, we provide the passports. We have specialist centres. At Chungking Mansions, for instance. There are others. When they pick up the document they're given a location, a date and a time for collection. Sometimes it's here, sometimes at one of the shops we operate on Flower Market Road, sometimes somewhere else.'

Stephanie remembered following Asim Maliqi. 'Flower shops?'

'For those going overland to Europe. The trucks that bring the flowers into the city early in the morning take the girls out. They get delivered to farms we own in the New Territories and across the border in China. We use them as holding centres. They wait there until it's time to leave. When they depart they go as a group. Through China, to the north and west. Up into Russia. There are gangs along the way. We have arrangements with all of them.'

Savic excused himself and headed for the cloakroom.

'So you and Milan go back a few years, then?'

Brankovic looked at her and nodded.

'You're from Serbia?'

A shake of the head.

'Bosnia?'

A shrug of the shoulders; *maybe*.

'A Bosnian Serb?'

A nod.

He was heavier than Mark and Stephanie reckoned he was a couple of inches taller, which made him six foot six. Everything about him was placid: his expression, the way he shuffled, or slouched, the glazed eyes.

'Do you like Hong Kong?'

Another shake of the head.

Savic was on his way back.

'Well, it's been nice chatting.'

Still nothing.

She asked Savic what route they used.

'We have several. From Kazakhstan or Russia, through the Ukraine, down into eastern Europe. Or across central Asia, through Turkey and the Balkans. It's the same when they fly. A document to get them to Kuala Lumpur or Bangkok, then something to take them on to Moscow, Istanbul, Karachi. Then a connection to Prague or Budapest. Or even Sofia. From there, anywhere ...'

'What about America?'

'They tend to travel by boat. These days we aim for Mexico, for two reasons. One: the United States coastguard is more proactive than it used to be. Two: once they're in Mexico they're not our problem any more. The Mexican gangs don't bother with any kinds of documentation. They prefer to try to run them across the Rio Grande and get them to a large metropolitan area, where they can disappear.'

An hour later they were at Club 151 in East Tsim Sha Tsui, a far larger establishment, almost completely deserted. Stephanie imagined the lacquer effect – predominantly black and red – looked good at night, under lights carefully dimmed and directed, but by day it was no less depressing than Kiss Kiss.

In one room there was a karaoke stage. The girl with the microphone looked bored and beautiful: a mini-skirt, rhinestone cowboy boots, a pale powder blue shirt, one tiny hand on a jutting hip, lips pouting. She didn't appear to have an audience. The backing track started and she began to sing. Hopelessly out of time and tune, she was half way through the song before Stephanie recognized it: 'A Little Less Conversation'.

'A little less singing wouldn't go amiss.'

Savic guided her towards the VIP lounge, placing a hand at the centre of her back. He left it there longer than necessary. When he withdrew it he ran a finger down a short stretch of spine. She didn't react at all. Somebody brought them cappuccinos in black cups with red rims. 151 had been sprinkled onto the foam in chocolate powder.

Stephanie said, 'There were a lot of Russians at Lai's place.'

'We work well with them. Everybody makes money. I've always had Russian contacts. Even before I came here for the first time. These days there is a noticeable Russian presence in Hong Kong. Mostly, the money is legitimate. Where it came from originally – who can say?'

Stephanie was thinking of Komarov when she nodded. 'You don't run the Russian routes yourself, then?'

'No. They wouldn't permit it. We'd be crushed if we tried. Everyone has their territory. There were some Russians from Vladivostok who tried to establish themselves in Macao a few years ago. They were running white Russian girls through the casinos, who turned out to be very popular with the customers. But not so popular with the local Triads. In the end it all turned to shit. There was a New Zealand lawyer who was living here – Gary Alderdice – and he fell in love with one of these girls. Natalia Samosalova. They went up to Vladivostok to try to buy her out of her contract for US$150,000. Both of them were murdered. After that the Russians were kicked out of Macao. Too much heat. The Triads made sure of that.'

'How?'

'They colluded with the police. At least that's the rumour.'

'Where do the local girls come from?'

'The poorer estates in Sham Shui Po, Cheung Sha Wan or Shek Kip Mei. Or from the mainland.'

'What percentage of your business do they represent?'

'The majority of those heading West are male. For us, females represent ten to fifteen per cent. For most groups, five to ten, I would say.'

'What do they pay?'

'It depends on where you want to go and how you're going to get there. Roughly speaking, between thirty and sixty thousand dollars.'

Stephanie raised an eyebrow. 'Not a bad return for a journey that would normally cost a few hundred dollars on an airline.'

Savic was annoyed. 'A few hundred dollars is a waste of money if an immigration official sends you home on the next flight. They're not buying an air ticket. They're buying a life.'

Over ten days, when she wasn't preparing for Waxman and Cheung, Stephanie spent more time with Savic than she'd expected. Since her agreement with Lai, Savic had relaxed and seemed happy to show her elements of the business. He took her to the site for the proposed Cyberport development beneath the village of Pok Fu Lam on the south-west of the island. Lai, he told her, would have a piece of it. Which meant he would too; the trickle-down effect.

They visited farms in the New Territories: chickens, pigs, beansprouts, flowers, all on an industrial scale. The chicken sheds were huge, the birds crammed into cages, fluorescent overheads ensuring it was light twenty-four hours a day. He took her to haulage depots in northern Shek Kip Mei and So Uk: cavernous warehouses filled with the sweet stench of diesel, echoing to the wheeze of sickly engines, lorries shunting in and out around the clock.

At first she thought she was getting close to him. He was star-struck, that much was clear. As taken with the physical reality of Stephanie as he was with the myth of Petra Reuter. Conversation revealed mutual acquaintances other than Marcel Claesen. Carleen Attwater, for one, and former US marine John Peltor. Peltor was a freelance assassin. The last time Stephanie had seen him was in the British Airways departure lounge at JFK. They'd had a couple of drinks over an hour of industry gossip; to the casual observer, a chance meeting between two executives on business. Peltor was on his way to Africa. A fortnight later, stranded between flights at Oslo airport, Stephanie read about the death of Prince Mustafa, the Mogadishu warlord, in a copy of the *International Herald Tribune*. Hit through the heart by a long-range sniper.

On the subject of Carleen Attwater, Savic said, 'Do you know her?'

'I've met her. I don't know her.'

'A strong woman.'

'That's the impression I got.'

'We didn't always agree – in fact, we argued a lot – but her opinions were never coloured by propaganda. For that I always respected her. At the time, that wasn't easy.'

'I can imagine.'

'Where did you meet her?'

For a second Stephanie wondered whether she should lie.

'London.'

'Yes, I remember. She and her husband were based there, I think.'

'They're divorced now. He's living in the States.'

'I'm not surprised.'

'Oh?'

'She told me they were separated. I think they'd been living different lives for a long time.'

That conversation occurred in an office in the Lippo Centre. Later, through a glass partition, Stephanie watched Savic and Brankovic together. They weren't aware that she could see them because of the angle, and she couldn't hear what they were saying, which forced her to look harder. It was the first time she'd seen Brankovic animated. Both laughed at something, then fell into conversation. She watched the body language – the gestures, the looks – and understood that the two of them were bound by something she couldn't penetrate: shared history.

She needed something more.

They were at his apartment in the Dragon Centre. Except it wasn't his. As Stephanie had anticipated,

Raymond Chen had traced ultimate ownership back to Gilbert Lai. Just like the villa in Marrakech.

The apartment was luxuriously uncomfortable: marble everywhere, ferocious air-conditioning, large rooms, mostly empty with white walls and gold fittings; it couldn't have been more impersonal. They moved outside to the terrace around the pool.

Savic said, 'Cheung's going to Shanghai.'

'When?'

'Thursday morning.'

It was Sunday afternoon. 'When does he get back?'

'Not for ten days. He's going on to Beijing and coming home via Taipei.'

'That leaves Wednesday.'

'Can you manage that?'

'Yes.'

'You could wait.'

He *wanted* her to wait. It wasn't his tone that betrayed him. It was his eyes.

'No. By the time Cheung gets back Waxman will have gone to Los Angeles. And he won't be coming back here for six weeks.'

'Six weeks …'

He let it drift. There was no reasonable justification for six weeks.

By Monday evening she had both men's schedules to compare. Waxman's was light – only a lunch at the Fullerton with an Israeli arms dealer and another lawyer – whereas Cheung's was busy; matters to attend to before Shanghai. There was a gap, however. Three hours blocked off. Another last-minute assignation before a period of enforced abstinence.

When she made her reservation she altered carrier,

choosing Singapore Airlines instead of Cathay Pacific. She picked SQ859 to take her to Singapore, arriving just after five in the evening, and booked herself on the first flight back to Hong Kong the following morning, SQ870, departing at half past seven, leaving her just over fourteen hours on the ground. Arriving back in Hong Kong at eleven fifteen in the morning, she reckoned there would be plenty of time.

That evening she met Raymond Chen in the bar at the Mandarin Oriental. Set against a wall-to-wall backdrop of bankers in button-down shirts, he looked even more preposterous than usual in a black silk polo-neck beneath a very light grey suit with shiny slip-ons of the same colour.

'I just wanted to know how things were going.'

Stephanie arched an eyebrow. 'That's why you asked to meet me here?'

'Sure. To see if you needed anything.'

'Like what?'

'Like … anything.'

'Raymond, doesn't working for Alexander bother you?'

At first she thought she'd insulted him. She took his blankness for offence. Then he said, 'Personally, I think he's a total asshole. But working for him keeps me in business and out of jail. What's your excuse?'

Just for a moment she could have kissed him. 'Let me buy you a drink. What are you having?'

'Strawberry daiquiri.'

The following evening she was at another bar, 1/5 on Star Street in Wan Chai: high ceiling, low lighting, stone for a floor and muted colour everywhere.

214

Catering largely to the after-dinner crowd, it was relatively empty at nine. Savic was drinking whisky, Stephanie was on vodka.

'Do you think you'll ever go back to Serbia?'

He laughed. 'Of course!'

'When?'

'Not for a while. But some day.'

'The climate might have changed by then.'

'I've heard that climate change is a bad thing. Personally, I agree. And the climate *was* changing in Serbia. Now we've changed it back.'

'What are you talking about?'

'Zoran Djindjic.'

Serbia's Prime Minister until Wednesday 12 March 2003.

'You had something to do with that?'

'No.'

'You mean, not directly?'

For a moment he wasn't sure. Then he smiled. 'Legija is an old friend.'

A shiver ran down Stephanie's spine. Legija was the alias for Milorad Lukovic, head of the ringleaders suspected of masterminding the assassination. Stephanie had come across his name before. He'd been responsible for a multitude of horrors, including the torching of the Croatian village of Dreznik in 1991 and the massacre of Albanians in Drenica in 1998. Lukovic had been the leader of the Red Berets. Officially a special operations unit within the Serbian Interior Ministry, in practice they operated death squads that rampaged through Croatia, Bosnia and Kosovo with the blessing of Slobodan Milosevic.

Since the end of the conflict Lukovic and his

right-hand man, Dusan Spasojevic, alias Siptar, had been prominent Belgrade mobsters involved in human trafficking, prostitution, illegal immigration, narcotics and gun-running. Lukovic was a good friend of Svetlana Raznatovic, better known as the popular singer Ceca, also famous for being the widow of Arkan, the most notorious Serbian warlord of them all. It was this that had prompted the shiver.

'Did Djindjic really merit it?'

Savic snorted with contempt. 'He was among the worst of them.'

'You mean, the ones who betrayed Milosevic?'

'Milosevic was a fucking idiot.'

In other words, yes.

'How come you left when a man like Lukovic stayed?'

Stephanie asked the question despite knowing the answer. Savic was on a list, Lukovic wasn't.

His version was more elaborate. 'The victors always write the history. In my position I could see that I was going to be … *misunderstood*. I knew there would be retribution. That's what happens. So it was time to leave. It's as simple as that.'

'Except becoming Martin Dassler can't have been that simple.'

'No harder than it is for you.'

'Not true. I'm used to not being anyone for more than five seconds.' He conceded the point with a shrug. Stephanie pressed on. 'I've heard there were others like you.'

Savic tried to feign indifference. 'Where did you hear that?'

'Let's just say that if it isn't true it doesn't matter.'

'It *isn't* true.'

'Then it doesn't matter.'

Except that she could see that it did. And he knew it. He lit a cigarette and changed tack. 'Do you have anyone?'

A question straight out of the blue. Stephanie's instinct was to answer too quickly, to blurt something out, *anything*, but she restrained herself. 'What about you?'

'Is that the way it's always going to be? I ask you a question and you answer it by asking me the same question?'

'Depends on the question.'

'I don't have anyone. I did, for a while. Sabine – we were both in Germany. But it was complicated.'

Sabine – we were both in Germany. Stephanie wondered where in Germany. Hamburg, perhaps, where Goran Simic had been sighted? She'd been expecting to hear details about Krystyna, the spectacular Slovakian lap-dancer.

'Why was it complicated?'

'We had a professional relationship before we had a personal relationship. Work was always in the way. Plus, I was here most of the time. In the end she started to work out of Moscow and we saw each other so little, it didn't seem worth the effort.'

'Business and pleasure, like oil and water.'

He nodded. 'You?'

Mark's sleeping face filled her mind. 'I don't have anyone.'

'Not at all?'

'You find that surprising?'

'I don't know. Maybe.'

'I can't afford the involvement. It's not worth the risk.'

If only Alexander could hear me now.

'Too many lies?'

'Not just that. I can't be involved with anything I can't leave in a second. That doesn't make for good relationships.'

'No baggage when you travel.'

'Exactly.'

He put his right hand on her left knee. She didn't remove it. She didn't encourage it, either. She just looked at it, then at him.

'As I was saying, business and pleasure, oil and water.'

Yau Ma Tei, Kowloon, seven in the evening, a cube of darkness opening directly onto the street. Suspended on a single hook dropping from the centre of the ceiling were five pig carcasses, the steel spike running through the hind leg of each, just above the trotter. Their bodies as pale and smooth as alabaster, heads pooled on the floor, jowl by jowl, light fluid oozing across the concrete towards an open drain. In the gloom to the rear she saw men hacking at a sixth carcass.

She stepped back and checked the number of the building. It was correct, so she ventured in. The men stopped chopping. One of them came towards her, a bloody blade in his right hand. She handed him the piece of paper with the Chinese script and he waved her towards the back. Down a narrow corridor, in almost total darkness, she came to a dead end in the form of a lift. She pulled open the cage, stepped inside, closed it and pressed the upper of the two buttons on the brass panel.

She rose two storeys and was disgorged into a total contrast: a salon of some sort, two plump sofas covered in purple velvet, scarlet walls with a damask inlay, a dimmed chandelier, its bulbs shaped like candles. On one wall there was a large oval mirror – the glass mottled – set in a baroque gold frame. The air was thick, sweet with the scent of jasmine. A Chinese woman in her fifties greeted her. Exquisite, in a black dress with gold thread, she beckoned Stephanie to follow her with a tiny curling finger. A heavy sapphire curtain swept aside, down a scarlet corridor to a door on the right. She smiled, pointed and vanished.

Stephanie didn't bother knocking. Inside there was dope and incense. The light was low, flickering gold. There were no windows. It looked like the inside of a tent, large folds of plum-coloured material gathered at the centre of the ceiling, falling away to the corners. Beneath, sprawled across dozens of cushions, was Viktor Sabin. On his left there was a girl in red underwear with milky skin, short, spiky platinum-blonde hair and green eyes. The girl to his right was naked; shoulder-length, dark hair, hazel eyes and an all-over tan betrayed by two light triangles. Sabin himself was resplendent in a cherry silk kimono that failed to reach the knees, exposing grotesque pink thighs. The dark girl's left hand was running through the sweaty folds and hair of his chest.

'Oh, Viktor,' Stephanie sighed, 'that really isn't a good look.'

He wasn't offended at all, breaking into a lecherous grin. 'But Katya and Irina seem to love it. Maybe it's 'true that beauty is in the eye of the beholder.'

'Maybe. Or maybe it's true that beauty is a bulging wallet.'

'Petra – *please*! How could you think such a thing?'

'Katya and Irina?'

'I've been here too long. I need simple pleasures to remind me of home.'

'That's where these two should be. Doing their homework.'

'They're not as young as they look.'

'Take it from me, Viktor. That's a line that only works on girls who *are* as young as they look. It's not something you should try on an adult.'

'Thanks for the advice.'

'Have you got it?'

'Behind you. The box by the wall. Do you want some tea?'

On a small lacquered table to her left there was a samovar, beside a bowl of fruit, some plates, several glasses, a bottle of Stolichnaya and two bottles of mineral water. There was also a copper ashtray containing four cigarette butts and the pinched remains of three joints. Stephanie shook her head, picked up the box and removed the lid; two phones, the gun, the silencer.

'What happened to the Browning?' Sabin asked.

'Nothing. This is for something else. A one off.'

Sabin raised a halting hand. *Enough. Don't tell me. I don't want to know.*

Irina, the brunette, rolled onto her side and propped herself up on one elbow. Katya lit a Mild Seven, then passed it to Sabin, who kissed her. Stephanie tried not to grimace but wasn't sure she'd succeeded. She took the manila envelope from her bag and tossed it onto

his lap. He ripped it open, withdrew the money –
American dollars only, please, no rubbish – and counted it.
Both girls perked up, eyes wide, lips licked. Sabin
found their reaction delightful and said to Stephanie,
'If you like, you can join us.'

'Tempting, but I think I'll pass.'

'Or I can organize a private room for you. You can
have either of them. Or both.'

'I wouldn't want to deprive any of you.'

By day Alexandra Park was an oasis of lush vegetation
in Singapore's steel and concrete desert. Now, by night,
it was an oasis of darkness in metropolitan light.
Cautious of roaming security, with only the rain for
company, she stayed among the bushes and trees, still
and silent, dressed in black from head to toe, including
a black balaclava. Waxman departed at eight, on schedule, in his dark blue BMW 740, returning shortly
before one in the morning, the car gliding within feet
of her, past a sign pointing to Eton Hall.

She waited ten minutes before heading for Russels
Road, at the heart of the estate. Waxman lived in one
of Singapore's earliest black-and-white plantation
houses; a small niche in local history. But the authorities in Singapore had never set much store by the past.
The future was what mattered, and so it was that
Alexandra Park had been earmarked for development
as a science park. Not dissimilar, Stephanie supposed,
to the proposed cyberport development that Savic had
shown her at Pok Fu Lam.

Set in a vast garden, raised on stone pillars,
Waxman's house had large, airy rooms and a huge
veranda. Stephanie opened the gate and crept close to

the house, the floor of the veranda a couple of feet above her head. On the other side of the house there was a small outhouse containing quarters for two servants, a laundry and a utility room. Waxman had a dog – an ageing Alsatian – but she generally slept on the lawn beyond the outhouse. Stephanie looked but there was no sign of her.

Above her, Waxman was on the veranda, the light of a lamp illuminating roof beams. Stephanie smelt cigar smoke and heard the clink of ice cubes in a tumbler. Waxman was talking to Judith, his second wife, a former lawyer from Miami. A skeletal exercise fanatic, when she talked it was a nasal whine that sounded like a mosquito. Waxman's first wife, Michelle, lived with their three children in Aspen.

Judith went to bed after quarter of an hour. Waxman followed at two. Around three it began to rain again. The downpour hammered roof-tiles and sluiced through branches, leaves and bushes. Gutters gurgled. Stephanie moved under the house for cover. She was still damp from earlier showers and couldn't afford to get any wetter; she didn't want to leave a trace. At three-thirty she decided to enter the house.

There was no barrier to the veranda; she passed through a wooden gate and climbed up stone steps to reach it. There was a large Turkish rug laid over the wooden floor, two sofas, two armchairs, a coffee table, three side-tables, all with ceramic lamps. The floor had been polished recently; she could smell wax rising off it. In the darkness she unzipped her black knapsack and took out the lock-pick that Cyril Bradfield had given her; handmade by Gustav Frunze of Basel, he'd told her. It had been a gift.

The lock was easy, the double doors barely worth the effort; without securing pins, they were loose anyway. Had noise not been a consideration, Stephanie guessed she could have rocked them open. For a man with his history, Alan Waxman lived with almost no home security. Then again, he'd never lacked confidence. Besides, burglaries in Singapore – and especially in a place like Alexandra Park – were still rare. That was part of the attraction.

The doors opened onto the main sitting room. Waxman had forgotten to switch off the fans, both rotor-blades circling slowly. She waited until her eyes had fully adjusted to the lack of light before moving into the kitchen. Small, tiled in white, it had a back door that opened onto steps, leading down to the outhouse. She peered through the window. No signs of life. There was a knife-block by the cooker. The blade she picked was six inches long. She'd decided that getting a gun in Singapore was going to be too complicated, under the circumstances. Especially since Iain Boyd had trained her to make use of everyday objects. A knife was a luxury.

From the kitchen she slipped down the passage to the master bedroom. To her left there was a lattice screen that looked onto the garden. She could just make out the edge of the large kidney-shaped swimming pool at the far end.

She opened the bedroom door slowly, pushing it back, inch by inch, ready for an unwelcome squeak. Nothing. She slipped through the gap. For several seconds she was completely motionless. The room was deliciously cool; the murmur of the Fujitsu air-conditioning unit above the window was just audible over the rain. Waxman and Judith were mounds beneath a single cotton sheet. Waxman was snoring.

Stephanie looked around: clothes on chairs, clothes on the floor, a towel draped over the end of the bed, a desk, books everywhere, an open briefcase, two tennis rackets, car keys, framed photographs, a small TV. Waxman's mobile was on his bedside table. Stephanie felt her pulse accelerate, so she waited, forcing it to slow. Then she began to cross the floor, the knife in her gloved right hand, ready.

She was half-way there when Judith shifted. Stephanie halted. More movement, the sheets rustling, then a deep sigh that drifted into renewed silence. She let fifteen seconds pass before moving forward. Waxman's mobile was recharging. She removed the cable, then tiptoed back to the passage.

From her knapsack she took the blue Motorola that she'd bought from Viktor Sabin. As far as she could tell, they were identical. She removed the SIM card from Waxman's phone, inserted it into Sabin's phone, then attached Waxman's phone to the transfer port, which bled the remaining information and the number. This task completed, she loaded everything into the new phone, sliding Waxman's Motorola into her knapsack.

Back into the bedroom, back across the floor, she attached the new Motorola to the old recharging cable. The screen illuminated for a second. Waxman groaned softly at her side, his eyelids fluttering. Stephanie put the phone down, bent over him and held the blade close to his throat, which he cleared, noisily. More grunting, a shift in position, then Judith moved. Stephanie wondered what exactly Waxman would see if he woke up now. Moving blackness and a glinting pair of eyes, then nothing at all.

They both settled down. Stephanie retreated, closed the door, returned the knife to the wooden block in the kitchen and left the way she'd come in. It was four fifteen. By five she'd left Alexandra Park and had hailed a taxi. She was wearing jeans, trainers, a plain purple T-shirt and a navy anorak. The knapsack was lighter than when she'd arrived in Singapore the previous evening, her damp black clothes now discarded. Her passport, ticket and cash remained dry in a pouch zipped into a side pocket. Just before five-thirty her taxi delivered her to Changi airport.

Five past one in the afternoon. In her bathroom at the Conrad she brushed her hair, applied some make-up and a generous swipe of ruby lipstick. In the bedroom she dressed in clothes bought at Pacific Place, beneath the hotel: a skirt and jacket by Armani, a blue shirt by Mango. The clothes she'd worn overnight were in a pile on the carpet. On the bed was the SOCOM, Mark 23 Mod0. Based on the Heckler & Koch USP, the gun was developed for the US Special Operations Command (hence SOCOM) in the 1990s and had a threaded muzzle that protruded from the slide to allow the attachment of the sound suppressor. Which lay next to it. She placed both parts in a Loewe handbag, then examined herself in the bathroom mirror and saw Petra looking back.

It could be worse. You could be Stephanie.

She caught a taxi to MacDonnell Road, ensuring that she was dropped off two hundred yards short of the building. Despite it being overcast and damp, she slipped on a pair of dark sunglasses.

The glass front door was locked. There was an intercom to the left and a key-pad. She punched in the four-digit number for Mr and Mrs Kuok on the thirteenth floor, a piece of neutral information provided by Magenta House. The lock released and she entered a lobby of polished stone and brass. There was a small booth on the left for visitors. Behind the glass a toothy man was watching a portable TV in a halo of cigarette smoke. Stephanie strode confidently past him. He turned to look at her, was sure he hadn't seen her before, yet she'd punched a correct entry code, so …

The lift doors opened. Stephanie stepped in before he'd made up his mind. She hit the button for the thirteenth floor. *Better to be consistent.* The doors closed. At the thirteenth she used the emergency staircase to take her up to the sixteenth. She checked the swing-door. It was unlocked and opened onto the space between the lift and front door. The building had one apartment per floor, which worked in her favour. She retreated into the stairwell, took the gun from the bag and attached the silencer. It was nine minutes to two. Cheung's programme for the day had a blank space between two and five.

Stephanie wedged the Loewe bag in the swing-door so that it offered a glimpse of the hall: a tiled floor, two pot plants on either side of a wooden door, a cheap mirror on the far wall. She wondered whether Daisy Yiu was alone in the apartment or whether she'd organized another girl for Cheung. Stephanie had watched him coming and going four times. Twice he'd been preceded by Daisy and another girl, one a leggy blonde, the other a dead-ringer for Naomi Campbell.

Cheung always entered the building alone. Normally, wherever he went, he was surrounded by

226

two or three men in cheap suits; a sure sign that he wasn't quite the model citizen he now claimed to be. But his protection never ventured inside Daisy Yiu's building. They escorted him to the entrance, then retreated to his black Mercedes 4x4 and parked a hundred metres down the street.

The stairwell was airless. Stephanie could feel perspiration on her top lip and beneath her armpits. Her stomach was tense; always the first part of her to register Petra's presence.

She heard the soft chime of the lift. She picked up the bag, stepped into the hall and hoped that Daisy Yiu wouldn't open the door. If she did, there would be no alternative. Since Cheung owned the flat, Stephanie assumed he had his own key, allowing him to arrive without warning if he wished.

She heard the whisper of rushing air as the lift decelerated in the shaft. It came to a halt and the metal doors clattered open. Felix Cheung was alone. He wore a Ralph Lauren Polo shirt, black trousers, lizard-skin shoes with a silver toe-cap and a pair of Ray-Bans.

Stephanie gave him her most dazzling smile. 'Hello.'

For a moment he wasn't sure. Stephanie read his mind: was she, perhaps, something off Daisy's afternoon menu? He never saw the gun.

Even with a twenty-five decibel reduction in noise, the shot sounded loud in such a confined space. The first bullet knocked Cheung back against the lift wall. He pitched to his left, his head smacking a rail. Stephanie stepped into the lift, fired a second shot into the skull and pressed the button for the first floor. As the doors closed she pointed the gun at Daisy Yiu's front door.

Please don't open.

227

As soon as she was on her way down she detached the silencer from the gun, put both pieces into the bag and took out the second Motorola that Viktor Sabin had provided. It was red, instead of blue. Sabin had made a point of that: *after all, you don't want to get them mixed up, do you?* When the lift reached the first floor she stepped out, then leaned back in and pressed the button for the top floor. Once it was on its way up she took the fire-escape to the ground floor. As she walked through the lobby she switched on the phone. By the time she was on MacDonnell Road she had a signal. She opened the address book. There was only one entry. She pressed 'OK' and put the phone to her ear. It was ringing as she strolled past Cheung's black Mercedes 4x4. Then there was a connection.

'Hello?'

'Is that Alan Waxman?'

'Yeah. Who's this?'

'I have a message for you from an old friend.'

'Who are you?'

Stephanie pressed the star button, then switched off the phone.

I step out of the shower and pull on a white towelling dressing-gown. I fasten the cord, go into the bedroom and call Mark. He's surprised to hear me, then even more surprised when I tell him I'm returning to London.

'When?'

'Tonight.'

'Fantastic.' Then there's a brief pause before the obvious follow-up. 'Why?'

I'm standing by the window. Dense cloud has descended. I can no longer see the ground from sixty-one floors up. Even the upper floors of the buildings closest to me are beginning to fade, melting into the greyness.

Alan Waxman and Felix Cheung are dead but am I any closer to Gemini? Am I any closer to freedom than I was yesterday? I should be but I don't feel it.

'It's a little complicated,' I say, not quite believing how lame I sound.

'Is everything okay?'

'Everything's fine. Anyway, look on the bright side: this time tomorrow I'll be home.'

The last apartment window vanishes. I'm now alone in swirling cloud.

The phone by my bed rings. I tell Mark to hold on, then answer it. It's Savic. He's heard about Waxman and Cheung. He's in the lobby and says we need to talk – can I come down? No, I tell him, it's not convenient.

'Then I'll come up.'

Before I can tell him that isn't convenient either, the line's dead. I finish my call to Mark as quickly as possible. When I open the door for him, Savic is like a small child on Christmas morning.

'I can't believe it! Waxman during lunch at Jade – incredible!'

I shut the door and follow him into my room.

There's real pleasure in his eyes when he says, 'Apparently his head went all over a plate of crispy suckling pig skin and foie gras.'

'That doesn't sound very Chinese.'

It's all I can muster but it makes Savic laugh.

'What was it?' he asks.

'Semtex with mercury droplets. Detonated by the star button on a dedicated handset.'

For five minutes we talk about what this means to Gilbert

229

Lai. And what it could mean for the future. Mostly it's Savic's monologue. He lights a cigarette to give him something to do with his hands. He waves it through the air as he talks; it only touches his lips twice. Then he stops. In mid-sentence. At last he's noticed what's on the bed. A suitcase, half-packed. It's as though I've pressed his star button; the good humour vaporizes in an instant.

'You're leaving?'

'Tonight.'

'Where are you going?'

'Home.' Then, before he can ask where, I add: 'Europe.'

'What about us?'

'I don't really do collaboration, Milan.'

'Why not?'

'Collaboration requires trust.'

'Not always.'

'For me, it would have to.'

'You don't trust me?'

'I'm not sure that you trust me.'

He considers this. 'I could. If I knew you.'

'But you don't.'

'Because you won't let me.'

'Do you find that surprising?'

'Of course not. You calculate everything so that you can eliminate risk. But trust is always a risk.'

'True. That's why I don't trust anybody.'

Which is when he reaches for my dressing-gown cord.

'You should try it,' he says. 'You might learn something.'

Time to pull a cord of my own. Except I don't. Or rather, Petra doesn't. Where I see impossibility, she sees an opportunity. And she recognizes the risk that he's taking. Whatever else he might be, Savic isn't an idiot. He knows he's not about to overpower me.

230

So everything depends on my reaction. This has been on the horizon for a while. I've had time to consider it. I hoped it wouldn't happen but imagined it probably would. As Petra, sex is a weapon I can't afford to ignore. Waxman and Cheung were an opportunity to get closer to Gemini. Sex is the same.

The dressing-gown falls open and he reaches inside with his right hand. Coarse fingertips touch my stomach. I'm looking into his eyes, giving him nothing. He runs his hand over my belly button, through my pubic hair and between my thighs. This is a contest he can't win. He presses one finger inside me, then two, before leaning into me and kissing me.

Petra does whatever it takes. That's the essence of her. I've killed two men today so the prospect of sex with Savic should feel inconsequential by comparison. But it doesn't, which is unsettling. I remind myself that I've done this many times before. That it's not sex. It's partition; I keep one part of me to myself, which makes it easier to allow the rest of me to be occupied. That's what I've learnt.

There's no tenderness when he pressures me to my knees, one hand fumbling with his zip, the other clutching my wet hair. But I don't protest. On the contrary. I take him into my mouth and do what used to come so naturally. Later he shoves the suitcase onto the floor, pushes me back onto the bed, spreads my thighs and presses his mouth between them, his frantic tongue and fingers everywhere all at once. I still don't give him anything. Even when we fuck, it's hard work. Devoid of emotion, we're rude and brutal. He takes me on the bed, against the wall, on the floor. But I match him for ferocity, pushing against him harder than he pushes into me. I'm burning, my sinews popping against my skin.

Now we're on the bed again. Savic is behind me, his hands clamped over my hips, his fingers digging into me, his thighs against my buttocks. Drops of his sweat drip onto my back. I hear the clinking of the gold dog-tags that hang from the chain around his neck. I can see a pale reflection of us in the window. We're fucking in the clouds. Every time I look at him I have to remind myself that I'm Petra. That this is okay because it has nothing to do with Mark. That it's business, not infidelity.

It just feels like infidelity, that's all.

9

London slid beneath her in perfect clarity. In the dawn the Thames was a ribbon of shimmering silver. She'd fallen asleep over China. When she woke up, over western Russia, she noticed the change. The reversion to Stephanie. At least, the start; it was a process, not a moment. Like a snake sloughing its skin. Now, as the aircraft completed its descent, Stephanie estimated it would take her an hour to reach Mark's bed. She caught a black cab to Queen's Gate Mews, dumped her luggage in the sitting room and tiptoed to the bedroom. Mark was asleep. She bent over him and kissed him lightly on the forehead. He stirred.

'Hey …'

'Go back to sleep.'

'Come to bed.'

'In a minute. I'm going to have a shower.'

'Shower later. With me.'

'I'll do that as well.'

'Mmm – come here.'

'No. I feel … you know … *disgusting*.'

'Even better.'

'In your dreams.'

She stripped in the bathroom and crushed her clothes into a ball in the corner. Beneath the jet, she turned up the temperature, steam filling the glass cabinet. For the second time in less than twenty-four hours she was wet and naked in the clouds.

She'd had a shower after Savic had left her room, then a bath, and she'd worn clean clothes for the flight, but she still felt contaminated. Now, her skin blushing, she scrubbed herself thoroughly, the soap stinging between her legs. She used Mark's shampoo to wash her hair twice.

She stepped onto the bath-mat and opened the small sash window to let the steam escape. Drying herself slowly, she caught her reflection in the clearing mirror. There were faint bruises over her hips and thighs. At first glance they were shockingly vivid. After consideration, she accepted they were faint. And easy to explain.

She used some Listerine to rinse out her mouth. Not strong enough; she looked in the medicine cabinet, found some TCP, used that, diluted at first, then neat, scorching the taste and feel of him from her tongue.

Mark was asleep when she returned to the bedroom. She slipped beneath the sheet beside him, as lightly as possible. Without waking, he reached for her, taking her left hand in his right. She stared at the ceiling. It was after seven before they were both awake. Yawning, he ran a hand through his dishevelled hair and said, 'That TCP is probably peeling wallpaper in Marble Arch.'

'Sorry.'

'Have you got a sore throat?'

'Not any more.'

When they made love, it hurt; that was Savic's legacy. But she showed Mark the pleasure in her head, the pleasure she *should* have felt. Only later did it strike her that it was a performance as fraudulent as the one she'd put on for Savic.

'*Jesus Christ!* An exploding phone in a public place? *And* Felix Cheung? What the bloody hell were you thinking?'

They were in Alexander's office, Stephanie as casual as she could be in frayed jeans and one of Mark's shirts. Alexander, as starched as ever, was apoplectic, the white of his collar setting off his beetroot face to full effect.

Earlier, in one of the conference rooms, she'd watched a montage of international news coverage with Rosie: CNN, PCNE Chinese, BBC World, TV Globo, Star News, Australia's ABC. The images were similar: the Fullerton hotel cordoned off behind a crush of police cars, a distant shot of paramedics carrying a stretcher towards a waiting ambulance, stills of Alan Waxman and his two lunch companions.

She'd seen the initial bulletins in the British Airways first-class lounge at Hong Kong airport. At that stage it had all been speculation. Besides, local news had dominated the evening's agenda: the cold-blooded slaying of Felix Cheung, the well-known and well-respected restaurant owner. According to sources, Cheung had just finished visiting the elderly mother of a business associate at the apartment block on MacDonnell Road. Stephanie had been unable to resist a wry smile: *so, not visiting his highly paid mistress, then, or any of her extracurricular assistants*.

Later there had been another item on the news that had grabbed her attention. It was almost an afterthought. The Hong Kong police were continuing to make enquiries following the discovery of a body at the edge of the Aberdeen Upper Reservoir. Identification was proving problematic; the body had been badly beaten and set on fire. They said they had reason to believe the man was an Albanian now living in Germany and that he'd come to Hong Kong as a tourist. They were appealing to anybody who might be able to help them with additional information.

Asim Maliqi. So he'd ignored her advice. As she knew he would.

She said to Alexander, 'I needed something to get me close to Savic.'

He looked utterly incredulous. 'So you did a contract for someone else? Without even consulting us? For God's sake, what's the matter with you?'

Stephanie's own temper was crumbling. 'The last time I sat in this chair I asked you how I should get close to him. You told me to think of something. Well, guess what? I did. And it worked. Spectacularly. So what's the problem?'

'The problem is *you*! Running around terminating civilians ...'

'Civilians? *Give me a break!* Waxman was already on the Limbo list. And Felix Cheung was hardly a model citizen, so ...'

In a moment of white hot fury, Alexander swept his arm across his desk, the backhand propelling his cup and saucer against the shelf to his right, drenching leather book spines with hot black coffee. Suddenly he was standing, his entire body trembling. Stephanie felt Rosie freeze beside her. Alexander slammed his palm onto the desk and shouted, 'Model citizen or not, he was one of *ours*!'

Which took the wind out of Stephanie's sails. 'What?'

'That's right. One of ours. A source. Not just for Hong Kong but for all of southern China.'

Now she was floundering. 'Raymond Chen never said anything about that.'

'Chen never knew.'

'*What?*'

'Given Chen's past, we thought it sensible to have another local source. Neither man knew about the other. We retained them separately.'

'Look ...'

'*You* look!' he screamed, jabbing a finger at her repeatedly. 'When I told you to think of something, I expected you to do what you normally do. Something sordid. You know, the kind of thing you're good at. I expected you to fuck him!'

For once, in Alexander's presence, Stephanie was completely speechless.

It was raining by the time she got back to Mark's flat. She grazed on the remains in his fridge, then made coffee. She put on a CD – *beautifulgarbage*, the third album by Garbage, her favourite band – and turned up the volume. She'd bought Mark copies of all Garbage's albums rather than not have them at Maclise Road. She found it was the same with paperbacks; she'd sooner buy one as a gift than lend her own.

She curled up on the sofa with her coffee mug and the remote control, repeating the song 'Drive You Home' seven times; the mood of the lyrics mainlining into her own mood.

Savic was the first man she'd slept with since she'd

started seeing Mark. Within the twisted parameters of Petra's world, that was something to feel good about. But she didn't. She'd tried to persuade herself in Hong Kong that it wouldn't matter. Because it hadn't mattered before. But it did. And even though she knew she'd get over it, she resented Petra for it.

In the middle of the afternoon she fell asleep. In her dream she was a young girl. She recognized Northumberland, the house, the field falling away from it, the stone walls. The wind was blowing, the family was outside. Her oldest brother, Christopher, was rolling in the grass with one of the boxers, the dog barking with excitement, slobber everywhere. Her father was by the crooked hawthorn tree, her mother was calling from the kitchen door. Nothing peculiar happened in the dream. It was just as it had been.

The spell was broken by a hand on her shoulder. As gentle a touch as it was, it ripped through her like lightning. For a few seconds she was disorientated. She looked up at Mark, then cast her blurred gaze around the room. She sniffed and rubbed her eyes. They were wet.

'Are you okay?'

'I'm fine.'

'You don't look it.'

She attempted levity. 'God, you're a smooth talker. Is there anything else you can do with that tongue of yours?' It failed. 'Seriously,' she insisted, wiping her face with the heel of her hand. 'It was just a dream. That's all.'

'A bad one, by the look of it …'

No. A beautiful one. The best ever.

238

They spent the evening together. Just talking, having a drink, preparing food, listening to music. As a snapshot, it was everything she'd imagined a normal relationship would be in the years when that prospect had been nothing more than a fantasy. Hiding in a broken storm-drain on a sub-zero night in Grozny. Suffering dysentery in a rat-infested hostel in Constanta. Even when she was with Kostya she'd wondered what love in the real world would be like. The two of them had existed in a private universe with no shortage of desperate exhilaration, but what of simple companionship?

She'd wondered whether she would ever feel comfortable with someone. Whether she could just be herself – whoever that was – and have them feel the same way about her.

Now she knew, and it made her nervous.

They reconvened the following morning. Alexander was reserve personified, his clipped Scottish as measured as ever. Stephanie noticed that the books which had been stained with coffee had been replaced by leather-bound editions of Walter Scott. It was as though the incident had never occurred. Which was exactly the way the Ether Division operated.

He said, 'The authorities in Singapore are saying it was a bomb but they haven't been specific about the type of device.'

'Are they blaming anyone?'

'Islamic militants.'

'Based in Malaysia,' Rosie added.

'Because Waxman was having lunch with Ari Gorodin?'

'Yes.'

'An Israeli arms-dealer,' Stephanie added, for emphasis.

Alexander said, 'What's your point?'

'They're not going to say what the device was because it's not the kind of device Islamic militants use.'

Rosie interjected. 'But somebody in the restaurant …'

'What? Would have seen the phone explode?'

That *was* the point she'd been going to make. This time Alexander was a step ahead. 'He's on the phone. A bomb goes off. You don't *see* anything. As far as those in the restaurant are concerned, it could have been a package under the table.'

'And as far as the authorities are concerned,' Stephanie continued, 'it's a gift. The truth will be suppressed for the greater good.'

An uncomfortable silence descended over the three of them.

Eventually Alexander said, 'What about the list?'

'Brankovic is alive. Goran Simic is alive. I don't know if there's an *actual* list but that's two names out of nine.'

'What about Savic?'

'He wants a collaboration. Which is why I had to take out Waxman and Cheung. Anything less wouldn't have got me close.'

Alexander ignored the bait. 'What kind of collaboration?'

Not the kind you suggested earlier. That was what she wanted to say. Even though it wasn't true.

'Savic is trafficking people into Europe, where he's

240

facing stiff competition. Mainly from Albanians, the way he tells it.'

Alexander took a Rothmans from the pack and began tapping it against his Zippo lighter. 'So, not content with ethnically cleansing Albanians from his own country, he's looking to do it elsewhere.'

'Savic by name, savage by nature. He maintains it's business, not political.'

'He would.'

'He wants me to take out selected targets.'

Alexander lit the cigarette. 'I see.'

'Obviously I can't run around Europe putting a bullet into every Albanian Savic doesn't like the look of, so …'

'Even though you *were* prepared to kill Waxman and Cheung?'

Stephanie throttled her immediate response.

Alexander went on. 'Supposing Savic's targets are justified?'

'Forget it.'

'Not so fast. Let's consider the kind of people we're talking about. Violent, hardcore criminals.'

'No way.'

'Come on. You know as well as I do the truth about the Albanians. They're the largest criminal menace in Europe. To the pond-life out there, Albanians are the wretched poor. They're displaced refugees, crossing mountains in winter, their malnourished babies wrapped in shawls. It's the same with the Chechens. Heroic freedom fighters, in the eyes of the media.' He narrowed his own eyes, drawing her in to their pale blue. 'Here we know better. They're savages, both groups.'

He was so devious she almost admired him for it.

The rage forgotten, here was a conversation engineered like a chess strategy.

'You're not listening to me.'

'You're the one who's not listening, Stephanie. Don't be emotional. Be practical. If a few Albanian criminals have to fall by the way to land Savic, that's not a monstrous atrocity. It's a sound investment.'

'If that's the way you feel, get someone else from S7 to do it.' She glanced at Rosie. 'Or perhaps you could lend him someone from the Ether Division.'

Alexander said, 'You're the one Savic trusts.'

'I'm not doing it.'

'Then we have a problem ...'

'You don't think I know what's going on here?'

Alexander and Rosie traded looks before he shrugged. 'What?'

'The whole idea of the list is just so attractive to you, isn't it? The moment you heard the rumour, you were desperate for it to be fact.'

'It *is* fact. Pearson provided the list ...'

'It doesn't detract from my point.'

'Which is what?'

'That the list is perfect for you. The names of war criminals who can never be allowed to see the inside of a court – not just one or two, but plenty – providing Magenta House with lots of work and absolute self-justification.'

'Absurd.'

'But true.'

He smoked a little, evaluating in silence, then changed direction; a familiar strategy to Stephanie. 'I hope you're not overlooking our agreement. You have a lot to lose.'

'I'll find another way.'

'I hope so.'

'I *will*,' Stephanie insisted.

He was nodding slowly when he said, 'Good. Because if you don't, every aspect of our arrangement is rescinded.'

They went through Victoria Embankment Gardens to get to the Embankment, the first of the falling leaves dancing around them. On the far side of the river the Millennium Wheel turned slowly, its pods brimming with tourists despite the murky weather. Rosie looked tired, dullness in her eyes.

'You know, Steph, you're wrong. We don't need Savic, or the list. We have plenty of work. Especially the Ether Division. To be frank, we have more than we can handle. Targets are a naturally occurring resource – like oil – and the fact is, we keep discovering new reserves. As it is, we've got enough to keep us in business for years to come, even allowing for a massive projected expansion.'

'You sound like the CEO of Shell.'

'To extend the metaphor, that's exactly who I am.'

'And is there a massive projected expansion?'

'It's under discussion.'

'Just what the world needs.'

'It's *exactly* what the world needs.'

Stephanie knew the argument: Ether Division targets didn't negotiate, the vast majority of them having surrendered the concept of personal responsibility to the most irresponsible authority of all: religion. They were beyond reason and they were multiplying. All of this she understood.

Rosie said, 'We're not choosing between alterna-tives.'

Stephanie had always accepted that. She just didn't like to admit it.

Rosie asked how she'd explained her departure to Savic.

'I said I had business in Europe to attend to.'

'And he bought that?'

'Why wouldn't he?'

'How did you leave it?'

'Pretty vague. I said he could call me when every-thing had died down.'

'And he was happy with that?'

'Seemed to be. Let me ask you something. If what you've just told me is right, why is Alexander so agi-tated about Savic?'

'Because he's still a legitimate contract.'

'There has to be more to it than that.'

'Well, there's always you.'

Nobody else within Magenta House had the volatile relationship with Alexander that Stephanie had. Nobody else had *any* relationship with him. Not even Rosie, the rising star. That was the point. As emotion-ally sterile as Petra, his judgements were never clouded by the human element. Except with Stephanie. In each other's company, neither of them could help them-selves.

Rosie had once said that Alexander was in love with Stephanie. 'That's why he hates you. Because he can't have you. In his universe he manages to bend every-one to his will. Except you. It's unrequited love.'

She'd told Rosie she was out of her mind.

They crossed the road.

'Are you sure you can get close enough to Savic?'

'I don't know. But I'll think of something.'

'Okay.'

Stephanie stopped walking. 'That didn't sound like "okay" to me.'

Rosie wouldn't look her in the eye. 'I thought perhaps you'd already thought of something.'

'Like what?'

'Like sleeping with him.'

As blunt as possible. Always a good idea.

Now it was Stephanie's turn to avoid eye contact. 'Why would you think that?'

'A hunch.'

She wanted to say something in her defence. Especially after Alexander's outburst the previous day. But there was no point in pretending. Not with Rosie. Resignation provoked an instant sense of deflation. 'Do you think he knows?'

It was the first question to come to mind.

Rosie's laugh was genuine. 'God, no! Alexander? Of course not.'

'What he said, though ...'

'That was just anger. A cheap shot in the heat of the moment. He knew it would get to you. That's the one thing he'll always have over you. You just have to accept that.'

'But it was obvious to you.'

'It was never obvious. It was instinct. *Female* instinct. And I think it's safe to say that's one quality he doesn't have in abundance.'

Stephanie tried to smile. 'Christ, Rosie ...'

'It's okay.'

She shook her head. 'It's definitely not okay.'

'All right – but put it in perspective. You've done worse in the past.'

'That's what I keep trying to tell myself.'

'It's true. And soon you won't have to do it again.'

'I know.'

'You've got to remember that.'

'I will. It's just that I'd hate to think that you thought …'

'Don't even say it, Steph.'

'I'm not even sure I made the right decision.'

'That was the nature of the decision.'

Saturday night. Dinner with Julian and Karen Cunningham, ten of them around the table, a lot of empty bottles, a few cigarettes, the sweet tang of a badly rolled joint. Stephanie looked around the table at the flushed faces in the candle-light. Justine Morgan was arguing with Karen about Robbie Williams. Did he have sex appeal? Or was he just grubby? Or was that the reason he had sex appeal? And would anybody remember him in ten years time? That was the only thing they could agree on.

No.

The question Stephanie wanted to ask was: does Justine have sex appeal? Or rather, does she *still* have sex appeal? Because she certainly had when Mark decided to sleep with her.

Justine had been a lawyer who'd traded ambition for two carats of flawless diamond and all that followed. In her more insecure moments Stephanie had often retreated to cliché: *I can't believe you had a fling with a lawyer.* Mark usually had the good grace not to offer the truthful reply, which was that he'd had an affair with a woman who was intelligent, beautiful, sexy and funny.

Rob, Justine's husband, was an investment banker. Stephanie liked him. He confounded the City stereotype. A little earnest, perhaps, he was a man who was perpetually concerned that he might not be concerned enough for others. Well read, widely travelled, broadly cultured, he had a wonderful sense of humour when he managed to shed the smothering cloak of shyness.

Rob was telling her about his job. Something similar to Julian's. A lot of travel, mostly in Europe, France and Germany in the main. *If it's not Paris, it's Berlin. Or sometimes Amsterdam. Very tedious, really.* Stephanie wasn't paying attention. She was watching Mark, who was at the other end of the table. He was in conversation with Alex, a dark-haired girl who was new to both of them. Whatever they were discussing, it was to the exclusion of everyone else. Mark was leaning towards her, his hands doing half his talking for him. Very slender, very pretty, she looked rapt, her head tilted up, her eyes never leaving his, even as his wandered.

Closer to Stephanie and somewhat drunk, Justine said, 'I'd let him do anything to me.'

Rob raised an eyebrow. 'I heard that.'

'We'll trade, darling. I get a night with Robbie. You get a night with … well, who would you choose?'

'Nobody. While you're with Robin Williams I'll take a night of uninterrupted sleep. That would be perfect.'

'*Robbie* Williams, not Robin Williams. God, what a thought … all that hair.'

When Karen asked Mark who he'd pick, Stephanie interjected. 'Cameron Diaz. And her tender hip flexor.'

247

Justine turned to Stephanie. 'What about you? One night with Robbie?'

Stephanie wanted to hit her. Not for the question. For sleeping with Mark. However many years ago it was. And for being his date while she was in Hong Kong. And because she felt guilty, even though that had nothing to do with Justine.

'I don't think so.'

'Come on. You've got to admit he's got something.'

'I'm sure he has, but I'm not sure I'd want to catch it. Anyway, I'd never sleep with someone famous.'

'Why not?'

'They seem so shallow and pointless. I'd sooner have a one-night stand with a complete stranger.'

She caught Mark's eye. They traded smiles. *Eight minutes past six.* Then he resumed his conversation with Alex, who hadn't stopped looking at him.

Rob was nodding. 'I agree. A stranger has infinite possibilities. A celebrity has none. We know far too much about them. And the more we know, the more we see how little there is to know.'

Mark had once said that only the vacuous found celebrity fascinating. At the time she'd disputed it. Later, once she'd considered it, she changed her mind. Sometimes, as Petra, she wondered why Alexander and his sort were so desperate to protect the nation and its people. 'Why bother? They're dull, ignorant and shallow. They're not worth it.'

In that way, Stephanie found Petra curiously liberating. Her views bypassed the contaminating filter of social opinion. Consequently she accepted Magenta House's existence because she rejected the idea that the public was entitled to know anything it liked. Liberal intellectuals could argue about freedom of expression and the sanctity of personal liberty, but Petra had once watched a young Saudi fanatic tear a dog to pieces with his bare hands, then bury his face in the carcass and eat its steaming innards, as a demonstration of devotion. She knew that as long as there were people who were prepared to surrender personal responsibility so readily, there would always be a need for Magenta House and its methods. Justice was a concept corrupted by law. Reason was a luxury. Rights were a fallacy.

In the real world nobody had rights. Not to cheap petrol, shorter working hours, food, or even life. Once born, there was only one right and it was universal: the right to die.

That was a truth Petra understood perfectly.

They took a radio-cab home and were stuck in traffic on Battersea Bridge when Stephanie said, 'Was Alex interesting?'

'Yes.'

'You two seemed to be having quite a conversation.'

'She has back trouble.'

Stephanie had never ceased to be amazed by the number of people who felt they could get a free consultation from Mark as soon as they learned he was a chiropractor.

'She had a car crash at the start of last year. Whiplash injuries ...'

'She's pretty.'

'She is, yes.'

'Although I think she could pluck her eyebrows a little.'

Mark smiled. 'Right.'

Stephanie punched him on the arm. 'Come on. She was all over you.'

'I wouldn't say that.'

'She *was*. I don't think I've ever seen such blatant flirting.'

'You're exaggerating.'

'I am not.'

'Well, I didn't notice.'

Stephanie felt her playfulness wearing thin. 'I'm serious.'

'Look, I don't agree with you. But even if she was, so what?'

'*So what?*'

'Did you see me flirting with her?'

'You don't think it matters?'

'Flirting? Not really. Especially when it's one-way traffic. I mean, it's not as though it's infidelity, is it?'

London, Monday morning, a pewter sky overhead, the first drops of rain falling. Stephanie was halfway across Hyde Park when her phone rang.

'Where are you?' Savic asked.

'Zurich. You?'

'Yekaterinburg.'

'What are you doing there?'

'What are you doing in Zurich?'

'Let's start again.'

'Can you come to Berlin?'

'When?'

'I'm arriving on Friday from Moscow.'

An hour later she was at Magenta House. Two days later she was standing on Charlotte Street, pressing the buzzer for Frontier News.

There was no response from the intercom.

'Hey. Stephanie.'

She looked up. Melanie, Gavin Taylor's assistant, was leaning out of the window. 'It's bust. I'll come down and let you in.'

KKZ, the graphic design agency that occupied the three floors beneath Frontier News, was undergoing renovation. Melanie opened the door, a lit Lambert & Butler wedged into the corner of her mouth. As usual, she looked ready for a hard Friday night – Bacardi Breezers and vomit before bed – dressed in a tight pink V-neck sweater and a pair of skin-tight black hipsters that dropped to the calf.

'Mind the mess. There's dust everywhere.'

They went up to the attic. The lights were out from the second floor, leaving them to feel their way in the darkness. Gavin Taylor was at a computer terminal in the far corner, perched on a swivel-chair leaking foam padding. A patch of plaster had come away from the ceiling; the tell-tale signs of damp were everywhere.

'I like what you've done with the place. It's very you.'

Taylor shook his head, despondent. 'Can you believe it? It's the third facelift those bastards downstairs have had in five years. Mind you, I could probably say the same for half the tossers who work there.'

'And here you are, just a good old-fashioned journalist mining the world for nuggets of truth in return for a hearty pat on the back.'

'Bugger off, Stephanie. You're hardly one to talk.'

'Harsh but fair.'

'Mind you, I've enjoyed watching the builders eyeing up the polo-necks.'

'The men or the women?'

'Both. They want to give the men a good kicking and the women a good shagging.' Taylor broke into a grin. 'The place reeks of fear.'

Stephanie sat down. Behind Taylor there were two easels either side of a Mercator map of the world. Small labels were pinned to the map, each with a number, which corresponded to notes on one of the easels. Frontier News assignments across the globe: Uzbekistan, Afghanistan, Colombia, Sierre Leone, Syria, North Korea.

He handed her four envelopes. Two were addressed to her at Maclise Road, two were addressed to him at Frontier News. The addresses were printed, not hand-written. All four letters had stamps, all had postmarks with different dates, all the envelopes had been torn open and were slightly creased.

'All you have to do is sign the two that you wrote.'

'What did I say in them?'

'You can read them, if you like. In the first one you outlined a proposal for a series of articles. I replied, saying it sounded good. In the second one you wondered if such a series might constitute a good basis for a book.'

'And you said?'

'Let's wait and see what you write.'

'And what did I write?'

'Take a look.'

He handed her a pile of papers that had been sitting on his desk. Finished articles, smartly edited, checked for errors, ready for distribution. She flicked through the headlines: *EU seeks to curb illegal immigration; People trafficking – Europe's new problem; OSCE condemns Balkans over enforced prostitution; Berlin – new hub for illegal immi-*

gration from Asia?; German police accused of ignoring vice trade from the East.

'How many other hard copies of these are there?'

'None.'

'This is pretty close to the bone.'

'That's why I wanted you to have a chance to read them. Just so you know what you're supposed to be doing. Before you leave I'll destroy them.'

'And the files?'

'Are on my computer. They've been encrypted and redesignated. Don't worry. They'll be well hidden. When you're ready, give me a call and I'll get a disk prepared. Then you can download straight onto your computer and produce it as your own work.'

'Picture files too?'

'Already assembled as part of the package. I wasn't sure you'd want to bother with them today ...'

It took her an hour to read the first set of articles that she was going to research in Berlin. Taylor sat with her, chain-smoking, answering questions where he could. Afterwards, as he was feeding the documents through a shredder, Stephanie said, 'When I saw you after Marrakech, you said you'd met Mostovoi.'

'That's right. With John Flynn of Sentinel Security.'

'Did you ever meet someone called Milan Savic with him?'

'I don't think so.'

'But you met in Berlin, right?'

'Once. I met Mostovoi twice.'

'What about a man named Martin Dassler?'

Taylor began to shake his head, then hesitated. 'Maybe.'

'Dark hair, slightly pockmarked skin.'

'Now you mention it … yes.'

'Remember anything about him?'

'I think he had a thing for Mostovoi's girlfriend.'

Which prompted something within Stephanie. 'You referred to her before.'

'Gorgeous. A real looker. Russian, I think. I don't recall her name. Flynn fancied her rotten but then he'll go for anything with a pulse.'

'You're sure about this?'

Taylor nodded. 'Now you've brought it up, yes. She was definitely with Mostovoi. But Dassler had his eye on her. No doubt about it. The strange thing was, Mostovoi didn't seem to care.'

'What about the girl?'

'Oh, she knew exactly what she was doing. Beautiful, yes, but smart with it. The kind who uses every weapon in her arsenal. You know … like you. Except better-looking.'

'Thanks, Gavin.'

'Berlin?'

'Yes.'

'I thought you were doing Chinese organized crime.'

'I am.'

'I thought after Hong Kong you were going to do something different.'

'This is an extension of the same story.'

'I see.'

'You don't believe me?' He doesn't reply, which I take to be 'no'. And like an idiot, I won't let it drop. 'Human traffic, Mark. From the Far East to Europe. It's a huge story, and if I …'

'Stephanie.'

'What?'

'Don't.'

Both of us lapse into silence. Once again I'm the one who breaks it. 'What are you thinking?'

'Do you really want to know?'

'Yes.'

As soon as I've said it, I'm not sure. My mother used to say you should never ask a question unless you're prepared to hear the answer.

'It's as though we're married and you're having an affair.'

My heart stops beating. 'What?'

He qualifies this immediately. 'I know you're not having an affair. Not in the literal sense. But I'm talking about the time when we're apart. The things you say to cover the things you do.'

'Are you accusing me of lying to you?'

'Do I need to?'

We're having lunch at Itsu, a Japanese restaurant in Walton Street, a short walk from his chiropractic clinic in Cadogan Gardens. Carefully prepared dishes pass before us on a conveyor-belt. We're surrounded by women who shop; pencil thin blondes in sunglasses with their never-ending conversations about nothing at all.

Mark is drinking miso soup.

My fury dissipates quickly, regret taking its place. 'Why do you put up with me?'

'Because I love you.'

'I'm sorry I've been such a bitch recently.'

'Forget it.'

'Impossible.'

I look around the room. Among the men I can see, there's no one remotely like him. It's not just his size – he's swamping the place allocated to him – it's his presence. Not the best-

*groomed man in the world and certainly not the best-looking,
I can see other women tuning in to him.* Here's something
you don't find on the menu every day. *And they haven't
even spoken to him. They know nothing about him. All of
which begs the question: why me?*

*In the beginning I thought I picked Mark. I did pick Mark.
It just doesn't feel like that any more. I was so cavalier back
then. Now I'm scared.*

Five past nine, a grey morning, the drizzle hanging like
mist. Stephanie was sitting with Cyril Bradfield in a
café on Wilton Road, close to Victoria Station. There
were two cups of milky tea between them. Stephanie
fingered a nylon buttercup in a plastic flowerpot.
Bradfield was rolling a cigarette with a dexterity that
shouldn't have belonged to such gnarled fingers.

'I'm tired, Cyril.'

'You're too young to be tired.'

'I'm serious. It's the lying. It's just so … *draining*.'

Bradfield nodded, then licked the paper and sealed
the cigarette. 'That's not entirely bad, Stephanie. It
means you're human.'

'I don't feel human.'

'What's wrong?'

She talked about Mark.

'Did he ask what you were really doing?'

'Of course not. He's too smart to do that.'

Bradfield lifted his cup to his lips. 'Well, what did
you expect?'

'What do you mean?'

'He loves you. It was bound to happen sooner or
later. And you love him. You live with him – you *relax*
with him.'

'I'm not with you.'

'He makes you feel normal, which is all you've ever craved. Ever since I've known you it's been painfully apparent. With him you can be yourself, as far as that's ever possible. But when you relax you let your guard down.'

'No.'

'Yes. Even you.'

'You don't know that.'

'On the contrary. It's been blindingly obvious. To be honest, I've been happy about that. It proves to me that it's not a façade. That even allowing for the strangeness of your arrangement, the relationship is genuine.'

'Cyril, if only you knew …'

He smiled and reached across the table, a father taking his daughter's hand. 'I think it's best for both of us if I don't know too much, don't you?'

Stephanie felt a tightness in her throat. 'I'm sorry.'

'Don't be sorry. Just be careful.'

10

Savic had offered to collect her from Tegel but she'd said she preferred to make her own way into the city. She thought she'd detected a hint of disappointment in his voice. What name was she travelling under? She told him she hadn't decided, which was untrue; she was Andrea Jakob, another Swiss, the surname borrowed from the patisserie on Gloucester Road opposite the junction with Queen's Gate Mews.

It was mid-afternoon. She took a taxi to the Pension Dortmunder on Pariser Strasse in Wilmersdorf, where she'd made a reservation for a fortnight, earning her a discount on the room rate. The proprietor, an elderly man with a club foot beneath a crumbling hip, led her up a dark staircase to the second floor. The room overlooked Pariser Strasse itself; dusty glass filtering sunlight, heavy bottle-green curtains, a loose parquet floor, peeling blue *toile de joie* wallpaper with pastoral scenes.

'It's lovely. Thank you.'

The proprietor smiled. *Nice of you to say so. There was a time …*

Alone, she called Savic.

'I'm here.'

'Where?'

'Where are *you*?'

He gave his address and she said she'd be there in half an hour. Then she switched on the Vaio, checked that the tamper devices were engaged, switched it off and locked it in her bag, which she pushed under the bed.

Savic's apartment was on Chamissoplatz, a square, east of Mehringdamm in Kreuzberg 61, the nineteenth-century architecture untouched by the Second World War or any subsequent development. There was an iron frame beside the entry-phone. Beside the apartment numbers each resident's name was painted in gold on a slim wooden disc, which was then inserted into the frame. The name by the number Savic had given her wasn't Dassler. It was Freisinger.

The apartment occupied the whole of the first floor. He was waiting for her at the door. They kissed and went inside, down a gloomy hall, into the living room, which overlooked Chamissoplatz. French windows opened onto a narrow balcony of wrought iron. A gentle breeze ruffled net curtains. The floor was wood; old beams, once stained, worn smooth over decades. But the furniture was contemporary; a plantation chair made of burnished cherry, a chocolate leather sofa, a Balinese coffee table. By one wall there was a Bang & Olufsen sound system with sleek speakers in each corner.

Stephanie stood at the window and looked out. A couple were talking on the corner. A BMW rolled past, music drifting in its wake. In another apartment a woman laughed, deep and uninhibited. Stephanie was aware of Savic moving behind her. She felt his breath on the nape of her neck, his hands settling on her shoulders. The touch sent an involuntary shudder through her that she hoped would translate as pleasure. He turned her around, kissed her again and reached for the top button of her black shirt.

Afterwards, lying in his bed, she looked at the two gold dog-tags on the chain around his neck. The first disc had *Forza Inter* on one side and a date on the other: 13.02.1999.

'The day you died.'

'I prefer to think of it as the day I was born.'

'Aren't you taking a risk wearing this?'

'I've survived this long. It's not something I lose sleep over.'

She looked at the second disc. On one side, a name: Prince Lazar. On the other, another date, beneath a place: Kosovo Polje, 28 June 1389.

The defeat of Prince Lazar at Kosovo Polje, the Field of Blackbirds, on 28 June 1389 remained the pivotal moment in Serb history. As a single event, the effect of the defeat on the collective Serbian psyche was unmatched anywhere in European history.

'How typically Serb to be so fixated on the wrong date.'

Savic propped himself up on an elbow. 'What are you talking about?'

'The Ottoman victory at the Battle of Maritsa River in 1371 was far more devastating to the Serbs in the long term than Kosovo Polje.'

Later, Savic said, 'Why are you staying somewhere else?'

'It's a bit early for me to be moving in, isn't it?'

'I'm serious.'

'You think I should stay here?'

'Why not?'

'Because I have another life, Milan.'

'I know that.'

'You're not part of it. Nobody is.'

'Doesn't mean you can't stay here.'

'Trust me, I don't react well to being confined. This is better for both of us.'

He lit a cigarette. 'Okay.' As though he couldn't care less. But he was so easy to read. A man like Savic could only ever reinforce what she felt for a man like Mark.

'A word of advice: when you send someone to go through my things ...'

He looked mortified. 'What are you talking about?'

'... you'd better tell them not to play with my laptop.'

Before he could persist with his mock offence, she offered him a way out: a smile that headed him off at the pass of denial.

'Why not?'

She told him. And saw him work it out all by himself.

At first he showed her where they lived and worked, his army of illegal immigrants, the invisible invading force in Wedding, Siemensstadt and Neukölln. He showed her the office blocks where cleaning crews of Kurds and Afghans took the night-shift. Baggage-handlers at Tegel, dish-washers in the restaurants on Friedrichstrasse, laundry-workers in hotels, hospital porters. Savic distanced himself from any of these transactions.

'I have men who take care of it.'

'Who?'

'Men I can trust. Men from the past.'

'From Serbia?'

'Who else would I trust?'

They ran businesses from mobile phones. No records, no offices, no conversations that could betray them. They worked in code, covering labour, quantity, price, delivery.

'You must be generating a lot of cash.'

'We are. Fortunately, the euro makes it a lot easier for us to launder.'

'How do you prefer to do it?'

'Here, mostly through restaurants and hotels. Restaurants, in particular, are good; high cash flow. Also, using immigrants for staff reduces the overheads so it doesn't matter if the restaurants don't generate too much income.'

'That works, here in Berlin?'

'Sure. Why not?'

'The authorities aren't vigilant?'

'Not very. Those that are … well, we offer them a holiday, maybe. And if they don't like the sound of that, we offer to cut off their balls. One way or the other, we work it out. Down in Italy and Spain you don't really have to bother. They're so corrupt, it's incredible. I thought it was bad in Belgrade but I promise you this: Italy is worse. There's a lawyer I know in Milan. I can walk into his office with two suitcases of cash – right into his office, *in broad daylight* – and just leave them there. Within forty-eight hours he will call me to tell me the money is clean.'

'What do you lose?'

'About twenty-five per cent.'

'That's quite high.'

'I know. But he makes it so easy, it's worth it.'

Brankovic and I are waiting for Savic to join us. We're sitting in a café, drinking coffee, watching rain slither down the windows. There are two other couples in the place, Sibelius playing quietly on a radio somewhere. As usual, the conversation has been flowing like a glacier. I find myself thinking about Savic's gold dog-tags when I see the chain around Brankovic's neck.

'Is it true they call you the Spoon because you wear one around your neck?'

He nods.

'Can I see it?'

He doesn't look happy but takes it off anyway and hands it to me. It's completely unremarkable. A cheap metal teaspoon, rather battered, with a crude hole drilled into the end to allow a chain to pass through.

'Why do you wear it?'

'It kept me alive.'

'How?'

He shrugs.

'You don't know?'

He shakes his head.

'So how do you know it kept you alive?'

'It just did.'

I drink some coffee. 'Where did you get it?'

'It's army issue. JNA.'

The Yugoslav National Army.

'You were a conscript?'

He nods.

'How was that?'

'Good.'

263

Said with genuine warmth.

'Why?'

'It was better, back then.'

'What was?'

'Life. It was simple.'

'In Bosnia?'

'Yes. In Bosnia.'

'Do you miss it?'

'Yes.'

'You don't like it here in Germany?'

'It's okay. Better than Hong Kong.'

'But you'd go home, if you could?'

He nods vigorously. Which is the first time I've seen or heard him do anything vigorously. 'Yes. I miss home. I miss the people. I miss the bakery. Not being able to go home is the worst thing that's happened to me.' He looks out of the window, almost in tears. 'I just want to go home.'

Friday night on Strasse des 17 Juni, a forest of artificial light. The pavements were crawling, the road congested. Stephanie and Savic were in a taxi, stuck behind a bus.

'Look at them all. Polish whores. They come here every Friday and Saturday night. By train, mostly. The Warsaw Express. They earn some money, then go home ready for Monday. You see them here, and along Lietzenburger Strasse and Oranienburger Strasse. Many of them are amateurs.'

'Amateur whores?'

'Girls with shit jobs in Warsaw, whores in Berlin. For some of them, a weekend on their backs here is worth more than a month's wages back home.'

'Are you involved?'

Savic shook his head. 'We looked into it. But it's too casual, too organic. Besides, interference was going to cause us problems.'

'Why?'

'Publicly, officials disapprove of these girls. Privately, they're not so quick to condemn. And the police don't mind too much. Most of the girls are independent. They're working tourists. They don't bring trouble over the border with them.'

'Trouble like you?'

'People like me reduce trouble.'

'Right.'

'Ask the police.'

'They'll vouch for you, will they?'

He was smirking. 'A lot of them, yes. You'd be surprised.'

As soon as he said it, she knew she wouldn't be.

'This is Berlin today.' They were on Wilhelmstrasse, south of Leipziger Strasse. It was a breezy morning, dense white clouds scudding across an intermittently azure sky. Savic was pointing to a huge cheerless concrete building on his right. 'The German Finance Ministry. And across the street you can see ...'

A wasteland. Behind a mesh fence topped with barbed wire was an abandoned concrete expanse, waist-high weeds rising through cracks between pools of stagnant water. A hundred yards beyond the fence was the rear façade of a large square building: red-brick, commercial, deserted, most of its windows boarded up, the rest broken.

'After reunification there was a huge programme of redevelopment, fuelled by an assumption that Berlin's population would grow massively. It never happened but in those boom years the demand for manual labour outstripped supply, which was good for us. We brought in as many illegals as we could and there was work for all of them.'

'And now?'

'Berlin is bankrupt. Apart from one or two prestige projects – the redevelopment of the Olympiastadion for the FIFA World Cup or the Lehrter *Bahnhof* – there is no new construction. As for all the deprived areas that were promised regeneration – tough shit. They have no chance. That's what gives this city its feel today; brand new designs full of futuristic vision right next to the decaying architecture of the past. I guess it's great if you're the Chancellor in the Neues Kanzleramt but not so good if you're living out in Hellersdorf in housing stock that was condemned when Honecker was still in charge of the GDR.'

'What about the illegals?'

'It's not as easy as it was, but it's still not too hard. There's always plenty of work that Germans won't do. There are even jobs that Turks consider beneath them.' Savic smiled mirthlessly. 'Can you believe that? *The Turks!*'

Gunther Katz was the first one to be identified, a week after her arrival in Berlin. As soon as she saw him, Stephanie knew she'd seen him before. But not in the prefabricated offices of Katz Europa, a haulage firm located on Motzener Strasse in Marienfelder, just inside the city boundary.

It was a functional business park, bound by a security fence, with a central depot and two modern warehouses, each with six drive-in loading bays. Stephanie and Savic were in Katz's office: a grey nylon carpet, black plastic chairs, a protective grille over the window. For decoration there was an Energie Cottbus team photo on the wall. The gasp of air-brakes and the grumble of diesel engines never ceased. Every time a lorry trundled past, the office reverberated.

Recognizing Katz was the easy part. He had shiny purple scar tissue over the right side of his face. Half his mouth was paralysed. When he spoke, it slurred his speech, making him sound intoxicated. Much of his right ear was missing, along with his right thumb and forefinger. The rest of the hand was a charred mess, but instead of using his left he preferred to wedge his Camel cigarette between the remaining stumps of the right, so that when he took a drag his fist covered his mouth.

Stephanie asked where he operated.

'Mostly through eastern Europe. I have commercial agents in Poznan, Warsaw, Kiev, Prague, Minsk, Moscow. But I will deliver anywhere.' A grotesque smile transformed him into a gargoyle. 'Location: not important. Route: not important. Cargo: not important. As long as my lorries are carrying, that's all that matters. I detest empty containers.'

Katz described the rest of his business. Every now and then he'd say something to Savic in Serb, which generally led to laughter or a wistful sigh. They drank coffee laced with plum brandy.

'You two go back a long way, then,' Stephanie said.

'Before Time itself. I knew Milan when he was in nappies.'

Milan, not Martin. They were casual with one

267

another, she'd noticed. As Savic had been with the others he'd introduced her to. That meant one of two things: Katz was either sloppy, or very secure. She knew which she thought it was.

Katz's real name – his pre-Gemini name – was Marko Kovacevic. The only official photograph of Kovacevic and his scars – the one she'd seen in London – had been taken seventy-two hours after the car bomb that had caused them. In it, he was half-bald, fifty per cent of his hair incinerated, his burns weeping, giving his skin a sickening gloss. Then, as now, he should have been one of the easiest Balkan war criminals to apprehend. But he'd escaped from his military hospital bed and had never been seen since. Yet here he was, living in Berlin, running a successful haulage company, trading stories with another target, both of them wanted, both completely unconcerned.

Kovacevic was a Serb who'd meandered into central Bosnia in the late summer of 1993 and had ended up serving with Darko and the Jokers, a predominantly Bosnian-Croat paramilitary unit who were fighting Muslims in what was essentially a civil war. A civil war that had nothing to do with Kovacevic. But it provided him with the opportunity to indulge his murderous talents with impunity, so their cause became his.

A highlight from the Lasva Valley: Darko's men had buried huge quantities of explosives in their own trenches and had then provoked a gunfight with local Muslims. A short while later they initiated a retreat. The Muslims, believing they had Darko and the Jokers on the run, pushed forward and overwhelmed the abandoned trenches. Which was when Kovacevic hit

268

the trigger, blowing them all to pieces, an event he recorded, using several carefully placed cameras. Edited into a single piece of film, Kovacevic later produced copies of the tapes and sold them for profit. The footage was particularly popular with Serb paramilitaries. Kovacevic had later boasted that the proceeds had paid for his white Mercedes.

There was only one problem. Marko Kovacevic was a veteran of the Gemini network but he was not one of the nine names on the torn list.

Savic was getting dressed. 'What are you thinking?'

'That I'm surprised you'd go for someone like me.'

'Why?'

'I pictured you with blondes. With surgically enhanced breasts. Like Ceca.'

'She's not blonde.'

Arkan's widow was olive-skinned and dark-haired. Savic's tone suggested he resented the implication.

'You know what I mean. The beautiful dumb ones you don't have to talk to.'

'I've had my fair share.'

Stated as a bald fact, not a boast.

'I'm sure.'

'And plenty of others. I don't have a type. I even dated a journalist once.'

'That's strange. I never pictured you as a pervert.'

Once he was gone she searched the flat, looking in all the places that were off-limits when Savic was around. It was the first opportunity she'd had. The apartment had two bedrooms. The smaller one was being used for storage. But in the corner, by the window, there was a small pine table and a laptop. She examined the computer without touching it, wondering whether Savic took measures of his own. And decided probably not.

Half an hour yielded nothing. No mention of Gemini, no names from the list, no business details. Not even hidden among the system files. She switched it off and turned her attention to the rest of the apartment.

There were photographs in frames, although none in Savic's bedroom. She looked at the ones on the mantelpiece in the living room: a family of four, two young girls in front of their parents, all of them laughing; a boy of about fifteen in a bad grey suit with a pencil-thin red tie; a house by the edge of a frozen lake; a Red Setter coming towards the camera with a branch in its mouth. Stephanie wasn't sure about the shots. She'd lived in too many places where the personal touches were the most impersonal aspects of all. Set props designed to give an impression.

There were two very large sets of shelves in the living room. Both were full. Rows and rows of paperbacks – Pasternak, Austen and Zola through to Suskind, Allende and Greene. Looking at the spines, she couldn't imagine Savic reading any of them. She could hardly picture him reading the sports pages of a newspaper.

Ninety minutes passed with no hint of Gemini.

There was a hint of something else, though. Another woman. In a chest of drawers under a dust-sheet in the second bedroom she'd come across underwear. In one of the cupboards there were two pairs of women's shoes. In the cabinet in the second bathroom there was a box of tampons and a small bottle of Chanel No.5.

It annoyed her that she'd been so slow. Petra never made such elementary errors. She was supposed to be too good for that. The paperbacks started to make sense. Why hadn't she seen it before? Nothing here belonged to Savic. She hardly knew him, yet she knew him well enough to know that these weren't his things. Except, perhaps, the Bang & Olufsen sound system.

She thought of the name-plate by the front door. Who was Freisinger?

It began to rain. They headed east, Savic driving a battered black Alfa Romeo with mud down each flank. The windscreen wipers squeaked on each return stroke. In Marzahn, close to the Springpfuhl S-Bahn, they came to a residential estate on Allee der Kosmonauten. A relic of the archaic Soviet system of planning, prefabricated concrete apartment blocks were clustered around a communal centre; asthmatic trees, balding grass, supermarket, pharmacy, bar. Stephanie had seen grimmer versions in Moscow – Bibirevo, for one – but the contrast seemed greater in Berlin.

Savic parked outside one of the blocks. There had been some remedial work to the exterior. 'See that? Typical. Dumps like this were supposed to be replaced. When they ran out of money they did a little work on the outside and said it wasn't so bad after all.'

On the ground floor the communal parts were spotless: an old grey linoleum floor, still shiny, institutional cream gloss on the walls, a list of regulations pasted to one of them. The lift was out of order so they took the stairs. The first floor landing was over-heated. On the second floor the front doors had been reinforced, cladding secured by iron studs. The higher they went, the worse it became: broken windows, smashed overhead lights, graffiti on the walls, litter everywhere.

They went through an apartment on the fourth floor. The front door was wide open. The only pieces of carpet that remained were those that were too heavily stained with … *what*? Oil, blood, excrement? All the fittings had been torn away: light switches, plug sockets, door handles, skirting boards. The smell of urine was as ubiquitous as the rubbish; discarded needles, broken bottles, crushed cans, a single shoe, half a phone-directory. On one wall, in a red as dark as dry blood, someone had scrawled in German: *Please kill me …*

'People just walk away. Then the junkies come.'

'Why here?'

'I'll show you.'

They went up to the top floor, passing more abandonment and decay, finally coming to another apartment with a secure door. Savic rang the bell.

'Who is it?'

'Milan.'

Stephanie noticed a small camera attached to a wall-bracket above the stairwell. It was pointing at them. She heard the clunk of heavy locks, then the door scraped open.

It was Brankovic. In his right hand Stephanie recognized a Korth Combat Magnum, a German gun – possibly the most expensive revolver in the world – notable for having no safety device. Behind him a stranger appeared, thin, pale, with light brown hair parted on the right, falling in a greasy slant over his left eye.

'Hey, Milan, how's it going?'

'Good. You?'

He sniffed. 'Not too bad. I was in Monaco last week.'

'Powdering European royalty?'

'You know what? The fourteen-year-olds are sucking for blow.'

'They don't have money?'

'They're loaded. It's got nothing to do with money. I swear to you, there's nothing I can teach them. Who's this?'

'Petra.'

'Hi, Petra. Klaus von Harpen.'

Stephanie noticed puncture scars running from his wrist to his elbow.

Savic said to Brankovic, 'How long have you been here?'

'Ten, fifteen minutes.'

'Is it all here?'

He nodded. 'In the pink bathroom.'

Von Harpen's squat was, in fact, two apartments. Or had been, when the building had first been erected. More recently – very recently, by the look of it – somebody had demolished the partition between the two. There was a rugged hole in the wall, approximately circular, plaster and dust everywhere. Savic stepped through and led her to the grimy window on the far side. Stephanie became aware of other people in the squat; music from another room, a squeaking door hinge, coughing, the flush of a toilet. A mobile phone rang but no one answered it.

She'd already seen the wasteland in front. The new view was only slightly different: a few shrubs over a mound of dead grass, a burnt-out block on the far side, a rusting car, pylons beyond and, in the distance, a smoking industrial chimney.

'Being able to see both sides is good for security,' Savic said.

'Apart from the fact that you're stranded on the top floor.'

'With access to the roof, though. We have entry-points into every block that is connected to this building. Also, we always have two cars parked somewhere in the centre and one right by Allee der Kosmonauten.'

Von Harpen followed them down a corridor lit by a single blue bulb to a room at the far end; a bedroom once, judging by the indentations on the carpet. The green curtains were drawn. There were narcotics on the floor, divided by class and quantity.

Von Harpen lit a Lucky Strike. 'Ecstasy is fifteen euros a tablet. We offer better purity than anybody in Berlin. Our average crack rock – about 150mg – is around twenty-five euros. Cocaine varies a lot, depending on purity and supply. From fifty euros a gram to more than one hundred sometimes. The majority of the business is heroin.'

The bags he showed her were mostly brown because they'd been cut. Probably with caffeine, she supposed, but she'd known dealers to cut with ground stone, or even pulverized glass. For those with more acute tastes there was also pure heroin: a soft, white powder, twice the strength of morphine. Von Harpen said cut heroin retailed between seventy-five and one hundred and fifty euros a gram depending on market conditions.

Stephanie watched in silence, learning nothing new. She recognized the drugs, she recognized the squat – a dealer's place, everything on the floor, squalid mattresses in some of the rooms, clothes and rubbish everywhere.

A phone rang. A male voice called out for von Harpen. Stephanie waited until he was out of earshot before saying to Savic, 'I didn't know you were into narcotics.'

'I'm not. This is von Harpen's business.'

'You seem friendly.'

'The guy's a fucking maggot. There are plenty like him in my line of work. You have to get on to get on. That's all.'

'Why are we here?'

'To collect some gear.'

'Gear?'

'Not that kind.'

In a small bathroom there was a large nylon bag lying in a pink plastic tub. Savic unzipped it and took out a selection of weapons, including four sub-machine guns – a Croat ZAGI M91, two Austrian Steyr TMPs and a Hungarian KGP-9 – plus three pistols and a revolver.

Von Harpen reappeared in the doorway. 'Everything okay?'

Brankovic replaced the weapons in the bag and zipped it shut. Savic reached into the pocket of his black leather coat and pulled out two fat rolls of euro notes, each secured by a rubber-band. He handed them to von Harpen, who began to remove the rubber-band from the first roll. 'You don't have to count it, Klaus. It's all there.'

Von Harpen opened his mouth to protest, thought better of it, then smiled lamely as though he'd never have considered such behaviour. There was something about him that reminded Stephanie of Marcel Claesen.

'How come you two know each other?'

'Serbia is a main transit route for heroin,' Savic said. 'All Klaus's heroin originates in Afghanistan and comes overland, via Iran, Turkey and the Balkans. He uses Serbia as a hub.'

'Like you?'

'Sure. Guns, narcotics, people – what's the difference?'

They ambled back into the living room of the first apartment. Which was when Stephanie began to feel claustrophobic. Two shapes emerged from a dim corridor, followed by a larger third. They stumbled into the partial light of the living room. A boy and a girl, both in jeans. The girl was gone; her skin had the peculiar bloodless sheen that Stephanie remembered too well. Eyes open but blind to everything, she could barely stand. The boy was supporting her, a bony arm around a bony waist. Stephanie smelt vomit coming from one of them; the girl's T-shirt had a damp patch over the chest. Between the bottom of her Levi's and her Reebok trainers she wore pink socks. There was darkness on the inside of one of them. Blood. A puncture point on the ankle. Which was why she was wearing long sleeves.

It wasn't the walls that were closing in on Stephanie. It was her past.

Outside, Brankovic put the nylon bag into the boot of the Alfa Romeo.

Stephanie said, 'What's von Harpen's story?'

'He's a fucking tourist,' Savic grumbled. 'Daddy's an industrialist with factories outside Hanover and Hamburg, manufacturing electronic components. He's got some huge estate between the two, a chalet in

Garmisch-Partenkirchen, a villa on Mallorca and an apartment in Paris. So what does Klaus do? Becomes a junkie, then a dealer.'

'With friends in Monaco.'

'Clients, not friends. The sons and daughters of Daddy's friends, all of them in a rush to end up like little Klaus. It's pathetic. I tell you, if I'd started off with one tenth of what that bastard has, I wouldn't be doing this shit, that's for sure.'

'What's the hardware for?'

Brankovic almost smiled.

Savic said, 'You'll see.'

They drove west along Allee der Kosmonauten, crossing intersections with Allee Märkische and Rhinstrasse. Suddenly the road narrowed to a lane. The buildings fell away, the traffic died and they were among trees and sprawling vegetation. She knew she was still in the heart of eastern Berlin but there was no longer any sign of it. Instead she was in some dark, menacing corner of the countryside.

Increasingly the trees encroached, scraping both sides of the Alfa Romeo until they came to a row of eight enormous greenhouses. Savic parked the car. Brankovic opened the boot, unzipped the bag, handed a Steyr TMP to Savic, took the KGP-9 himself and offered Stephanie a Ruger P-85.

'Sub-machine guns for the boys and pistols for the girls? Isn't that sexual discrimination?'

Savic laughed. Brankovic didn't.

They entered the first greenhouse. It was vast, larger, somehow, on the inside than on the outside. There was an aisle down the centre with rows of concrete cultivation benches on either side. All that was growing, however, were weeds. Strong enough to puncture the concrete floor, they were flourishing. Swamped by two or three rampant bushes, the far end of the greenhouse could barely be seen. The rain was loud, coming through gaps in the glass roof. Stephanie estimated two thirds of the panes were missing. Many of them lay shattered on the ground.

In the second greenhouse there were colossal pieces of diaphanous pink nylon draped from iron struts suspended from the roof. Here all the cultivation benches had been removed. There was a thin blanket of dirt on the ground, almost all of it dry. The roof was intact despite the fact that the tops of the trees along the right-hand side were pressing against the glass. In the next greenhouse, which was also dry, there were a dozen arc lamps on tall stands, arranged in a broad circle. Power cables snaked through the dirt to a diesel generator outside.

One by one they went through them, all in various states of decay except for the last two. Beyond these was a concrete cube of a building.

'What is this place?'

'It used to be a flower factory. Industrial flower farming. It was during the time of the GDR. The flowers that were grown here were distributed to Party offices throughout the country. And to the homes of high-ranking officials.'

'This was just for the Party?'

Savic nodded. 'And when the GDR died, so did this place. A classic white elephant. A symbol of the GDR, in its own way.'

'But there are flowers being actively cultivated in two of the greenhouses.'

'Sure. People still want flowers. Demand and supply. It's just the scale that's changed. I'll show you.'

Six, large, rusting pipes protruded from the concrete cube, high enough to allow a lorry to pass beneath, before dipping vertically into the ground.

'Heating pipes,' Savic explained, 'pumping hot water to all the greenhouses. It used to be a different temperature for each. Now, for most of them, it's whatever temperature Nature decides.'

There were workshops beyond, also abandoned, except for the last one. As they got close, Stephanie saw shapes moving inside.

'We provide fresh flowers for the stalls and stores in the city but we also press dried flowers here.'

'I can't believe you're telling me this with a Steyr MTP in your hand.'

Savic grinned. 'What can I say? The flower business has never been more cut-throat.'

They entered the workshop. There were two wooden benches running down the centre beneath suspended fluorescent lamps. Stephanie estimated there were twenty workers. All female, all young. A portable radio was playing europop, the tinny sound echoing off hard walls. A few of the girls were treating dried flowers with some kind of chemical. Others were arranging them, copying designs from printed templates set in front of them. The rest were packaging. It took Stephanie a moment to realize that German wasn't the predominant language being spoken. She looked at the girls more closely: the clothes they wore, their faces, their demeanour.

They came to an adjoining office, where an older woman sat behind a desk. She had too much make-up and wore lipstick like a wound. She was on the phone. As soon as she saw Savic she finished her call and kissed him on both cheeks, leaving crimson prints that she didn't bother to wipe away.

'Milan, my darling. You look wonderful.'

'You too, Tamara.'

'Liar.'

'I could never lie to you.'

'Listen to him!' she shrieked.

'Is everything ready?'

She nodded. 'The boys will be here by six.'

Stephanie looked at her watch. It was half past four. Through a window on the other side of the office there were five more girls, sitting around a portable TV perched on a chair. They were all smoking.

'Can we wait upstairs?' Savic asked.

Tamara nodded. 'If you like, one of the girls can bring you tea. What time do you want them to leave?'

'In about half an hour. Are any of them included?'

Tamara inclined her head towards the five next door.

'Where are they from?' Savic asked.

'Three from Chisinau, one from Bucharest, one from Sofia.'

Upstairs there was another small office: one desk, some shelves – mostly empty – and a filing cabinet that had been pushed onto its side. Brankovic decided to use it as a seat.

Stephanie said, 'Your flower-pressers downstairs – they're all female.'

Savic pulled a face. 'It's not really a man's job, is it?'

'And young.'

'It's delicate work. You need nimble fingers.'

'And pretty.'

'You think so?'

'Their German isn't very good, either.'

'You said you wanted to see everything. So now you're going to see.'

Shortly after six, two battered Volkswagen vans pulled up outside. Stephanie, Savic and Brankovic went downstairs. Tamara and her girls were nowhere to be seen. A dozen men climbed out of the vans; surly, in leather coats and stubble, all dark. Most were already armed. Brankovic supplied those that weren't. A quarter of an hour later a third van pulled up, more men spilling out. At seven Savic addressed them as a group. *Sweep the area, then take your positions. No sub-machine guns for those on display.* The meaning of which became apparent when half the men melted into the darkness of the surrounding vegetation. At eight the rest congregated in the greenhouse with the arc lamps, which were now ablaze.

Soon after, the first of them arrived. Three Turks in a Mercedes 4x4, two fat ones and a thin one with a black beard. They parked beside a long shed with a corrugated-iron roof, then checked their guns with two of Savic's men.

'In some places,' he murmured to Stephanie, 'we don't have to be so cautious. But here, in Berlin, it's better to avoid violence. Especially *loud* violence.'

Savic greeted the Turks stiffly. Clearly there was no love lost between them. It was the same with the other groups: Albanians, fellow Serbs, Russians, more Turks, more Albanians, and five Chinese. By eight-thirty

Stephanie guessed there were thirty men in the greenhouse, including Savic's eight. She remained on the periphery, keen not to be too visible.

The door at the far end of the greenhouse opened and a man appeared. Behind him there were three girls. Behind them another man, as large as the first. They approached in procession until they reached the circle of white light. The girls were nudged into it, blinking, uncertain. One of the men arranged them in a line. Two blondes – one fake – and a brunette. The fake blonde was tall and slender. She wore jeans and a crop-top. The brunette, taller and larger, wore a PVC skirt and purple T-shirt. The other girl was tiny. She wore a flimsy dress with a floral print. It reminded Stephanie of a cheap motel curtain. It fell half way between her waist and knees. She didn't seem aware of anything, whereas the larger girls looked frightened.

Most of the men gathered on the rim of the light, half of them muttering into mobiles, shrouded in cigarette smoke. Savic himself withdrew to the darkness, allowing someone else to take over. Stephanie recognized him immediately but couldn't recall his name or where she'd seen him. A bull of a man, coarse black hair running off his scalp, down his neck and into his shirt without a trace of thinning.

Moving towards the centre of the circle of light, he said, in German, 'I won't waste any of your time.' He waved a large, hairy hand at the three girls. 'From the left, then, one to three. Starting with one – twenty years old, Russian, from Nizhniy Novgorod. No German, no English, no certificates. Three thousand euros?' There was a pause, then he spotted a reaction in the blackness. 'Three to you. Three five, anyone?

Yes, you. Four? Four thousand. Back to you – four five?'

Stephanie became aware of Savic standing just behind her left shoulder.

'An auction?' she whispered.

'How did you imagine it happened?'

She knew the auctions existed but was still stunned. She shrugged, hoping it conveyed indifference.

Shardov, she remembered. Aslan Shardov. He'd been one of Gilbert Lai's guests at Deep Water Bay. Stephanie had talked to his girlfriend. Julia from Moscow, six foot tall, blonde, green eyes. She'd said that she'd worked in Berlin before Shardov took her to Almaty. Stephanie had asked her what line of work he was in and remembered the answer: construction, transport, banking. In other words, anything and everything. Including, it now seemed, auctioneering.

The first girl went for six thousand euros. The brunette, a Ukrainian, went for four thousand five hundred. The girl in the floral dress went for nine thousand.

'Why so much more?' Stephanie asked.

The girl was smaller than the other two but no more attractive.

'She's got medical certificates proving she's clean.'

'Authentic?'

'I doubt it. She's from Belarus. Mind you, perhaps it's the novelty.'

'What do you mean?'

'Most girls from Belarus are from the countryside. Raised on farms. Like pigs. Plain and fat, but good in winter. Especially in somewhere like Irkutsk.'

Later there were Chinese and Thai girls, all of them

283

bought by the Albanians. For the London market, Savic told her. Stephanie felt strangely detached from the process. Except for when a mousy-haired girl from Slovenia started to cry. One of the escorts marched her out of the greenhouse. She was paraded again at the end of the auction when interest was waning. She'd put on extra make-up. Stephanie assumed that was to hide a blossoming bruise. The Chinese stepped in when no one else was prepared to meet the starting price.

'They pick up anything white for the Far East market,' Savic said. 'It doesn't matter how ugly they are. It's the colour of the skin that counts. They'll probably make her dye her hair blonde, just to emphasize the fact she's white.'

Stephanie didn't need to suppress a reaction. She was numb, the blur of sold faces rendering her senseless. They were girls, not women. None of them were beautiful but they'd all been attractive. Even the Slovene reject. Stephanie knew that was because the ugly ones never made it to northern Europe. Wealthy Europeans had money and that meant they got the best.

She spotted Tamara on the other side of the light circle, standing beside a man in a black suit and white T-shirt. His silver hair was pulled into a pony-tail and he had a trimmed goatee beard. He was scribbling notes into a pad. Tamara appeared to be dictating to him.

'Dieter Maier,' Savic said. 'Tamara keeps track of everything. She gives the information to Maier – the girl, the price, the purchaser – and Dieter works out the back end.'

Of the five who had been smoking in the room next to Tamara's office, three were bought by the Turks; two of the Moldovans and the Bulgarian. The thin Turk with the beard demanded a closer inspection of the Bulgarian, a willowy girl with long black hair, dark skin and a large, pointed nose. She'd kept her arms firmly crossed during the bidding so he checked her elbows for signs of drug use. They were clean. Then he pinched her waist for spare flesh. She didn't wince. He pinched harder. Nothing. So he slapped her across the mouth. Still nothing. Which pleased him a lot. He grinned at her, then looked across at Shardov and nodded. Tamara whispered to Maier, who scribbled on his pad.

'They're not looking for fresh girls,' Savic told Stephanie. 'Or girls with attitude.'

They were looking for compliant, experienced ones who *looked* fresh, but who would have sex with ten or more men daily without complaint. That was a working asset. Girls who got tired or upset were a liability. Not that they tended to remain that way for long. Instruction was painful, protest was pointless. It was better to be a quick learner. Which was something that remained true for Stephanie; standing there, in the greenhouse, with the butchers in the meat market, it was all she could do to hold herself together.

It's as though I've got some kind of eating disorder. Every time I swallow a mouthful of food I want to regurgitate it. We're sitting in Margaux, on Wilhelmstrasse. It's one of Berlin's most expensive restaurants.

The auction finished abruptly at ten. As soon as the last girl was sold – a slender, shivering Chinese, purchased, predictably, by the Albanians – everyone vanished. First the traders, then Savic's security, emerging from the bushes, dripping, sullen and silent. They climbed back into the Volkswagen vans. Five minutes later the arc lights were out, the last car was gone, all evidence destroyed. Brankovic drove the Alfa Romeo, dropping Savic and me at the restaurant. In the boot there were two bags: one containing the guns, the other containing cash, every euro accounted for by Dieter Maier.

Now, an hour later, there are six of us at the table: Savic, me, Dieter Maier, Aslan Shardov, Wim Frinck and Else Brandt. Frinck is a senior police officer and is the reason why the auctions occur without interference. Brandt works in the mayor's office. When Savic tells me this, she doesn't bat an eyelid. Both of them appear quite happy to be seen in public with the businessman Martin Dassler, not to mention the pony-tailed financier, Dieter Maier, or the Kazak industrialist, Aslan Shardov. Or even me, the Swiss tourist, Andrea Jakob.

We're drinking champagne, Dom Pérignon 1962, and claret, Chateau Margaux 1953. It's not that surprising, really. We have so much to celebrate. According to Maier, sixty-five girls have generated over half a million euros, all of it in cash. Not bad for ninety minutes' work.

'Any problems?' Wim Frinck asks.

Savic waves his hand one way, then the other. 'Only with the Albanians. They never want to pay up front. But you can't deal with them any other way. They never pay afterwards.'

'Is the situation resolved?'

'I think so.'

'By force?'

'Not at the moment.'

Frinck looks concerned. 'Is it a possibility?'

'There are some other issues. But I think it'll be okay. Even baboons have some kind of brain.'

Frinck peers into his glass. 'On a related subject, I have something for you.'

'What?'

'Farhad Shatri is in Berlin.'

Savic stiffens. 'That prick.'

'Arrived last week from London.'

'You couldn't have told me then?'

'I only found out last night.'

Shardov summons a waiter then waves an empty champagne bottle at him.

Savic says, 'That explains why those dogs were so slippery this evening. I swear, Milosevic may have been a useless bastard but he was right about the Albanians. They'd sell their mothers to cannibals. Where is he?'

'It's being looked into. There's a rumour he's got a safehouse, on Hobrechtstrasse.'

'Aren't there some Kosovar places on Hobrechtstrasse?'

'I know. It's a little too convenient. Maybe it's just someone adding two and two to get five. Let me deal with it. I'll let you know.'

Shardov says, 'I owe that bastard a good kick in the balls.'

Frinck looks surprised. Savic shoots Shardov a warning glance that the police official misses. So does Else Brandt. But I don't.

Shardov lets Savic explain. 'Aslan was in Hamburg. There was a small problem and he had to leave earlier than expected. That's all.'

The new bottle makes a timely intervention. It's trivial chit-chat until the cork has been popped and our glasses are brimming. Then Savic steers the conversation towards business and I find myself thinking about the Slovene reject. Will she end up greasing the poles in Club 151 in East Tsim Sha Tsui? I doubt it. Not attractive enough for that crowd. But she'll have plenty of Chinese customers who will pay much more for her than for far prettier Chinese girls.

I've known so many like her. Maybe she has a violent

father and a broken mother. Or a father who vanished when she was young. Or a mother more interested in drugs and other men than her daughter. The reasons are never that different, the outcome is almost always the same. I have a strong mental image of the Slovene's mother: small, dark-haired, tired eyes, a chain-smoker, she's clinging to the lie her daughter told her – that she's a waitress in Berlin. Soon it'll be Hong Kong. Wherever, whatever.

It doesn't make any difference whether the girls come from Carlisle or Minsk. They're on the run and very few of them would go back, given the chance. For most, prostitution is better than what they've left behind.

I look around the restaurant, avoiding eye-contact with everyone at my table. By force of will I push their contaminated conversation into the background. Other diners are coming to the end of their evening. The place resonates with a pleasant hum; it's the murmur of the self-satisfied. Rosy cheeks glisten in dimmed light, fawning waiters collect platinum credit cards. The last of the cognac swirls around the bottom of huge glass balloons. Cigar smoke hangs like low cloud, obfuscating the ceiling.

He's looking at me.

I look away. Because I'm avoiding eye-contact. Except he's not at my table. He's at a table by the window at the back, almost in shadow.

When I look back he's still looking at me. Except it's more than that. He's staring at me. Again, I look away. In a heartbeat my mouth turns to dust while my palms turn to liquid.

I look back. It can't be true, I tell myself. But it is. It's him.

Konstantin Komarov.

11

In the cloakroom, she stood in front of the mirror, shaking. Komarov. In Berlin. In *this* restaurant. She took a deep breath. Could shock leave a scar?

You look like you've seen a ghost.

Which was exactly what he should have been. That was the arrangement. Or, at least, a clause within it: no contact between them and he stays alive. Alexander had insisted on that and she knew why. One of them had to die. Without him, it was her.

Apart, there had been times when he might as well have been dead. Which, in turn, had left her dead on the inside. But she knew where he lived, the places he went, the things he did. She could close her eyes and be with him. Eating at Aragvi. Or with the children at the former state orphanage in Izmailovo that he'd bought. And to which she had contributed.

Time had eased the ache. At first she hadn't believed it would. She thought he'd be different. But working for Magenta House dulled the senses. Slowly he'd slipped away, the passing months softening the focus of memory. Until, eventually, she stumbled across Mark, and Komarov was relegated from active to archive.

She opened the cloakroom door. He was standing outside. 'Stephanie.'

For most of the time they'd been together she'd been Petra. It was only after he was gone she'd realized that when she'd been with him she'd been Stephanie all along.

'What are you doing here?' she asked.

'Eating. Although, in my case, alone.'

'I mean, in Berlin.'

'What are *you* doing here?'

He was in a grey single-breasted suit, a white shirt, open at the neck, black shoes. She guessed the suit was either a Canali or a Brioni. Probably Brioni. That was what he'd always favoured. She recognized the watch. It was the same Breitling he'd been wearing in New York, the first time they met.

'Oh God, Kostya …'

'Am I safe?'

'Can we talk?'

'Yes.'

'Tomorrow?'

'No. I'm going back to Moscow. It has to be tonight.'

She ran a hand through her hair. 'When I saw you I thought I was hallucinating. What are the chances of this?'

He shrugged. 'It's a coincidence. That's all.'

'Alexander says a coincidence is an oversight.'

'What else does he say?'

She closed her eyes for a moment. 'We *do* need to talk.'

'Come to my hotel.'

Four words that produced a very peculiar sensation in her stomach.

'I need to go back to my table.'

'Afterwards.'

'Where are you staying?'

'Just on the other side of Pariser Platz. At the Adlon.

It's a minute's walk from here. What's so funny?'

The smile took her by surprise. 'I'm staying in this weird little place on Pariser Strasse and you're staying on Pariser Platz.'

'What would Alexander say about that? Another coincidence, another oversight?'

'No. He'd say that two coincidences are a conspiracy.'

Five minutes later, back at her table, her mobile rang. She answered it. Komarov said nothing, as agreed. Stephanie nodded, chose Russian for a few murmured phrases of no significance, then terminated the call.

She rose from the table. 'I'm sorry but you're going to have to excuse me.'

Wim Frinck said, 'Nothing bad, I hope.'

'Not bad, just urgent.'

Savic rose too, putting on a face for their benefit – *nothing unusual, no need to worry* – then followed her across the restaurant. He didn't say anything until they were out of view. 'What's going on?'

'I have to leave.'

'Where are you going?'

'It's work.'

She collected her coat and pulled it on.

'You have to leave right now?'

Stephanie turned to face him. 'This is what happens. It's who I am. When a client needs me, I go.'

'And what if I need you?'

'You're not a client.'

'If I was?'

'That would be different. That would be business.'

He glanced at his watch. 'It's quarter to midnight ...'

'It's quarter to midnight *here*. Most of my clients aren't even based in this time zone. And there's certainly no reason for them to expect me to be in it. I could be anywhere. I'm on call twenty-four hours a day, three hundred and sixty-five days a year, Milan. I have to be ready to go anywhere in the world at a moment's notice. I told you – I'm not good at being confined.'

He held up his hands in defence. 'Okay, okay.'

'I thought we were starting something special. I hope I wasn't wrong. Because if you want a regular lover you'd better go back to the pneumatic blondes. You're not going to change me.'

It was five past midnight when Komarov opened his door to her. She hesitated for a second. *What am I doing here?* Then she entered, brushing his sleeve on her way past. He closed the door and followed her into the room.

For a second or two they stood there, not knowing what to do. A hug, perhaps, or even a kiss on the cheek? Could they risk that?

'Would you like a drink?'

'Oh yes.'

There was a bottle of cabernet sauvignon on his desk, already open, two glasses beside it. He poured for both of them.

Stephanie wasn't sure she could detect any changes in him. She recognized the small scar above the mouth. And she knew what lay beneath the shirt. A physique that was hard to the touch and a shock to the eye. The tattoos he'd acquired during the years he'd lost to the brutal prisons of the Soviet penal system covered most of his body. Predominantly blue and green, his torso had been a piece of sculpted jade.

'How are you, Stephanie?'

What a question. It was the way most civilized conversations started. But, as ever, it was never that simple for them. She could give him the civilized answer, of course. *I'm well. How about you?* But they'd never done that to each other because they'd never had the luxury of time. Some things, it seemed, never changed.

'I'm a mess. You?'

'Right now? Confused.'

'Thank God.'

'You want to go first?'

Stephanie cupped her glass between both hands. 'No. You go first. Tell me how it's been.'

'It's been okay.'

'Really?'

'Actually, no. Not really. Sometimes it's been okay, sometimes not. When I think about you it's difficult. When I don't it's easier. That's the truth.'

'I'm sorry.'

'When I worry about you I worry about myself.'

That made sense. 'I'm sorry about that as well.'

'I often wonder where you are, what you're doing. Who you're doing it to. Because I know that if anything happens to you, my protection evaporates. I won't hear about it – not unless you make the papers – which means that one day somebody is going to appear out of the blue and I'll be dead. Chances are, I won't see it coming, but it's a strange sensation. Like knowing that you have a fatal gene defect. It lies dormant but it's always with you. It's *part* of you. And sooner or later it'll become active and that'll be that. No warning, nothing.'

She bit her lip, then decided to do the wrong thing and tell him. 'Maybe not.'

'Maybe not what?'

'When you asked whether you were safe, I said no. But I wasn't being entirely honest. There's a chance you could be. Not now, but soon.'

'Go on.'

'Alexander might let me go.'

'Why?'

'I don't really know. But if he does, you'll be free.'

'Are you sure?'

'It was part of the deal we made.'

'Will he stick to it?'

She paused. 'He gave me his word.'

They both knew that wasn't an answer.

'What do you have to do?'

Another pause, this one longer. 'Does it matter?'

She could see that he wanted to say that it did. But he restrained himself, then changed the subject. 'That looked like an interesting table at the restaurant.'

'Christ, don't …'

'The woman – I've seen her before. Here in Berlin.'

'She works in the mayor's office. Else Brandt.'

'And the man to your left – I've seen him somewhere too.'

Stephanie flinched. 'Where?'

'I'm not sure. Who is he?'

'Here, in Berlin, he's Martin Dassler. In Marrakech he was Lars Andersen.'

Marrakech sparked something in Komarov. He struggled with it for several seconds, then shook his head.

She said, 'He's a Serb. Milan Savic.'

'Yes ... I thought I recognized him.'

Stephanie's heart sank. 'You know him?'

'No. But I know an associate of his. That's why Marrakech rang a bell. Maxim Mostovoi?'

Now she wasn't sure what she felt. Relief, certainly, that Komarov hadn't been contaminated by Savic's acquaintance, but what was she to make of the Mostovoi connection?

'How do you know Mostovoi?'

He shifted awkwardly. 'Through business.'

'How well do you know him?'

'Well enough.'

'What's he like?'

'Max? He's an animal. But everyone loves him.'

Gavin Taylor at Frontier News had said something similar.

Komarov said, 'Okay. This is what he's like. A couple of years ago he decided he wanted to go on safari. You know that he does a lot of business in Africa?'

'Yes.'

'So he books this place in Botswana. A five-star camp in the bush. Total luxury in virgin wilderness. Max pays for the whole place, which can take about thirty or forty people. Except he's going with three or four friends and a dozen hookers.'

'Classy.'

'That's Max. When the time comes, he flies every-one down in one of his planes. They take the best wines, a sand dune of coke, tons of caviar. By day Max and his friends go into the bush, looking for wildlife, while the girls sit around getting a tan. At night the wildlife is *inside* the camp. Everyone's getting drunk – the way only Russians can – and doing staggering quantities of coke. Then it's sex until dawn with these top-of-the-line hookers before going out again a couple of hours later. Say what you like about Max, you can't deny his stamina.

'The owner of the camp and all his staff, they've never seen or heard anything like it. They don't know whether to be appalled or just amazed. They're wilder than the animals they've paid to come and see. But they're also charming. They're fun. And they treat the people looking after them with respect. Also, they're paying way over the odds for all of this.

'Then the owner's little boy – he's about six or seven – gets a nasty eye-injury. Something really serious. The owner decides he must drive to the nearest town to get it treated. Which is fine because he's got competent staff who can easily take care of Max and his friends. Except that Max gets to hear about the boy. When he sees how distressed he is, he insists on flying father and son to the town. It'll be quicker, he says. And, on second thoughts, they better make sure he gets the right attention. He makes some calls and finds out the name of the best eye-doctor in southern Africa. Turns out the man they need is based in Johannesburg. So, in no time at all, the plane is fuelled and Max is flying the father and son to Johannesburg. But it's the weekend; the eye-doctor is playing golf. While they're flying, Max gets a connection to this man's cellphone – he's actually on the fairway when it rings – and speaks to him directly. It takes about two minutes to persuade him to take the case.'

Stephanie raised an eyebrow. 'Persuade?'

'Money, not menace. He says to the doctor, I'll pay twice your going rate. The doctor's making enough money to say no. Max says, fine, what's the one thing your business could use that you don't have? The doctor comes up with the name of some piece of specialist equipment. Max tells him that he'll have it as soon as it can be delivered *and* he's going to pay *three* times the doctor's rate. The doctor meets them off the aircraft, they go to the hospital, the boy gets treated and the sight in his eye is saved. If he'd been taken anywhere else, he'd have lost it. After the operation Max sits up all night with the father, at the boy's bedside. The father, overcome with gratitude, suggests he might want to return to the camp. He says they can make other arrangements for his son now that the worst is over. Max declines. He waits in Johannesburg until the boy's pronounced fit to travel. Then they all fly back to the camp together. From that moment on there wasn't anyone – father, son, staff, even the hookers – who wouldn't have walked over broken glass for him. That's Max: the girls, the drugs, the gun-running, the smuggling of conflict diamonds, the man who takes the time to look after the boy rather than just write the cheque. It wasn't a stunt, Stephanie. That's who he is.'

She nodded slowly, then said, very softly, 'I almost killed him.'

'I know. Marrakech. He told me.'

'When?'

'About a month later. In Moscow. That was the last time I saw him.'

'Do you know where he is now?'

'No.'

'Or where he was headed?'

297

'He didn't say. Are you still after him?'

She shook her head. 'His contract was suspended.'

'Why?'

'I was never told.'

Komarov lit a cigarette. 'Tell me about Savic.'

A request that sent a shudder of sobriety through her. 'A Balkan war criminal. He ran a Serb paramilitary unit in Croatia, Bosnia and Kosovo …'

Komarov nodded. 'Inter Milan.'

'You know this?'

'We're quite sophisticated in Moscow these days. Our newspapers do more than report on Ukrainian wheat yields. What's your interest in him?'

'Need you ask?'

'I mean, what's the reason?' She hesitated. Then felt ashamed. He noticed both the pause and the reaction. 'It doesn't matter. Go on.'

'Apparently he established an escape network for other war criminals.'

'Apparently?'

'I haven't come across any evidence of a network. Have you met Savic?'

Now it was Komarov's turn to hesitate. 'Actually, yes.'

'With Mostovoi?'

'No.'

Stephanie's skin began to tingle. 'Where?'

'In Moscow.'

'How?'

'Through a business associate of his.'

'Who?'

'Sabine Freisinger.'

Freisinger; the name belonging to Savic's apartment.

298

The first name had resonance, too. Sabine. It was something Savic had said to her. It took a moment to download it from the memory. *I don't have anyone. I did, for a while. Sabine – we were both in Germany.* They'd been drinking at 1/5 on Star Street in Wan Chai. He'd gone on to say that when Sabine had moved to Moscow it had been the perfect opportunity to end it.

'Yes, he's mentioned her before. They had a relationship here.'

'So I've heard.'

'Do you mind me asking what kind of business you were doing?'

The frown formed slowly, keeping pace, perhaps, with the dawning realization of her ignorance. 'You don't know who she is, do you?'

'He only mentioned her once. And it was just Sabine. He didn't tell me her surname.'

'Sabine Freisinger is Dragica Maric.'

In an evening of surprises, this is the knock-out punch.

Dragica Maric.

First and foremost, a Serb. Also, one of the most beautiful women I have ever met. When I first saw her she was Natalya Markova, a Russian trophy girlfriend draped over the arm of a Russian gangster. We were in a casino in Atlantic City. The last time I saw her was also in the United States. In New York.

In the perverse parallel universe in which Petra exists, all of this begins to make some kind of sense. We were in a dimly lit passage in the decaying ruin of the Somerset Hotel on West 54th Street. She made me sink to my knees. She stood behind me, pointed a gun at my head and prepared to fire.

Before deciding to let me live.

I still don't know why. Even though it turned out we had something in common – we were both in the lobby of the Hotel Inter-Continental in Belgrade on 15 January 2000 – there was no reason for her to let me live. On the contrary. For what happened on that day, she should have killed me as soon as she had the chance.

The painful truth is this: I'm only alive because Dragica chose to let me live.

There's something else I remember about those final few moments before I expected her to kill me. She asked questions. About Kostya. About what it was like to love him. And I told her. Expecting to be dead in a moment, there was no reason not to. And I remember the response. She was jealous of me. She'd wanted him too. All the time she'd been Natalya Markova, first on the arm of Oleg Rogachev, then Vladimir Vatukin, what she'd really wanted was to be in Kostya's bed.

And now, it turns out, the two of them are doing business in Moscow.

She tried a smile but knew it was crumbling. 'I'm not surprised you look a little awkward.'

'It was just business, Stephanie.'

'Right.'

'I promise you. I was never interested in her …'

'Of course not. After all, she's so unattractive and she wouldn't look twice at you, so that makes perfect sense …'

'I have someone else.'

A low blow, right to the pit of the stomach. Stephanie felt winded.

'Her name is Ludmilla.'

'Oh, that makes it so much better, Kostya.'

Immediately she regretted it. The cheap assumption, then the bitterness.

An image flashed in her mind. A photograph, black-and-white, three people outside the Hotel Lancaster on Rue de Berri in Paris. Beneath the photo there had been a caption. She couldn't remember the name of the third man, or what he looked like. She remembered the way Komarov looked, though. A little dishevelled, his jacket billowing in a stiff breeze. What she remembered most, however, was the stunning blonde in the sable coat by his side. And the name on the caption: *L. Ivanova*. L for Ludmilla. Alexander had provided the photographs. As leverage, naturally.

Then there was the secondary reaction. The female reaction. Why would he need Dragica when he already had Ludmilla? Both beautiful, although in different ways, they nevertheless had one thing in common: they made Stephanie feel ugly.

She drained her glass and focused on the concept of Dragica Maric, rather than the physical entity. *First and foremost, a Serb.* Working, somehow, with Savic. Suddenly the idea of a network didn't seem as unlikely as it had earlier. In Serbia, Maric had been connected, right from the start. Milosevic, Frenki and Badza, Arkan. And now Savic. Why Moscow, though? She'd been in Germany, then moved.

'What does Sabine Freisinger do, Kostya?'

'I couldn't tell you. We only transacted one piece of business.'

'Which was?'

'Is this what you want to talk about in the time that we have, Stephanie?'

'Which was?'

301

'I was setting up a company in the Russian Far East. For financial reasons that I won't bore you with, it was advantageous not to register it anywhere in Russia.'

'Let me guess. Primorye Air Transport.'

He worked his cigarette for a good while. 'Looks like I'm not the only one handing out the surprises.'

'I saw your name on the list of directors at the Companies Registry at Hong Kong's Central Government Offices.'

'I see.'

'Apparently you run quite a decent airline.'

'It's not an airline.'

'Whatever. I met someone in Hong Kong who was a fan. Can't remember his name. A German. From Berlin, as it happens. An oil man …'

'Dieter Hausmann?'

'That's it.'

Komarov smiled. 'Dieter's an old friend.'

'He said Primorye Air Transport had a reputation for reliability and safety.'

'We do.'

'I don't recall you being involved in oil and gas.'

'It's something new for me. The Russian Far East is where the future lies.'

So did a great deal of the past. Of *his* past. He'd spent a decade in the prisons of the Russian Far East, including a stretch on Sakhalin itself. She wondered how that felt. To be reminded, constantly. Then again, perhaps it didn't bother him at all. Like her, he adapted to any environment. Sakhalin was no longer a prison. It was a treasure chest.

'Tell me about Hong Kong.'

'There's not much to say. I was advised that there

were good legal and financial reasons for registering the company there. I needed some local directors for representation. I didn't know the Far East so I asked Mostovoi. He's always had contacts out there. He introduced me to Sabine Freisinger.'

'Let's call her Dragica.'

'Okay.'

'When was this?'

Another smile. 'When Max was still visible. Before 9/11. Anyway, Sabine – sorry, *Dragica* – set me up with some locals to make sure everything looked right. The man who organized it for me is called Tsang Siu-chung.'

Stephanie remembered the name from the registry. He'd also been a director of Victoria Entertainment International, the company that controlled the three nightclubs: Kiss Kiss, Gold Cat and Club 151.

'That's it? That's the connection?'

'That's the connection.'

She sat on the edge of his bed, deflated. 'God, I feel such an idiot. I'm sorry.'

It was two thirty-five in the morning. Komarov had ordered a second bottle of wine. The uniformed man who'd delivered it had been the essence of discretion, barely noticing the woman sitting on the guest's bed.

Now it was Komarov who was sitting on the bed, sleeves rolled up, the tattoos on his forearms clearly visible. Stephanie was on the chair by the desk, hugging her legs close to her body, her chin on her knees, her shoes kicked off.

'Tell me about Ludmilla.'

'I was wondering how long it would take you.'

'I didn't want to appear too keen. Is she attractive?'

He reached for the pack of Marlboro. 'She's not unattractive.'

Stephanie smiled. 'You're not being entirely honest, are you? I've seen a photograph of her.'

'Then you're not being entirely honest, either. Where was the photo taken?'

'Paris. Outside the Lancaster. With a third man.'

Komarov nodded. 'Yevgeny Paskin. A friend.'

'Don't stray from the subject. She's gorgeous ...'

'Where did you see the photo?'

'Magenta House.'

Stephanie regretted the slip instantly. Too many surprises for one night, too much wine, too much emotional bruising – the reasons barely mattered. It was only the consequences that counted.

'Am I safe?'

That was the second time he'd felt the need to ask the question.

'Yes.'

'Are you being entirely honest with me now?'

'I'd never lie to you.'

A lie in itself, it nevertheless had the intended effect. Komarov relaxed a little. Stephanie asked him about Ludmilla.

'We met in Moscow. At Café Pushkin, actually. Do you remember?'

'Of course.'

'She was with someone else.'

'But couldn't resist you?'

Komarov squirmed a little. 'It wasn't quite like that.' In other words, it was *exactly* like that. 'She's a geologist.'

That came as a surprise. From the image of her,

Stephanie had been quick to construct a very detailed profile, based on a stereotype she knew all too well. It was the template Dragica Maric had used when she'd been Natalya Markova.

She took a guess. 'Who works in the oil business?'

'Correct.'

'Mixing work with pleasure?'

Like I am with Savic? Oil and water?

'She works for Yukos.'

'Do you see much of each other?'

'Not as much as we'd like.'

This time he winced. She knew he'd meant it. And that he hadn't wanted to hurt her. Stephanie pretended to shrug it off. 'I can imagine.'

'What about you? Do you have someone?'

'Yes. Mark. He's a chiropractor in London.'

Straight out with it. The two worlds she'd worked so hard to keep separate, merging in a careless moment. After the jolt, though, there was no regret. Telling Komarov was not a risk. Of that, she was absolutely convinced.

'Do you love him?'

'Yes. I do.'

'And he loves you?'

'Yes.'

'I'm glad.'

'Although I thought I'd never love anyone after you, Kostya. Truly I didn't.'

He didn't say that he'd felt the same way. He just nodded. She was going to ask him if he loved Ludmilla but he got in first. 'Can I ask you an ugly question?'

No one had ever put it quite like that. 'Okay ... but I can't promise you that I'll answer it.'

'Savic – are you sleeping with him?'

First Rosie, now Komarov; the only two people in Petra's world that she trusted. Her outrage was genuine. She glared at him but he wasn't going to justify it without provocation. Finally she said, 'What kind of question is that?'

'An ugly one. Like I said.'

'Why would you think that, Kostya?'

'Because I saw the way he was looking at you. And because I know that sometimes you have to do terrible things.'

When they'd been together she'd had sex with Salman Rifat, the Turkish arms-dealer, in order to procure information. The memory of Komarov's reaction to her infidelity still haunted her.

'No.'

His stare was as intense as hers. 'No?'

'No.'

I'm the first to wake. I'm in his arms. That's not how we fell asleep. At least I don't think it is. We're both fully dressed, lying on top of the bed, not in it. Delicately, I extricate myself and examine myself in a mirror. I look like a tramp.

I feel like a tramp. I feel as though I've been unfaithful to Mark. The thought of sex with Savic leads me back to the lie. Why couldn't I tell Kostya the truth? Perhaps that's a form of infidelity itself. Besides, I don't know if he believed me. I got the feeling he saw right through me. Which might explain why both of us were so eager to move on.

We talked about Mark and Ludmilla. Not about us. Maybe that would have been too dangerous. Then again, maybe I'm kidding myself. He has Ludmilla now. A geologist, fluent in four languages, a fellow Russian. And so beautiful. I know it's childish but it's that, as much as anything, that hurts.

'Are you okay?'

I turn round. He's rubbing an eye with the heel of a hand. The drug squat, the auction, the restaurant, the Adlon. No wonder I feel drained. I look at my watch. It's five past six. We've had an hour's sleep.

'I'll order some breakfast. Why don't you have a bath?'

It feels like a trick. Me, in his hotel room, naked. I make it as hot as I can stand, then strip and slide into it. Bliss. I lean back and close my eyes. I could be anywhere. As I relax, it's not just the steam that washes over me. It's the past. It's us. We're in New York again, then Moscow. Or even Paris. And I'm still able to delude myself that I can escape Magenta House and that he can relinquish his past, and that we can slip away and build a secret future together.

And as I'm thinking about all of this, I'm also wondering what would happen if he came into the bathroom now. If he stretched out his hand to take me to bed – would I go?

I never find out. Because it doesn't happen. And there's one part of me that's overcome with relief. I dry myself slowly and get dressed.

'Better?'

'You have no idea.'

There's coffee and orange juice for me. He's drawn the curtains. From his window I can see the Brandenburg Gate and the top of the new Reichstag.

'How are the children at Izmailovo?'

The smile that spreads across his face is perhaps the warmest I've ever seen from him. 'The money you gave, Stephanie … if only you could see what it's done.'

One million and eighty thousand dollars, give or take. The money I made as Petra in my first stint at Magenta House.

Soiled money that needed to be put to a good use in order to redeem it.

'We've constructed another building, next to the original, doubling the capacity. As for the facilities – well, you wouldn't recognize the place.'

'I knew you'd do something good with it, Kostya. You've always been good with money.'

Breakfast is lovely. Somehow the pressure is off. But it's over too quickly. He has a plane to catch. Back to Moscow. Back to work. Back to Ludmilla.

'What about the future?' he asks.

'The future?'

Both of us realize that our wires are crossed.

The Pension Dortmunder on Pariser Strasse, seven in the evening. The proprietor gave her one smile – *I know you didn't stay here last night* – so Stephanie gave him a slight smile of her own, with a little shrug, and his second smile was warmer.

In her room, she took the Vaio out of her bag, switched it on and sent a message to Stern at one of his Hotmail addresses.

I need to speak to you immediately.

Within half an hour they were together in the ether.

Sabine Freisinger – does the name mean anything?

Not instantly. Do you want a profile?

Yes. Thumbnail first, deeper later.

One hour.

One thing she knew for certain was that Dragica Maric was Serb to the core. Stephanie wondered how she existed in Russia now as Sabine Freisinger, having once been Natalya Markova there. She wasn't sure she believed that Komarov hadn't slept with her, if only because she knew how Maric had felt about him. On the other hand, Komarov knew how Stephanie felt about Maric and she liked to think that, had the opportunity arisen, some sense of loyalty would have prevented him from succumbing to such obvious pleasures. Then again, he was a man.

When it came, Stern's thumbnail sketch was a good start. Sabine Freisinger was renting an apartment in Moscow on Bryusov Lane, between Tverskaya and Bolshaya Nikitskaya, and was registered as the owner of Lazar, an import–export company with offices in a building on Novokuznetskaya Street. Lazar had subsidiary offices in Berlin and Belgrade.

According to her passport, Sabine Freisinger's birthday was in three days' time. Stephanie wondered whether Dragica Maric used her own birthday for Freisinger. Stephanie had always kept hers separate. Others, she knew, always used their own date to ensure they were never caught out. After all, by itself, a date of birth was worth little, and yet a false date was such an easy thing to forget.

She'd spent one of Petra's birthdays with Komarov. They'd stayed at the Atlantic Hotel in Hamburg and he'd asked whether she'd go back to New York with him. It had been the first hint of a possible future together. She'd spoilt it by wondering why she should be the one to make the sacrifice. A pointless row had followed, which she'd regretted before it was even over.

Stephanie stopped the memory. There was something gnawing away at her. Something to do with Hamburg. Or was it the Atlantic Hotel? She tried to cast her mind back to the time they'd spent there. That wasn't it. Slowly, though, there was another idea forming. Somebody was emerging from the fog. She recognized the face, heavy-set, brutish. And the hair, thick, black, *everywhere*.

Aslan Shardov. That was right. Shardov had been in Hamburg. That's what Savic had said when they'd been in Margaux. Shardov had said he owed Farhad Shatri 'a good kick in the balls' and Savic had shot him a silencing look, before going on to explain that Shardov had been in Hamburg, had encountered a problem, and had been forced to leave sooner than planned.

But why was that resonant? It was more than just Hamburg. It *was* something to do with the Atlantic Hotel. She was increasingly sure of it.

The answer came an hour later, when she'd stopped thinking about it. It was the conversation she'd had in Hong Kong with Asim Maliqi after she'd chased him from his hotel. They'd been in that plastic patisserie, she recalled, the rain hammering down outside, the cut beneath his eye still raw. Maliqi had told her that he had a friend named Hamdu who'd worked at the Atlantic Hotel.

She ran through Maliqi's story in her mind, then contacted Stern again.

I'm looking for a face.

Who?

Goran Simic. A Serb who served in the JNA under Ratko Mladic. In 1992 he was a prison guard at the Serb camp in Omarska. He stayed there until the end of July. He was also one of those implicated in the 1995 massacre at Srebrenica.

Forty-five minutes later she had her answer. She downloaded the photograph. All that had changed was his weight. There was no doubt about it. Aslan Shardov was Goran Simic. Shardov was the identity Gemini had

310

provided for Simic. Which meant he'd also been Paul Ullman, a German from Bremen. That was the identity he'd been using at the Atlantic Hotel in Hamburg when he was recognized by Hamdu.

Another name from Gemini but how much closer was she to the list? Her post-Magenta House future was like gold at the end of a rainbow; the closer she got to it, the further it receded.

She sent a message of thanks to Stern and set about making payment; this time a dollar transaction, transferring from one of Petra's Mexican accounts – at Banco Aurelio Gutierrez in Oaxaca – to a company in Bermuda named Redman Realty.

It was nine in the evening when she pressed the button next to the name-plate marked Freisinger. Savic looked tired when she entered the apartment.

Stephanie said, 'Is everything all right?'

'Where have you been?'

They'd had no contact for twenty-one hours. Easily enough time for her to travel to the furthest corner of Europe and back again. In fact she'd spent all but the last two hours in Komarov's room at the Adlon. Needing to stay invisible, she'd asked him for a favour. Anything, he'd said.

'Buy me another day in this room.'

He'd seemed disappointed that her request wasn't more significant. She'd said she couldn't ask him for more than that because she already owed him too much. Later she watched him pack in silence. When it was time to leave, she brushed imaginary fluff from the lapel of his jacket.

'You should look your best for Ludmilla.'

They kissed by the door; a light brush of the lips, and he was gone.

She sat on the crumpled sheets. The hotel staff would assume they'd made love. There was a part of her that felt as though they had.

She watched TV, then fell asleep. In the afternoon she sat by the window, in a daze, watching the rain, her thoughts alternating between Mark and Komarov. So different but with something in common: the ability to tolerate her, to absorb her and not react against her. To let her breathe. The ones who'd never attempted to hold on to her too tightly were the ones she'd wanted the most.

Unlike Savic, who was still waiting for his answer. He wanted to possess her. Despite the warning she'd given him, she knew he thought he still could. She'd come across so many men like him. Predictable and aggressive, yet easy to manipulate.

'Too far from you,' she said.

When they went to bed she closed her eyes and pretended it was Mark. Then Komarov. Then Mark again. As though the two were different versions of the same man. One face, two names.

Gemini.

Now that she knew who Sabine Freisinger was, it felt peculiar to be in her apartment, in *her* bed. With her ex-lover. When she faked her orgasm Stephanie wondered whether Dragica had too. Or whether she hadn't needed to.

It was still raining at six in the morning when the phone rang. Savic answered. Stephanie was aware of him tensing beside her. He listened, nodded, then

312

said he'd be there in fifteen minutes.

'Come on. Get dressed.'

'Where are we going?'

He was pulling on a pair of trousers. 'To a breakfast meeting.'

A slate grey dawn, the streets still quiet; they drove in silence with just the spray for sound. Stephanie put on a cold front. Like wearing black, she found it was good for all occasions.

They turned into Hobrechtstrasse in Neukölln, a cobbled road lined with trees and a mixture of buildings – nineteenth century and post-war – all residential above street level. The wheels grumbled over the cobbles as Savic slanted the car into a diagonal parking space, the bonnet beneath dripping branches. He looked over his shoulder.

'Good. Vojislav is already here. The red Fiat on the other side of the street.'

The car was empty. Brankovic was nowhere to be seen. Stephanie noticed the names above four shops in a row – Kosovare, Prishtina, Illyria Travel, Café Tirana – and felt her pulse flutter.

Savic took out his mobile, made a call, spoke in Serb, presumably to Brankovic, then said to her, 'We can go up.'

They got out of the Alfa Romeo and crossed the street. The plain brown door between Prishtina and Café Tirana looked closed but Savic reached out and pushed. It swung open.

They entered a gloomy, airless hall, then climbed creaking stairs to the second floor. The doors on the first floor landing were nailed shut behind wooden boards.

Savic produced a Mauser 90DA from the waistband of his trousers and rapped the butt against the door. When it opened they were in a small, unloved apartment: functional furniture – none of it new – paint peeling from the walls, the smell of damp everywhere. In the living room, masking tape ran across one of the windows, following the line of a crack.

Six men and a woman were squeezed into the kitchen. Around the edge, an old, electric two-ring stove, a grill, a sink and some cheap seventies fitted units in avocado. At the centre, a table with a yellow Formica top. Beside it, a chair, which one of the men was tied to, his wrists secured by duct tape. One of the other men was sitting on a chair in the corner, cupping his nose. Blood was running through his fingers, splattering his lap. Both eyes were puffy. The woman, who stood beside him, tried to help but was prevented by a man Stephanie had seen at the auction.

Savic looked at the two men who were sitting, then at Brankovic. 'Where's Shatri?'

'He's not here.'

He glared at the man taped to the chair. 'Who's this?'

'Says he's called Sevdie.'

'And the two over there?'

'They own the café downstairs. Bobo recognizes them.'

A squat figure with bad blond highlights bristled at the mention of his name.

'And you haven't seen this one?'

Before Bobo could answer Brankovic held out a manila envelope. Savic emptied the contents: some papers, a passport, an airline ticket.

314

Brankovic said, 'From London. Doesn't speak German. Came in last week. Same as Shatri.'

'Well, there's a coincidence.' Savic looked at the man and said, in English, 'You a friend of his?'

Nothing.

Stephanie thought Savic would throw a punch. But he didn't. He just sighed and turned away. There was a pot of coffee simmering on the stove. He helped himself to a cup. 'I can see this is going to take some time.' He sat on the edge of the table and lit a cigarette. 'Sevdie – is that right?'

Still nothing.

'This will be easier for you if you talk to me.'

Black hair pushed back over the scalp, greasy skin stretched over prominent cheekbones, his darting, deep-set eyes were full of fear. He wore a crumpled grey suit over a dark blue-and-brown checked shirt with a frayed collar.

'Where's Farhad Shatri?'

He shook his head.

Savic took a drag from his cigarette. 'But he was here, right?'

'No.'

Brankovic took a tea-towel from the rail by the cooker.

Savic tapped ash into Sevdie's lap. 'I know he was here.'

'I don't know anyone called Farhad Shatri.'

Brankovic moved behind Sevdie.

Savic smiled but there was nothing warm in his eyes. 'Let me explain something to you. Farhad Shatri arrived at Tegel last week. With someone else. A male, more or less like you. And I know that Shatri came

315

here with his friend. Who may or may not have been you. This ticket, though, tells its own story. You were on the same flight.'

Sevdie was pulling against his restraints, trying to look over his shoulder to see what Brankovic was doing.

'Sevdie, pay attention.'

'Please …'

'Look at me.'

Reluctantly he turned back to Savic, who said, 'Let's start again. Where is Farhad Shatri?'

'I don't know where …'

Before he could complete the sentence, Savic threw his cup of coffee into Sevdie's face. A second of silence was followed by the start of a scream. Which was muffled by Brankovic who secured Sevdie's head in an arm-lock and rammed the tea-towel into his mouth with the force of a punch.

The Albanian rattled from side to side, skinning his wrists on his bindings, the veins rising off his throat. By the window, the café owners whimpered. When the scream had subsided to a quivering moan, Savic yanked the tea-towel from Sevdie's mouth and said, 'Was Farhad Shatri here?'

Sevdie nodded, the movement barely discernible over the tremble. Steam was rising from his scorched skin.

'I can't hear you. Was Farhad Shatri here?'

Through scalded lips, Sevdie mumbled, 'Yes.'

Savic stared hatefully at Sevdie. 'Bobo, that seemed a little cool. Turn up the heat. I like my coffee boiling.'

He stood up and turned his back on Sevdie. He circled the room in silence, no one else daring to move.

Then he put a hand on Brankovic's shoulder and led him to the door, where he whispered an instruction that Stephanie overheard.

He said, 'This isn't going to work. Call Gunther. Tell him we're coming. Tell him we need some place where no one can hear you scream. And tell him we need a bolt-cutter.'

Brankovic's eyes began to sparkle.

12

Stephanie arrived before Savic. At five to midday it was drizzling but several determined Berliners persisted in taking coffee outside. Swathed in overcoats, they sat at small circular tables on Unter den Linden beneath a large canopy. Stephanie entered Café Einstein and chose a table at the rear, beside a window. She ordered black coffee.

Savic had called at half past eleven. He'd sounded breathless, anxious even. He'd been walking as he talked; she'd heard shoes clicking on concrete, the rumble of an engine, the rattle of heavy gates.

Three tables away, two women sat opposite one another. The older woman was in her seventies, Stephanie guessed, or even her eighties. Her hair was completely white and her skin was alabaster pale, without a single obvious blemish, as though she had never seen sunlight. She sat bolt upright, in a dress with a frilly collar, a triple string of pearls around her throat, her hands in fingerless gloves of white lace. She was smoking Lucky Strike, which seemed a little incongruous.

Stephanie felt she could use a cigarette herself. It had been years since her last smoke. Every now and then, though, the urge rose, Phoenix-like, from the cigarette ash. It was the mention of the bolt-cutter that had done it. That, and the look in Brankovic's eyes.

She'd told Savic she wasn't going to the Katz Europa depot in Marienfelder. He'd nodded, not offering a view in front of the others, but the message was clear enough: *I don't blame you.*

When he arrived he appeared to have aged five years in five hours. His skin was almost as pale as that of the woman in the fingerless gloves, the effect made more dramatic by the dark stubble over his jaw. He shrugged off his leather coat, resisted a waiter's attempt to take it from him, and draped it over the back of the chair. Another waiter brought Stephanie's cup of coffee.

Savic said, 'Vodka, no mixer, no ice. Make it a triple.'

When the waiter had gone, Stephanie said, 'Sevdie?'

He shook his head. She wasn't surprised. The kind of interrogation that required a bolt-cutter was unlikely to yield useful information.

'I need you, Petra.'

'Personally? Or professionally?'

'Both.'

She took a moment to decide how to play it. 'I don't want to work for you.'

'Why not?'

'It'll come between us.'

'Not necessarily.'

'It came between you and Sabine.'

'That was different. *She* was different.'

'I've been thinking about what you suggested in Hong Kong. I don't want to get drawn into a … *programme*. I value my professional independence. I've only ever done single contracts and that's the way I'd like to keep it.'

'You did Waxman *and* Cheung.'

'Essentially they were one person.'

319

Gemini, again.

'I only want one.'

Stephanie picked up her cup and took a slow sip. 'Farhad Shatri?'

Savic nodded. 'And I don't want you to kill him. I want you to find him.'

'Because you can't find him yourself?'

'That's right.'

'What makes you think I can?'

'You found Mostovoi when no one else could.'

'Who is Farhad Shatri?'

'It doesn't matter. Once you find him I'll deal with him.'

'That's not the way I work, Milan. Gilbert Lai didn't want to explain why Waxman and Cheung were important to him. And I had to explain to him that I don't go into anything blind. That's why I'm still in business.'

The waiter returned with Savic's drink.

'This is different,' he told her.

'Why?'

'Because it's me. Because it's *us*.'

'So it's a question of trust, then?'

'Yes.'

Stephanie's smile was measured. 'What are we going to be, Milan? Two strangers who have sex because they like the look of each other? Or something more? Because, if we're being totally honest, there are other strangers around. I see them everywhere. On the street, in the airport, in a shop. Maybe even in here. And if that's the way it's going to be, why bother with the commitment?'

She saw this was the last kind of conversation he

wanted to have. Certainly not now, probably not ever. Which meant the timing was perfect.

'We could be something special. Look at us. Look at what we've done. We broke away from our pasts and created something new – something *better* – out of ourselves. Both of us. Now we have our own lives, our own reputations, but the question is this: can we have a life together?'

'Why not?'

'Because I'm Petra Reuter. And I won't accept anything less. And because you're Milan Savic. And I still won't accept anything less. If we're going to be together there can be no half-measures. It's everything or nothing.'

The blood was returning to him. Perhaps it was the vodka. Perhaps not. She decided to gamble. 'Think of how it could be for us. The two of us, both dominant in our own way. What a couple we could make, Milan. Like Arkan and Ceca. Only better.'

At first she thought she'd gone too far, both names a punch to his solar plexus. But once the shots were absorbed they seemed to energize him. Tired eyes became revitalized. He polished off the vodka and lit an American Spirit.

Time to push home the advantage.

'I'll do this for you, Milan. But not for money. I'll do it for *you*. The way I do things for you in bed. I'll do it for *us*. But in return, I want something back.'

'Name it.'

'Trust. You have to tell me what I need to know. You have to show me. And then let me show you.'

He was completely motionless. 'Everything or nothing?'

'Everything or nothing.'

Stephanie could almost see the creaking cogs turn with the vodka acting as lubricant. The idea of Arkan and Ceca coloured everything. They'd all been together: Milosevic, Arkan, Savic, Frenki and Badza, Ratko Mladic and Vojislav Seselj, organizer of the Serbian Chetnik movement. But of all of them it had been Arkan and his paramilitary Tigers who'd been the touchstone. He'd been the one with the flair, the one with the trophy wife, the one who'd inspired the most fear among Serbia's enemies.

An image was forming in Savic's mind: of Savic himself, the criminal entrepreneur with a business stretching from the Far East to Western Europe, and Petra Reuter, the wraith spirit. She didn't have Ceca's voice, or her extraordinary breasts, or even her smouldering, angular beauty, but she had a reputation. And what a reputation it was. Not one that could be publicly paraded through the best nightspots in Belgrade or Moscow, but among Europe's criminal *cognoscenti* Petra would outclass Ceca and all the others. Arkan and Ceca had been Balkan giants. Petra Reuter was universal. That was the bottom line.

Savic said, 'I'm hungry. Let's eat.'

He ordered veal, she ordered carrot and coriander soup. He steered clear of alcohol, ordering Coke instead. Stephanie drank sparkling mineral water.

He was like a child's toy. She'd wound him up. Now she let him go.

What was most striking was the casual drift from Belgrade gangster to hardcore paramilitary leader. At first they'd all been seduced by Milosevic's romantic vision of a greater Serbia. He'd come to the presidency on 8 May 1989, but it was his speech, on 28 June of that year, to one million people to mark the 600th anniversary of the Battle of Kosovo that truly made him. Savic had been there, at Gazimestan, part of the historic battlefield where Prince Lazar had perished in 1389.

Recalling the speech, Savic submitted to the fog of nostalgia. Milosevic told them that throughout their proud history Serbs had never conquered or exploited others. He played on the heroism of Serbs over the course of six centuries and pointed out that they were now engaged in modern quarrels. And that although they were not engaged in battle, it could never be ruled out.

With Mira Markovic, his wife, then a professor of Marxism at Belgrade University, at his side, they surrounded themselves with Serbian intellectuals who were prepared to regard Milosevic as the great Serbian messiah. Through mass manipulation of public and political life, they managed to impose direct Serbian rule over Kosovo and to install a pro-Milosevic regime in Montenegro.

'After that it just seemed there was too much momentum. Previously Serbs and Slovenes had always got on. Suddenly that was no longer the case. And although our fight with Slovenia was over almost before it had started, it was obvious that Croatia was going to be a problem.'

The transformation from gangster to paramilitary leader was organic. The leaders of the SPS, the Socialist Party of Serbia, *were* gangsters, Savic said, in all but name. Jovica Stanisic had been head of the SDB, Serbia's secret police. He'd realized that the SDB would not be able to incite Serbian insurrection in Croatia by itself. He brought in his two top men – Franko Simatovic, *aka* Frenki, and Radovan Stojicic, *aka* Badza – to help. They selected and recruited generals from the Yugoslav National Army, to help arm those who were ready to rise up, and they formed links with sympathetic criminals, Arkan and Savic among them.

'I founded the unit in 1989. It was about 1991 or 1992 before people started to call it Inter Milan. Arkan set up the Serbian Volunteer Guard – the Tigers, as they became known – a little later. 1990 or 1991, I think. Among other things, he was the head of Delije.'

'What's that?'

'The official supporters' club for the Red Star Belgrade football team. They were regarded as the Serb team. When Arkan set up the Tigers he recruited a lot of men directly from Delije.'

'And you?'

'Most of the ones closest to me – with the exception of Vojislav – were with me from childhood. We grew up together. We made money together. We had a bond that you can't buy. Inter Milan was merely the formalization of a tight group that already existed.'

'I thought it became known as Inter Milan because of the unusually high number of foreigners you recruited.'

'True. I wanted that blend. The ones who'd always been with me – the ones I knew I could trust with my life – and the ones who weren't interested in the politics or the history. Complete outsiders, only interested in money. They were there to fight. And we respected that in them. As a mixture, I would say it worked well.'

Over the course of lunch he took her through a

decade of war. Croatia, Bosnia, Kosovo. Milosevic couldn't stop. He needed to be pressing constantly. To have stood still would have been to retreat. And to collapse.

Eventually Savic came to the network.

'Even when we were in the Krajina, back in 1991, there were some who thought it would end in tears. In 1992 I was in China. Lai asked me that very question. *What will you do when it all goes wrong?* I'd always assumed it might, but that was when I started to believe it *would*. This was five years before the British handed Hong Kong back to the Chinese. A lot of people in the colony were making their own preparations, assuming the worst. So that was what I started to do too.

'At that time, apart from my links to Hong Kong and China, my businesses were based in Belgrade. It was clear that if we lost, everything I'd worked for in Belgrade would be at risk. So I decided to diversify. Lai suggested human trafficking. Whatever happens, he said, the Balkans will be a lucrative transit region. And he was right. He was to provide the raw material – the people, in their thousands – and I was to provide the network for dispersing them across Europe.'

So he'd started to strike deals with other criminal organizations. At the same time he expanded his own. Even as he did this he realized that in the advent of the worst-case scenario he was going to need to reinvent himself. Stephanie didn't bother pursuing the atrocities perpetrated by Inter Milan; they both knew what he meant.

First he made preparations for himself. Then for those closest to him within Inter Milan. The ones he wanted at his side after the war. It took time and money to source those who could provide documentation – real or forged. Having established the basic network – courier routes, finance, contacts and safehouses – Savic then simply recognized a commercial opportunity: to extend the service to those who could pay. Or, occasionally, to those who couldn't, but who had something he wanted in return.

'We called the project Gemini. One face, two names – an only twin.'

'And where did they go, these solitary twins?'

'Anywhere. Everywhere.'

'Give me an idea.'

'I could name the owner of a car dealership in Atlanta, Georgia. Or a director of a plastics factory in Cubitão, on the outskirts of São Paulo. Or a Brisbane-based airline pilot for Qantas. I can think of four in New York: two investment bankers, a lawyer and a cab driver. There's a cleaner at the British Library in London who runs three crack houses. Or an orthopaedic surgeon in Buenos Aries. Or a dry-cleaner in Chicago. Off the top of my head I could name five restaurant owners: two pizzerias in New York, a sushi bar in Rio de Janeiro, another pizzeria in Cape Town and a steak-house in Frankfurt. Tell me when you've had enough …'

'How many of them were there?'

'Fifty-four.'

'And the details are all in your head?'

'Yes and no. They *are* in my head. But they're also written down and locked away. In separate parts, in different places.'

'So that if anything happens to you …'

'That makes it sound worse than it is. I don't really need the protection. These people are bound to me in the same way that I am bound to them. We're glued together by history and commerce. It goes beyond the service I provided. On the other hand, it only needs one of them to feel nervous.'

'Because you're the only one who can link them with their former lives.'

'Correct.'

Stephanie smiled ruefully. 'The carrot and the stick.'

'Exactly.'

'You said history *and* commerce.'

'Gemini is ongoing.'

'How?'

'Not on a day-to-day basis. But those who benefited from it have always accepted that they are obligated to it. So, for example, if we have a problem that needs attention in Brazil, I can call São Paulo or Rio, and the factory director or the restaurant owner will sort it out. The jobs they have are legitimate and full-time. But so is the debt owed to Gemini.'

'Tell me about Farhad Shatri.'

'He was a leading member of the KLA. He was involved with the Homeland Calling fund, too. To be honest, I admired the way those bastards organized that. Very efficient.'

'I know he's connected somehow to the Albanians who were at the auction.'

Savic nodded. 'They're family. Albanians are impossible to penetrate because they run their enterprises around a family unit. They take the idea of blood being thicker than water *very* seriously. The Albanians you saw are cousins of Shatri. I can't say that they were buying directly on his behalf but I can say that he heads the clan.'

'Why do you need to find him?'

Savic paused a good while. 'Because there's a list.'

Stephanie hoped the kick in her chest didn't show. 'What kind of list?'

'The complete kind. All fifty-four names from Gemini. Who they were, who they are now, plus the people who helped it happen.'

'How could such a list exist?'

'I don't know.'

'Has there ever been such a list?'

'Not to my knowledge. When I recorded aspects of Gemini I did it in sections. Different areas of the project, recorded in different ways, stored with different people. People who don't know each other. In different walks of life, in different countries.'

'You don't think there's any way that somebody could have collated the sections to form an overall picture?'

'Not a chance. I was the only one in a position to do it. And I didn't.'

'So Farhad Shatri is … *lying*?'

Savic shook his head. 'I've seen evidence of part of the list. A scrap of paper with nine names. And I've seen the other half: the new names for the original nine. The tear matches. Both sets of names were on one piece of paper.'

'Just nine?'

'The lateral tear ran through the tenth.'

'And you're sure he has the full list?'

'The rumour is that he has access to it. He's not in actual possession of it. But he's in a position to negotiate.'

'So he's not the vendor?'

Savic smiled humourlessly. 'I wouldn't say that. If he's offering it, there's a ninety-nine per cent chance that he *is* the vendor. By saying he's not, he discourages someone like me from putting him out of my misery.'

'If you could find him.'

'Exactly.'

'Do any of the people on the list know about it?'

'No.'

'And the other people on it, the ones you said had helped it happen – who are they?'

'Bankers who processed money for us. Government officials who sold blank documents. Police officials and politicians who've taken bribes ...'

'Would Wim Frinck and Else Brandt fall into that category?'

'Certainly.'

Stephanie frowned. 'If Shatri is putting this list on the market, how come nobody on the list has heard about it?'

'It's not an *open* market.'

'You think he has potential buyers singled out?'

'Yes. And not too many.'

'Who?'

'Enemies of mine, obviously. Look at it this way: if I was Shatri and in possession of such a list, what would I want from it? Firstly, money. Because Shatri always wants money. Secondly, me out of the way. That would leave a vacuum. In my world a vacuum never lasts long. There would be other pretenders, but Shatri would be well placed to fill it.'

*   *   *

Zoo station, mid-afternoon, a gun-metal sky overhead, a cold wind whipping functional concrete, glass and steel. Serving long-haul passengers and commuters alike, the station is constantly busy; scurrying locals, ponderous tourists studying city maps, the aimless dispossessed, loitering police. Inside, it's the usual mix of news-stands, fast-food outlets, bars and luggage lockers.

When I asked why we were coming here, Savic would only say that it was a surprise. Now that we're here I don't find anything surprising at all. It's a depressingly familiar scene, to be found in dozens of cities across Europe. But there's wonder in his eyes.

'This is where they came.'

'The fifty-four?'

He nods. 'Once they'd escaped they made their way to Berlin to be reborn. And this was where it happened. Zoo station.'

He explains the procedure. Before leaving the Balkans, the runner would be photographed and have information recorded: height, weight, hair colour, eye colour, languages, medical conditions, scars. The information and the runner then took separate paths to Germany. Savic had been smuggling illegal goods into Yugoslavia for years. He was using most of the same routes throughout the war. All that really changed was the cargo: fewer Chinese TVs, more Chinese-made AK-47s. Those in flight took the same routes in reverse.

All the elements of Gemini were kept separate for their own protection and for the overall protection of the programme. By the time the runner arrived in Berlin, the photographs and information he'd provided in south-eastern Europe had been transformed into the cornerstone of a new identity. Zoo station was the collection point.

They arrived in the city with a phone number. One call would yield a contact, the contact would yield a key. And the key would yield a bag, to be collected from the luggage lockers at Zoo station. Whether the runner was destined for Frankfurt or Buenos Aries, everything necessary was contained within the bag: clothes, money, passport, travel documents, letters of introduction, phone numbers.

'A completely new start in a bag,' Savic says with pride. 'And this is where it happened. This is where they passed from one life to the next.'

An airlock, then. Like my flat at Maclise Road. And like other flats I've known. Or safe-deposit boxes that have contained emergency identities.

More than Savic, more than any of his fifty-four, I understand what it's like to be stranded between two worlds, between two lives. In that sense I've spent my whole adult life at Zoo station.

Stephanie called Mark from the Underground as the train sat between stations, west London to either side, a collage of terraced housing, offices and gasworks.

'I wasn't expecting you back for two or three days.'

'I wanted to surprise you.'

'You always do that. I'm well. Look, I'm with a patient at the moment. We'll speak later, okay?'

'No need to be so abrupt.'

'Sorry. But I'm running late ...'

'Fine. Bye.'

She switched off the Siemens and waited for the train to move. The driver apologized for the delay but offered no reason.

Stephanie ached with fatigue; Petra had given an

overnight performance that could have left Savic with no doubt about her plans for both of them. During a stolen weekend in Paris, Komarov had once told her that the reason Russian men tended to treat their women so badly was to compensate for the punishment they took in the bedroom. Stephanie had dismissed that but never forgotten it. And with Savic she'd tried to make it so.

At one point, with Savic pinned to the bed beneath her, she'd risen and fallen to the phrases she whispered in his ear. 'I'll find him … you'll get what you want from him … then we'll kill him … *together*.'

Later, as he tried to sleep, she reached for him again.

'Please, Petra. No.'

She'd bitten him on the shoulder. 'You can't say no to me.'

And he hadn't.

In the morning, as he watched her dress, he said, 'You're the devil.'

She'd beamed at the compliment. 'Of course. What did you expect?'

The carriage was almost empty. There wasn't anyone within earshot. She turned on the Nokia and dialled Magenta House's number.

'Good morning. Adelphi Travel. My name's Helen. How can I help?'

'Can I speak to John Brown?'

'Transferring you now.'

She waited for the bleep. Then: 'Market-East-1-1-6-4-R-P.'

In the past her security clearance code had been enough. These days her voice was subjected to instant analysis as an added precaution. Which was fine when it worked. But in February she'd had laryngitis and it hadn't recognized her.

A minute later Rosie was on the line. 'You've landed?'

'Landed and stranded. Somewhere near Acton Town, I think.'

'Lovely.'

'Should I come straight in?'

'Yes. S3 has a profile for you. The old man wants to see you afterwards.'

'The old man? I hope your phone's not bugged.'

They were in Rosie's office. She was on her computer while Stephanie introduced herself to Farhad Shatri, a former member of the Kosovo Liberation Army. In the early eighties he'd been part of an underground movement based in Pristina that had organized demonstrations and distributed anti-government propaganda. Harassed by the authorities, he fled to Romania in 1982 then to Germany. In 1990 he settled in London and made contact with other dissidents.

He got a job working for the Caledonian Cab Company, on the junction of Caledonian Road and Gray's Inn Road. By then the KLA were already established as an entity. Pleurat Sejdiu was their London spokesman. By 1995 Shatri was travelling to Kosovo four times a year, via Albania, to make contact with the KLA's 'active' force. Even as late as 1997, that amounted to no more than a hundred and fifty men. At that time there was still no expectation of an uprising.

Two things changed that. The first of them had already occurred: the Dayton Conference on Bosnia,

333

which took place in November 1995. Before Dayton the Kosovo Albanian leader, Ibrahim Rugova, had advocated a path of passive resistance, believing that moderate behaviour would be rewarded by Western intervention. The Dayton Conference was judged a success because it brought the war in Bosnia to an end. But to the Kosovo Albanians it appeared to prove that Serb aggression had been rewarded and that nobody was going to intercede on their behalf. Consequently, from 1995 onwards the KLA began to agitate for armed struggle. This, however, was not regarded as a serious threat to stability.

The second event occurred in the spring of 1997, when there was a complete breakdown of law and order in Albania. The descent towards anarchy started with the collapse of the *Ponzi* schemes. These were pyramid saving plans, which promised enormous rates of interest. Completely unsustainable, the implosion was as inevitable as the fall-out was catastrophic.

There were riots. The government lost control, the police dissolved, the army fragmented and the mafia consolidated to take advantage. State arsenals were looted. Suddenly Albania was awash with weapons available for free. With no one to constrain them the KLA built up huge stockpiles, an activity partly coordinated by Farhad Shatri, who travelled to Albania just as the discontent was reaching boiling point.

By December Shatri had moved into Kosovo, becoming a full-time military officer, organizing smuggling parties over the mountains to Albania, bringing in men and weapons as the crisis in Kosovo deepened. Injured twice, he fought to the end, resisting the ethnic cleansing of Serb forces during the retreat, then helping to implement the ethnic cleansing of Kosovo Serbs during the return; initially heroic, subsequently barbaric.

Alexander had arrived in Rosie's office. So had lunch: a silver tray laden with sandwiches and rolls, a flask of coffee, two bottles of mineral water and a selection of cups and glasses.

'Ciabatta instead of Mother's Pride? Your budget must be fatter than I imagined.'

Rosie smiled despite herself.

Alexander said, 'Savic doesn't think Shatri has the list himself?'

'He didn't say that. He said it was a possibility. On balance, he thinks Shatri *does* have the list and is just trying to cover himself.'

Alexander nodded and looked out of the window, lost in thought.

'Apart from the biography, what's the deal on Shatri from S3?'

Rosie finished her mouthful, then said, 'He came back here as soon as the war was over. Others in the KLA chose to stay, but Shatri had too much of a good thing going on here.'

'Driving cabs?'

'Not any more. These days he *owns* the Caledonian Cab Company. And that's the least of his interests. His family are into slum rentals and prostitution. He's a leading figure in the new wave of Albanian criminals who've seized control of London's vice trade. They're running all the walk-ups in Soho now.'

Alexander was looking at her. As inscrutable as he was, she had a pretty good idea what he was thinking.

Do you remember them, Stephanie? Or rather, Lisa. That was the name you used back then, wasn't it? Rosie had been right when she'd said it was something he'd always have over her. He lit a Rothmans, still staring at her.

'What now?' she asked.

He narrowed his eyes. 'For you?'

'Yes.'

'Nothing.'

Out of the corner of her eye she noticed Rosie frowning at him. He didn't see it. Couldn't see it. Because he was *still* staring at her.

After Magenta House, she dropped Petra's things at Maclise Road then walked to Queen's Gate Mews, taking advantage of a cold and blustery afternoon.

Alexander hadn't forgiven her for Waxman or Cheung. That was the conclusion she'd come to, but she wasn't sure about the primary reason. Was it the loss of the asset, or the fact that she'd acted independently? One thing was certain in Stephanie's mind: she was no longer on the inside. In the past, despite their mutual antipathy, Alexander had kept Stephanie at the core of Magenta House.

She was being sidelined. Rosie had denied it emphatically, when Stephanie had asked her, once Alexander had gone.

'You're being paranoid.'

'That doesn't mean I'm wrong.'

Alexander had expressly stated this: she was not to pursue Farhad Shatri. When she'd asked why, he'd said there were other sections within Magenta House that were better suited to the task. She couldn't deny that. But the manner in which he said it carried a subtext.

Either Rosie had missed it or she wasn't being honest.

If she was being frozen out, what would that mean? An easy end to her Magenta House career? Or a technical failure to meet her obligations giving Alexander the opportunity to rescind their agreement?

It was half past five when she reached Queen's Gate Mews. Mark wasn't back from work. She made tea, kicked off her shoes and lay on the sofa for half an hour. She thought about Komarov. About the first time they'd made love in New York, and how startled she'd been by his tattoos, as they undressed. The first time she made love with Mark, in their hotel in the Dolomites, had been equally startling. But not because of the way he looked. Because of the way he made her feel. More than pleasure, it was security. A complete stranger, and he'd made her feel safe. Being naked with him had seemed entirely natural.

She had a bath. It was almost seven when he returned. Stephanie was still wrapped in a towel, her skin pink from the wet heat.

He kissed her. 'I didn't mean to sound rude earlier. But I was way behind. Appointments stacking up like aircraft over Heathrow.'

Stephanie cast off her towel. 'Well, you can make it up to me now.'

'I'd love to but I can't. Not tonight.'

'Why not?'

'I'm going out. And I'm already late.'

'Where?'

'To the RGS with Larry, Michael and Karel. Oh, and Nobby.'

Some of Mark's climbing friends. A different crowd to the rest of his friends. In that sense he was similar to

337

Stephanie: two distinct aspects to his life, both kept well apart from the other.

'What are you doing there?'

He'd shed his suit and was tugging his shirt over his head. 'It's a documentary on K2.'

Feeling foolish, Stephanie picked up the towel from the bed and wrapped it around herself. 'Can I come too?'

'Sorry. Larry organized it. Five tickets, no spares.'

He was already half-dressed. Stephanie sat on the edge of the bed. 'I was hoping for a quiet night in.'

'You didn't tell me you were coming back today.'

She wanted to ask him whether he could cancel. And was glad that she didn't. 'What time does it start?'

'Seven thirty.'

'You're going to have to run. Do you know what time it ends?'

He shook his head and pre-empted her next question. 'We'll be going out afterwards. A few drinks and a bite to eat, I expect ...'

Stephanie nodded slowly. 'So, not a late one, then. Or an alcoholic one.'

He grinned. 'Wouldn't dream of it.'

Although they were both essentially solitary climbers, Mark enjoyed the few climbing friends he'd retained over the years. When he was with them Stephanie detected a slight shift in character. From widely different backgrounds, and ranging in age from late twenties through to early fifties, they were bound by shared personal history. Just like Savic and Brankovic, or any other member of Inter Milan.

'I'll be here,' Stephanie sighed. 'The downtrodden dutiful homemaker ...'

'You've done a great job,' Mark said, surveying the dirty clothes littering the bedroom floor.

She laughed. 'All I want is someone to make me feel like a real woman.'

'Well, I've got a pile of shirts that need ironing.'

'Bastard.'

'Bitch.' He kissed her, then slapped her on the backside. 'Keep it warm.'

'*Keep it warm?* My God, you're in trouble ...'

'Promises, promises.'

Once he was gone she took a bottle of red wine from the wooden rack in the kitchen and opened it. She'd never subscribed to the idea that drinking alone was bad. On the contrary. She usually found it was very good.

For an hour or so she channel surfed and found nothing to tempt her. The more TV there was, the less there was to watch. So she switched off and put on some music: a compilation by The Clash – one of Mark's favourites – and *Red Square* by Laurie Anderson, one of hers.

All along, Alexander had lusted after the list. Now that she'd provided positive proof of its existence, he didn't want her to pursue it. But Savic did. And she'd promised him she'd do her best to find it. He needed it. Alexander needed it. Perhaps she needed it too.

Around nine she went to the kitchen to make something to eat. She put on a pan of water and poured in some penne. Which was when she remembered ... *what*? It was a germ of an idea that took time to grow. Something about Farhad Shatri ...

The phone rang at just the wrong moment. She put her fingers to her temples, squeezed her eyes shut and tried to think past the noise. The answer-machine took it.

Asim Maliqi.

That was it. In Hong Kong, Asim Maliqi had mentioned Farhad Shatri. In passing, a casual remark. She tried to recall the context but her recollection was too vague. Still, she knew that was it. Maliqi knew Shatri. Or had met him, at least. Sadly, Maliqi was dead. But it was a starting point. She remembered that he'd worked for Deutsche Bahn in Berlin.

That was something she hadn't mentioned to Alexander or Rosie.

She went into the living room and hit the 'play' button on the answer-machine, hoping it was Mark, post-film, pre-dinner. It wasn't. The voice was female.

'Hi Mark. It's me. I hope it's okay for me to call you at home. I left a message on your mobile earlier. I hope you got it. Anyway, I just wanted to say … thank you … for yesterday. It was really good. And it was lovely to see you again. And thanks for calling this afternoon … the day after tomorrow's fine. Or the day after that. Whatever's best for you – any time's good for me. I'm a lady of leisure at the moment … as you know.' There was a nervous giggle. 'Call me when you can. Lots of love … bye. Oh, it's Alex, by the way. In case you couldn't guess. Take care. Bye.'

My first instinct is to erase it. But I don't. Instead, I play it again. Three times. Alex. The flirt. I drink some more wine. She was all over him like a rash. He'd denied it, said he hadn't noticed, accused me of over-reacting. And I let it go. I should have trusted my instinct. When I looked at her, I knew

340

what she was thinking. The same thing I've seen other women thinking once he starts to talk to them, once his hands begin to move. He doesn't even need to touch them to make them feel him.

I rein myself in a bit, refill my glass and play the message once more. She hasn't actually said anything that incriminates either of them. But the tone of it ... she's purring with pleasure. Almost gloating. And when I remember the look she was giving him, the way she stared at him even when he was looking elsewhere. Not many women are truly predatory, in my experience. But the ones who are tend to be more ruthless than any man I've ever come across.

I dial his number. His phone isn't switched on. I'm pacing furiously. The room isn't big enough. There's a pile of his wretched biographies by the sofa. I give them a good kick, scattering them across the kilim.

How could he?

Not a good question to ask myself. As soon as I have, I'm flooded with legitimate reasons. I know what I told him at the start of our relationship, about areas of my life being off-limits, but that seems absurdly redundant now.

I finish the bottle and want to open another. I want him to come back. I want to fight. But I don't do any of these things. Instead, I leave and catch a taxi back to Maclise Road.

It's ages since I've slept here. The bedroom smells damp. There's dust on the pillow and duvet. I go into the kitchen. There's no alcohol in the fridge. There's some cooking brandy in one of the cupboards, though. That'll have to do.

It's almost one in the morning when he calls.

'Stephanie? Why aren't you here? What are you doing?'

By now I've had far too much to drink. The room's moving. 'What am I doing? Jesus Christ, Mark! You've got a fucking nerve. What am I doing?'

'Stephanie …'

'Have you checked your messages since you got back?'

'I haven't had the chance …'

'Fine. Do it. Then call me.'

I end the call. Less than a minute later the phone rings.

'That's it?' he says. 'That's what this is about?'

Which provokes a gasp of amazement. Then I say, 'Just tell me this. Alex – is that who I think it is?'

There's a long pause before he answers. 'Yes.'

No explanation offered. Just a confirmation.

'Do you want me to come over?' he asks.

'No.'

'Do you want to talk?'

'I'm going to bed.'

'Stephanie …'

'Fuck off, Mark.'

For the second time in as many minutes, I cut him off. Then I reach for the cooking brandy and wait for him to call again.

But he doesn't.

She woke at four, nauseous, dehydrated, a thumping headache. She took Nurofen, drank water and wondered whether to call him, before crawling back under the covers. She tried to convince herself that she would feel better in the daylight.

It was after eight the next time she woke. Her eyes were stinging and she still felt lousy. More water, a hot bath and coffee constituted the first step on the march of a thousand miles. Still he didn't call. She tried Queen's Gate Mews, before realizing that he'd already left for work. She rang his mobile. Not on. She began to dial the practice before changing her mind. She

342

couldn't face a chirpy conversation with one of the receptionists; they were always so nice to her.

She turned to work. The great saviour in times of personal crisis.

Asim Maliqi via Stern. She sought a meeting, got one, made her request, received a price, agreed to it and waited. When Stern got back to her, he was armed with a surprise.

Reports of Asim Maliqi's death have been greatly exaggerated.

Are you sure?

Are you doubting me, Petra? Anyone other than you and I'd be very offended.

I'm just surprised.

You won't be surprised, perhaps, to learn that there aren't very many Asim Maliqis working for Deutsche Bahn in Berlin. He's at work as we speak. Checking track. That is what he does, isn't it?

It is.

I imagine you'd like his address.

Alexander had always thought she was crazy to place so much trust in Stern. You've never even met him, he'd say. And he's never met me, she'd reply, and neither of us has ever let the other one down. All true, she imagined, but how could she be so sure?

It was possible she already knew Stern. Eric Roy, perhaps, in Groningen, or Bruno Kleist, in Vienna. Or even Marcel Claesen, God forbid. She wasn't sure she'd ever be able to contain her disappointment if Claesen turned out to be Stern. More than once it had occurred to her that Alexander might be Stern. The more he criticized her arrangement, the more perverse the possibility, so the more she was inclined to consider it. As a method of controlling her, what could be better? Relying on their mutual contempt to drive her towards Stern, where Alexander himself would be able to drip-feed her the information he wanted. Certainly, it was true that nothing Stern had provided for Stephanie had ever resulted in an action that was detrimental to Magenta House.

13

Karen was waiting for her at a table close to the bar. She was relaxed and tanned; the sun had bleached her blonde hair so that it was almost white.

Stephanie sat down opposite her. 'You look great.'

'That's ten days of pointless luxury in Thailand for you. You look like shit.'

'That's cooking brandy for you.'

They were in a pizzeria on Swallow Street, between Regent Street and Piccadilly. Stephanie had called her an hour earlier and suggested lunch. Karen had said she already had plans. And then said she'd change them.

'I spoke to Mark.'

'Did he tell you?'

Karen shook her head. 'He's far too discreet for that. I read between the lines.'

'I don't know what I've done.'

'Tell me.'

'Either I've made a complete idiot of myself, or I've caught him out.'

Karen raised an eyebrow. 'Another woman?'

'Alex.'

Stephanie told her about the message. And about his failure to explain it. Or even to call her.

'You know, Steph, I love both of you. But I really don't want to come between you. This is something you should sort out face to face. I will say this, though:

if Mark's been unfaithful to you, I'd be amazed. I know there's no such thing as the "faithful type" but, if there was, that's the type he'd be. I've known him long enough to know that.'

'How long have you known Alex?'

'Not as long as Mark. Or even you. Look, I like Alex a lot. But I also recognize that she does have a rather – how shall I put it? – *voracious* appetite when it comes to men. I know that's not what you want to hear, but I'm just being honest.'

'Thanks.'

'But it takes two to tango. No matter what you heard on the tape, you should remember that.'

'I will.'

The waiter arrived with their drinks, a large glass of white wine for Karen, a large Coke for Stephanie.

Karen looked at the glass. 'My word, you really are in bad shape, aren't you?'

'You have no idea.'

'I've only got one more thing to say on this. Mark once asked me if I thought you'd ever be unfaithful to him. All I could say, Steph, was that when you were together I saw that you loved him. When you're apart … well, I know you're not entirely forthcoming with him.'

'He told you that?'

She shook her head and smiled sadly. 'Same as before. I read between the lines. You're forgetting how long I've known him. The point is, if it's true, then I can only vouch for one part of you. And that's what I told him.'

Which was truer than she could possibly have realized.

Karen said, 'Talk to him, Steph. You two are made for each other. Don't screw it up through neglect.'

Maclise Road, four in the afternoon. Stephanie was in the kitchen, leaning against the sink, watching workmen drill a hole in the road for no good reason. Rosie was on the phone to her with more questions about Farhad Shatri.

'How's it going?' Stephanie asked.

'So far he's proving rather elusive.'

Stephanie wanted to tell her about Sevdie. Sevdie had been a member of the Shatri family. Even as his Achilles tendons were severed by a bolt-cutter, he hadn't whispered a word. That was the way they worked. She wanted to tell Rosie about the *besa*, the oath that Albanian recruits had given on joining the KLA. More than a mere promise of allegiance, it was a pledge of one's life. A total commitment. Contained within it was the understanding that if a recruit betrayed the cause his comrades had the right to kill him. She wanted to tell Rosie that the concept of the *besa* permeated many areas of Albanian life. But she mentioned none of these things to her.

'Good luck. I hope you find him soon.'

Rosie didn't answer immediately. When she did, there was caution in her tone. 'You don't think we will?'

There was a knock at the front door.

'I don't think you'll find it easy.'

'Is there something you want to tell me, Stephanie?'

'No.'

There was another knock. She finished the call and opened the door to Mark.

347

She said the first thing that came to mind. 'No phone calls?'

He said, 'I thought this would be better. After we'd had some time to cool down. Can I come in?'

She stood to one side, then followed him into the living room. He was wearing a suit, as he always did to work. Stephanie found that strange, but he'd told her that it projected professional competence.

'A light afternoon?'

'I had Linda reorganize my schedule.'

Stephanie perched on a sofa arm. 'So …'

'So.'

'Was I wrong? Is that what you've come to tell me?'

'Yes.'

'Go on, then.'

'I'm treating her.'

Stephanie snorted with contempt. 'The same way you first treated me?'

'As I recall, my treatment of you was first class. What followed was provoked by you.'

'And you put up such a fight, didn't you?'

Mark ignored the bait. 'Alex has a chronic spine problem due to whiplash injuries sustained in a car crash at the start of last year. After we met at the party she called the clinic and made an appointment. She came for an initial consultation last week, then for a session of treatment the day before yesterday …'

'A session?'

'Grow up, Stephanie.'

He didn't raise his voice. He didn't need to.

'She was booked in for an appointment at five this afternoon. Which I've now rescheduled for ten tomorrow morning so that I could come here to talk to you.'

348

'And the nervous giggles? The lovey-dovey voice?'

'I haven't erased the message. You're welcome to come and listen to it again. Perhaps a little factual analysis wouldn't go amiss.'

'I'm running on instinct, Mark.'

He raised an eyebrow. 'And your instinct about me leads you to this conclusion, does it?'

She felt a stab of panic. 'My instinct about *her* leads me ...'

'What about *me*?'

'I saw the way she was looking at you. And the way other women look at you. She didn't just want to have you. She wanted to devour you, Mark. And you told me that you hadn't noticed.'

'I hadn't.'

'Hadn't?'

He hesitated before confirming it. 'Hadn't.'

'But now?'

'Now ... well, you were right.'

'And?'

'And that's it.'

'What do you mean?'

'I mean, I'm not interested in her. Yes, you were right. She probably was flirting with me at the party. Alex *is* a flirt, I admit it.'

'But not when she's half-naked in your room at the practice?'

'Nothing happened.'

'I see. So when she's been with you and you've put your hands on her body – the way you first put them on me – she's made no move at all?'

'I'm telling you that there's nothing between us.'

'That's a pretty unfortunate choice of phrase. Let me

349

get this straight. On the two occasions you've seen her, she hasn't tried it on?'

'Yes.'

'Yes, I'm right? Or, yes, she has?'

'Yes, she has.'

Stephanie faltered. It wasn't the answer that tripped her up but the way in which he gave it. It couldn't have been more direct.

'And I told her that I wasn't interested.'

'And that was it? She was happy with that?'

'No.'

'*No?*'

'She's a flirt. She wanted something to happen. But it didn't.'

'I can't believe I'm hearing this.'

Mark spread his hands and said, 'I know what you're thinking. Why am I still agreeing to see her?'

'That's *one* of the things I'm thinking.'

'I can help her.'

'I'm tempted to say that she seems well capable of helping herself.'

'I'm serious, Stephanie. I've told her categorically that nothing is ever going to happen between us. She may not like that but she's accepted it. I told her that if she ever made another move I'd stop treating her. And she's accepted that too.'

'It didn't sound like it on the answer-machine.'

'She's a flirt. A player of games. It's in her nature. But she does know that nothing's going to happen. And that's all there is to it.'

All Stephanie's evangelical certainty was gone. Now there was only confusion. 'I don't know what to say.'

'Look, I've told you the way it is. Either you believe

350

me or you don't. That's something only you can decide. I've agreed to see Alex because I can help her. If you ask me not to see her I'll drop her from my list. But I won't be happy about it. She's in constant pain.'

'You're not the only chiropractor in London.'

'No. And if you ask me not to see her, no doubt she will go to one of them, now that she's starting to see what can be done for her. All I'm saying is this: since we know where we stand, I don't see there's any reason not to treat her. But it's up to you.'

Stephanie shook her head. 'Making me the villain of the piece.'

A comment that annoyed Mark more than any other. 'If you don't trust me, Stephanie, you should say so now, so that I don't waste any more time with you.'

'Hold on a minute ...'

'No! *You* hold on! I love you very much. But if there's no balance, there's no point. Trust doesn't insulate you from doubt. It's what gets you *through* the doubt.'

The glittering truth. And she'd managed to miss it.

She couldn't believe herself and, for once, couldn't blame Petra. Not this time. Fidelity, honesty, trust – who was she to cast doubt? He was right. Her genuine instinct had never suspected him of infidelity with Alex. But she hadn't paid attention to it. Instead, she'd done the cheap thing and had looked for a way to shift her own guilt. He'd never questioned her. He'd never attempted to possess her, or restrict her in any way. He'd let her be herself. The only thing he'd wanted – expected, perhaps – was a little reciprocity.

And this was how she'd handled it.

Having offered his defence, Mark was turning away

from her. He was heading for the front door. He was leaving her.

'Stay,' she said.

'You need some time to think, Stephanie.'

'No. Stay with me.'

'I'm serious ...'

'*Please*. Don't go.'

He stopped and turned round. 'Why?'

'Because you want to.'

'You know I want to. But we're beyond that. I need a better reason now.'

Panic was starting to choke her.

'Because it's eight minutes past six.'

At first he's not sure. It sounds like a cheap sentimental trick. Even to me. But it isn't. I know that if he walks out now, we might not be able to repair the damage. And I can't let that happen. Because I now know with absolute certainty that I don't want to lose him. In that sense we're strangers in the Dolomites again and I'm selecting a stranger to give me an intermission from my loneliness.

I kiss him so hard, our teeth clash. But it's symptomatic of what follows. We're making love but it's more visceral than anything I've ever experienced. At first we don't manage to shed all our clothes, or even move out of the dirty hall. Against the wall and on the floor, the hard surfaces suit us.

I remember Karen once saying to me that there had been times with Fergus, her baby, when she honestly thought she could eat him. 'He's so delicious, Stephanie. When I kiss his little toes I just want to bite them off.'

That's what happens to Mark. I'm on the floor, splayed. He looms over me and I reach up to kiss him, taking his lower lip between my teeth. I bite. Softly, at first. Then a little too

352

hard, drawing blood. He flinches but I don't let go. And he carries on regardless.

We do it in the kitchen, in the living room. Even in the bedroom. Our bodies are slippery with sweat. We reek. I can taste his blood on my tongue. Our mouths look as though we've got lipstick smeared all over them. When he comes, there are tears in my eyes.

Afterwards we lie on my mattress, cooling, drying. Apart from the cut, which is still running. I kiss it softly, as Mark rolls onto his back and pulls me on top of him.

'How did this happen?' he asks.

The truth is, I'm not sure. I feel the same way I did the first time we made love. Simultaneously exhausted and energized. Later we share a shower. There isn't much room. There isn't much hot water, either. We don't care. And we don't bother getting dressed, content to wrap a towel around ourselves.

We'd both like a drink but I advise Mark against the remains of the cooking brandy. I watch him drift through the flat as I prepare green tea. Although I'm in the kitchen I can see him in the living room. He flicks through a pile of papers on my desk: preparatory notes of mine, created by Frontier News. He examines a couple of battered cameras, a Nikon F-80 and a digital Nikon D-100. These are my props, not Petra's. He's been here so rarely, it's as though none of these things belong to me.

Later, while we're drinking tea, my Nokia rings. Mark is sitting cross-legged on the other end of the sofa. He hands me the phone. Without thinking, I answer it.

'Petra, it's me.'

I freeze. Mark notices and mouths a silent word at me. Okay? I recover some composure and nod furiously. But my heart is rocking in my chest. Fortunately, Savic is speaking German, a language Mark doesn't understand.

'Are you in London?'

'Yes. You?'

'Berlin, Tiergarten.'

Remember who you are.

I'm looking into Mark's eyes when I say, in German, 'I miss you when I'm not with you. I miss the things you do to me, the way you make me feel.'

In Berlin, Savic says, 'I feel the same way, Petra. I want you back here as soon as possible.'

In London, on the other end of this sofa, Mark appears to have understood that I've said something to him. *He puts down his cup of tea and moves towards me. Savic is still speaking. Still telling me how good I am, how great we're going to be together. Mark loosens my towel and lets it drop to one side. Silently, he kisses me on the mouth while Savic talks to me. Mark lets his mouth roam over my breasts, down my ribs, across my stomach. One part of me is on auto-pilot – mumbling something about Farhad Shatri and how I've got to go back to Berlin – the rest of me is in total submission. By the time Mark's mouth is between my legs, it's a miracle I can make any sense at all. When the call's over I let the phone drop to the floor, reach down, grab his hair and pull him against me as hard as I can, splitting his lip again.*

Later, he asks about the call. 'Berlin?'

I nod.

'When?'

'As soon as possible. Tomorrow.'

He smiles. 'Better make the most of tonight, then.'

Of all the ways he could have reacted …

I throw myself at him, wrap my arms around him and kiss him. 'I love you, Mark. I love you to death.'

'Sometimes that's definitely what it feels like.'

'I want to tell you everything.'

Spurting out of me before I have a chance to think about it,
that's a sentence that sobers up both of us.

'Now?'

'Why not?'

'Are you sure?'

'One hundred per cent. I should have told you at the start.
But I wasn't brave enough. So I had to make all those silly …
conditions.'

'You didn't know me then, Stephanie. You couldn't tell
me.'

True enough.

I say, 'You're a bit of a smart arse, aren't you?'

'I like to try.' We lie there for a while, his pulse coming
through my skin, merging with me. Eventually, he says, 'I've
got a better idea. Why don't you tell me when you get back?
Tonight, let's just keep going like this and see what happens.'

Landing at Tegel on a blustery afternoon, she took a
taxi directly to Asim Maliqi's address, a block of flats on
Allerstrasse in Neukölln, just beyond the eastern
perimeter of Tempelhof airport, close to the corner of
Schillerpromenade. Maliqi's building was proof that
the GDR hadn't monopolized grim housing: a functional concrete box, partitioned vertically and horizon-
tally to produce living units, not homes.

It was a cobbled street with a few trees and an abandoned set of roadworks. The trees were circled in dog-
shit. There was a cannibalized Passat outside the
entrance to 30/31. All that remained was a rusting
frame and the front passenger seat, which was badly
charred. Inside the building, the communal areas smelt
of institutional disinfectant and spicy cooking.

Maliqi's apartment was on the third floor, along a

dark corridor, walls painted mustard, six khaki doors along each side. Noise echoed off hard surfaces: a baby crying, a dog yapping, music – German rap, an Arabic love song – a couple arguing in a language she didn't understand. She used the Gustav Frunze lock-pick to let herself into Maliqi's apartment.

One bedroom, a bathroom and a living space, with a sink and cooker along one wall. There were clothes hanging from a cord strung between the curtain rail and a nail banged into a partition wall. Small puddles had formed on the linoleum floor. She touched a grey wool shirt; still damp. She peered into the bedroom, which was dark, a dust-sheet nailed to the window frame. The single bed occupied almost all the floor: a mattress with no sheet, a pillow with no cover, an old bedspread for a blanket.

Maliqi was neat. Then again, with so few possessions, it was easy to be neat. Apart from the clothes on the line, there was a small drawer for underwear and socks, one shirt on a hanger in a cupboard, a spare pair of trousers and no shoes. She checked the fridge: pitta bread, haloumi cheese, yoghurt, a few vegetables.

She waited in the bedroom. Maliqi returned just after six. When she heard the scrape of his key in the lock, she moved into the bathroom. The front door closed. She heard rubber soles squeaking on linoleum, keys placed on a table, a tap running, water filling a pan.

She emerged from the darkness. 'You're supposed to be dead.'

He dropped the pan, spun round, then reversed, clattering the edge of the sink, then scrambling away from her towards the window.

'What are you doing here?'

'The Hong Kong police found a body by the Aberdeen Upper Reservoir.'

'So?'

'I thought it was you.'

Maliqi's shock was dissipating swiftly. He frowned. 'Why?'

'From the description.'

'Because all Albanians look the same?'

'I'm glad you're alive, Asim. I really am.'

Anger stepped aside for regret. Stephanie let him take the time he needed. 'It was Hamdu.'

Now, it was Stephanie's turn to be on the back foot. It had never occurred to her that Maliqi wasn't acting alone. She couldn't imagine why she hadn't considered that possibility. There was no reason for it.

Hamdu. Maliqi's friend. A fellow survivor from the camp at Omarska. Hamdu, who'd worked at the Atlantic Hotel in Hamburg, and who'd seen through Paul Ullman from Bremen, recognizing him as Goran Simic, one of the Gemini fifty-four. A man Stephanie had first known as Aslan Shardov.

Maliqi gave her the details. After their encounter he'd tried to persuade Hamdu not to confront Savic. But he'd already talked Hamdu out of not killing Simic when they'd the chance in Hamburg, a decision both men had come to regret. Hamdu wasn't about to let that happen again.

'We should have taken your advice and come back here. We should have tried to leave the past behind.'

'Easier said than done.'

'Maybe. But you were right.'

'What happened?'

Maliqi scratched his jaw. 'We argued. Hamdu told me I was a coward. Then he left and I never saw him again.'

'You're not a coward, Asim. You're just not hot-headed. That isn't a crime.'

'I *feel* like a coward.'

'I understand that. But it's not true.'

She could see he wasn't convinced. He picked up the pan from the floor, took a rag from the cupboard beneath the sink and began to mop up the water. When he'd finished, he said, 'Why are you here?'

'When we were in Hong Kong you said you'd met Farhad Shatri. I need to find him.'

A request that provoked a wry smile. Maliqi made instant coffee for them, spooning powdered milk and sugar into both cups without asking her.

'I don't know him well enough to do that.'

'Do you know anybody who does?'

'Why do you need to find him?'

'I'd rather not tell you.'

'You break into my apartment, demand assistance and don't want to tell me why? You're not asking for much, are you?'

'It might be better for you if you don't know.'

'I survived Omarska. I think I can handle a little information.'

Stephanie had called Rosie earlier in the day and had enquired, as casually as she could, whether Magenta House were any closer to locating Farhad Shatri. Rosie had said they were making progress. Stephanie wasn't sure she believed her. Now she felt she had to assume it was true. Rosie had then asked her how she was intending to fill her days. Another question masquerading as a spur-of-the-moment thought. Stephanie had said she was considering a few days away. Somewhere nice and quiet. Somewhere well out of the way.

Maliqi was waiting.

Stephanie decided to gamble. 'I'm close to Savic.'

Maliqi's eyes widened with alarm. 'Why do you want Farhad Shatri?'

She told him. It took an hour. She left nothing out. She answered every question as honestly as she could. Petra and the unadulterated truth; she wasn't sure they'd ever been in such close proximity.

When it was over, Maliqi said, 'You're a risk-taker. Like Hamdu.'

'Not usually. But if I'm wrong about you I'll end up like Hamdu.'

'Very true. And you swear that Simic is on this list?'

'Yes.'

Maliqi considered this. 'When you said you were close to Savic, what did you mean?'

'Exactly what it sounds like.'

'How close?'

'Far too close.'

It hurt to admit, and Maliqi seemed to sense that.

'I'll see what I can do. But I can't promise you any-thing.'

They met in the bar of the Four Seasons hotel on Charlottenstrasse at nine. After the monstrous marble of the lobby, the bar was an oasis of taste and quiet; muted light, wooden panelled walls, leather armchairs. Savic was with two men who didn't belong there. They melted as soon as Stephanie arrived. Fellow Serbs, she guessed; they *were* wearing leather coats, after all. Savic slid off his stool and pulled her into a full-blooded kiss. The bartender blushed. Stephanie would have been embarrassed too, if she'd felt anything at all.

Savic said, 'I have something for you.'

He reached into his coat pocket. *Whatever it is, it's going to be the best thing you've ever received.* It was a box wrapped in black paper secured by gold ribbon. It felt heavy. Inside, there was a gold cross fashioned from miniature ingots, the vertical as long as her little finger and just as dense. On the reverse, a date. Hong Kong, the first time they had sex. She thought of the watch Mark had given her – forever eight minutes past six – and the comparison made her feel sick. Grossly ostentatious, it was precisely the sort of thing Savic would have liked.

From somewhere, she found a smile of beatific pleasure, before pulling him into a kiss as intense as the one before. Just to make sure. Then Savic took it from the box, as Stephanie held up her hair, allowing him to encircle her throat with it, fixing the clasp over the nape of her neck.

'It looks beautiful on you.'

It felt like a hangman's noose.

Later there was dinner at the Paris Bar on Kantstrasse, the stuffy staff fawning over Savic as unpleasantly as they ignored other diners.

When Savic asked about her search for Shatri, she said, 'Don't worry, darling. I'll find him.'

'How far have you got?'

She reached across the table and put her hand on his. 'Trust me. I'll deliver. I always do.'

Back in the apartment, he asked her to strip for him. 'Leave the gold cross on. Take off everything else.'

They were in the living room. The lights were off. Stephanie was silhouetted against the street-light coming through the French windows. She did what he wanted, following every murmured instruction until he could no longer help himself. Then he fucked her on the floor. Just like Mark had twenty-four hours earlier. Just as hard, just as long. But completely different. There was only one thing the two had in common: they both reduced her to tears.

She slept deeply, drifting towards the waking shore slowly, where she reached out, hoping to touch Mark. Then she remembered where she was. In Berlin, in bed with Savic. Except he wasn't there. Her eyes still closed, she ran her hand across the bed to check. She was alone. Or maybe not. She smelt coffee close by.

Her senses began to sharpen. There was no one in the bed but there was someone in the room. She couldn't see who it was but she felt a presence. Slowly she looked around. Beyond the foot of the bed there was a chair by the wall. A woman was sitting in it. On the table to her right, a mug, steam rising from it. On her lap, a SIG Sauer P226, Petra Reuter's gun of choice.

Dragica Maric.

Or Sabine Freisinger. Or even Natalya Markova. Tall, slender, angular, Stephanie had forgotten quite how beautiful she was. Runway calibre, at least. Not that Maric could have cared less. She wore a thick black jersey, jeans and a pair of walking boots. Her raven hair was chopped short and crudely parted on the left. On her right wrist she wore a chunky sports watch. As ever, she made androgyny look stunning.

She smiled at Stephanie. 'I never expected to find you in my bed, Petra. Although I have to confess, I've occasionally thought about it.'

Maric was looking at Stephanie in exactly the same way that Stephanie was looking at her. With cautious wonder. There was a difference, though. Stephanie was naked. She'd kicked off the duvet in the night. At least, she supposed that was the explanation. In any case, only her calves and feet were beneath it. She pulled the duvet up, so that all but her arms and shoulders were covered.

'Where's Milan?'

'Out.'

'What are you doing here?'

'I think that's a question I should be asking you. You're in my bed. In my apartment.' Her good humour vanished. She picked up the gun. 'That's a tasteful bit of bullion you're wearing. I'll bet it's got a date on the back.'

Stephanie said nothing.

'Say what you like about Milan, at least he's consistent. I gave mine to a tramp in Mexico City.'

'Why are you here?'

'To see for myself.'

'See what?'

'You. And him. Together.'

'Why?'

'You're smart. You tell me.'

'You're not sure.'

'I'm sure about him.' She took a sip from her mug. 'I believe *he's* in love. It's easy to tell with a man like

362

Milan. His tone changes. He can't help it. As for his critical faculties ... well, they've completely disintegrated.'

'What are you talking about?'

'Getting you to find Farhad Shatri.'

'You don't think I can?'

'I have no idea. The point is, Milan's not that bright. But it would still be better if he did his thinking with his brain, not his dick.'

'You don't trust me?'

She waved the gun at her. 'I haven't decided yet. That's why you're still alive.'

Her bed. Her apartment. Her *decision*.

Savic answered to Dragica Maric. Stephanie had never considered that. There had been no evidence to suggest it. Since his teenage years Savic had been a leader. It had been *his* street-gang in Belgrade. Inter Milan had been *his* paramilitary unit. Gemini had been *his* idea. Where and when had Dragica Maric entered his life?

'Does Milan make you happy?'

An echo of another question Maric had once asked. *Do you love him?* Another time, another gun, another city: New York. Another man: Komarov.

'Yes.'

Maric just looked at her, the stare rendering words redundant.

'You don't believe that either?' Stephanie asked.

The tone of the reply couldn't have been more scathing. 'Sure. Why not? Once you had a man like Kostya, now you have a man like Milan. Why wouldn't you be happy?'

'He's different, that's all.'

Maric laughed loudly. 'Different? He certainly is! Having had both of them, I can confirm that.' Stephanie flinched. Maric had been looking for it and it spurred her on. 'Milan is exactly what you'd expect. Basic and unimaginative. An agricultural thruster. Not like Kostya. He's a little rough round the edges too, but he has a certain … *something*, don't you think?'

Stephanie wanted to accuse her of lying. She didn't think being naked had ever felt so uncomfortable. It was as though the duvet didn't exist.

Maric sighed wistfully. 'Maybe it's all those tattoos. How much is Milan paying you for Shatri?'

'Nothing.'

As soon as she said it she knew it was a mistake.

'Nothing? You're doing it for *him*?'

Stephanie stayed silent.

Maric's eyes narrowed. 'Well, well. He must be a lot better than he used to be. Perhaps I should try him again. Either that, or your standards have dropped, Petra. Maybe any passing prick is enough for you these days.'

Stephanie could see that Maric didn't believe that either. 'Why don't you tell me what you're thinking?'

'I think you're fucking him because you need to.'

'Really?'

Maric nodded. 'Which is the worst option of all from my point of view. But that's the kind of person you are. I wonder if you'd have sex with me, if you felt you needed to. My feeling is, you would. My feeling is, you'd do anything.'

'You're talking about yourself, Dragica.'

'No, Petra. I'm talking about *us*.'

* * *

She's pointing the SIG Sauer P226 at me. Her choice of gun isn't a coincidence. She knows it's what Petra uses. If she has to kill me, it's the perfect weapon. But she doesn't want to. She likes me.

'Can you find Shatri?'

'I think so.'

'What's in it for you?'

I take a long time to answer. 'That's my business.'

'Not when I'm pointing this at you.'

'Yes. Even then.'

I know she won't pull the trigger. She couldn't in New York and she had more reason then than she has now.

'I need to be sure about you, Petra.'

'Is that why you came here from Moscow?'

She nods.

'You don't have to worry,' I tell her.

'How can I be sure of that? How can you *be sure of that?'*

I look into her eyes. 'Trust me, Dragica. Our worlds won't collide. Savic has something I want. When I get it, I'll be gone.'

'What is it?'

'Like I said before, that's my business.'

'Not good enough.'

'It will be when I deliver Farhad Shatri and the list.'

'Go on.'

'There's no need. We've reached the end. If you shoot me you won't get Shatri or the list. You're the one with the gun. You choose.'

Slowly she eases the safety back on. Then she takes another sip from her mug and suggests I get dressed. My clothes are scattered throughout the apartment. I slip out from beneath the duvet and get up. The floor is cold. Maric goes into the bathroom and returns with a dressing-gown, which she throws to me.

It's hers. I pull it on.

Half an hour later we're in the Atlantic, a café on Bergmanstrasse. I'm taking my first sip of black coffee. I ask her what she's told Milan.

'That we had business in the past and there were things we needed to sort out if you were going to be involved.'

'And he went for that?'

'Of course.'

Dragica's too clever to cause trouble without a reason. She opens a pack of Marlboro Lights. 'Did you know that Milan and Arkan were friends?'

A hand-grenade casually lobbed into the conversation.

'He's mentioned that he knew him. I didn't know they were friends.'

'More than just friends, Petra. Comrades. Kindred spirits.' She lights her cigarette. 'I wonder how Milan would react if he discovered that you killed him.'

We're both in the lobby of the Hotel Inter-Continental in Belgrade on 15 January 2000. Arkan is walking towards me, Ceca close by, his so-called protection everywhere and nowhere. The lobby is crowded. Somewhere, among the throng, Dragica is watching. I don't know that, though; I only discovered that later, in New York. Arkan sees me. Just for a second, our eyes connect. And he knows.

I've never forgotten it. Fear fuelled by premonition.

Dragica blows smoke in my face. 'Milan asked me once if I saw the gunman.'

'What did you say?'

'I said I had. He asked me what he looked like. Typical ... to assume that it had to be a man. You know how I described you?'

'How?'

'Short and fat with a beard.'

Despite myself, I laugh. And everything changes. Dragica laughs too and a barrier breaks. A waitress saunters over to the table. I order another cup of black coffee and a croissant. Dragica dithers, then chooses hot chocolate. I can't picture her dithering. Then again, in my world, reputation and reality rarely match. John Peltor – once a US Marine, now an assassin – makes marmalade in his spare time.

The table we're sitting at is made of wood. Square in shape, there is a pane of glass set into it. Beneath that are hundreds of roasted coffee beans, tightly packed. I'm reminded of the one million tiny figures beneath the glass floor at Gilbert Lai's house at Deep Water Bay. I wonder if Dragica has been here too. Does she know Lai? Or is she one of the European contacts – the best imaginable, he'd said – that Savic provides for him? There are a couple of men on a table on the other side of the café. They've been watching us since we came in.

'What do you reckon they make of us?' I ask.

Dragica tilts her head one way, then the other. 'I think … you'd be a magazine editor and I'd be … an architect. We're in the right part of town for it. We look okay. What do you make of them?'

Both skinny, one with a trimmed goatee beard, the other with a thick polo-neck, a shaved scalp and natty little glasses with a dark blue frame. 'The same.'

She laughs again. 'You're right! We should leave.'

And so it goes on. Dragica Maric and Petra Reuter together over breakfast. It is, possibly, the most surreal experience of my professional life. Despite every decent instinct within me, I have a good time. She's bright and funny. We talk about work and we talk about other things. Countries we like, cities we hate, fashion, music, politics, mutual acquaintances. We don't talk about men.

I avoid Gemini but ask her about the Balkans, and she's candid. The most surprising thing she tells me is that she felt catastrophe was inevitable the moment Milosevic became president. 'Arkan, Mladic, Karadzic – they all believed in the bullshit. At least, at first. And, in Mladic's case, right to the end. But there were many who knew it was going to be a disaster before it had even begun. We were fighting fires before the arsonist had struck a match.'

'How come?'

'Because we didn't have a cause. And we didn't have a leader. We had a bureaucrat; Milosevic was a gifted organizer. He was good at reacting to events but he could never shape them. He had no vision. No long-term plan. Kosovo was a matter of political expediency. He picked it up and ran with it for short-term gain. Sure, it was a problem. The Serbs in Kosovo were being brutalized by the Albanian majority. It needed fixing, certainly. But there was never any doubt over Kosovo's place at the heart of Serbia. Now, however, the concept of independence for Kosovo is closer to being a reality than it was before. That is Milosevic's legacy. We are worse off, in every possible way. Do you know what it's like to be a Serb today?'

'What?'

'It's like being a German in 1945. You're guilty by association.'

'Dragica, you're guilty by deed.'

She smiles. 'I know. And I accept that. But I'm talking about ordinary Serbs. Milosevic and his cronies sold them out. Look at the Zemun gang in Belgrade today. Still ruining the lives of regular people. Is it a surprise they killed Zoran Djindjic? No. The only surprise is that they didn't manage it earlier.'

'They came close.'

'Amateurs. Neanderthals.' She can't mask her contempt. 'Compared to you or I, Petra, who are these people? Nothing. Not even the shit on our shoes.'

She tells me she heard about Waxman and Cheung while she was in Los Angeles. Finally, we come to New York. The only moment in my life when I knew I was going to die. When I'd got beyond thinking I might. The only moment when I was ever resigned to it.

'Can we leave it in the past?' Dragica asks.

'It is in the past.'

'Can we keep it there?'

'There's no reason not to.'

She nods slowly. 'And is there any reason not to talk about the future?'

'What future?'

'Any future. Our future.'

'You and I?'

'Why not?'

'Milan's already tried to tempt me.'

This surprises her. 'With what?'

'A long list of Albanians.'

She giggles like a teenager. 'Some men ... I don't know. It seems cruel to say it. Or even to think it.'

I am thinking it. We're in tune.

She says, 'I had in mind something a little more imaginative.'

'Like what?'

'I don't know. I just think we'd be good together.'

What was it that Claesen had said in Marrakech? That Dragica and I were a reflection of one another? Superficially, perhaps. And sitting here, having a good time with her, I might even believe it. But I have to remind myself of the critical difference between us. Dragica is real. I'm not.

'It's a neat idea. But I think I'll pass.'

She smiles. 'Another time, maybe.'

'Maybe.'

'You don't mean that.'

'No,' I admit. *'I don't.'*

'You're wrong, you know.'

'Not to mean it?'

'Not to believe it.'

'To believe what?'

'That we'll work together. That we'll be together. We will. *One day …'*

At six she met Asim Maliqi at Gorlitzer U-Bahn. They headed up Oranienstrasse.

'I can't get you close to Farhad Shatri. It's impossible.'

'I thought it might be. But I had to ask. Thank you for trying.'

He shrugged off her gratitude. 'If you were to obtain this list, what would happen to Savic?'

'That would depend on what I did with it. At the very least he'd be arrested and prosecuted. More likely someone would have him killed.'

'What about you? Would you do it?'

'Again, that would depend.'

'But you wouldn't exclude the possibility?'

'What are you driving at, Asim?'

'I can't deliver Shatri but I have something else. Maybe it's useful. Maybe not. If I give it to you I want something in return.'

'What?'

'If this information helps lead you to the list, I want you to promise me that you'll kill him. For Hamdu.'

They walked in silence for a while, until they reached Oranienplatz. Then Stephanie said, 'If your information helps, Milan Savic is a dead man. You have my word on it.'

Maliqi nodded. 'There was an intermediary between Shatri and the vendor of the list.'

'Who?'

'I don't have her name. But she knows Savic well. And she flew from Hong Kong to London to meet Shatri.'

'*She?*'

Maliqi nodded. 'The intermediary was a woman.'

'What else?'

'She might be a journalist. That's all.'

'How do you know this?'

'Please don't ask. As it is, I'm betraying a family confidence.'

Which was as much evidence as she needed. He shook her hand formally, then walked away in the direction of Moritzplatz.

She spent the night with Savic, fuelling the same fantasy as the night before, distracting him from the subject of Dragica Maric. She found it less easy to distract herself from the same subject. It was harder to play the slut after Maric because Savic was diminished. Yet he was the one who needed the list. Maric didn't. And that was why he remained vital to Stephanie because she needed it too. In that, at least, they were united.

It was almost three in the morning when he hauled himself off her back, leaving sweat along her spine. He rolled onto one side, panting heavily, scratching his hairy belly.

'I love you, Petra.'

Sore and sweaty, she said she loved him too, and wondered if he'd ever said it to anyone else. Or was it only to her, his very own Ceca?

'What are you thinking?' he asked.

I'm wondering about all the different ways in which I could turn Asim Maliqi's wish into a gruesome reality.

She was smiling. 'Nothing.'

In the morning she caught a Lufthansa flight to Heathrow, then called Mark at work. He was busy so she left a message on his mobile.

'Darling, I'm back. It's time to tell you everything. I'll see you tonight. I'll bring something special to drink. Call me when you get a chance.'

Dragica Maric was back in Moscow. And back in perspective, too. Calculating and ruthless, she was the *de luxe* version of Petra. Stephanie remembered that now, having somehow overlooked it when they were together. Then again, that was one of Maric's weapons; in her presence, people were rendered defenceless.

At Maclise Road there was a message on the answer-machine. 'Hi, Steph. It's Rosie. I just want to have a word. Call me when you get a moment.'

Stephanie ignored it and erased it.

In Kensington Gardens autumn was in full cry, a strong wind ripping gold and ruby leaves from the trees. Between the showers there was sharp sunlight, peeping through racing cloud. Autumn had always been Stephanie's favourite season.

It was raining again by the time she reached Poplar Place, off Bayswater Road. She pressed the buzzer and a woman answered.

'DHL. I have a delivery for you. From Mr J. Barrie in New York. I need your signature.'

'Come up. Top floor.'

It was dark inside, the communal parts old but well cared for: a plain navy carpet, striped wallpaper – two shades of very dark red-framed watercolours on each landing, flowers in vases.

The front door was ajar. She entered, closing it behind her. Carleen Attwater stepped out of the kitchen, both hands in oven gloves.

'Could you hold on a minute. I just have to … we've met, haven't we?'

'I didn't think you'd agree to see me again.'

Attwater noticed there was no sign of a DHL package. 'Stern. He gave you my name …'

'Is something burning?'

She followed Attwater into the kitchen. The American took a dish from the oven, the pastry on the top slightly burnt. She placed it on a mat, then shed the gloves.

'I'm sorry. I don't remember you.'

'Stephanie.'

She tried to imagine Attwater as she would have been then. A little lighter, perhaps – war zones tended to assist weight loss – with more of a tan and a few less lines. In all, not much different. She was still a good-looking woman. Earthy, sexy, *vital*.

'That was a neat trick, using my ex-husband's name like that.'

'Neat but cheap.'

'Coffee?'

'Thank you.'

'Is instant okay?'

'Fine. Black, no sugar.'

She watched Attwater busy herself with the kettle and mugs. On a blustery weekday morning in west London, in her well-appointed kitchen, in her comfortable flat, it was hard to picture her drenched in mud and blood. Absorbing the dead, living the nightmare.

'I wonder why you'd think I wouldn't want to see you. Are you still looking for Milan Savic?'

Stephanie felt the chill wind of Petra blowing through her. 'No. I've found Savic. I'm here for you.'

Attwater froze. She turned round slowly, perhaps expecting Stephanie to be armed. She offered the coffee mug. Stephanie was careful, knowing exactly what Petra would do in Attwater's situation.

'What do you want?'

'When was the last time you went to Hong Kong?'

Instantly Stephanie saw she was going to lie.

'I've never been to Hong Kong.'

'Not even when your husband was the *Time* correspondent there?'

'Well … obviously then, but …'

'You said never.'

'What I meant was …'

'Never, as in recently?'

She gathered herself for a counter-offensive. 'What are you doing here?'

'Tell me about the last trip you took.'

'I asked you a question …'

'Where you went, who you saw, what you brought back.'

Nothing. That was the word that formed in her mouth.

'Please leave.'

'Tell me what you gave Farhad Shatri.'

Her eyes were letting her down.

'You've got a lot of nerve coming here like this.'

'Is that right?'

'You're so wide of the mark, it's unreal. I don't know what you *think* you know but ...'

'Savic wasn't a professional assignment, was he? You were in love with him.'

She took the blow like a seasoned professional; rolled with it, then struck back. 'Just wait a god-damned minute!'

'And you thought he loved you.'

The first one had winded her. The second one injured her.

'You don't know what you're talking about!'

'I do now.'

Attwater was trembling. She just stared at Stephanie, stranded somewhere between rage and heartbreak. While Stephanie herself felt only pity. In Berlin she'd goaded Savic, suggesting he was the type of man to go for a certain type of woman – big-breasted blondes with as little intellect as possible – and he'd denied it. *I don't have a type. I even dated a journalist once.*

'In the end it wasn't too much CNN or too much alcohol that did it for you, was it? Despite everything, it was love. Not a great catch, for sure, but in war, standards differ. He was a one-man cyclone and you got sucked in. It's not hard to imagine. You, an older woman, high on danger, high on accelerated living. High on the testosterone-fuelled attention coming from this younger man, who seemed to be at the centre of everything. What was the phrase you came up with? Heroin for the soul?'

'You *bitch*.'

'Heroin for the soul. That's what Savic was, wasn't he? Destructive and addictive in equal measure.'

'Please – just leave.'

A request, not a demand. The venom gone, weariness in its place.

'As for Milan … well, he'd had sex with every surgically enhanced bimbo in Belgrade by then. You were something different. An American, for a start, and intelligent too. Always a challenge for a man like Milan. And even if you were quite a bit older than him – so what? You're not without physical appeal. And in war you take your pleasures wherever you can find them. Right?'

Her eyes were glassy, the surrendered truth welling up inside her. 'Right.'

They settled in the sitting room. It was cool and dark, the heavy plum curtains half drawn. Attwater sat on one end of a sofa with a bold floral print. Stephanie was in a high-backed chair by the fireplace. On the table to her right there were photographs of Attwater with her ex-husband. Younger, happier, both in love with adventure as much as each other, the backgrounds featured as prominently as they did: Beirut, Hong Kong, Baghdad, Beijing.

'Straight after our divorce I headed for the Balkans. Turns out, there couldn't have been a worse place in the world for me at that time. We were both so confident we could make it work, but we were too career-minded. That's why we never had kids. Too selfish to compromise, I guess. We really loved each other. But just not as much as our work. Too many assignments, too much travel, too much time apart. We thought we could handle it. But being apart is never a good thing if you've got a good thing going. That's the truth.'

The divorce was amicable, their relationship improving almost instantly, and ever since. But Carleen Attwater's sense of loss and guilt ran deeper than she realized. Crippled by both, she headed for Belgrade just as the trouble began.

'I couldn't have cared less what happened to me. Being in the Balkans made it worse. There was no trip too hazardous, no drink too many, no fling too seedy. Depending on your point of view, it was either perfect or catastrophic. For a decade I was on the verge – of euphoria, of suicide, of both at once.'

Savic was coming into context. Intelligent and feisty, her recklessness masquerading as courage, it wasn't so hard to understand what he'd seen in Attwater. But it was doomed to fail. As Kosovo crashed, Savic needed to vanish. There was no prospect of Attwater going with him. She'd understood that from the start. By the time it became a reality, however, she couldn't accept it. She was addicted to the nomadic brutality of the life they'd led.

The parting was pitiful. 'I was on my knees, begging him, all dignity gone.'

The worse it got, the more revolted Savic was. Eventually there was a fight. It started with a slap, which he returned with a punch. But that wasn't enough for him. Once he'd started he couldn't stop himself. He beat her the same way he'd beaten so many other women: with pleasure, and to a pulp. He left her battered and bleeding in the corner of a squalid motel room in northern Bosnia.

'The last thing he did was empty his gun. Except for one bullet, which he left in. Then he tossed it onto the bed. His final words to me were: "You disgust me, you old whore. Do yourself a favour. Use the bullet." And you know what? I almost did. I took the gun, I put it in my mouth and ... I just couldn't. I don't know why. But it was the turning point.'

It's a turning point for me, too. It makes perfect sense. She's a woman scorned, which is why I tell her the real reason for my visit. And which is why she then opens up to me. The tears dry, the quiver fades from her voice.

'I met Farhad Shatri in a house in north London. Wood Green.'

'*How was that arranged?*'

'I made contact with him and ...'

'*Wait. You did?*'

'That's right.'

'*I didn't think anyone knew how to find him.*'

She looks a little cross. 'I'm not anyone.' The way she says it begins to reveal another dimension to her. 'Why do you think I was approached?'

Of course. Because she knew both men. That was what made her ideal. 'Did you give him the list?'

'There was no list. At least I certainly didn't see one.'

'*But he was selected to put it up for sale.*'

'Naturally. He has all the reasons in the world to see harm come to Milan.'

'*And you were happy enough to assist ...*'

She smiles bitterly. 'It was the least I could do.'

'*Who's the vendor?*'

'I don't know.'

'*So how did Shatri know the offer was legitimate?*'

'A code I used.'

'What was it?'

She writes it down for me. 0006302/QRT/Vlore/77.

'What does it mean?'

She shrugs. 'Vlore is a port on the Albanian coast, favoured by people smugglers. The rest of it, I don't know. But I memorized it anyway. Just in case.'

'And it satisfied Shatri?'

'Seemed to.'

'Who gave you the message?'

'A contact in Hong Kong.'

'How did that come about?'

'A phone call from someone I used to know.'

'Who?'

'This Belgian guy …'

'Not Marcel Claesen?'

She looks startled. 'You know him?'

I can't believe it. Claesen. Again. Like McDonald's and dog-shit, he gets everywhere. 'Sort of. Go on.'

'He asked if I'd be interested in a courier job. Hong Kong to London, first class both ways, a room at The Peninsula and fifty grand in cash. Four days from start to finish. I asked what I would be carrying. When he said information, I said okay. In Hong Kong the contact showed me that it was a document but didn't let me read it. He placed it in an envelope and secured it with a wax seal. It was only when Farhad opened it that I discovered what the document referred to.'

'Gemini.'

'Yes. Farhad was very excited. And I'm ashamed to admit, I was too.'

'Whoever selected you must have known that you'd be able to contact Shatri.'

'Yes.'

'So someone who knows him too, perhaps.'

'Perhaps.'

'Then what?'

'Then nothing. Farhad paid me the cash ...'

'He *paid* you?'

'That was the way it was supposed to be. If it wasn't his money, I guess someone reimbursed him. Frankly, I didn't care that much.'

'Why would you?'

'Exactly.'

'And you don't believe your contact in Hong Kong was the vendor?'

She laughs. 'Lord, no! He was some local guy. Definitely an intermediary. And not a very classy one, either.'

'A Chinese Claesen?'

'Now you mention it ...'

She gives me the location for her rendezvous but can't provide a name. When I have everything I need, I get up to leave.

'I'm sorry I was so hurtful.'

'Forget it. I've been trying to.'

As we walk towards the door she puts her hand on my arm. 'What are you hoping to do, Stephanie? Can I ask you that?'

'I need the list.'

'I was talking about Milan.'

'Put it this way: if I get the list, Milan's in trouble.'

'What kind?'

'The terminal kind.'

'Then there's something else you need to know. You don't have much time.'

'Why not?'

'Farhad has offers. At least two, possibly three. All of them have met the asking price. The only reason he's waiting is to find out who will go highest.'

'How long have I got?'

'I don't know.'

'Can you make an educated guess?'

'A few days, maybe. Less than a week, for sure.'

'How do you know this?'

At first she says nothing, inviting me to figure it out. But I can't.

'Let's just say that since I made contact with Farhad he's made contact with me.'

It still takes me a while to get it. When I do, I can't help myself. 'You're joking.'

My astonishment makes her giggle. 'Is it really that hard to believe?'

On Bayswater Road she switched on her Nokia and decided to walk back through the park to Queen's Gate Mews. She was by the pond when the phone rang: Rosie Chaudhuri.

'Where are you?'

'Kensington Gardens.'

'We need to talk.'

'Can it wait?'

'What were you doing in Berlin, Stephanie?'

They met at a large pub on Victoria Street that was busy at lunch and immediately after work. In the late afternoon there were only a handful of customers: a few bar-flies wreathed in cigarette smoke, two of them hunched over the *Racing Post*, and four stragglers from lunch, ties loose, sleeves rolled up, cheap jackets draped over their chairs. Rosie picked a table close to the fruit machines, their incessant and irritating squawking good for swallowing conversation.

'How did you find out?'

'I called Mark. Don't worry. I said I was an assistant at Frontier News. He said you were in Berlin and that you'd be back in a day or two.'

Stephanie peered into her vodka and tonic. 'Why are you checking up on me?'

Rosie tried to shrug it off. 'Alexander thinks you've become ... erratic.'

'He's a fine one to talk.'

'What were you doing there, Steph?'

'My job.'

'You were told to take some time off.'

'I wonder why.'

'I've just told you why. You've become unreliable. *Unstable.*'

Stephanie turned over the idea in her head. 'Alexander thinks he's close to the list, doesn't he? That's why he's asked you to keep an eye on me. To make sure I don't screw things up.'

'You're way off the mark.'

'I wonder if he knows that Farhad Shatri doesn't actually have the list.'

Rosie couldn't smother her surprise but resisted the obvious question. 'You can't get involved.'

'I'm already involved. And you can't stop me. I can walk out of here and disappear. You know that.'

'There's always Mark.'

'I don't think so. If Alexander thinks I'm unstable at the moment, he'd be in for a shock if anything happened to Mark. Or Komarov, for that matter.'

Rosie drank some wine. Stephanie saw she was struggling with herself.

'Does he know that I've been to Berlin?'

She shook her head.

'You decided not to tell him?'

No response.

'But he can't actually do anything until he has the list, can he? Just in case …'

Again, no verbal response. Instead, Stephanie took her cue from Rosie's eyes.

'Supposing I get the list first?'

'Please, Steph. You can't expect me to do this.'

'Would he honour our original deal?'

'Stephanie …'

'*Would he?*'

Rosie took a long, deep breath. 'That would depend.'

'On what?'

'On whether it was the *only* list.'

In other words, only if he had to. He was looking for a way not to. Stephanie knew what that meant: he wasn't going to renege on their deal. He was going to redefine it so that she broke it by default.

'How long have I got, Rosie?'

She couldn't look Stephanie in the eye. 'If only we'd had this conversation a week ago.'

This morning, Berlin. Now, London. Tomorrow, Hong Kong. I ring British Airways. They have two flights this evening. There's space on the second of them, BA027, leaving at ten to ten. That leaves me just enough time to see Mark, to explain my predicament, to beg his forgiveness – and possibly lay down a physical down-payment on that, if I'm lucky – before heading for Heathrow.

At Queen's Gate Mews I find Mark in the kitchen. He looks exhausted, as though he hasn't slept for days. When we kiss, he's a cold fish.

'Are you okay?'

'I'm not feeling a hundred per cent.'

'You're not looking it, either.'

There's no pleasure in his smile. 'Well, there you are …'

'Look, I know what I said earlier in my message so I'm not quite sure how to put this but I'm going to have to blow you out tonight.'

'Oh?'

'It's important.'

'Back to Berlin?'

'Hong Kong.'

Clearly surprised, he raises an eyebrow, then folds his arms and leans back against the sink. 'Hong Kong? I hope you're collecting air miles.'

'I know. I've been up and down like a yo-yo.'

'And who is it in Hong Kong?'

'Sorry?'

'Who are you seeing in Hong Kong?'

'Nobody.'

'Nobody?'

'Well, obviously somebody. What I mean is …'

'You know Rob Morgan, don't you?'

Justine's husband.

'Of course.'

'Do you know what he does?'

He's told me so many times and it's never stuck. 'Something in banking, I think.'

'He's an investment banker.'

'I remember now. Why?'

'When his clients come to London he has to entertain them. You know the sort of thing. A few drinks at a chic bar, dinner at a posh restaurant, maybe a nightcap somewhere else.'

There's a really unpleasant sensation forming in my

stomach. 'Mark, what are you getting at?'

'What I'm saying is this: that's how Rob treats his clients when they come to London because that's how he gets treated by them when he's abroad. As you know, he travels a lot. Last week it was Paris and Amsterdam.'

My heart is slowing to a halt.

'This week it was Berlin.'

14

Stephanie couldn't move, could barely breathe. All she could do was look at him, six foot four, dark hair all over the place, irregular features that were as familiar to her fingertips as they were to the eyes.

'The bar at the Four Seasons,' he said.

Pleading the Fifth. Wasn't that what it was when you stayed silent so that you didn't incriminate yourself? She couldn't imagine a silence more damning than hers.

'That's where Rob's clients took him. For a couple of drinks before dinner. You know … happy hour.'

Stephanie felt utterly numb.

'You were with some low-rent gorilla in a leather coat. You kissed him. Then he gave you a gift. *A piece of tasteless gold crap that you'd generally expect to find on some retarded rapper.* Rob's description, not mine.'

She wanted to say something. *Anything*.

'The two of you were all over each other. Poor Rob. He couldn't believe what he was seeing. Or how he was going to tell me. You know how concerned he always is about other people. Initially he tried to play it down, make it sound less tacky than it was, but in the end I got the director's cut.'

Mark wasn't fooling her. He hadn't raised his voice but she could hear the pain. The colour had drained from his face as comprehensively as the life from his eyes.

'Is it true?'

She couldn't bring herself to admit it directly. 'Why would Rob make up something like that?'

'I've been trying to think of a reason. Because I can't believe it. I thought I understood you, Stephanie.'

'You do.'

'Evidently not.'

But he was wrong. He *did* understand her. Completely. The problem, as ever, was Petra, and there was no adequate way to explain her to Mark.

'I thought we'd be together, Stephanie. That first morning, when I woke up beside you, I really believed you'd be the one.'

I am the one. And so are you.

'Who is he?'

She shook her head.

'Are you in love with him?'

She couldn't prevent a desperate cough of laughter. '*God*, no!'

Mark frowned. 'Is that supposed to make me feel better? That you're *not* in love with him, so it's not so bad somehow?'

'You don't understand.'

'Do I need to?'

'Don't you want to?'

He bought himself time by taking a bottle of Macon Villages from the fridge. He offered her a glass. She would have been happier if he'd hit her with the bottle, but she nodded anyway. He poured for both of them.

'In all the time we've been together I've accepted the empty spaces. I didn't need an explanation then. Why would I need one now?'

'So that you could know.'

'Know what? That when you were away you were sleeping with other men? What possible explanation could you give me that would make that all right?'

'None,' she conceded.

He turned away from her and headed for the living room, a glass in one hand, the bottle in the other.

'You've made an idiot of me. I gave you the benefit of the doubt. Of *every* doubt. Because I trusted you. And you took advantage of that.'

'Please let me try to explain, Mark. You owe me that much, at least.'

'I owe you *nothing*. The excuses, the secrecy, the evasion – I put up with all of it because it was better than being lied to. I always said that. That was the one thing I wasn't prepared to accept, Stephanie. The *one* thing. Why? Because I loved you.'

'I love you.'

'Do you love them as well?'

'There is no *them*.'

'One, a dozen, a hundred – what difference does it make?'

'I couldn't tell you the truth!'

'I didn't ask you to.'

He was right. That was *the* point. He knew when not to ask a question. More times than she cared to remember, he'd curtailed any natural sense of curiosity to save her from that predicament.

Stephanie wanted to kiss him. Wanted him to hold her. To say that he could forgive her. To allow her to promise that it would never happen again. To let her show him how completely she loved him.

She held open her hands. 'So ... what now?'

'Don't you have a plane to catch?'

'I'm serious.'

'So am I.'

'Mark … whatever you're thinking … don't. There must be something I can do. Or say. *Please* …'

'It's too late.'

'*Anything* …'

He drained his glass, then refilled it. 'Anything?'

'Anything.'

'You'd give up … whatever it is?'

'In a heartbeat.'

'Then stay.'

'I will.'

'Now.'

But she couldn't. There was a single thought pulling her through the maelstrom: without the list, she was lost. The list was her only bargaining chip. Without it, there was no future. Not for her, not for Komarov. As for Mark, who could say?

'I can't.'

'I don't think I've ever asked you for anything, but I'm asking you now. Stay.'

'Mark, you have to believe me. If I could, I would.'

He shook his head. 'I don't have to believe you. Not any more.'

At the door she handed him his keys. That was when reality began to cut through the fog of shock. It was the finality of it that was so crushing. When Mark told her to take care, she began to cry. And despised herself for it. He looked as damaged as she was. She saw no hatred, just disappointment. Somehow that was worse.

At Maclise Road she tried to summon Petra but she

wasn't available, so she had to pull herself together alone. Assuming her flight landed on time, and assuming she got what she wanted from the address Carleen Attwater had given her, she felt it should be possible to go straight back to the airport and catch one of the late flights to London. With as little as six hours on the ground, she could be back at Heathrow in under thirty hours.

That was the plan. She shuffled round the flat on auto-pilot, throwing a few bits and pieces into a small carry-on bag, to make it look as though she intended to stay at least a short while. She chose the Claire Davies passport she'd used for her last trip to Hong Kong. Then she'd been a tourist. What would she be now? Still a tourist. Who, if anyone bothered to ask, had received tragic news on her arrival and was consequently taking the first available flight home. She collected the Siemens and Nokia phones, a couple of Claire Davies credit cards, two thousand US dollars in cash and the Sony Vaio laptop.

The bed was exactly as she and Mark had left it, after the night they'd spent in it before her trip to Berlin. One part of her wanted to crawl into it, to wrap what remained of him around her aching body. The other part wrenched everything off the mattress, rolled it into a ball and hurled it into the corner.

She caught a black taxi outside Olympia. The driver was the perky type. He caught her eye in the rear-view mirror and resorted to cliché.

'Cheer up, love. Might never happen.'

She shot him her most withering look. 'It already has.'

*   *   *

During the night she saw a thunderstorm thousands of feet beneath her, circular ripples of brilliant white light spreading out from a central flashpoint in the clouds. Her favourite photograph of Mark was taken during a climb of the Eiger, the summer before they met. In it, he was perched on a ledge in such a way that it made him look as though he was floating. Above, it was a beautiful, clear day, the sky dark blue with altitude. Below, there were clusters of pristine white cloud, the spaces between them clear enough to reveal the land beneath.

Now, with her face pressed to the window, watching the light-show, she tried to convince herself that it made no difference. That if she *had* missed the flight Mark would still have told her to go.

She wanted to tell him everything. Now that the worst had happened, she wanted to plead her case, if only to prevent his memory of her from being incomplete. She accepted she was guilty but there were mitigating circumstances.

She didn't sleep at all. By the time her aircraft began its descent into Hong Kong she was dehydrated and exhausted. Under the harsh light in the tiny aircraft toilet she looked at her reflection in the mirror. It wasn't good; her skin so pale it was almost blue, set against the whites of her eyes, which were as red as the rims surrounding them. Standing in line at Immigration she felt dizzy and tried to remember when she'd last eaten anything. In Berlin, probably. Dinner with Savic. She couldn't quite work out how many days ago that had been. Two or three? It seemed like weeks.

She took the Airport Express to Kowloon. Once the train was out in the open she turned on her Nokia and called Mark. She'd thought about it on the flight. She knew she should wait. In another eighteen hours she would be back in London. But she didn't care about doing the right thing. She had to say *something* to him.

She got his answer-phone. The first message was an incoherent ramble: a string of apologies linked by pauses and repetition. Ten minutes later, having composed herself, she left a second message.

'Sorry, it's me again. About the other message – if I were you I'd disregard it. I just wanted to say this. You asked if there was any explanation that would make what I've done all right. The answer is no. But there *is* an explanation for why I did it. And I'd like you to hear it when I get back. I can't really think of a good reason why you should. If you decide not to, I won't think anything less of you. And if you do decide to listen, and it makes no difference at all, I'll understand. Because what I have to tell you is something I would never tolerate from anyone. Probably not even you. Mercifully, though, you're not like me. Anyway, it's up to you. I still love you. Whatever happens, you can't change that. Take care.'

The call made, it was time to cast Stephanie aside and to be Petra. Despite the way she felt, she needed clarity. Just for a few hours. On the flight back she'd let pills and alcohol do their worst.

At Jordan station in Kowloon, it was just a few minutes walk through the neon forest to Woosung Street. The Nikita Studio was on the second floor, above a Nepalese restaurant. The entrance was sandwiched between the restaurant and Sum Fai Photo Services. Large illuminated billboards protruded over the street, advertising Fuji, Pentax and Minolta. Stephanie entered a hall barely shoulder-wide, rose to a half-

392

landing, where there were battered metal mail-boxes nailed to the wall, before taking the stairs to the second floor. The first floor seemed deserted.

The door to Nikita Studio was locked. There was no light seeping from beneath it. She pressed the buzzer, then knocked several times, but got no response. Nikita Studio was painted in gold on the door above the name of the photographer – Anthony Yu – and the studio number. She dialled it and got a recorded message. The place was shut for three days.

Three days. Stephanie couldn't afford days. She was measuring her future in hours.

To the left of the door was an empty display case. There had been sample photographs in it once; dark rectangles on red felt marking out their positions against the rest of the faded material. In the bottom right hand corner were two business cards. Or, rather, two sides of the same card; one in Cantonese, the other in English. Yu's mobile number was included. Stephanie rang it.

'Is that Mr Yu?'

'Who's this?'

'A friend of mine gave me your number.'

'Who?'

'You took some photographs of her. They were *really* good. I need some the same.'

'You call me tomorrow.'

'That's the thing. I need them now.'

'Tomorrow. Not now. Not possible.'

'It's urgent. I'd be happy to pay extra.'

'Where are you?'

'I'm at your studio in Woosung Street. But it's shut.'

'I'm not there.'

No shit, Sherlock. 'Where are you?'

'Macao.'

Stephanie swore silently, then said, 'This is an emergency. If I came over to Macao tonight would you ...'

'Not possible. Call me in the morning.'

'But the message on your answer-machine says ...'

'Back in the morning. Eleven.'

He ended the call. She tried his number again but he'd switched off his phone.

She stood there, in the rank gloom of the second-floor landing, and whispered curses that echoed around her. Then she took a deep breath and reached for perspective. She wouldn't be flying home tonight. A setback, but hopefully not a catastrophe. In any case, there was no point in worrying about it. Yu could be anywhere in Macao.

There was nothing to do until morning. Which meant she needed somewhere to stay. Her first instinct was to choose somewhere cheap and close by. But she ignored that and opted for her second instinct, taking a room at the Ritz-Carlton on the other side of Victoria Harbour. If they were surprised by her dishevelled appearance, Claire Davies's platinum American Express card reassured them.

Alone in her room, she flopped onto the bed. She felt disgusting; she was still wearing the clothes she'd been in the last time she'd kissed Savic. He was still on her skin. But she was too tired to bother with a shower. Instead she stripped, raided the mini-bar for alcohol, took two tablets of Melatonin, then crawled beneath the sheets.

* * *

She woke at half past six and spent forty-five minutes stretching, easing the stiffness away, welcoming the warmth that liquefied her muscles. By the time she'd finished she was perspiring, sweating the last of Savic out of her body.

She ran a hand over the firm ripples of her stomach and promised herself that once she was free of Magenta House she would let herself soften. She'd lived in the south of France for a while, leading the kind of idyllic existence she yearned for now, and had enjoyed a fuller figure then: a little extra on her hips, heavier breasts, the slight suggestion of a belly – it had felt so right, so *her*. All that remained of that version of Stephanie was the length of hair. For most of her life as Petra she'd worn it short. Lately she'd made a conscious effort to grow it. Something different, something to make her feel less like Petra.

She rang room service, ordered breakfast, then had a long, warm shower, soaping herself thoroughly, washing her hair twice. She was in a white towelling dressing-gown when her food was delivered. After she'd eaten she poured herself more coffee, hooked up the Vaio to her phone and checked Petra's Hotmail accounts. There was a message from Stern. Half an hour later they were together.

I've been looking for you everywhere. Where have you been, Petra?

After all these years, Oscar, and you try a cheap shot like that?

One day I'll get lucky.

Not with me. What's on your mind?

You're in demand.

Without wishing to appear immodest, I usually am.

Not like this.

What are you talking about?

Waxman and Cheung. What a spectacular. Your profile has never been higher. I have three firm offers and five maturing enquiries, two of them from governments.

Will I make the cover of Vogue?

I'm serious. You can confine the days of the six-figure contract to history.

I'll bear it in mind.

You're not interested?

Not at the moment. I'm working on something else.

Please tell me it'll be as good as Waxman and Cheung.

Oscar, what are you going to do when I retire?

Wear black for a year. I hope that was a rhetorical question.

Stephanie poured the remains of the coffee into her cup. Stern lasted almost two minutes.

Please tell me you're not retiring, Petra.

She switched off the Vaio without replying.

Woosung Street, ten to midday. The Nepalese restaurant was closed. Stephanie saw someone sweeping the floor towards the rear. She entered the narrow hall and took the stairs to the second floor. The front door to Nikita Studio was still locked but she saw muted light coming from beneath it. She heard faint sounds – a male voice over bad pop music – and pressed the buzzer.

Nothing.

She tried again, keeping the button depressed until she heard footsteps and curses coming her way. One chain, a second chain, then a bolt, and finally a key, before the door swung open.

Carleen Attwater had been right. Anthony Yu was a Chinese version of Marcel Claesen. Shorter, but no less emaciated, his skin as waxy, his cheeks as hollow, his hair as greasy, though Yu's was pulled into a pony-tail. He wore an effeminate gold charm bracelet around his right wrist. His crimson silk shirt was undone to the stomach, revealing two gold chains and a corrugated rib-cage.

'Anthony Yu?'

'What?' he snapped, his teeth clenched, keeping a cigarette in place.

'We spoke last night.'

'Busy. Call tomorrow.'

He started to close the door but Stephanie moved forward, barging past him into a cramped reception area, a desk occupying a third of the available space, no one behind it. Half the ceiling panels were hanging down; she could see pipes and wiring above. Yu told her to leave. She ignored him and opened the door to her right, revealing a dim storage area and a foul-smelling toilet beyond.

'Get out!'

There was only one other door and it led towards the music. Yu slammed the front door shut, then scampered after her. At the end of the stunted corridor she flung open the door. The studio windows overlooking Woosung Street had been blacked out, three of them with blinds, two of them permanently, plywood panels nailed to the frames. There were two cameras mounted on tripods – a Fujifilm FinePix and a Minolta – two light boxes and a selection of reflector panels. At the centre of the floor a gaudy purple satin sheet had been laid over a mattress. A young Chinese girl was lying naked on top. As soon as Stephanie entered the room she sat up and wrapped the satin sheet around her body.

'What you want?' Yu shouted.

Submitting to Petra completely, Stephanie spun round, took a step towards Yu and elbowed him in the face, extinguishing the cigarette on his lips. He dropped to the floor with a surprisingly meaty thump. The girl squealed.

Stephanie pointed at her and said, 'Stay there. Don't move.'

Then she grabbed Yu by the collar and hauled him to his feet. He was cupping his mouth, groaning into a bony hand. Stephanie marched him towards a chair and pushed him into it.

When he finally looked up her eyes were waiting for him. 'Questions.'

He shook his head. 'I don't know.'

'I haven't asked yet. But you *do* know. And you *will* tell.'

The room was hot and stuffy. It smelt of baby oil and stale cigarette smoke. Something sickening by Celine Dion was coming from a portable radio-cassette player on the floor in the far corner.

'A few weeks ago an American woman came here. Early fifties, blonde hair, good-looking.'

He was already shaking his head.

'You remember her. She's not the type you normally see here. She came to collect something. You had to show her it was a document before putting it in an envelope and sealing it in front of her.'

Yu took his hand away from his mouth. The burn on his upper lip looked like a monstrous cold sore.

There was a measure of rage in his eyes but there was a far greater measure of cowardice.

'Who brought you the document?'

'I can't tell you.'

The backhand swipe was so fast, he never saw it coming. It split his lip and was all Stephanie needed. Yu took pictures of naked girls. He wasn't made for physical resilience. Between theatrical sighs he told her everything.

Every month he paid protection to a 49. About a week before Attwater appeared his 49 phoned him and told him he would receive a call from a man he'd never met. It didn't matter who he was. Yu was to follow his instructions to the last detail. In return, this man was going to pay a month's premium. It never occurred to Yu to argue with the 49. Stephanie understood that.

The man called. He was sending round a document in an unsealed envelope. Yu was not to read the contents. He was to wait for a foreign woman to call, who would then come and collect it. He would show her that it was a piece of paper, then he would close it in her presence and use the wax seal that the man would provide.

'That was it?'

'Yes.'

'And everything happened the way it was supposed to?'

'Yes.'

'Who was the man?'

'He didn't deliver the envelope himself. He used someone else.'

'Why did he pick you?'

Yu shrugged. 'I don't know.'

Stephanie could tell he was lying. 'I'm going to break your nose if you try that again. The man on the phone and you – what's the connection?'

Yu's shoulders slumped. 'The girl who brought the document.'

'She knew him?'

He nodded.

'How did you know her?'

'I photographed her.'

'Do you have a print?'

'Please ...'

Stephanie was already helping him out of the chair. 'Show me.'

He sorted through half a dozen large portfolio cases, selected one and laid it on a work-bench. He unzipped the case and began to flick through one laminated page after another. When he found the girl, there were two things about her that surprised Stephanie. Firstly, she wasn't Chinese. Secondly, she recognized her.

Stephanie parted the bead curtain and stepped inside. There were only three tables in front of the counter. There was a green light overhead between two rotor-blade fans that were spinning as fast as possible. They did nothing to disperse the poaching heat but were effective at recycling the fragrant air: curry, Turkish tobacco, body odour. Only one of the three tables was occupied. The small Indian in the avocado suit saw her first, peering over the shoulder of the much larger man opposite him, who then turned round.

'This time, Viktor, you *do* need to be worried. This time you *are* the business.'

Viktor Sabin blanched. 'What are you doing here?'

'Can't you guess?'

'With you it's impossible to tell.'

Sweat was pouring off him. His pale blue polo shirt was saturated, the dark hairs on his arms slick to the skin. Stephanie glanced at the table: two glasses of beer, a selection of plastic plates, mostly picked clean, and a small square of paper. At the centre of it, three stones.

'Rubies, Viktor?'

'For a friend.'

'What a coincidence.'

She moved round, pulled a metal chair across from another table and sat down between Sabin and the Indian.

'Aren't you going to introduce me?'

'Javinder, Petra. Petra, Javinder. How did you know I was going to be here?'

'I went to your office. Your secretary was very helpful.'

'Did you leave her in one piece?'

'Viktor, I'm offended.'

He waved a fat hand at her. 'She's not the brightest star in the night sky but she has other qualities.'

'So I saw. Are these for her?'

'No, no, no. These are real.'

'Very classy, Viktor.'

Sabin apologized to Javinder, who was politeness itself – *if there's a sale, I'm happy to wait* – and then asked Stephanie if she wanted something to eat. 'Don't be put off by the apparent lack of hygiene. The food is very good here.'

'I'm not hungry but if they can run to a cup of coffee …'

'Good idea. The best coffee in Hong Kong.'

Six floors up in Chungking Mansions? Stephanie doubted that. The café was a less appetizing prospect than any of those she'd seen in the arcade during her previous visit. On that occasion she'd confronted Savic for the first time. She wondered whether there was a connection, or whether it was coincidence. And when she considered that, she tried to imagine what the oversight might be.

'The stones aren't for Irina, are they?'

Sabin stayed mute.

'The last time I saw you, Viktor, you were entertaining Irina and Katya. You remember, don't you?'

Amazingly, his face began to turn redder than it already was. But then the recollection appeared to mellow into fond remembrance. 'How could I forget? Although I have to admit that I had forgotten that you interrupted us.'

'I wish I had too.'

'Don't be cruel. Why are you here?'

'The list, Viktor. The one Anthony Yu passed to Carleen Attwater.'

'Ah.'

'Anthony Yu didn't know who you were. All that linked you was your choice of courier. You could have hired anyone. You could have picked a neutral. Then I wouldn't be here and you wouldn't be in trouble. Why Irina?'

He peeled the wrapper off a pack of Viceroy. 'Laziness, I guess.'

'Come on.'

'I mean it. And if that disappoints you, I'm sorry.'

He lit the cigarette. Stephanie's coffee arrived. In the

kitchen there was an argument, raised voices just audible over the grind of a pointless extractor fan.

'Who is it, Viktor?'

He looked her straight in the eye. 'Mostovoi.'

'That doesn't make sense.'

'Don't ask me to explain it to you. I don't know the details. Just the name.'

Stephanie cast her mind back to Marrakech. Mostovoi in the Mellah but, before that, Savic masquerading as Lars Andersen at the villa in Palmeraie. They were close. Or supposed to be.

'What's Mostovoi doing, Viktor?'

He shrugged. 'Making a move.'

'Farhad Shatri and Carleen Attwater make sense. They have a vested interest in seeing harm come to Savic.'

'True.'

'What about you?'

Sabin looked offended. 'Absolutely not.'

'So why did he pick you?'

'We know each other. I seem to remember telling you that before.'

'So you're doing it for friendship, then?'

'Of course not. I'm doing it for the same reason I do everything. I'm doing it for money.'

There was a swish as the bead curtain parted again. A small man entered the café, wearing a grey short-sleeved shirt, filthy trainers and nylon black slacks. In his right hand there was a Beretta. He was followed by a second man, carrying a Czech Skorpion. There were nine of them. They fanned out because they had to; there wasn't enough space for them to congregate on the customers' side of the counter. Seven of them were

Chinese. Stephanie noticed that two of them had thick chopping scars on their forearms.

The Indians who ran the café stuck their hands in the air and said nothing. The Indian in the avocado suit attempted to scrape the rubies off the table until one of the gunmen stuck the tip of a LA France M16K submachine gun behind his ear. Then he raised his hands.

The tenth man to enter looked like a clean-cut teenager: small, round glasses, the latest Nike running shoes, Calvin Klein jeans, a white Lacoste tennis shirt. There was a nylon duffel bag over his right shoulder. The last man was Vojislav Brankovic.

In the sickly green light of the café his skin looked paler than ever. His blond hair was in need of a brush and he was sweating as furiously as Sabin. Stephanie could see how much he hated it. It was hard to imagine anywhere on earth more distant from rural Bosnia than Chungking Mansions.

It was Stephanie who wanted to do something but it was Petra who knew that six of the nine guns were pointing at her. It was Petra who kept still.

Brankovic walked up to her and said, 'Milan sends his love.'

The first blow knocked her out of her seat, catching her on the right cheek and eye-socket. In two strides Brankovic was at her side, his boot thumping into her stomach, punching the breath from her lungs. She curled into a ball but Brankovic was too experienced for that. He grabbed her by the hair, hauled her up and drove his knee at her, aiming for the face, catching the collarbone instead.

She did her best to protect herself and nothing to provoke him, knowing that was the best she could do. For a while he devoted himself to her. Between strikes, Stephanie wondered if he'd ever devoted himself quite so fully to any woman. When he'd had enough, one man was assigned to the bead curtain. The two cooks, the server and the Indian in the avocado suit were corralled into the next-door unit, which was vacant. Two men watched over them.

Brankovic left the rubies on the table. 'Troy, open the bag.'

Troy, the clean-cut teenager, opened the duffel bag, took out her Sony Vaio, then emptied the rest of the contents onto one of the other tables: cash, a few toiletries, her passport, the Siemens phone.

Stephanie and Sabin were dragged through the kitchen. It was an inferno. The two gas-rings were no longer on but since there was almost no ventilation – the air-extractor being almost cosmetic – the temperature was excruciating. The rings were fed by a rubber pipe that disappeared through a ragged hole in the wall. Opposite the cooker and microwave was a sink that hadn't been cleaned in ages and a humming fridge. The space between was so narrow, one person could barely pass by another. Especially if they were the size of Viktor Sabin. There was an ultraviolet fly lamp in one corner. The collecting tray was full.

They ended up in the store-room at the back. Brankovic switched on the light. One of the men brought a chair from one of the tables at the front. Stephanie looked along the shelves: cans of vegetable oil, small sacks of rice and flour, spices, dried vegetables, pastes.

There were two men behind her, both armed. There

was blood in her mouth and seeping from her nose. Her stomach and ribs ached, her legs trembled. Brankovic pressed Sabin into the chair so that he was facing Stephanie, the Bosnian Serb's mighty hands weighing heavily on his shoulders. Not for the first time, Stephanie thought Sabin might be about to have a heart attack.

Brankovic said, 'Who is selling Gemini?'

He was looking at Stephanie but it was Sabin who answered. 'Mostovoi.'

Brankovic continued to look at her. 'Maxim Mostovoi?'

'Yes,' gasped Sabin.

'Is it true?' he asked Stephanie.

She shrugged. 'Sure.'

Just casual enough to cast doubt. Brankovic was good with pain but not with questions. He glared at her, the menace flaring in his eyes, just as it had with Sevdie in the apartment on Hobrechtstrasse.

'Is it Mostovoi?'

'That's what I said, wasn't it?'

Savic's driver, Figueiredo, the Macanese, pulled a knife from the waistband of his trousers. The handle was swathed in a leather strap, the blade a tapering crescent.

The remains of Sabin's fragile nerve failed. 'It's Mostovoi. I swear it! *It's Mostovoi!*'

Figueiredo grabbed a handful of Sabin's polo shirt, then cut it, vertically, shredding it. In effect, skinning him as he watched, the blade never quite touching him. Sabin looked as though he was about to vomit. Stephanie was sure his heart wouldn't resist for much longer.

Figueiredo took three strips of the material and used them to secure Sabin's wrists behind the back of the chair. Brankovic then moved behind Sabin.

He said to her, 'Right from the start I knew you were trouble. I could smell it on you. Milan, though, he smelt something else. Something that went right to his head. The bitch on heat driving him crazy. But he's back to normal now, thinking straight.'

Brankovic reached inside his shirt, pulled out the spoon on the chain and lifted it clear of his head. He smiled at her – the first time she'd seen him do that – and then cast Sabin in a ferocious head-lock, the biceps swelling horribly, the sinews rippling along his forearm. Sabin gasped, his eyes bobbing with fear, completely restricted by the grip. The sweat was rolling off Sabin's chin onto Brankovic's arm.

'Like tendon cutting, this is a Balkan speciality.'

Very slowly, he dug the spoon into the edge of Sabin's right eye. Sabin screamed, then froze, not daring to move, the impulse to protect the eye greater than the pain. Or the fear. Stephanie felt sick.

The Spoon revealed. He wasn't a novice, she could see that; he was itching to go deeper, to plunge the spoon into the socket, to gouge the eye out.

'Okay. It's not Mostovoi.'

Through clenched teeth he muttered, 'I don't want to know who it *isn't*. Tell me who it is.'

'Simic.'

No matter how discordant, the name struck a chord. 'Goran?'

Stephanie nodded. 'Or Aslan Shardov.'

'His Gemini name.'

'That's the name Farhad Shatri knows him by.'

407

Brankovic's grip of Savic remained unyielding. 'I don't believe you.'

'You don't have to. I have evidence.'

'Where?'

'On my computer.'

Brankovic stared at her, not blinking. 'Explosive evidence, I expect.'

Petra matched his look. 'Shatri's made a down-payment to Simic. I've got bank records, transaction details. I've got two phone transcripts. I've got ...'

'Why would you have such things?'

She looked away, prompting him to repeat the question more forcefully.

'Because I have a buyer.'

It took Brankovic time to work it out. 'That's what this is about? Money?'

'Don't be naïve. It's *always* about money.'

'Not with us.'

'Not true. Milan opened up Gemini to those who could pay.'

'He opened it up to those who could help.'

'Who could help his interests. That still translates into money. It's the same with Simic. He's processing Afghan opium in Kazakhstan and running it down to the Caspian. Shatri has connections there. They're making money. You should see the palace Simic is building for himself in Almaty. You should see his girlfriend. It's all perfect. Except for his past. Except for Milan. Except for Gemini.'

'You're lying,' he growled, giving Sabin's eyeball a sharp prod.

The Russian yelped.

Stephanie focused on Brankovic's eyes. 'Why don't

you get your geek to have a look?'

'And blow us all to pieces?'

'I'll deactivate the tamper.'

'Stay there. Tell him how to do it.'

'He can't.' She held up her right hand. 'It's palm recognition.'

'Bullshit.'

'Fine. Give it a go.'

Brankovic hesitated, then released Sabin's head and said to her, 'If you screw this up I'll take out your eyes and make you eat them. Then I'll kill you.'

As the two Chinese walked her through to the front of the café, she could almost feel the invisible thread that ran from the tips of their guns to the centre of her spine. Troy was sitting at the table, in front of the laptop.

Pressing the power button, she said, 'Just as well you're not the curious type.'

He looked at her blankly. Brankovic was behind the counter, watching. Stephanie nudged Troy out of his seat and waited for the screen to materialize. Then she pressed a dozen keys, including three simultaneous depressions of two keys, one of which deactivated the tamper. Afterwards she pressed her palm to the screen, an entirely cosmetic touch for Brankovic.

On the screen a password box formed, the cursor winking. She punched three random letters, then 20, then another three random letters and hit 'enter'.

'It's all yours.'

'Move away,' Brankovic ordered her, before she could delete anything.

She got up and stepped aside.

'Come back here.'

She moved behind the counter.

'Where's the evidence?'

'Hidden in the system files. The file name has a two-letter designation. KP. For Kosovo Polje.'

Brankovic wasn't amused. He turned his back on her. Which was when she dropped to the floor and pulled herself into a ball. In Berlin she'd told Savic about the tamper device to help win his trust.

She'd never mentioned the timer.

For a split second it occurs to me that I've miscalculated. Or that the device is faulty.

Then it goes off.

I've seen how little explosive goes beneath the keyboard. But the force of it is stunning. A moment later a second explosion rips through the café: the gas cylinder serving the rings in the kitchen. The solid air punches into me, driven by a pulse of scorching heat. It feels as though it's coming from below, the shockwave bursting through the floor.

For several seconds I'm too dazed to do anything. There's blood everywhere. It could be mine. It could be someone else's. I'm caked in dirt. All I can see is debris, dust and smoke, punctuated by tongues of fire. The ringing in my ears is painfully loud. When I breathe, I cough.

Petra rises to the surface and takes charge of me.

Viktor Sabin is lying motionless on his front. Beside him there's a hole in the floor. It's dark, almost every light blown. I can just make out Brankovic's feet, the soles of his boots twitching. Two partition walls have completely vanished. Part of the ceiling has come down. An overhead light has fused, sparks dripping off the connection, black smoke swirling around the plastic box. The counter that stood between me and the computer has disintegrated. I can just see one of Troy's feet protruding from a mound of rubble, smoke curling off it.

My right hand is a bloody mess, a grid of cuts across the palm. Much of the skin over the back has been scraped away. I get to my feet. There's a sharp pain in my left hip and I have no left shoe. My head feels like it's stuffed with cotton wool. I wish my nose was. Blood is dribbling over my mouth and down my shirt. I lurch towards a source of dim light.

Got to get out. Got to lie low. Got to recuperate and reorganize.

In the corridor people are scurrying in both directions, some running for their lives, some carrying what they can: a half-made suit, a cash-box, a glow-in-the-dark Madonna and Child, a widescreen TV.

Figueiredo is on his hands and knees, spluttering. I grab the Russian PSM from his side. Behind me Brankovic shouts, the sound peculiarly distorted to me. I look over my shoulder at the empty space where his twitching boots once were.

The stairs are to my right but there are two armed Chinese blocking my path. They haven't seen me yet. I go left. It's even darker down here. Behind me shouts cut through the ringing. Then gunfire, some of it tearing away a loose panel. A stray bullet pierces a water-pipe, water gushing down one wall. Thick black smoke snakes along the corridor, hugging the ceiling.

A single shot whistles over my right shoulder, past my right ear, and smacks into a door. I spin round, drop to a crouch and fire back. Three bullets. At least one of them connects; I feel the thump and hear the gasp.

I try the nearest door: an empty waiting area. Through the next door, into an acupuncturist's treatment room, the bench vacant, the needles laid out on trays. Through another door, into another passage. I can't stop. I don't have a clue where I'm going. It's like a dream, where you run as hard as you can but you barely move. No matter what you do you can't escape. Left and right, in and out of darkness, my body screaming, my senses scattered.

Breathless, I lurch through an open door into a small workshop. The owner, an elderly Chinese man, is filling a leather holdall with ivory carvings. On the work-bench, there are magnification glasses, small chisels, a screwdriver, a saw, an array of fine brushes, six pieces of ivory.

I kick the door shut. He yells at me to get out. I point the PSM at him and put a finger to my lips. The ringing is subsiding a little and I'm just able to hear my pursuers charge past the door. We wait in silence. I try to catch my breath, then kick off my right shoe; one is worse than none.

I look around. There's another door on the opposite side of the workshop. But before I can try it, the men are back. They're not running. They're creeping, trying to be quiet. I turn to the man and motion him to the floor with my hand. He sinks to his knees and crawls under the work-bench, mouthing silent curses at me.

The door gets kicked in. Three men charge into the room. The lack of space works to my advantage. I shoot the first one before he can fire. The other two run into him, the second one discharging his gun accidentally into the man I've already shot. I fire once more before the PSM is knocked out of my hand by the second man, who lunges at me. I flatten myself against the wall, taking him with a blow to the throat. Choking, he falls on top of the first. The third skips over both of them, as I retreat. He unleashes a series of blows which I parry with battered arms. The second one is rising. I duck and swivel, lash out with my injured left foot, driving the heel into the third's mouth. He spirals backwards. I'm exposed long enough to allow the second to land a massive blow to my bruised ribs. As I crumple, he throws a kick. I do just enough to avoid the full force. Stumbling, I scoop a chisel off the work-bench. He doesn't see it and throws himself at me. Coming in from the side, I drive the chisel between his ribs to the depth of the handle.

He hisses through his teeth as though he is, quite literally, deflating. I grab his Steyr TMP instead of my Russian PSM — it has an eight-round magazine and I've already fired five — then plunge through the far door into a lightless passage. There's another door at the end. I can't see a handle but I find a lock and shoot it, then kick the door with my right foot. It flies open at the second attempt.

Another cramped workshop, this one illuminated by dim ultraviolet. The owner has fled. And it's a great shame he didn't take his stock with him.

I'm surrounded by snakes and spiders. In cases of glass, of many sizes, stacked from floor to ceiling, on free-standing aluminium shelves. It's intensely hot and humid, the air rich with eucalyptus.

Some of the snakes are solitary, others are two or three to a case. The spiders are social, small or large, patterned or plain, or just hairy, there are dozens per case. The shock of my entry has excited them. In the eerie purple half-light, entire cases of glass are alive, flickering legs and trembling bodies. The room is quivering around me. Even though my ears are still ringing I can hear the collective rustle, and it's the most sinister sound I've ever heard. I look straight ahead, walk to the workshop's front door and open it.

I can't believe it.

Brankovic.

What's he doing here? Then again, where is here? Perhaps I'm back where I started.

His nose is badly broken, his face burnt. I can smell the singeing; his eyebrows are completely gone, along with much

413

of the hair from the front half of his head. In the ultraviolet his skin glistens, the eyelids grossly swollen. His blood looks as black as tar.

Before I can shoot him he lunges at me with Figueiredo's knife. I recoil. The tip misses my wrist, clattering the gun, knocking it from my hand. For a large man he's incredibly nimble. I've come to think of him as a lumbering brute, but put a weapon in his hand – a bolt-cutter, a spoon, a blade – and he mutates into a dancer. The tapering crescent leaves incandescent arcs of light in the ultraviolet.

He surges forward again, feints a swipe, then tries a jab. I throw myself to the right but the blade rips through my shirt and skin, just below the ribs. I crash into display cases, my face momentarily pressed to the glass, several dozen agitated legs stuck to the other side. He thrusts again, misses, hits the corner of a case, cracking it; a spider's web for the spiders inside. A shudder reverberates through all the shelves. An upward drive misses my nose by millimetres and allows me an open shot with my right foot. It catches him between the legs.

Behind me there are shouts, voices echoing in the passage. The sound of reinforcements. The sound of time running out

Brankovic rides the pain and attacks. I throw myself back against the same cases as before. The cracked glass buckles. For a second he's off balance and I kick him with as much force as I can muster. He falls and crashes against the wall of glass on the other side. Several display cases shatter on impact. He falls to the floor, the knife spilling from his fingers. Serpents, spiders and glass cascade onto him. Destabilized, the aluminium support structure wobbles, then topples, all the cases sliding off all the shelves, burying him.

Barefoot, I scramble for the door, collecting the Steyr TMP from the floor. I feel something biting into my feet. Not just once, either.

No time to check. In the corridor I turn round. Brankovic
has managed to get to his knees, rising out of the glassy
rubble, clutching his dagger defiantly. In the ultraviolet he
looks as though he's wearing a crawling cloak. The spiders
shimmer on his skin.

I shoot him, then empty the magazine into other display
cases. I drop the gun and confront the passage. It's deserted,
nobody around to indicate which way I should go. I'm com-
pletely disorientated. Left or right?

Left. There's an open door at the end: an abandoned recep-
tion area, a small sign on the desk. It's a guest house. I smell
burning as I go from room to room. All empty. The one at the
end of the corridor has a window. When I look out of it I can
see another building just yards away. I can also see that it's
not part of Chungking Mansions. Which means I made the
wrong choice.

This is a dead end.

Outside, it was pouring with rain, torrents sluicing
from ledges. She wanted to lie down. Just for a minute.
Just for a second. Her hands stung, her side stung, her
feet stung. She saw blood trailing through the doorway, potentially a trail for her pursuers. She sat on the
edge of the bed and examined the soles of both feet:
filthy and cut but not bitten, she decided, the glass to
blame. She picked out the obvious pieces. She sneezed,
clotted black blood spilling from her nose.

Eight minutes past six, the broken watch, the same
time forever.

Time to move.

She hauled herself off the bed. The window was
bolted shut. She took the bedspread, wrapped it
around her right hand and forearm, then punched the

glass out of the window, before scraping clear the remaining splinters. Over the rain she heard the first siren.

Using a chair, she eased her top half through the gap, then grabbed the exterior portion of the air-con unit to help herself onto the ledge. Curling toes over the bottom of the frame and fingers under the top, she leaned back a little, looked left and right, then up and down. Through two sheer walls of narrowing darkness she recognized a thin slice of Nathan Road to her left. Which meant the building on the other side of the drop was the Imperial Hotel.

She looked for a route down and saw a diagonal descent over three storeys. After that she'd need to traverse. She looked up, in case a rise of a floor might lead to something more direct, but the pummelling rain and lack of light made it almost impossible to see.

The downpour made filthy surfaces slippery; grease, dirt, oil, bird-shit, all smothering overflow pipes, air-con units, extractor fans. She spanned a five-foot gap to grasp a vertical drain. Only when she'd transferred her weight did the couplings start to pull free from the rotting wall. She made another transfer, propping one foot against a beige extractor outlet, the other against a corroded overflow pipe. With each move her cuts were investigated a little further.

She climbed cautiously, aware that her judgement was as impaired as the rest of her. The chorus of sirens grew louder. So did the rain, as she neared the ground; it was hammering the corrugated iron and plastic awnings that partly covered the alley. She made her final drop from ten feet, her bleeding soles crunching onto filthy concrete. Above, thick black smoke billowed from a wound in the building.

With Chungking Mansions rising on one side and the Imperial Hotel on the other, and with the awnings shutting out most of the remaining light, she could almost believe it was night. Out of this darkness, shapes emerged. From both ends of the alley, closing in on her.

They were armed. And in uniform.

15

Her face in the dirt, they closed in on her slowly. But Stephanie was too exhausted to hold any surprises for them. She placed her hands in the small of her soaking back, ready for the cuffs.

Sirens everywhere, a helicopter hovered overhead, the thud of its blades reverberating through her. A searchlight flickered over Chungking Mansions, its penetrative beam occasionally lighting up the alley.

There were two plain-clothed detectives among the uniformed officers. They marched her to Mody Road, which had been sealed off at the junction with Nathan Road. There were three police cars at the kerb, lights flashing, and two plain Toyotas. Stephanie was bundled into the back seat of the first of them. No handles, no locks, a perspex partition separated her from the front. One of the detectives sat in the passenger seat, the other rode in the brown Toyota behind. The driver of each vehicle was a uniformed officer.

The cars pulled away, swishing through the rain. Time to regroup. For a while, silence would be the best policy. But not for long. Because she didn't have long. What she had was a name. Mostovoi. And the only other man to whom that would have meant something – Brankovic – was dead. So Mostovoi was still currency. For the moment.

Goosebumps rose on her skin, bruised muscles

began to stiffen. As the last of the adrenaline faded, so fatigue staked its claim, and the cuts began to sting.

They headed into the Cross Harbour Tunnel for Hong Kong Island.

She wondered about Raymond Chen. Was he the man to contact? A Magenta House source – and not one they trusted fully, either – but perhaps her only option. If Alexander had been angry over the death of Felix Cheung, he'd be beside himself with rage now. But she still had the bargaining chip. On the other hand, if she used Mostovoi now, that left her with nothing. But if she didn't, she might be left to languish in some police station while time slipped away and his value degraded.

They emerged from the Cross Harbour Tunnel and ran into traffic.

Other questions formed. Who'd sent Brankovic to Hong Kong? *Milan sends his love.* Savic's work? Or Dragica's? Why not? Stephanie wasn't blind to her true nature. She would have taken pleasure in betraying Petra to Savic. Pleasure in the consequences for Stephanie. Pleasure in the pain Savic would feel. Not that he'd sacrifice her lightly. He'd need to be persuaded. But who better than Dragica? She could persuade anybody of anything ... one way or another.

Finally free of traffic, they entered the Aberdeen Tunnel to the South Side. Which was when Stephanie began to pay attention. Where were they going? On the other side of the perspex the detective and the officer seemed relaxed, the detective smoking, the officer laughing at something she couldn't hear. When they exited from the tunnel and forked left

419

on Wong Chuk Hang Road, Stephanie took a guess.

And was right.

Gilbert Lai was dressed for golf, despite the torrential rain: cream slacks, lime shirt, red and black golfing shoes. He peered at Stephanie through tinted lenses and then at the marble floor onto which she was dripping. He made no attempt to hide his disgust.

At first she'd been surprised. And was then surprised at herself. Of course Lai would have a presence among the Hong Kong police. How naïve to imagine otherwise.

The two detectives and the two uniformed officers stood behind her, by the front door. Behind Lai were two bodyguards, dressed in black Mao suits with purple collars, both armed. Her hands were still cuffed. She could feel blood oozing from the slice in her side and the cuts on her feet. Small puddles were forming around her toes. But she stood as upright as she could, returning Lai's stare with interest.

'It's very considerate of you to try to destroy Chungking Mansions. Demolition is long overdue. It's not only a revolting eyesore but an excellent development opportunity. Sadly, you don't seem to have succeeded.'

He twisted a Philip Morris cigarette into a tortoiseshell holder. One of the bodyguards stepped forward to offer a light. Lai smoked a while. *What am I going to do with you?* The view through the wall of glass behind him could not have been more different from the last time she'd seen it; then, a brilliantly sunny day, now, a solid slab of slate grey.

'I didn't expect to see you again.'

'The feeling's mutual.'

'I imagine it is.' He spoke in Chinese and one of his bodyguards disappeared. Then he said, 'Are you injured?'

'I'm standing.'

'By the look of it, only just.'

'I'm fine.'

'Are you fit enough to travel?'

Not the question she was expecting. 'Where am I going?'

He took a drag from the cigarette, then exhaled theatrically and returned his gaze to the dark puddle on his marble floor. 'I hope you're not going to leave a stain.'

A maid showed her to a bedroom, then waited for her outside. On a clear day there would have been a spectacular view of Deep Water Bay from the window. The king-size double bed had a gold bedspread. The bedside tables were carved from large blocks of solid soapstone, lamps rising seamlessly from the centre of each. The floor was still marble but there were three huge Persian carpets on it. Stephanie avoided them. In the bathroom the walk-in shower was polished granite with gold taps and a bronze dragon for a showerhead.

Twenty minutes later she emerged, pink and steaming. Bandages and plasters had been left beside the sink. The slice below her ribs was still bleeding. Some of the cuts on her feet had stopped, while others persisted. She dried herself, then did the best she could, slipping into the blue silk robe provided, pressing a bandage between the material and the cut. There were black silk slippers. Putting them on hurt.

421

The maid was waiting for her and took her to Lai's study. Teak floors and walls, a dozen vases, none of them the same size, all of them creeping with jasmine. On top of a huge rosewood desk there was a plain white pot with a wicker handle and two small cups. He poured tea for both of them.

'A doctor will be here shortly. Someone is fetching you something to wear.' He handed her one of the cups, then sat down in a large swivel chair on the opposite side of the desk. 'You and I have something in common.'

Looking at him, it was hard to see what.

'We are both people of our word,' Lai said. 'These days that's increasingly rare. A man like Milan Savic wouldn't understand the value of that. Over the years our arrangement has been mutually lucrative but we have never enjoyed each other's company. Fortunately we've never had to, and so we've never pretended to. We differ in many ways, generally, but in one aspect, in particular: I have evolved and Savic hasn't.'

'He's come a long way from Belgrade.'

'On the contrary. He's still there, on the street-corner. An ignorant thug. He just has more money.'

'What's on your mind?'

'As I've grown older I've attempted to leave my past behind. For a man like me, with my history – not to mention my fortune – that's a natural instinct. In Hong Kong I'm almost respectable now.' His bloodless smile took her by surprise, the lop-sided droop parting for yellow teeth. 'But it's taken nearly thirty years. Now that Alan Waxman and Felix Cheung are no longer with us, he's the only one left to bind me to the past.'

'This is starting to sound like a sales pitch.'

'It's a trade. You live and Milan Savic dies.'

'And if I say no?'

'I can have you on an aircraft to Europe tonight, no questions asked.'

'And at the other end?'

'You're on your own. My influence is local, nothing more.'

'You're too modest.'

'Local is Asia. My interests have evolved. Europe is no longer a priority. It's better for me to focus on regional ventures and to let others take care of business further afield.'

'But isn't that precisely what Savic does for you in Europe?'

He narrowed his eyes while he considered how much to say. 'I've formed a partnership with Russians in Vladivostok. They take care of everything. They're represented from the Russian Far East through to Moscow and beyond. I don't need Savic's contacts in Europe any more. Which means I don't need to tolerate him here. He's outlived his usefulness. What's more, I can't risk being associated with the kind of chaos we've seen today. Not even by insinuation. You, of all people, will understand this. After all, in your profession, as in mine, reputation is everything.'

There was a car to meet her at Heathrow, eighteen hours later, at quarter to six in the morning. The cabin crew made sure she was first off the aircraft. She was escorted out of the umbilical, down the steps to a waiting black Range Rover; two men in front, one in the passenger seat beside her, none of them familiar. From the aircraft to Magenta House in thirty minutes,

London still wrapped in slumber.

She'd made the call at the airport in Hong Kong, just before boarding, knowing it would give Alexander no option. He wouldn't risk her at Immigration. Not if he thought she was unstable. Who could predict how she'd react?

Now, in a subterranean conference room, she wasn't sure what she felt. Other than tired, sore, confused and anxious.

She'd been waiting alone for twenty minutes. There was a tray at the centre of the oval table: a pot of coffee, croissants, rolls, a jug of orange juice, four glasses, four plates. She didn't have an appetite but she helped herself to coffee.

They came in together. Alexander wore grey flannel trousers, a crumpled white shirt, the sleeves rolled up to the elbow. There was no sign of a tie. Or a razor; for the first time, Stephanie saw stubble on his jaw. Despite the early start, Rosie looked less tired than when they'd last met.

Stephanie braced herself.

Both of them looked at her, both startled. Her right hand was bandaged, two stitches in the largest cut on her palm. Her right eye was grazed and swollen with a bruise beneath. Under her shirt there were three stitches in her side. On her skin she wore a girdle of black and blue. The sixth stitch was on the sole of her right foot, the other lacerations treated with plasters.

Alexander poured himself coffee, sat in his custom-ary position at the head of the table, and lit a Rothmans.

'It's over, Stephanie.'

No outrage, which was a surprise. Just the basic fact.

She nodded. How could she dispute it? Alexander didn't say anything. The longer the silence persisted, the more apprehensive Stephanie became.

'Is one of you going to tell me what's going on?'

Rosie glanced at Alexander, who gave the merest nod. She said, 'It's Mark.'

'Sorry?'

'He's okay ...'

Which she took to mean, *he's not okay*. 'What do you mean? What's happened to him?'

'Stephanie, are you listening to me? He's okay.'

'What are you talking about?'

Her voice was rising with panic.

'He was attacked.'

'*What?*'

'Yesterday afternoon.'

'Attacked?'

'He's fine, Stephanie.'

'What happened?'

'There were three of them.'

'Where?'

'At his clinic on Cadogan Place.'

'Who were they?'

'Savic's people, we think. Anyway, they tried to rough him up and ...'

'Rough him up? What are you talking about? *Rough him up?*'

Rosie told her to calm down and listen, then told her how it had happened. The men had barged into the practice in the middle of the afternoon, terrorizing the other patients. They said nothing. When one of the receptionists tried to intervene she was punched. When they found Mark they tried to break his hands.

Stephanie felt sick. 'His hands ...'

'They failed, Steph, because they underestimated him. He fought back and gave them a real beating.'

Just as he had that night in south London. Rosie filled in the blanks. The police had been called, which was how Magenta House had been alerted. Two of the men were in hospital, the other was under arrest. None of them was saying anything. Rosie assured her they would, just as soon as they could be transferred to Magenta House custody. Stephanie didn't doubt that for a second.

His hands. Of all the things they could have chosen. Which was precisely *why* they'd chosen them. Premeditated violence dressed up as a casual act, the fear almost worse than the act itself. Nothing spontaneous about it, it was a message for her.

'How is he?'

Rosie tried a smile. 'In better shape than you, by the look of it.'

'His hands?'

'Bruised but not broken. Most of the damage was from the punches he threw.'

'I want to see him.'

Alexander spoke up. 'Not now.'

'Where is he?'

'Somewhere safe.'

'*Where?*'

'You can't see him, Stephanie. It's for his own good.'

'Don't give me that!'

He pointed a finger at her. 'I told you a dozen times, at least. One slip is all it would take. But you never listened. Which is why we're here now. You've compromised yourself, Stephanie. Which means you've compromised us. And him. He's safer where he is, in quarantine from you.'

Exactly the sort of thing she'd expect Alexander to say. But the tone was a surprise. There was no savagery, no subliminal pleasure. Instead, she thought she detected concern.

'What's he been told?'

'Not a lot. Does he know what you do?'

'No.'

'You've never mentioned it? Never let it slip in a loose moment?'

'Absolutely not.'

'That's not the impression he gives.'

On the inside, she managed a smile. How typical of Mark. And how revealing. He hadn't known, exactly, but he'd made an educated guess. And he'd been happy to accommodate it. Or, if not happy, able to overlook it. Which only cast her current situation into greater relief.

'What a fucking mess.'

'I'm sorry, Stephanie,' Alexander said.

She shrugged it off. 'What happens now?'

'Someone else will finish it.'

She nodded. 'And me?'

'You're not in much shape to do anything.'

'What about our deal?'

'We'll work something out. In the meantime I'd like you to stay at a safe-house for a few days. Just until this is resolved. Arrangements are already in hand. We'll transfer you later today.'

'Why?'

'Because you can't go near anything familiar.

427

Hamilton's flat, your flat at Maclise Road, the friends you made through him – they're all compromised. You don't have anywhere else to go.'

They provided a room for her at the top of Magenta House. Now that most of the leaves had fallen from the trees she had a clear view of the south bank and the Millennium Wheel. In the early afternoon Brian Rutherford, a doctor with a private practice on George Street, came to check her injuries. He diagnosed the pain in her left hip as a strain of the flexor.

'Just like Cameron Diaz,' Stephanie said.

'I'm sorry?'

'Never mind.'

Rosie visited her later in the afternoon. 'You're going to a flat in Paddington. It'll be fine for a couple of days. Get as much rest as you can.'

'What about Mark?'

'We've got him at a hotel, under protection. That much I can tell you. He's staying in considerably more comfort than you.'

'What's going to happen to him?'

Rosie frowned. 'Nothing. When this is over he'll be able to pick up his life again.'

'What's left of it.'

'Don't be melodramatic, Steph. You're the one who needs to think about that.'

From anyone else, Stephanie would have been offended. 'What's the story?'

'Mistaken identity.'

'That's a little lame, isn't it?'

'In a few days it'll be over. In a fortnight it'll be history.'

'Have you spoken to him?'

Rosie nodded. 'Last night, after he'd been discharged from hospital. I took him to the hotel.'

'How was he?'

'As you'd expect. Shocked. Confused. Angry. Can I ask you something?'

'What?'

'Any idea how they found out?'

'No,' she said. It wasn't a lie, exactly, but it certainly wasn't the truth. 'I took so many precautions, Rosie. I didn't think I'd left anything to chance.'

Ten past ten. It's a cold wet night as I step onto Adelphi Terrace. The way I look, the way I move, there can be little doubt that I'm defeated. I had it all within my grasp and now it's gone. The fight has deserted me. That's what I'm hoping they'll see.

Rosie puts her hand on my arm, before I climb into the same Range Rover that brought me here from the airport this morning. 'It'll work out, Stephanie. One way or the other.'

Again, there are two men in the front and one beside me. I don't recognize any of them. They all look in good condition. In other words, nobody is taking any chances. Alexander wants me in a safe-house while the end-game is played out. His reason? I'm no longer able to participate in it. Or, I need to recuperate. Or, I'm even more unstable than he initially thought.

Perhaps there's another reason. Alexander's nervous. When I consider his conciliatory tone, I wonder whether that's complimentary or contradictory. My feeling is, he's trying to pacify me. Just for a day or two. Just until he has what he wants.

As for Rosie, she's stranded between friendship and obliga-

tion. As incomprehensible as I find that, it's crucial to recognize it. If she has to go one way or the other, which will it be? I thought I knew. Now I'm not sure. The more I think about it, the clearer it becomes. I still need the Gemini list.

Up Charing Cross Road and into Tottenham Court Road, I sit slumped in my leather seat, my face pressed to the glass. I was so sure I could keep Mark safe. That I could have a real life to make this other life bearable. But my existence as Stephanie is no more authentic than my existence as Petra. They're both built upon a foundation of dishonesty.

Except that what I feel for Mark is genuine. Just like it was with Kostya. In both cases, love cuts through the lies and protects the truth. No matter what Alexander might say, he can't compete with that.

Park Lane is busy, so's the Bayswater Road. We're close to Paddington. I know there will only be one moment for me. My head still lolling against the glass, I let my eyelids flutter with fatigue as we slide to a halt.

In the end they make it absurdly easy. We're in Hyde Park Square. The flat is in a mansion block. I know the type; mostly owned by foreign nationals, only occupied a month a year, good security and eighty per cent empty. The two men in the front enter the lobby to check that everything is all right as the man sitting beside me comes round to open my door.

Sometimes the luck runs against you, sometimes not. I slide onto the pavement, shoulders rounded, despondent, submissive. He closes the door, glances at the lobby and waits for the signal. The two inside are talking to the porter.

My minder's about the same height as me, which makes it easy to head-butt him when he looks my way. His nose pops. As he stumbles back against the car I kick him hard, on the side of his right knee. He crumples. Once he's down I stamp on his right ankle with as much force as I can.

I don't bother waiting to see if they've noticed.

*By the time I hear the first shout I'm into Strathearn Place.
I don't feel the cuts on my feet opening up again. I don't know
what's fuelling me but I'm running as fast as I've ever run.
Into Sussex Place, across Sussex Gardens and into London
Street. Several seconds later I hear squealing brakes on Sussex
Gardens, which tells me how far ahead I am. It's enough
because now I'm into a small grid of interlocking streets. I can
cut one way, then the next, knowing that every time they turn
a corner and I'm not there, their doubt will grow and their
pace will drop.*

Bleached by the white light overhead, Stephanie sat at
one end of the carriage as it rattled through the darkness between Euston Square and King's Cross. The
Underground late at night had always been a curious
interface between the general public and the city's
underclass – the dispossessed and the deranged – with
only the drunk crossing between the two. These days
she felt like a tourist. A voyeur. Once she'd been one of
them. Although perhaps she looked like one of them
again, drenched as she was.

She surfaced at King's Cross. Victoria was the nearest station to her destination but she had to assume
that within hours station CCTV tapes would be under
scrutiny at Magenta House. A sighting at King's Cross
would mislead and simultaneously present a number
of options. Had she used the main line to leave
London? Had she melted into the surrounding area?

She knew that recordings from street cameras could
also be sequestered, as S3 tried to narrow down her
whereabouts. Which was why she avoided as many
main roads as possible, picking a largely residential

431

route to Longmoore Street in Victoria. The variable hazard remained patrolling police, but she expected to spot them before they spotted her.

Longmoore Street, the familiar façade: bricks blackened by dirt, rotten window-frames, blue paint peeling from the front door. Cyril Bradfield opened it and peered at her over half-moons, surprised then confused.

She said, 'I didn't call. I couldn't risk it.'

He glanced up and down the street. 'Come in.'

'Cyril, I'm sorry. I'd never do anything ...'

'I know.'

Alexander had said she had nowhere to go. He'd almost been right. But this remained the one place that nobody knew about. It was warm inside, the air thick with sweet tobacco. She waited for him in the sitting room while he fetched her a towel. An open book was resting on one arm of an old leather armchair: Peter Hopkirk's *Quest for Kim*. Classical music was playing. Stephanie picked up the empty cassette case: Khachaturian.

'Tea?'

She took the towel – once yellow and fluffy, now off-white and threadbare – and managed fragments of an unconvincing smile.

'Something stronger, perhaps?' he suggested.

He interpreted her silence correctly, collecting two cheap tumblers from the kitchen and a bottle of Bowmore from a cupboard beneath the bookcase.

'I've been waiting for a special occasion to open this.'

'I'm not sure how special this is.'

Stephanie sat on a sofa that tilted from one end to the other. She began to dry her hair. Directly ahead of her, on the wooden mantelpiece there was a black-

and-white photograph in a silver oval frame. Ellen, Bradfield's wife, dead for almost twenty years. In the years before that she'd been his portal to the world, allowing him to submerge himself fully in his peculiar art. In those days Stephanie would have conducted her business with Ellen.

He handed her half a tumbler. 'It's fine stuff, this. Do you a power of good.'

'Whisky usually crucifies me.'

'Looks like somebody's already taken care of that.'

She cupped the glass in both hands. Bradfield sat in the armchair, slipped a marker between the pages of his book and placed it on a side table beside a brown Bakelite telephone.

'So, what's happened?'

She dropped her gaze into her glass as her vision blurred. The first drop peeled away, falling into the gold below. And once they started they wouldn't stop, streaming down her cheeks, down her nose. Bradfield began to haul himself out of his chair. Between lurching breaths she told him not to. She held the glass tightly, the liquid dancing to her convulsions.

Eventually, the worst of it passed, sobs subsiding to sniffs. She wiped her face, smearing wetness across it, then took a sip that became a slurp. The heat erupted in her chest. When she looked, half the whisky had gone.

The morning suited her mood perfectly: a lead sky overhead, a sharp wind rattling her window with volleys of rain. Her headache made her nauseous. She lay in bed for a while, listening to the worst of the weather, trying not to think about Mark. Or Berlin. Or Hong Kong.

Around eight Stephanie kicked off the coarse blankets and got dressed, a chilly draught to encourage her. The cuts on her feet were black and dry.

It was a small first-floor room at the back of the house, a single bed pushed against one wall. The wallpaper had daisies and dandelions and patches of damp. The overhead bulb was in a cream shade stained sepia with age. Sepia, Stephanie thought, was the colour that best described the spirit of the house. It was the colour of the past.

She could hear Bradfield in the kitchen below; a door shutting, a cough, the rush of water from a tap, then the sound of the morning's news on the radio. She tried to remember what they'd talked about from the top of the bottle to the bottom. Not her predicament, that much she knew. They'd started to but she'd lost control, descending into a chaotic stream of consciousness, part conspiracy theory, part self-pity. And there was nothing she disliked more than self-pity. Bradfield had brought a stop to it. Not tonight, he'd told her, leave it until the morning. Daylight will bring clarity. Not much, as it turned out.

A phone rang. She heard Bradfield answer it.

Which prompted something within her. Another phone. One that *didn't* ring. A phone that went straight to the answer-machine.

'The thing she'd missed.'

She'd called Mark twice on the Airport Express between Chek Lap Kok and Kowloon. On the Nokia phone. *Petra's* phone.

She'd imagined the mistake had been committed the night they'd spent together at Maclise Road before she went to Berlin. Savic had called her while Mark had undressed her. She couldn't think how that might have backfired, but it had seemed the only possibility. Until now.

Was it possible that Savic had a trace on the Nokia? Technically, of course it was. How likely was it? Harder to say. How likely was it that Dragica Maric had been involved? That seemed easier to believe. The incident had occurred after they'd been together in Berlin. There would have been plenty of time to tamper with the phone.

Which meant that the measures she'd taken *had* been sufficient. The mistake had been hers. Human error; Stephanie, as ever, Petra's weak link.

In the kitchen there was tea. Russian Caravan, naturally. Bradfield turned down the radio and offered her something to eat, which she declined. Then they sat at the table while he poured for both of them. As he did so, she began. He listened in silence until she'd finished, twenty minutes later.

'Alexander was right,' she concluded. 'The truth is, Stephanie and Petra can't coexist.'

'Don't be too hard on yourself.'

'That was last night, Cyril. Whisky and emotion. This morning it's headaches and facts. I thought I could live both lives because I thought I was good enough to do it.'

'It was one mistake, Stephanie, that's all.'

'That's another thing he was right about. *One slip is all it'll take*. That's what he always said. Something as insignificant as using the wrong phone for the wrong call. And all because I was tired and upset, and not paying attention.'

'What will you do now?'

'I don't know.'

'Why don't you just vanish? You could run. They'd never find you. You're good enough for that. Others might slip. You wouldn't. Not by yourself.'

'But they'd find him.'

'Mark?'

'Komarov.'

'Why?'

'The moment I ran, I broke ranks. I'm no longer Magenta House. I'm on the outside. I might even be a target. I don't know. What I do know is this: by running, my agreement with Alexander is over. Komarov's protection is gone.'

'That doesn't mean they'll kill him.'

Stephanie wanted to believe that. 'It doesn't mean they *must* kill him. But he's on a list. Like the rest of us. It just depends which list you're on. But that's all it takes. It means they can.'

I place a blank cassette into his ancient machine in the sitting room. I press 'play' and 'record' simultaneously. The spools creak into life. I mumble a few words into the tiny fixed microphone, then play the tape back. The sound quality is dreadful but it works.

Ever discreet, Cyril's made some fatuous excuse about urgent work that needs his attention in the attic. Sometimes his attempts at subtlety are so painfully clumsy I wish he'd be more direct. But that's not his nature. Just as confession isn't mine. This won't be my first, but that doesn't make it any easier. I press both buttons again.

'Mark … by the time you hear this I'll be gone. I have no idea how you'll feel about that, after what's happened. Before

436

I go back to the beginning, there is one other thing I'd like to say now. My love for you was genuine. Is genuine. Please remember that, no matter what you hear on this tape. You rescued me. Falling in love with you, learning to trust you – you made me human again.'

I speak without pausing, forty-five minutes one way, forty-five back. It's not cathartic, exactly, but at least it's a gesture. Which is what I'm reduced to, where Mark is concerned. There's nothing else I can do.

Later Cyril asks me whether I'm ready to start my transformation. Not yet, I tell him. I need to deliver the cassette first.

Just before four I cross Pont Street. It's a dark, wet afternoon, which helps. I'm wearing an old donkey jacket of Cyril's with the collar turned up, a pair of jeans and some boots. The coat swamps me, making me look smaller. I've also borrowed an umbrella, which I hold low, hiding my face. I stand on the corner of Pavilion Road, a long, narrow lane, running parallel to Sloane Street, south of Knightsbridge.

At five past four a front door opens. Again the weather works in my favour. Usually, the women coming out would linger for a few moments, exchanging kisses and gossip before dispersing. Today, because of the rain, that ritual has taken place inside. Umbrellas up, they scatter.

Karen is the sixth to leave the mews house. Twice a week she comes here for yoga. There are more convenient studios closer to home, but she knows everyone in this class. She's been a regular since she was single. These days the sessions are more than an attempt to reclaim her physique; she says they maintain her sanity. They're mini-breaks from motherhood.

I follow her to Draycott Place. Her green Golf is parked on a meter. I hang back a bit, as she unlocks the car. When she climbs in I let down my umbrella and scurry to the passenger *door. As the engine coughs to life, I jump in.*

She freezes, then sees who it is. Now she's not sure if she's frightened, or just shocked.

'Get out!'

I don't do anything.

'What the hell are you doing here?'

'Twice a week, three until four.'

'Get out.'

'I wanted to call you first but I couldn't.'

'Get out of my car, Stephanie.'

'I couldn't come to your house, either …'

She takes her mobile from her coat pocket. 'I'm calling the police.'

I snatch the phone and switch it off. Now she looks scared, not angry.

'Leave me alone.'

'Drive.'

Desperation creeps into her voice. 'Please, Stephanie …'

'Drive.'

'… don't hurt me.'

'What?'

'Think of Fergus.'

Her baby son. In a mental snapshot, he's gurgling in their garden on a hot afternoon as we drink Pinot Grigio.

'Karen …'

'Please don't hurt us.'

I must be losing my touch. It's so obvious.

'I'm not going to hurt anyone, Karen. I just need to talk to you.'

I can see she doesn't believe me. When I try to place a reassuring hand on her arm, she flinches.

'Let me guess. In his late fifties, well dressed, well mannered, clipped snow-white hair, clipped Scottish accent.'

The answer is in her eyes.

'What did he tell you?'

She doesn't want to say, which points me in the right direction.

'When did he contact you?'

Her voice is no more than a whisper. 'This morning. Just after Julian left for the office.'

Impressively swift, I have to admit. 'At least it proves I'm not completely out of touch. I was right to intercept you here.'

'Why?'

'Because your house is under surveillance.'

Karen shakes her head. 'He never said anything about that.'

'He wouldn't. But you can take it from me, it is. They'll be reading your e-mails too, and listening to your phone calls. Land-lines and mobiles ...'

Her mouth is open but there's no sound coming out.

'Karen, as long as they believe you've had no contact with me you've got nothing to fear,' I tell her, wishing I could feel as confident of that as I sound.

'Can they do that?'

'What?'

'Tap our phones?'

'Easily. Especially the mobiles ...'

'I mean, legally.'

There's no simple way to answer that. If an entity doesn't exist, aren't matters of legality redundant?

She shakes her head and buries her face in her hands. 'I can't believe I'm even listening to this! For God's sake, Stephanie ... what have you done?'

'Nothing.'

'What's happened to Mark? They wouldn't say ...'

'He's okay.'

'Where is he?'

'I don't know. But he'll be fine. I promise you.'

She needs me to confess. And then to offer an explanation. For a few seconds we sit in silence, with only the patter of the rain on the windscreen for sound.

'What have you been told?'

She's still scared. 'That Mark was attacked and that you were involved.'

'What else?'

'That your name isn't really Stephanie Schneider.'

'Go on.'

'I didn't believe him. Not at first. I didn't want to.'

But Alexander had produced evidence. For a start, photographs. Me, with other men, in foreign cities, each shot explained, simultaneously plausible yet incredible. He'd shown her a reproduction of the Gilardini passport bearing my image. That was the one I used in Marrakech. Later he'd asked if Karen and Mark had ever discussed me. Naturally, she'd said they had. He'd asked her if Mark had ever said that I was secretive about my past. Or whether I'd ever been forthcoming about my family.

As she's telling me this I find a part of me admiring his craft. He didn't force-feed her information. He introduced her to it gently. Vaguely. He made accusations by asking questions, allowing her to come to the conclusions. *His* conclusions, though they must have felt like hers.

We end up in a café on the King's Road, where we take a table at the back. Karen drinks a large glass of white wine. I have water. By the time I've finished my attempt at an explanation, we've both reordered. Karen wants to ring home to tell the babysitter that she's going to be late.

'Not yet,' I say. 'Not until you leave.'

'Why not?'

'The moment you switch your phone on they'll know where you are.'

'Are they listening to us?'

'Karen, look. Soon this will all be over. One way or the other.'

'How do you know?'

'You'll just have to take my word for it.'

Which, for the first time, she does. 'What do you want, Stephanie?'

I reach into my coat pocket and put the cassette on the table. 'This is for Mark.'

'You want me to take it to him? I don't know where he is.'

'Not yet.'

'When?'

'When it's all over.'

'How will I know when that is?'

'You'll get a call.'

'From you?'

I shake my head. 'This is the last time you'll see me. Someone else will call.'

'What's on the tape?'

'An apology. An explanation. A love letter.'

She takes it and puts it in her pocket.

'Hide it, Karen. Not just in a drawer. Somewhere really secure where no one's going to stumble across it. And you can't say a word about this to Julian.'

'For God's sake, Stephanie …'

'It's for your safety, not mine. I can look after myself.'

'What if they come back?'

'They?'

She nods. 'There were two of them. The man you described – he called himself Mr Ellis – and a woman. I didn't catch her name.'

A cold fist squeezes my heart. 'An Indian woman, good-looking?'

'That's right.'

I close my eyes and pinch the bridge of my nose.

Karen says, 'Are you all right?'

'Just give me a moment.'

I need to think it through. It takes a couple of minutes. Then I say, 'I'm going to call you tomorrow. At the house. Mid-morning. Will you be in?'

'I can be.'

'I'll talk about Mark. I'll try to persuade you of many things. About how it's not my fault but that I can't go into details. String it out as long as you can. When I've finished, call the number he gave you and tell him about our conversation in as much detail as you can.'

'But if you're right, he'll hear it.'

'That's what I'm hoping.'

After Karen, she called Ali Metin, outlined her problem and asked if he could help. Sure, he told her. When did she want it?

'Tonight.'

'I was thinking a few days, Steffi.'

'I'll pay for delivery.'

'Tomorrow morning?'

'As long as it's early.'

After the call she travelled to the Cromwell Road in west London, rented a room in a dilapidated house that had been converted into bedsits, then returned to Cyril Bradfield, taking the bus, not the Underground.

She found him in the attic, perched on a stool, hunched over a Cuban passport, craggy fingers using tweezers to peel a photograph of a young black woman from the dog-eared document. He didn't look up when he said, 'So you've decided, then.'

'Sort of.'

'What do you need?'

'One document.'

'Where to?'

'I'm not sure yet.'

'I have a Russian passport available. Legitimate and unused.'

'Fine.'

'Appearance?'

'I need a change.'

'Age?'

She smiled at him. 'Early twenties, if you can.'

'You're not in shocking shape, so it might be possible. Permanent or temporary?'

'Temporary.'

'Let's change the hair. Cut and colour.'

'Blonde?'

'Or dark red. It's up to you. And your eyes. Lots of eye-liner, drawing attention to them. It'll make your skin look paler.'

'I thought I was going to be a Russian. Not a corpse.'

'If I put your place of birth as Norilsk, you can be both.'

At seven the following morning she met Metin at Warren Street. She got into his second-hand BMW carrying a black grip containing items borrowed from Bradfield. They parked on Howland Street, which was quiet, and Metin reached over to the back seat and grabbed a sports bag. He unzipped it and handed over two pieces of equipment. One was a hand-held monitor. The other was a transmitter, attached to a length of

443

ultra-thin cable with a tiny lens at the end.

'It's like the cameras they use in surgery. It's just the base unit that's different. Switch on the transmitter, place the probe, switch on the monitor and off you go.'

'Range?'

'The transmitter's good for five hundred metres.'

By eight-thirty she was in the room she'd rented on the Cromwell Road. A gloomy place, with a view straight into the back of a cheap hotel, virtually no natural light in the room. The sash window was loose, the wooden frame rotten. Stephanie pulled a chair over to the window, stood on it, then drilled a diminutive hole through the top right-hand corner, just wide enough to accommodate the cable. Next she opened the window, eased herself out onto the ledge, threaded the cable back through the hole, before taping the transmitter to a drainpipe. She switched it on. Inside, she adjusted the lens so that it sat snugly in the window frame. Only four millimetres across, it was almost invisible.

At ten she called Karen. As their conversation drew to a close, Stephanie said she had to go out but might call her when she got back, around midday. She made Karen promise not to tell anyone that she'd called. Karen swore she wouldn't.

She had her answer at eleven-thirty. From Karen's phone they'd traced her mobile, homing in on her as the conversation progressed. She'd given them easily enough time to locate the building. After that it would be simple. Enquiries would be made, quickly establishing that a woman fitting her description had taken a room the previous evening. Since they knew she was due back at midday, all that remained was to get someone installed before then.

Now, standing on the Cromwell Road, just a couple of hundred metres away, Stephanie looked at the black-and-white image on the hand-held monitor. Although the picture lacked clarity, she recognized the man waiting for her.

Alan Carter. An S7, just like her. The hunter and the hunted.

Dazed, she walked for a while. After seven years, she was on the outside. There had been a period when she'd been independent, but even then she'd known that part of her belonged to Magenta House. With hindsight, it hadn't been that much of a surprise when Alexander appeared to reclaim her.

For seven years she'd wanted to be free. But not like this.

It all came down to lists. She'd been on one, now she was on another. And needing a third. That was the only option that remained. There was no way back. Not for her. Not for Komarov. Not for Mark. Even as she'd recorded her message on the cassette, she'd imagined she might get an opportunity to explain – face to face – and to plead for a shared future. Now that she was a target, she knew that couldn't happen.

She was a disease. If she came into contact with Mark again, she'd infect him. Terminally. The list was the only possible antidote.

She bought a BT phonecard and made a call from a public phone. A man answered and Stephanie said, 'It's me.'

'Where are you?'

'I need to see you.'

'When?'

'As soon as possible.'

'Where?'

'Wherever I can find your safari friend.'

'Berlin.'

That surprised her. 'Berlin?'

'It's always been Berlin. Tomorrow?'

'Yes. There's one more thing. I need you to bring something for me.'

She reached Longmoore Street in the late afternoon. Bradfield was in the kitchen. She put her shopping on the table and took a box out of the chemist's paper bag. She handed it to him. He turned it over and read the label. 'Ruby Fusion, from the Féria Color 3-D range, by L'Oréal. It promises you rich auburn red hair.' He looked up at her, smiling. 'Sounds lovely.'

He cut her hair, then she dyed it before he took photographs of her and went to work on the passport. 'When are you going?'

'Tomorrow morning.'

'When will you be back?'

'Soon.'

But he'd already seen the truth in her eyes.

Never.

Bradfield looked wounded, which hurt Stephanie. 'Promise me one thing,' he said.

'Anything.'

'Whenever you get to wherever it is, promise me that you'll make a real life for yourself.'

16

Berlin was cold and grey. Stephanie ached, her sense of loss more acute than her bruises. Rosie was right. Mark would resume his life. It wouldn't be so different to the life he'd led before her. He'd treat people, he'd climb, he'd spend lazy evenings with their friends. And he'd miss her. She knew that. But there would be the occasional Alex to distract him – willing and breathless yet ultimately pointless – until, eventually, he found someone to eclipse Stephanie herself.

She wanted to believe they would suffer by comparison but knew she was deluding herself. She'd given him as much as she could but Mark deserved more. He deserved the openness and trust that he'd given her. It was painful to acknowledge the truth: that there were women out there who'd be better for him than she'd been.

She took a taxi from Tegel to Treptower Park then walked. It was misty, a penetrating damp gnawing at her bones. She crossed Puschkinallee and picked her way along the dusty path to the rough wooden gate. Stone steps took her down to the water's edge. Freischwimmer was a café on the Flutgraben, a water run-off next to the Landwehrkanal. It bore a faint resemblance to a boat-house, or even a barge, with small tables and cheap chairs set on wooden decking beneath a canopy.

Konstantin Komarov was the only customer, in a dark blue suit beneath a black overcoat, a grey cashmere scarf around his neck. He got up, hugged her, then kissed her. Still holding her, hands firmly planted on her shoulders, he took in the shorter, redder hair.

'Russian?'

Stephanie's smile was weary. 'Very. Svetlana.'

'I always knew being Russian would suit you. You *are* Russian.'

'Only with you.'

They sat down. A waitress appeared: tattooed tears over her left cheek, studs in her right nostril and lower lip. She wore a large sheepskin coat over ripped denims and military-issue boots. Stephanie ordered coffee, then said to Komarov, 'This isn't the sort of place I'd expect to find you.'

'No?'

'It's a bit … casual.'

'You think I'm too old?'

'Too serious. It has a bohemian feel to it. That's not you.'

'You wanted to meet somewhere discreet. So here we are. Mid-morning, mid-week, in the cold. No one to disturb us.'

'Too right.'

'Freischwimmer doesn't usually open until two,' Komarov explained.

'Who was she?'

'Who?'

'The girl who brought you here.'

'What makes you think it was a girl?'

'You didn't discover this place yourself, Kostya.'

'You sound like a wife who's caught her husband

448

with lipstick on his collar.'

'And you sound like a husband who should have gone to the dry cleaners.'

'A Norwegian. She was a student here.'

Stephanie raised an eyebrow. 'A Norwegian student?'

His shame fell short of regret. 'It was entertaining while it lasted.'

'Aren't they all?'

'Tell me about Mostovoi.'

'He's in trouble.'

'From you?'

'Maybe. And if not, then from someone else.'

Komarov looked out across the water. 'What about you?'

'I'm in trouble too.'

'And me?'

She nodded. 'I'm sorry.'

'Well, it's better this way. To have some warning.' He lit a Marlboro. 'What about Mark?'

'It's over.'

When he turned to her, she couldn't look him in the eye.

'What happened?'

'What usually happens to people when they get close to me. He got hurt.'

'You loved him.'

Half a question, half a statement.

'He's better off without me, Kostya. Just like you.'

Komarov smiled thinly. 'Not true. For either of us, I suspect.'

'Don't kid yourself. Ludmilla is the one for you.'

'You've never met her.'

'I don't need to. The people who fall for me suffer

for it. They can't help it and nor can I. That's the truth, Kostya.'

The girl arrived with her coffee. Stephanie cupped her hands around the mug, trying to infuse some warmth into her stiff fingers. Away to their left beside a Nissan dealership there was a large red-brick building on the waterfront, its façade plunging straight into the murky water. A former factory, Komarov told her. During the Cold War the Wall had run down the Flutgraben. The windows on the lower floors of the building had been covered by metal panels, the interior patrolled by East German guards.

'It's strange to think of it now, us sitting here, drinking coffee. When that was a reality, I was on Sakhalin, in a camp I thought I would never leave. This would have seemed impossible then. Yet here we are. I don't take anything for granted, Stephanie. Good or bad.'

'What will you do?'

'If I have to, I'll relocate. Maybe to Sakhalin itself. Or Vladivostok. They'll find it harder to get me there.'

'What about Ludmilla? Would she be happy to go with you?'

He looked faintly amused. 'Maybe you arranged this on purpose.'

She tried to look cross but failed. 'Is that what you think?'

'You want to know what I think? I'll tell you. I think you're the strangest woman I've ever met.'

Just what Mark had said.

'Nobody can change that,' Komarov continued. 'Not even Ludmilla.'

'I'll bet she takes your mind off it.'

He spread his hands. 'I won't deny it.'

450

'I can't believe you're taking it like this.'

'Do I have a choice?'

'I'm ruining your life, Kostya. Again.'

'If you hadn't saved it before, I wouldn't even be alive for you to ruin it now.'

'Very smooth.'

'I'm not scared, Stephanie.'

'I am.'

'I don't believe you.'

'Not for me. For you. For Ludmilla.'

'And for Mark?'

'He's safe.'

'Are you sure?'

What a question. She didn't know. Rosie had given her word. Until now, that had always been good enough. It wasn't that she didn't trust Rosie. She didn't trust Alexander and so wasn't sure that Rosie was in a position to offer guarantees of any sort.

Komarov looked around, then reached into the grip he'd brought with him and pulled out a Walther P88 with a full magazine of fifteen rounds. Stephanie tucked it into Bradfield's donkey jacket.

'When you said Mostovoi was in Berlin, I was surprised.'

'His connections here go back many years. Before reunification, he flew here regularly when he was a cargo pilot for the Soviet air force. He made a lot of contacts. Max makes contacts wherever he goes. More than anything else, he's a networker. He bought property here in the mid-nineties, trying to capitalize on the development boom. He sold most of it before the collapse but he still owns two commercial buildings in Mitte. He also has a house in the countryside, somewhere out near the Polish border, and an apartment in Charlottenburg. I couldn't get the address, though.'

'So where can I find him?'

Komarov took a card out of his wallet and wrote on the back. 'Twice a week, when he's in Berlin, he goes to this place for lunch. Same time, same companion. Valery Malenkov. Ex-Red Army, an old friend.'

'Thank you.'

'One other thing. He always arrives on foot.'

'Walking distance?'

Komarov shrugged. 'I can't say. But that address is also in Charlottenburg.'

She took the card. 'Is Mostovoi going to be a problem for you?'

He shook his head. 'Max is a rogue. People like him. *I* like him. But we were never friends. It was always business.'

Just as Komarov had once been. She remembered sleeping with him and wondering whether she would have to kill him. She'd done the same with Savic yet the two experiences could not have been less similar.

'After I saw you at the Adlon, I saw Dragica Maric.'

'You went to Moscow?'

'She came to Berlin.'

Komarov considered this for a moment, then nodded. Stephanie said, 'You don't seem surprised.'

'You're doing business with Savic. That means you're doing business with her.'

'She said you slept with her, Kostya.'

'And you believed her?'

'I didn't say that.'

'You don't have to. Normally I think you would accept my word on anything. Yet on this matter you're

452

prepared to take her word instead...'

Entirely true. Stephanie winced, feeling idiotic and cheap. She took a sip of coffee. 'Sorry. Force of habit. Always believe the worst.'

'Listen to you. More Russian than Russian.'

'When are you returning to Moscow?'

'Tomorrow afternoon.'

'Back to Ludmilla.'

It came out wrong; too quick, too bitter. Komarov gazed at her for a while. 'I didn't have to come, Stephanie. The address, the gun, I could have got them to you without leaving Moscow. I *chose* to come.'

She shook her head. 'Then you've made a mistake.'

'Probably. But I don't regret it.'

We sit in the gun-metal gloom, order more coffee, and allow ourselves the indulgence of brief reminiscence; Moscow, New York, Paris, Vienna. It seems so long ago but it wasn't. It's just that so much has happened since then.

All the time I was with Mark, I was working for Magenta House to keep Kostya alive. From one point of view, that seems almost noble. Seen from another point of view, it looks like perpetual infidelity. Either way, the arrangement now feels perverse. At the time, I never thought about it too much because I was partitioned and it was effective. Two worlds, two identities, neither encroaching upon the other, black and white with no grey between. That's all gone now. Everything is grey.

'What happens now?'

I shrug. 'I wish I knew. If Mostovoi doesn't work out, I won't have anything left. We'll have to run. Both of us.'

Kostya sniffs the air. 'I've been running all my life.'

'So have I.'

'We're alike, Stephanie. Which means you'll survive. You always do. You'll run, then you'll find somewhere and you'll reinvent yourself and start again.'

'I don't want to, Kostya. I've had enough.'

'I know. But you won't have a choice.'

'Neither of us will.'

'Unless it works out.'

'True.'

'Then what?'

'Until now, I imagined a future with Mark.'

'Perhaps there still could be?'

'No.'

'Why not?'

'Firstly, I don't think he'd take me back. After what I've done, there's no reason for him to.'

'Apart from love.'

'Secondly, I can't do it to him.'

'What do you mean?'

'It'll never be over. No matter what happens with Mostovoi. Or even afterwards. Mark and I could build a life for ourselves and it would be lovely. I know it would. But there would come a day when the past would knock on our door. Mark's too good for that. He's a real person, Kostya. A good person. You should see what he does for people. Being with me puts him in danger and probably always will. I can't do that to him. Or to the people he treats. Or to his friends.'

'There was a time when you thought you could do it to me.'

'You're different. You're like me. We're from another planet.'

Kostya smokes a while, then appears to agree.

I say, 'I tried to absorb him into my life. To make him fit. And to make myself fit into his life. All so that I could pretend that I was normal. That I could be normal. But it was an

454

illusion. A beautiful illusion, but an illusion nevertheless.'
'So, no matter what happens, you'll let him go?'
I smile sadly. 'I love him. What else can I do?'

Café Dollinger on Stuttgarter Platz. Stephanie strolled past the window. The last time she'd seen Mostovoi he'd been sweating into chinos and a polo shirt in Marrakech. Today, in Berlin, he wore a navy tracksuit that looked like velour, a grey sweatshirt and a pair of purple and white Nike trainers. Valery Malenkov, by contrast, was in an ill-fitting brown suit, a plain grey shirt and black lace-ups.

The men left Café Dollinger at half past two. On the pavement they bear-hugged, then parted. Stephanie watched from across the street. Mostovoi struggled to relight a cigar in the stiff breeze, then began to waddle up the cheap pedestrian precinct of Wilmersdorfer Strasse before turning right onto Goethestrasse. Mostovoi's apartment was close to the junction with Knesebeckstrasse in a building with an ornate façade of crumbling baroque balconies. Although smarter than the buildings at the Wilmersdorfer Strasse end of the street, it still didn't look like a likely home for a man with $200 million. Perhaps that was the point. He disappeared through a dark arch into a cobbled courtyard. Stephanie kept her distance. There was another arch on the far side of the courtyard with a door set into the right. Mostovoi went through it. Stephanie sprinted across the courtyard and skidded to a halt by the door.

Peering through a pane of etched glass, she saw Mostovoi collecting his mail from a varnished wooden pigeon-hole on the wall to the left. The lobby was small and dark with a cage lift at the far end.

Instinctively, she clutched the Walther P88 in her coat pocket. Mostovoi puffed on his cigar, the tip flaring orange as smoke billowed from his nostrils and mouth. Stephanie looked both ways through the arch. There was no one around. Mostovoi was heading for the lift. But he paused, reaching into his tracksuit pocket. Stephanie heard the shrill tone of a phone. Mostovoi put it to his ear. Stephanie pulled up the collar of her donkey jacket so that it concealed as much of her as possible. Her hands thrust into coat pockets, she leaned against the door, which swung open.

Mostovoi was pulling the first of the two gates on the cage lift. His conversation was in Russian. Now he was pulling open the second gate. Stephanie hurried across the tiled floor. He stepped in, leaving plumes of blue smoke in his wake. Stephanie reached the lift just as he was closing the inner gate.

'*Entschuldigung.*'

He looked at her, irritated. In her pocket, she tightened her grip on the Walther. Any moment now...

Perhaps it was the hair – shorter and a different colour – or perhaps it was a question of context. But in the second he spared her, he didn't recognize her. Instead, he half-turned away and resumed his call. Stephanie closed the gates and pressed the button for the top floor. Mostovoi leaned across her and pressed 2. The lift began to rise. Stephanie withdrew the gun from her coat but kept it at her side.

The lift shuddered to a halt at the second floor. Without casting her another glance, Mostovoi yanked open both gates and stepped onto the landing. Which was when Stephanie raised the gun and aimed at the base of his skull.

In Russian, she said, 'Don't turn around or I'll shoot you.'

Mostovoi froze mid-sentence.

'Turn off the phone, Maxim, then drop it on the floor.'

He did.

'Who's waiting for us inside?'

'No one.'

'If you're lying, I'll kill them before you get a chance to explain.'

'There's no one, I swear it.'

'Let's hope not. Open the door.'

His hands were trembling. It took three attempts to slide the key into the lock. Stephanie picked up his mobile. The front door opened onto a huge open-plan living area. There was a kitchen at the far end; halogen spots, slate worktops, cupboards of frosted glass.

'Turn round slowly.'

Mostovoi did. Stephanie let him have a good look. Gradually, like a breaking dawn, recognition washed across his face. Followed by dread.

'Petra Reuter,' he whispered.

'Give me one good reason not to kill you.'

He thought about it then shook his head. 'I can't.'

'You know what Marcel Claesen said about you after Marrakech?'

'What?'

'He said you were a cat who used up eight of its nine lives when you were with me.'

'He wasn't even there.'

'That's Claesen for you.'

'What do you want?'

'This moment.'

She eased the safety-catch off, watching him watching her.

He shook his head in resignation. 'Why?'

That had been his chosen last word in Marrakech, the last thing he'd uttered before her gun had jammed.

'Because we both deserve it.'

She began to squeeze the trigger.

'Wait!'

Her smile was as sinister as she could make it. 'Why? To prolong the pleasure?'

'We can make a deal.'

The smile faded.

'Whatever you're being paid, I'll double it!'

Her eyes went dead.

'Okay, okay ! *Ten* times!'

'You're a maggot, Max.'

'*Please…*'

She stared at him, letting the silence elongate. The only sound was coming from Mostovoi; shallow, halting breaths. Sweat erupted across his forehead. The eyes that had been shielded by dark sunglasses in Marrakech were dancing in their sockets, a pinprick of fear for each pupil.

When Mostovoi could stand it no longer, Stephanie said, 'One chance.'

'Anything.'

'I'm serious. One chance.'

He was nodding vigorously. 'I understand.'

Her eyes were still riveted to his. 'Gemini.'

He blanched. 'Gemini?'

'The list.'

She thought his instinctive reaction – despite her threat – would be to deny any knowledge of it. Instead, he was mute.

Stephanie said, 'It's the list or the bullet. The choice is yours.'

She watched him running through as many permutations as he could, searching for an alternative.

'Is this what you were after in Marrakech?'

'I'll ask the questions.'

'There isn't a list.'

'I'm going to count to three. One…'

'Okay, there is a list. I admit it. But it's not here.'

'Two…'

'It's in Moscow.'

'Three…'

'I can get it for you in twenty-four hours.'

'If you don't want to see it coming, close your eyes now.'

'*Fuck!*'

They got into Mostovoi's metallic blue Mercedes, which was parked in the courtyard. Stephanie sat in the back, the Walther in her lap.

'Drive carefully, Max. Don't get pulled over. Don't hit anything.'

He glared at her in the rear-view mirror. 'You want to drive?'

'And when we get there, don't try to be clever.'

'What are you talking about?'

'Airport security. Take it from me, if I get the slightest sense that something is wrong, you'll be dead and I'll be gone before anybody has time to react.'

Out through the first arch, they turned onto Goethestrasse. It had started to rain. Mostovoi switched on the windscreen wipers which squeaked with each return stroke.

'Who told you I had the list?'

'Viktor Sabin.'

'Fat bastard.'

'Coming from you, that's rich.'

'How did you find him?'

She ignored the question. 'Savic knows you have a copy of the list, doesn't he?'

Mostovoi arched an eyebrow at her. 'Copy? It's the original.'

'Who made it?'

'Savic.'

'He told me he never made a list.'

'He's a liar.'

'Didn't he ever confront you?'

'Of course he did!' Mostovoi snapped. 'When the rumours of a sale started, I was the first person he came to.'

'And?'

'And what do you think? I told him he was out of his mind. Why would I put the list on the market? As soon as it becomes common currency it has no value. It would no longer be an insurance policy.'

'Quite. So why do it?'

Mostovoi looked a little bashful. 'Well ... by persuading Milan that I had as much to lose as he did, I removed myself from the list of possible vendors.'

'But you *do* have as much to lose as him.'

'Superficially, yes.'

He let her work it out. Which, gradually, she did. 'Unless he dies.'

Mostovoi nodded.

Stephanie said, 'If Savic is dead you don't *need* insurance.'

'Correct.'

'So why not just hire someone to kill him?'

'Because there's something else I need.'

'What?'

'Immunity.'

'From prosecution?'

He snorted with contempt. 'That I should be so lucky to see a courtroom. No. Immunity from people like you. Immunity from the assassin's bullet.'

Stephanie was puzzled. 'Is that a condition of the sale?'

'That and Savic.'

The Gemini list in return for his removal from another list.

'How many bidders does Farhad Shatri have?'

'Three.'

'And they're in a position to guarantee you that immunity?'

'Yes.'

'So we're not talking individuals, then?'

He shook his head. 'I'm tired of being on the run.'

'My heart bleeds for you.'

'I don't even care about going back into business. I just don't want to spend the rest of my life waiting for someone like you to put a bullet in my back.'

'You made a mistake and thought you could rectify it with this list?'

He nodded. 'I never intended to transport weapons for al-Qaeda. They were anonymous end-users. I didn't know.'

'Not an argument that goes down well at the State Department, I don't imagine.'

'I thought the list would help pay for the error. I just want to be left alone.'

'Like Greta Garbo?'

'Very funny.'

'So that's what this is all about? Right from the start, this is what you planned? A scheme to get you off the hook with the Americans and their allies? With the added bonus of getting rid of Savic?'

'Yes.'

'Playing both ends at once.'

'There was no other way.'

Stephanie sat back. Was Magenta House one of the three? If so, had they really offered such a guarantee? Knowing Alexander, it seemed unlikely. On the other hand, he'd make any kind of promise in return for the list. She already knew that. But once he had it in his hand, would he deliver? She wanted to ask who the bidders were but bit her tongue, not wanting to give Mostovoi the impression that he still had a card to play.

The fourth largest building in Europe with more than ten thousand rooms, Tempelhof airport, near the centre of Berlin, was a vast structure synonymous with the massive arrogance of Nazi architecture, although it actually predated the Third Reich by a decade. The car park was almost empty. So was the colossal terminal building. Down the right hand side there were check-in desks, only two of which were staffed. Down the left hand side were airline and administrative offices.

They went down the steps to the terminal floor, Stephanie slightly behind Mostovoi, her hands deep in her pockets. It was eerily quiet. They came to an office half way down the left-hand side. Mostovoi pulled a set of keys from his shimmering trouser pocket and began to sort through them. On the plate glass front was the name of the company – First Aviation – and a list of services: individual charter, business charters, express small cargo. First Aviation was a subsidiary of Air Eurasia, his Qatar-based cargo transport business, he'd told her.

Inside, he closed the door behind them. The office was small and dusty: two desks, with an old IBM terminal on each, a calendar – two years out of date – and three telephones, none connected. There was a dirty coffee cup by one of the terminals. On the walls were four faded posters, each featuring a bright red Pilatus aircraft with First Aviation painted in gold German Gothic along the fuselage.

There was a tiny storage room at the back of the office. Not much larger than a cupboard, it had four filing cabinets along one wall. Mostovoi turned on the light, a single overhead fluorescent tube. He went to the third filing cabinet, opened the middle drawer, and sorted through bulging files before eventually selecting one. Back in the office he put it on one of the desks and began to rummage among the paperwork.

'1998 invoices, March and April.'

'This is where you keep it?'

'Sure. Why not?'

Stephanie shrugged. 'I was expecting somewhere more secure.'

'You'd have to look hard to discover that First Aviation was owned by Air Eurasia. For a start, you'd have to travel to Qatar. Not even Savic is that persistent.'

'Still…'

Keen to prove his point, Mostovoi held up the key to the door and said, 'Apart from this, that's the only thing that ties me to this office. Technically, First Aviation is owned by a German. Ernst Kessel. A Bavarian domiciled in Monte Carlo who spends most of his time in Vancouver. To be honest, I can't think of a better place to lose any kind of document than in a file of ancient invoices. Especially if they belong to a company with which one has no connection.'

He had a point. Why bother with a safe?

The list was on three pieces of paper, printed in landscape format rather than portrait. The first two pages detailed the fifty-four names of Gemini. Reading across the page: original name, new name, date of collection from Zoo station, country of destination, first address, first bank details, passport details. The third piece of paper contained the names of those who had helped Gemini to operate.

'Shatri was a good idea,' Stephanie said.

'An obvious choice. Like me, he stood to benefit.'

'Like you, he still might.'

Mostovoi permitted himself a small smile. 'That's what I'm thinking.'

'What about Carleen Attwater? Presumably you knew about her and Savic.'

'Naturally.'

'Did you know that she knew Shatri?'

He nodded. 'Not just knew him. She spent time with him. Milan never knew that.'

'But you did?'

'Sure. I know Farhad. The code that I gave Attwater to pass onto Farhad – 0006302/QRT/Vlore/77 – that was an invoice to transport weapons out of Kosovo and into Europe after the conflict. An invoice for machine parts, actually, but an invoice all the same.'

'But if you know him, why bother with the other intermediaries?'

'I needed distance. Farhad was never going to be a

problem. Nobody gets close to him unless he wants them to. I picked her because she knew them both, but the two of us had never met. And I needed Sabin to keep someone between me and her.'

Stephanie took the list, folded it twice and put it in her pocket. Outside, there was an announcement over the public address system. A dozen passengers shifted from the bank of seats at the centre of the terminal and gathered their hand-luggage.

'What happens now?' Mostovoi asked.

'That's up to you. Without the list, you're still on the run. If I were you, I'd climb into one of your planes and head for Patagonia.'

'Maybe I will.'

'I've got to hand it to you, Max. You're taking this pretty well.'

Mostovoi shrugged, then rubbed a hand over his chest. 'When I saw it was you, I thought I was dead. An hour later, I'm still alive. Why would I be upset?'

Back in the Mercedes, they headed up Mehringdamm. Mostovoi tried to make conversation but Stephanie told him to be quiet. She knew what he was thinking. That she might kill him anyway. Why not? She had the list. There was no reason not to. Not for a woman like Petra Reuter.

They crossed into Wilhelmstrasse. At the first set of lights Stephanie got out of the car. She never said anything. She just opened the door and melted into the pedestrians on the pavement. Mostovoi never saw her leave.

She took the U-Bahn to Alexanderplatz and entered the Venezia Pizzeria. Cheap and gaudy, catering to

tourists, it was a good neutral location. There was a pay-
phone in the back. Her first call was to Asim Maliqi, survivor of Omarska, Deutsche Bahn employee. They spoke
for twenty minutes. For her second call, she dialled a
local number and was answered after the fifth ring.

When she spoke, her voice was barely a whisper.
'Vojislav sends his love from Hong Kong.'

There was a long pause. 'Where are you?'

'What your people did in London was a mistake.'

'Making an idiot out of me was a mistake.'

'Don't kid yourself, Milan. You did that all by yourself.'

'What are you doing?'

'I've got your list.'

Another pause, this one even longer, the same cogs
turning as slowly as ever.

'What do you want?'

'Money, since it's no longer for love.'

'How much?'

'A million euros.'

'Fuck you.'

'From what I've read so far, you're dead without
this. That makes a million a bargain.'

'Five hundred thousand.'

'This isn't a negotiation.'

'You're out of your mind.'

'A million euros. In cash. Tomorrow. If you don't
show, you won't hear from me again and I'll sell this to
somebody else for twice as much.'

'Who do you think you are?'

'I know who I am. And so do you.'

'I can't get that kind of cash together. Not by tomorrow.'

The first hint of panic in his voice.

'Then you're already dead.'

She terminated the call and dialled the third number. It was two minutes before Alexander came on the line, her location presumably already becoming clearer at Magenta House.

'What are you doing?'

'You tried to kill me.'

'Nobody tried to kill anybody.'

'You sent Alan Carter after me. He's S7. An assassin, like I am. I recognized him in the bed-sit on Cromwell Road.'

There was no denial, just an accusation: 'You're out of control, Stephanie.'

'One of us is, that's for sure.'

'Where are you?'

'Haven't you discovered yet? Let me give you a hand. Berlin.'

'We need to talk.'

'We're well beyond that, believe me.'

'What do you want?'

'What I'm owed.'

'Okay.'

'Not good enough.'

'Look, stop fucking around, Stephanie. There's too much at stake here.'

'I know. I've got the Gemini list.'

Alexander's pause was longer than either of Savic's. Stephanie looked over her shoulder. Logically, she knew she was safe but she couldn't shake the anxiety.

'I don't believe you,' Alexander said.

'You don't have a choice.'

He hesitated. 'What are you proposing?'

'A trade. Tomorrow. Here in Berlin. I give you the list – and Savic if you want him – and you give me what you owe me. Then we're done.'

It's two in the morning. I can't sleep. I'm in a cheap hotel off Kurfürstendamm. The walls are paper thin. I can hear a man snoring in the next room. There are drunk Scandinavians passing by in the street. The thin tangerine curtains are drawn but the neon sign beneath my window radiates sickly green light into the room.

I look at the Gemini list again. And at the photocopy I've made.

Fifty-four names plus the names of those who made it happen. The list doesn't help. It hinders. By its very existence, it suggests that these are somehow the worst, and that those whose names do not appear here, are not guilty. Or are less guilty. But it isn't true. The Balkans is littered with monsters who never made this list.

That's the point about lists. They're essentially dishonest. They exist to make life easier for bureaucrats. Whether the bureaucrats work for Magenta House or for a high street bank, the lists they use rob you of individuality and make you easier to process. Nobody knows the number of lists they belong to, or what they mean. Are you a bad credit risk? Or a poor insurance risk because of a genetic predisposition to cancer that you don't even know about yourself? Are you on the Limbo list? Will the Ether Division pay you a visit because your name has erroneously appeared in a specific column in a file? Will you die because of administrative error? Because of a misplaced stroke of the keyboard?

It happens. I should know.

17

At five to ten, she entered Zoo station from Hardenbergplatz. It was a bitter morning, frost underfoot, a clinging mist and clouding breath. The concourse was busy, a constant stream of human traffic moving up and down the main stairs to the platforms above. Stephanie circled the hall once; newsstands, a pharmacy, Tie Rack, a souvenir stall, the Nordsee coffee shop. Then she took the stairs to the first level and entered the InterCity restaurant, picking a table by the sloping window. It offered her a clear view of Hardenbergplatz with its crush of taxis and buses. She ordered a cup of coffee from a waitress.

Zoo station was the perfect place to trade the past for the future. For the beneficiaries of Gemini it had been the gateway to a new life. One way or another it would be the same for Stephanie.

As scheduled, Alexander arrived at ten, dressed as he always appeared in her mind; navy suit, white shirt, polished black shoes, magenta tie, gold cufflinks. The cold had forced him into a dark blue overcoat with a black felt collar. He scanned the restaurant, saw her, hesitated, then came over.

He said, 'It never needed to come to this.'

'I know.'

'You look a wreck.'

'Coming from you, I'll consider that a compliment.'

He surveyed their surroundings with a grimace then sat opposite her. 'Good venue, Stephanie. Nice and public, very busy. Less chance of fireworks.'

'I needed something to restrain me.'

'You're armed?'

'I'm armed when I'm naked.'

Alexander winced. 'So I've heard.'

'Here's what's going to happen. At precisely eleven o'clock, Savic is going to enter the station from the Jebenstrasse entrance. He'll be carrying a hold-all of some sort, which he'll take to the luggage lockers. He'll place the hold-all in locker number 885 and take something out. Then he'll leave the same way he came in. At five to eleven, I'm going to call you and tell you where you can find the key to the luggage locker containing the Gemini list. It won't be 885. That gives you five minutes to make a choice. You can have Savic if you want him. Or you can forget about him and leave. Either way, you'll have the list before he appears. It's up to you.'

Alexander stared at her coldly. 'Very neat.'

'I'm just doing what I said I'd do.'

'What about you?'

'I'm leaving now.' She glanced at her watch. 'That gives me just over fifty minutes before I call you. By then, I could be anywhere. I thought it would be best this way. Frankly, I couldn't picture us doing an emotional farewell.'

Alexander reached into his overcoat pocket, took out a pack of Rothmans and placed it on the red paper tablecloth. He placed them on the table-top then produced a stainless steel Zippo lighter, which he turned over and over.

'You'll have your deal, Stephanie. But not until I have the list.'

'At five to eleven, you will.'

'I want you to hand it to me. In person.'

'What difference does it make?'

'I don't know. That's why I want you to do it.'

'Where's the logic?'

'Forget logic. If you walk out now, I walk out too. That means there's no deal.'

'You don't trust me?'

'I'd sooner trust Milan Savic.'

'Now you're hurting my feelings.'

'At least he's predictable.'

'Then the two of you are made for each other.'

'Why don't you get the list now?' Alexander suggested.

'I don't know which locker it's in.'

'Why not?'

'Somebody else is involved. Nobody you know. I'm going to get a call from them just before five to eleven to tell me which locker it is and where the key is located.'

She could see that he wanted to say that he didn't believe her but they both knew there was no point.

'Then we'll wait. Together.'

'What a prospect.'

'All you have to do is sit where you are for fifty minutes. Have a cup of coffee. Talk, if you must. Or pick your nose. I don't care. It shouldn't be a problem for you, Stephanie. You're good at spending time with men you dislike.'

She ignored the barb. 'You're being paranoid.'

471

'In our world, paranoia is precaution. You know that as well as I do.'

Fifty minutes. He was right. She could hand him the list and still vanish in a moment. Especially in a place like Zoo station. She understood his caution because she understood his nature. Everybody was a liar. Honesty was weakness or stupidity.

Alexander took a Rothmans from the pack and began tapping it against the Zippo. 'It seems strange that this will be the last time we ever meet.'

'Strange is good.'

'Grow up, Stephanie. You may not like me but at least give me some credit.'

'For what?'

'For turning you into the woman you are today.'

'Firstly, I don't regard myself as a wonderful work of human art. Secondly, I am who I am despite you, not because of you.'

'That's what you say but we both know it isn't true. You were excrement in a gutter when we first met. Less than human. Dead on the inside, the rest of you decaying.'

'That may be true but only a man like you would regard a woman like Petra as an improvement.'

'Sentimental crap. And predictably disappointing.'

'The parts of me that are worth anything are nothing to do with you.'

'If you believe that, you're deluding yourself. You were a machine, Stephanie. That's why Petra was so good. You were programmed. You were never independent. Magenta House occupied all of you.'

'Nobody has ever occupied all of me. The flawed machine who sits opposite you now was flawed from the start. I won't deny I was good. You know why? Because I thought for myself. Intellect and instinct. Part of me has *always* been independent of you.'

The restaurant began to tremble as a train passed overhead. Alexander lit his cigarette. Stephanie checked her watch. Twenty-five past ten. She looked around. No sign of Savic lurking, which was good. Two uniformed *Bahnpolizei* officers sauntered through the restaurant, both bored. Passengers shuffled in and out; tourists with rucksacks, businessmen with briefcases and overcoats, a mother with three small children in tow.

Alexander said, 'What will you do?'

'Nothing. Petra Reuter is retiring.'

'You'll get bored.'

'You may find this surprising but I don't get a great deal of satisfaction out of killing people.'

'It's not the killing. It's the life. The adrenaline.'

'I don't need it.'

'Not today. Or next week. But you will.'

'If that's what you think, you know me even less well than I thought.'

'On the contrary. *You're* the one who knows you less well than I thought.'

'You'd like to believe that, wouldn't you?'

'At your best, you're too good for normality, Stephanie. You'll never settle down. Petra is in your blood. You'll never get rid of her. Be realistic. What would you do? Marry a man like Hamilton? A chiro-practor? Please...'

'He's more of a man than you'll ever be.'

'You'd be a mother to his children, would you? Changing nappies and baking cakes? Come on,

Stephanie. What a waste. What would you talk about in the evenings? Back-ache and cracked nipples?'

'Is that really how your mind works?'

His smile was cruel. 'We're different, you and I.'

'I'm different to you, that's for sure.'

'You're different to everybody. And there's no way back for you. You can't suddenly reinvent yourself as a regular person. You tried and look what happened. It was a fraudulent performance that ended in disaster.'

'You've made your point.'

'The only surprising thing is that it took so long.'

'At least I fucking tried!'

As soon as she'd snapped, she regretted it. Alexander leaned back a little and took a long slow drag from the cigarette, satisfaction seeping from his pores.

'What about you? Are you married? Have you got children?'

He smirked through the smoke.

'Perhaps your tastes are more exotic.'

Still nothing.

'What's your first name?'

'What do you suppose it might be?'

'Don't tempt me. Just tell me.'

'No.'

'Where do you come from? Where do you live? At Magenta House itself? Perhaps you're not married, after all.'

'Perhaps not.'

'Perhaps you're gay. Or perhaps you love me.'

'Now you're straying into the realms of fantasy.'

'You wouldn't be the first man to end up hating the target of their unrequited love.'

Alexander grinned at her. 'Very amusing.'

'If not me, then Petra.'

The humour evaporated in an instant, catching her by surprise. He shook his head and muttered, 'You should listen to yourself, Stephanie. It's pathetic.'

Having found the nerve, she decided to investigate it. 'Isn't Petra the physical embodiment of Magenta House? And isn't Magenta House the one thing you love?'

Alexander glared at her.

'Having created Petra, didn't you long to have her? To taste her? To be inside her? Perhaps even to *be* her...'

He couldn't bring himself to answer or even to deny.

When Stephanie spoke, her sneering contempt was unrestrained. 'Well, well. What do you know? It's true. One way or another, you've always wanted to fuck me.'

Alexander asks for a cup of coffee from a passing waiter. He won't drink it though. He only bought it to break up the conversation.

Ten forty-two. Not long now.

There's a man at a table by the food counter. He's flicking through a magazine. Or rather, not flicking. Even though he's only at the periphery of my vision, I'm aware of the fact that he hasn't turned a page. Every now and then, he casts quick glances at us.

Alexander is still talking but I'm no longer really listening to him. Instead, I'm tuning into my environment the way I was taught to.

Black trousers, running shoes, grey sweatshirt and a heavy dark brown coat. Shaved scalp, between five ten and six foot, about one hundred and sixty pounds. He's still on the same page.

Now that Petra is in charge, I'm seeing without looking. My attention is drawn to a table on the far-side of the restaurant, where there's a single woman in frayed jeans and a bottle-green fleece that's too large for her. The fleece has a hood which is down. She's reading a paperback. On the floor, by her feet, there's a khaki canvas satchel. There's not much in it. It could even be empty. On the table, by her cup, there's a portable CD-player. There's an earphone in her left ear but not in her right.

Magenta House? A third party? Or paranoia? It's impossible to know. And impossible to ignore.

Ten forty-five. It won't be long before the call.

Alexander takes a second cigarette from the pack and begins to play with it but he's become clumsy and drops it. He's nervous now. Over the public address system a female voice announces an imminent arrival.

I look out of the Intercity restaurant at the first level concourse. Tourists head for the stairs to take them up to the platforms. A Rastafarian ambles by, a bright red knitted wool knapsack slung over his left shoulder. Two Japanese move in the opposite direction. They're followed by a tall woman with short dark hair in a long grey coat. I've got a partial view of her. She's wearing sunglasses despite the gloom outside. She moves beautifully and I'd like to watch her but my attention is hijacked by a shorter man now crossing the concourse.

He wears the orange and white uniform of a Deutsche Bahn employee. He goes to the luggage lockers, opens one, sticks a token in the slot, places something inside, shuts the door, withdraws the key and walks away.

I glance at the woman reading the paperback. She hasn't

moved. The man by the food counter continues not to read his magazine.

Alexander lights his cigarette and checks his own watch.

Ninety seconds later, my phone rings.

'Yes?'

Asim Maliqi says, 'Are you ready?'

'Yes.'

'It's locker 343. The key is an envelope in the men's toilets. Third cubicle along, taped to the rear of the bowl.'

'Fine. You're happy with the rest?'

'Yes.'

'Good luck.'

'And to you,' Maliqi says. 'And thank you.'

'No need.'

'Not true. Hamdu's family will be grateful. As I am.'

I press the red button.

Alexander shifts awkwardly on his stool. 'So?'

Ten fifty-three.

Over his right shoulder I see something that throws me into confusion. It's the tall woman in the grey coat and sunglasses. I've got a full view of her.

Dragica Maric.

Alexander senses my confusion and looks round. Maric might be looking right at us. It's impossible to tell because of the glasses. The woman reading the paperback on the other side of the restaurant is reaching for a bookmark. The man in the dark brown coat is putting coins on the table.

Ten fifty-four. I feel as though I'm back in the lobby of the Hotel Inter-Continental in Belgrade on 15 January 2000.

'Time for the list,' Alexander says.

'How many are there?'

'What?'

'How many people have you got here?'

'None.'

'You're lying. I've made two already.'

He looks truly surprised. Or cross. It's hard to tell which. 'I don't know what you're talking about. They're not Magenta House.'

Dragica Marie has vanished. 'The locker number is 343. The key is in the toilets. Third cubicle along, taped to the back of the bowl.'

'You're coming with me.'

'The men's toilets.'

'So?' Alexander's demeanour hardens. 'I don't trust you, Stephanie. You're going to get the key, then open the locker and hand me the list. If you don't you can kiss goodbye to our deal, to Komarov and to Hamilton. Do you understand?'

I want to punch him.

We leave our table. I glance at the woman on the other side of the restaurant. She's slipping her paperback into her khaki canvas satchel. Deep within me, the first hint of panic makes its presence felt.

We go down into the main hall and head for the toilets. Through the Jebenstrasse entrance, a familiar figure materializes, almost in silhouette against the steel daylight behind him.

Milan Savic. I check my watch. Ten fifty-six. He's four minutes early. I don't think Alexander has noticed him but I can't be sure.

Savic is wearing a black leather coat as usual. In his right hand there's a navy hold-all. There should be a million euros in it. He turns left and heads down the corridor towards the luggage lockers. At this end of the corridor is the entrance to McClean, the washroom. When Alexander and I reach it I look down the passage and have a clear view of Savic. He's searching for locker 885.

Suddenly, he spins round and he's looking straight at me. Or not. It's hard to tell; the distance, the light, the lattice of passers-by between us. Alexander and I head down the steps to the station basement.

McClean is a privately run washroom. It's spotless; a cleaner runs a sopping mop over pale blue tiles that are already gleaming. Two tough looking women in white are behind a desk stacked with towels for the shower stalls. There are turnstiles for the toilets. Alexander presses E1.10 into the slot and enters the male section. Ignoring a bemused look from the cleaner, I do the same.

There's an aisle of urinals to the left and an aisle of cubicles in front of us with two stone basins at the far end.

'Go ahead,' Alexander says.

I push open the door to the third cubicle. Alexander stays by the basins opposite. I drop to a crouch, reach round the back of the toilet bowl until my fingers find paper. I tear the envelope away from the porcelain and hold it up for him.

'Show me.'

I stand up and take out the key.

'Okay. Let's go.'

Which is when the door opens. Milan Savic bursts in, his hand already inside his jacket. Before I can pull out the Walther P88, he's pointing a Beretta at me. I freeze, then slowly raise my hands.

One of attendants shrieks. Savic yells at her to be quiet, then orders both of them to lock themselves into a female toilet cubicle, before swinging the gun at the cleaner. He orders the man to join them. Too terrified to move, he does nothing.

'Now!' Savic shouts. In Serb.

And the cleaner understands.

Of course he does. I don't know if Savic has recognized the face itself, or just the type. But he knows exactly who the

479

cleaner is. A footsoldier in the invisible immigrant army. Perhaps even a veteran of one of Savic's trans-European smuggling routes. He joins the two women on the female side and they lock themselves into a single cubicle.

Then Savic looks at Alexander and asks, in German, 'Who are you?'

Alexander does nothing. He looks back at him, utterly blank.

Savic says to me, 'Who's the old man?'

'I don't know.'

'Lying whore.'

'He followed me in here.'

'What are you doing in here anyway? This is the men's toilet.'

'Don't judge a book by its cover.'

'I don't have to. I've read you from the first page to the last.' *Which, coming from him, would be laughable under different circumstances.* Then he sees the key in my hand. 'What's that?'

'Does it matter? You've got your list.'

Alexander chooses this moment to speak. In flawless German. 'He's got the list?'

It takes me a moment to realize that's he's speaking to me. I had no idea he knew German.

Savic frowns. 'What's going on? Who are you?'

'Have you got the list?' Alexander asks him.

Savic turns back to me, visibly losing control. 'Petra, what the fuck is he talking about?'

Alexander looks just as ragged. 'Where's the bloody list, Stephanie?'

Savic's voice rises to a shout. 'Stephanie? Who's Stephanie?'

Disintegration: there's nothing I can do about it.

480

The door opens.

And everything speeds up. Into slow-motion. That's how it always feels. A blur of breathless action that moves like a glacier. It's amazing how much can pass through a mind in a millisecond.

I recognize the face coming through the door. He's Magenta House but it's neither the man with the magazine nor the girl with the paperback. It's the man who was waiting for me in the bed-sit on Cromwell Road. Alan Carter, an S7 assassin.

Carter goes by the book. He scopes the room and picks the preferred target, shooting the man with the gun first. Two shots into Savic, one in the chest, one in the head. Savic crashes against the change dispenser bolted to the wall. Carter then turns to me. By now I've yanked the Walther P88 from my coat pocket. I fire just before he does. The bullet rips through his throat. He flies back and his gun goes off, the round shattering a mirror. He pirouettes then collapses against the turnstile, his head smacking against a metal prong with a sickening thud.

Alexander is pulling his hand out of his overcoat pocket. But he's nowhere near as quick as the woman he created. We both know it. He hesitates, then I fire, a fraction of a second between the two.

The door opens again. Alexander is falling, his right hand springing free from his overcoat pocket, a snub pistol spiralling onto the tiles. I swing my gun onto the entering figure. It's Dragica Maric, a Heckler & Koch by her side in her left hand.

She doesn't even try to raise it. She knows she'll never make it. My finger tightens on the trigger.

First Belgrade, then New York, now Berlin.

Dragica says, 'Whatever you're going to do, you better do it quick.'

'Why are you here?'

'For the list.'

'And for Milan?'

'Milan was dead anyway.'

It's now or never. We're back in Manhattan. Except this time I have the gun. I'm the one holding the power of life or death. We are also back in Belgrade in the lobby of the Hotel Inter-Continental. Gunfire, bodies dropping, the wildfire panic. Arkan and Ceca. Milan and Petra.

I put the safety back on and lower the gun. If I'm wrong about Dragica, she'll shoot me but I know I'm not. She couldn't then, she won't now. She'd sooner kiss me.

She crouches beside Savic and takes the Gemini list out of his coat pocket. When she stands, her smile broadens as she surveys the three bleeding bodies on the floor.

'It looks like the geneticists are right,' she says. 'Men are becoming redundant.'

They used public chaos as cover. Outside Zoo station they headed left along Budapester Strasse. Five minutes later, they were on Kurfüstenstrasse and completely clear. Behind them, the first of the sirens cut through the rumble of the city. They crossed the road so that they were walking beside the traffic heading away from Zoo Station, not towards it.

Maric buttoned her grey coat to the throat. 'Where will you go?'

'I haven't decided yet.'

Maric lit a cigarette, took a deep drag and exhaled slowly. Coming down after the high. The sensation was etched into Stephanie's memory. The adrenaline rush. There was no feeling like it. In that respect, at least, Alexander had been right.

Stephanie said, 'Milan was marked?'

'He was in love with you. As much as a man like Milan can be in love with anyone other than himself.'

'So?'

'That made him even more of a liability. It was obvious he would have to go.'

'What about Gilbert Lai?'

'We have mutual acquaintances.'

'In Vladivostok?'

'Naturally.'

'And the list?'

'I'll destroy it.'

'Why?'

'It's worthless. I don't need any of them. Not any more.' She hailed a taxi. 'I'm going to miss you, Petra.'

They were at the junction with An der Urania. Dragica Marie climbed into the back. Before closing the door, she leaned out and said, 'By the way, I never slept with Kostya.'

'I know.'

'I'll see you around.'

'I doubt it.'

Stephanie watched the traffic swallow the taxi.

Between Kielganstrasse and Genthiner Strasse a familiar voice called out to her. 'Steph. Over here.' Rosie Chaudhuri was in the back of a black Mercedes parked at the kerb, the tinted window wound down. Stephanie stopped short, a little confused. Rosie said, 'Look behind you. And across the road.'

Thirty yards in her wake was the man from the restaurant. On the other side of Kurfürstenstrasse, another twenty yards behind, was the woman with the paperback.

Rosie opened the car door. 'Jump in.'

Stephanie remained on the pavement. 'Alexander's dead.'

'I know.'

'Did you know about Alan Carter?'

Rosie nodded. 'Alexander's been using him for special tasks.'

'What does that mean?'

'Work beyond the remit.'

'What remit?'

'Get in.'

'What remit, Rosie?'

'You're in the clear, Steph.'

'I want to believe that.'

'I promise you.'

'I'm sorry but my sense of trust has been badly eroded.'

'The two behind you – they were there to protect you.'

'They weren't anywhere to be seen when it went wrong.'

'I know. I had to pull them. It was too public.'

'Leaving me to sink or swim?'

'It wasn't that much of a gamble. It never is with you.'

'They're Ether Division?'

'Come on, Steph. Get in the car.'

'Not yet.'

'He was going to kill you. Then Komarov. Then Mark.'

'Why?'

'To be thorough. That was his justification. Sever all ties, erase everything. You know how it is. Power corrupts. And absolute power corrupts absolutely.'

'I don't understand.'

'He overestimated himself. Alexander regarded Magenta House as his personal fiefdom. But it wasn't his creation. It was never his to own. It was set up by others.'

'Who?'

'Trustees. They appointed him. They gave him control. His power was a gift. In time, he forgot that. And for most of that time, it didn't matter because he ran the organization beautifully. Magenta House has always been brutally efficient.'

'Who are the trustees?'

'Forget about them. You're on the outside now, Steph.'

'Unlike you.'

'That's right.'

Stephanie got into the Mercedes and pulled the door shut. They didn't move.

'Tell me about Alexander.'

'I went to the trustees. I told them what he had in mind and they agreed it was time for a change. To be honest, it's been coming.'

Small moments suddenly came into context: Rosie contradicting Alexander in front of her; Alexander struggling with doubt; Alexander tired; Alexander resigned.

'What about the Gemini list?'

Rosie shook her head. 'The list doesn't matter. Alexander was never going to work his way through it. He wanted it for leverage.'

485

'Leverage?'

'He didn't give a toss about Balkan war criminals. They're yesterday's news. And tomorrow's. His view – and he was probably right about this – is that they'll be at each other's throats again in ten or twenty years. Or in ten minutes. Who knows? Who cares? What he wanted was the list of those who'd assisted in the Gemini project.'

'The bankers, the politicians…'

'Exactly. The trustees weren't happy with that. It's not what we do. They didn't want to see Magenta House expanding into other areas.'

'I thought you said an expansion was being considered.'

'Only in our volume of work. Not in the variety. We only offer one service.'

'Elimination.'

'*Bespoke* elimination.'

Rosie was smiling. Despite herself, Stephanie smiled too. 'God, you sound even more sinister than he did.'

'Believe me, Stephanie, I'm under no illusions about the nature of our work. But at least now it'll be strictly controlled and as professionally administered as possible.'

'Because you're in charge?'

Rosie nodded. And Stephanie found that she couldn't disagree. She took the Walther P88 out of her coat pocket and laid it on the seat between them. Beside it she put the key.

'Locker 343 if you're still interested.'

'What are you going to do, Steph?'

'I don't know.'

'If you're ever short of work, give me a call.'

'If I call you again, it won't be for work. It'll be for wine and gossip.'

'Even better.'

Stephanie opened the car door. 'Tread lightly, Rosie.'

'I will. By the way, what happened to the money Savic put in the locker?'

'It was collected by a Deutsche Bahn employee.'

'Who?'

'You don't need a name.'

'Can I ask what it was for?'

Stephanie got out of the Mercedes. 'War reparations.'

The following morning, Svetlana Asanova caught a EuroCity train from Lichtenberg station bound for Vienna. After collecting documents held for her in the strong-room at a firm of lawyers on Rotenturmstrasse, she intended to spend the night in Vienna before flying to Zurich the next day for a meeting with Albert Eichner at Guderian Maier bank in Zurich.

On the empty seat beside her were two newspapers, the *Berliner Zeitung* and the *Berliner Morgenpost*. Both covered the Zoo station outrage to the point of exhaustion. Although the police were still collating their evidence there seemed to be a measure of consensus among the speculation: the violence was the work of Balkan criminals, two of whom had died. The third man to be killed was thought to be a British businessman although his identity had yet to be established. One thing was certain though: he was an innocent victim.

Stephanie had smiled when she read that. Alexander the innocent victim. It was hard to imagine a less suitable epitaph.

An hour and a half south of Berlin, her phone rang.

'Where are you?'

'On a train to Vienna. You?'

'Back in Moscow. What are you going to do in Vienna?'

'Pass through.'

'Are we safe?'

'Yes.'

'No need to relocate to Sakhalin, then.'

'No.'

'What are you going to do after Vienna?'

'Nothing.'

'Sounds good. Where?'

'Somewhere warm.'

'Even better.'

'I'll call you when I get there.'